How to Bury the Undead

Undead

A Cadence Galloway Mystery

J.J. Brown

For Ashley the 1st
8P
Cea-fully yours, ☺
J Brown
11/26/21

No Problem! Press

Front cover photo: J.J. Brown
Back cover photo: J.J. Brown
Author photo: Elizabeth Victoria Photography
                elizabethvictoriaphotography.com

No Problem! Press
1129 Maricopa Hwy, #242
Ojai, CA 93023
noproblempress.com

ALSO BY J.J. BROWN:

The Wolf's Head Bay Mysteries
  Secrets & Howls

DEDICATION

My friends and family, for their patience as I wrote this
tale – and re-wrote and revised.

Judith Tarr, who helped me when I was stuck in the
middle and ultimately helped me find the ending.

Jeanne Kalogridis, who helped me polish and refine what I
ultimately had.

How to Bury the Undead

Vampire Vespers

It wasn't until I'd finished my jambalaya and pushed my dish to one side that I realized that the scruffy-looking man at the far end of the counter was a vampire.

The diner was Deke's Place, little more than a hole-in-the-wall shack that serves the best jambalaya in New Orleans. It was hidden within the surrounding neighborhood and a well-kept secret among the locals. On my second night in the city nearly a year ago, Mama Louise had introduced me to her cousin Deke Tremont and his famous jambalaya. Deke Tremont was a distant cousin to Mama Louise, who acted as my mentor, and she was the main reason I was having dinner here tonight. The second was the jambalaya. The third and most important was the vampire troubling Deke's establishment.

Mama Louise, aka Louise Tremont, brought this to my attention earlier in the day. She's a lean, black woman in her early sixties and a fifth-generation hoodoo priestess. She holds a business degree with honors from Princeton, has a fine-tuned sense of the theatrics that thrills the tourists and lives in the same house her five-times great-grandmother had been born in. It was one of the luckier structures – any damage it had suffered from

Hurricane Katrina more than a decade ago had been minimal.

Over breakfast, she insisted that I help Deke out with his vampire problem that had begun earlier in the week. That request resulted in an ongoing argument over whether or not I had the ability to pull magic from my surroundings. It was the only bone of contention between us – she insisted that I had untapped magic the likes of which she hadn't seen before. I was equally insistent in my refusal to accept that I had anything beyond Crafting a few spells, deciphering charms and the ability to see ghosts.

The latter, I felt, was quite enough.

Louise sipped her coffee, eyes thoughtful as she looked at me. "You have magic in your blood, powerful magic, Cadence. You deny it, but it's there, all the same."

"Isn't it time to let that go?" I asked, mixing creamer into my own coffee before taking a sip.

"Your stubbornness is going to get you killed," she said, mild annoyance in her voice. "It's blocked and untapped, and yet, you have no interest." She paused, added, "Much like that birth certificate you've got hidden in your pack."

"That's a little extreme," I said, adding more creamer. "Since I talk to ghosts and can work a protection spell, I don't have to prove anything, do I? And do I even have to ask how you knew where I hid my birth certificate?"

"The Undead like human blood, but they yearn for magic blood," she said, ignoring me. "It is magic blood that gives them a taste of their former existence, rekindles their memory of what it was to be alive, with breath in their lungs and blood coursing through their veins." She eyed me, thoughtful. "Deke says they've been walking again."

"What do the Undead have to do with anything?" I quipped facetiously. "Are they having a convention here, to celebrate Anne Rice's birth or something?"

It went downhill from there.

"You are an *imp*…." When Louise gets irritated, she sometimes slips into Creole-French, as she did now. I understood only the first part.

"I don't understand what you're saying," I said. Really, it just sounded like a joke – I'm an imp? Was that it? Weren't imps like fairies or something? Even though I had learned a few simple spells like unlocking doors under her tutelage, seeing ghosts was enough for me. I wasn't interested in encouraging things by entertaining her idea that I had actual magic.

"You will go and help Deke tonight," she said. It was not a request.

My taste buds tingled at the thought of jambalaya for dinner. "Okay. And for the record, I did send in a request for a new birth certificate yesterday. It'll take a couple of weeks to process, but that should make you happy."

Louise only rolled her eyes at me and went to the front room, where she held her readings, and began to prepare her space. I stayed in the kitchen and finished my breakfast. Dinner would be at Deke's and I was going over to see if the vampire would show up. If it did and sensed me over the evening crowd, I would take care of it. There would be no question as to how it would know me from a normal human.

"It will name you what you are," she called back when I asked.

I didn't pursue that topic and I finished my breakfast in relative quiet.

Which is how I ended up at Deke's place. When I'd first met him a year ago, I had been more than a little surprised that he didn't put more effort into advertising. Since his diner was in an out of the way spot, far from the more crowded and touristy cafes in New Orleans' famous French Quarter and its foot traffic, it seemed prudent to let people know he was in business.

Over time, however, I'd come to appreciate this hidden gem and on any given night, music could be heard, either from the Quarter or from a neighboring street. It was only a couple of blocks from St. Roch Cemetery No. 1, one of my favorite places to volunteer at when I'm not helping Louise at her shop. The ghosts occupying the booths along with the living convinced me that Deke's place was also popular among the non-corporeal population of New Orleans.

My seat at the counter was close to the kitchen and gave me the perfect view of the dining area. Now that I'd finished my dinner, I concealed my observation of the diner by glancing through the travel magazine I'd picked up on my way over. Leafing through it, I watched surreptitiously as Junie the waitress served a fresh bowl of jambalaya to a near-by table, the scent of spice and peppers making my mouth water all over again. The scruffy man at the far end of the counter was flirting with Junie, who flirted back casually and without much interest as she drifted between the tables. Fingering the four-point Celtic knot charm on its chain around my neck, I began reading a piece on Maurier County, California.

The writer, Naughton, knew the area well – well enough, I suspected, to be a native and had done what the travel magazine had paid for. I studied the article closely, taking in every detail with more than a traveler's curiosity about the area. I'd spent my whole life believing I'd been born in Massachusetts, but the birth certificate I kept stashed in a secret pocket in my backpack said otherwise.

There was a shout of surprise, accompanied by hoots of laughter from more than one person and I looked up. A couple of booths had been taken over by ten or twelve teenagers, sharing a couple of bowls of gumbo and jambalaya and fries. High school, I thought, a mix of classmates who probably lived on the same street. My gaze settled on the only occupied table in the center of the dining area.

The sole living occupant of said table was Junie the waitress. Next to her, trying to get her attention, was a woman in her late thirties. Despite the fact that she seemed to be of a decade or two earlier, I could see enough of a resemblance between the ghost and the waitress with the vivid purple and blue hair to suspect that they were related.

I studied the waitress closely. She was clearly on break, whether or not Deke wanted her to be, and was currently scowling at the screen of her cellphone, stabbing out a reply to whatever message she had received.

Turning back to my magazine, I noticed for the first time that, beneath the scruff, the man at the end of the counter was actually good-looking in a young Robert Redford sort of way. He caught me looking at him and favored me with a smile, a lazy curling at the corners of his mouth that exuded a barely hidden sexuality. His lips were full, the lower one curving in a sensuous line. Idly, I wondered what he would taste like.

My whole body suddenly flushed with a heat so intense that I forced myself to look back down at the magazine article. I could feel my face grow bright red and an unfamiliar, yet potent, desire pooled between my legs. I crossed them reflexively, hoping my red face wasn't noticeable under the poorly lit space.

Vampire on the prowl. My fingers twitched, restless, wanting to touch his hair, so I picked up my pen and began to doodle.

Sitting to my left, Harriet Douglass gave a dreamy sigh, matched only by the expression on her face. Harriet was a seventeen year old black girl who loved Elvis Presley and Little Richard and had just discovered Ella Fitzgerald. The singed flesh on the right side of her face and the smoke stains on her pink poodle skirt came from a fire that had occurred on this spot in the summer of 1958, in which she had died. We had met on my second visit to Deke's place and became friends of a sort.

Harriet the spectral teen's attention was on the vampire. "He's one cool cat, isn't he?"

I flicked another glance at the man at the end of the counter, then scribbled a note, pushing the paper over to her. *He's a vampire.*

Harriet nodded, still dreamy. "Uh, huh. Still a cool cat."

The vampire's expression had gone from speculative flirt to thoughtful predator. A dim warning tickled me and I looked to see what had caught his attention.

Junie the waitress.

The long-dead relative looked up, saw me watching. "You have to keep her safe."

I let my breath go, dipping my chin in a casual nod as I flipped through my magazine. I was acutely aware of the vampire as he slid from his seat at the counter in a casually graceful move and walked the short distance to the table.

Junie didn't look up. "I'm on break. Deke can help you."

From the kitchen there was a low string of curses. Deke didn't appreciate being volunteered to take care of the register when his place was clearly over the fryer. Out of the corner of my eye, I tracked the vampire as he sat down across from Junie.

One of the many subjects Louise tried to teach me about was vampires and some of the folklore. There had been a lot about seduction, unearthly physical beauty and a sort of magical mind manipulation. In some cases, they traveled in groups of three or more. Fortunately, it seemed to be just him.

At the moment, the vampire was just scouting, but that could change in the time it took a muscle to flinch. Now that I wasn't the focus of his attention, I could see how it affected the waitress.

Harriet the spectral teen sighed.

Being careful not to draw attention, I turned to a fresh page in my notebook and, with quick strokes, I wrote two words – *Distract him.*

Then I slid it towards my ghostly companion. After a couple of coughs, I finally got her attention and she looked down at my note.

"How do I do that? He can't see me anymore than Junie can."

I nodded, to show I understood, keeping my movement minimal. Then I wrote again. *Do what you can.*

She read my second note, brightened and popped out, reappearing again next to the vampire, casting a quick look in my direction. Keeping my face turned to my magazine, I gave a small nod and observed the spectral teen from the corner of my eye.

Apparently, she found something that was falling out of his back pocket. Her expression went from mildly curious to extremely focused and she twitched her fingers. A worn, leather billfold flew out of his pocket and hit the nearest living customer in the head, a big man with muscles and a scorpion tattoo curling out of his t-shirt collar and around his neck.

The tattooed man was up and out of his booth in seconds, his muscular frame towering over the vampire. He leaned in close to the vampire, his demeanor threatening. "You got something to say to me?"

The vampire's eyes narrowed, not moving. I kept my eyes locked onto my magazine from my place at the counter, acutely aware of the tension in the air. A vampire's physical strength outstripped any mortal's, but this one seemed to operate on discretionary use of his powers and, after a minute, backed down easily. He smiled, his expression relaxed as he made several humble apologies and offered to pick up the table's tab.

The tattooed man was going to take it. Even half-way across the dining room, I could feel the vampire's charm work on him. Either Junie the waitress had some latent ability to sense the supernatural or she simply wanted to get away from the conflict before it started, because she immediately got up from her table and walked back to the counter.

She grabbed the coffee carafe and came over to me. "Wanna refill?"

"I had iced tea," I said, startled.

"Oh, right," she said, laughing, nervous. "Sorry."

She took my half-full glass of iced tea and went to re-fill it, leaving the coffee carafe on the counter next to me. Junie's relative smiled at me and faded out. It was time for me to go.

I had confirmed that Deke had a vampire problem, but it would be bad manners to try and solve it here. Best to get the vampire out of the diner first. He'd already made me as a potential victim and, having his attempt at dining on Junie thwarted, I was pretty sure he'd follow me out to try and get his dinner. Shoving the magazine into my pack, I put down some cash to cover my bill, along with a generous tip. Then I took my leave, slipping out the back through the kitchen.

Junie the waitress was leaning up against the double-sink, scowling down at her cellphone again. She never looked up as I walked right past her and out the door. My iced tea sat on the counter next to her, forgotten.

Stepping out into the cool evening, I paused just outside the kitchen door, an over-flowing dumpster to my left. It took a few minutes for my eyes to adjust to the sharp relief of light from the streetlight and black-blue shadows it cast around the back. From the French Quarter, I could hear the low buzz of music and laughter. New Orleans always came alive at night.

I started walking towards Elysian Fields Avenue, hoping to catch the next streetcar back to Louise's. The St. Roth cemetery was just ahead and to my left and I quickened my pace to a fast walk, curious. Sometimes the residents of the cemeteries can be just as loud and raucous as their neighboring and living counterparts. Tonight, as I walked past, however, they were silent, almost watchful.

The night air was humid, typical for this time of year in the south, much like my first night in New Orleans, the air acting as a thin layer on my skin. I'd met Louise that same night, when I passed by her shop as she was closing up. Within five minutes, she'd hired me on and gave me a place to stay.

The neighborhood surrounding Deke's place was quieter than usual as I walked – either most of the residents had gone out to enjoy the evening or they had decided to turn in early. A flutter of shadows from above caught my eye as I walked past the cemetery and I paused, looking up at the stone wall that separated me from the dead. Something moved among the stones, pale and willowy, intangible. Pressure began building behind my eyes, indicating that the spirits were restless. This was not unusual.

With some reluctance and a quick glance over my shoulder towards Deke's place, I walked through the cemetery's entrance. Because of the time I'd volunteered here, it was easy to find my way around the moonlit paths and shadowed crypts to the spot that had caught my attention on the street side. Soon, I found myself at a small crypt that tickled my memory only because I'd worked on the larger, more ornate one next to it the day before.

I felt in my pocket for the old silver coins I kept for any potential interaction with ghosts – I had six that I could leave as a gift. Reaching out, I touched the time-roughened stone surface, my fingers finding and tracing out a name carved into the stone.

Elias Pierce Johnson. He had been a former slave who had found his way to freedom and a new life in New Orleans. He shared only so much with me, which, all things considered, was a lot and I respected his wishes not to get close to a white woman. Even though he was a spirit now and I meant him no harm, old lessons died hard.

"Anything you need to say, Mr. Johnson?" I asked the crypt, my voice soft.

There was silence, then a light thud. I looked up and froze.

The vampire was standing in the pathway leading back to the cemetery entrance, directly in front of me. He blocked my route back to the street and safety beyond. As expected, the vampire had followed me. Studying him, I didn't move, didn't even dare to breathe, my thoughts chasing themselves – this was consecrated ground, even without a church. How was it possible for the vampire to be inside the cemetery walls?

"*Bon jour, ma petite*," the vampire drawled, his dialect a light mixture of Louisiana bayou and genteel French. I wondered how old he was and when he had settled in the area. He couldn't have been more than a century Undead. Lifting his face, the vampire tasted the air. "I've some business to discuss with you."

"I've got business with you, as well," I said, focusing on his chin, being careful not to meet his eyes. Vampires use eye contact to hypnotize their victims – that's part of their glamour when on the hunt. I didn't want to take my eyes off of him and I felt that flush again as it warmed up my face. He was working his glamour or charm or whatever you wanted to call it. I could feel it, but unlike earlier, I was clear-headed, not overwhelmed by his false charm. As long as I didn't meet his gaze, I'd be fine. "State your purpose."

"I was just about to order up a meal from that succulent waitress," he said, his words a caress to my ears, "when you somehow managed to disrupt the exchange."

"Well, too bad for you," I said, "and lucky for her that plans changed."

He considered me, thoughtful. "What is your business with me, *ma petite*?"

"I'm here to stop you from bothering Deke Tremont," I said.

"I will do so," he said, "if you allow me a taste of your sweet blood."

This was not an unexpected request. It was an obvious 'no', in any case. "You will leave Deke Tremont alone without tasting my blood."

"It seems we are at an impasse," he said, his tone reasonable.

"Seems that way," I agreed, keeping my gaze focused on his chin.

The pressure that had been a mild discomfort earlier was now a deep, painful throbbing and I wished fervently for a stake, preferably ash, another tool to use that I remembered from Louise's lectures. My fingers on both hands throbbed, deep into the bone, and I felt something cold and metallic slither into my left palm.

The vampire stroked his chin in a light caress. It was taking every ounce of willpower to not look into his eyes. My pulse pounding in my ears, I risked a quick look at my surroundings, wanting to find anything to fend him off with. Or a helpful ghost or living human to distract him so that I could make my escape. The metallic chain slithered around my fingers, tightening.

Glancing at my hand, I opened up my fingers to see a cross attached to a string of metal beads wrapped around them.

The vampire tilted his head again, still tasting the air, eyes closed. He was practically purring, now. "Ah, an *impremere*." He moaned the word in a deeply primitive and sexual sound, caressing my ears. There was a sudden, responding heat between my legs and I ignored it. "He did not say that that was what you are, *ma petite*." He moaned that word again and again my body responded to his seduction. I bit the inside of my mouth hard – the sharp pain broke his hypnotic tone. "Your blood will taste far sweeter with your magic in it than most mortals." He gave an almost orgasmic sigh. "It will be a pleasure to drink you."

I flinched, the throbbing in both hands unbearable now. He'd named me as an *impremere*, which Mama Louise had said he would. My fingers ached down to the bone and I tried to flex them, seeking relief. Even my fingernails seemed to hurt. The thin, metallic, snake-like cross and chain, bit into my palm, my grip was so tight.

"I don't know who sent you, but I have no magic," I choked out. "I'm just like everyone else."

He smiled, revealing the sharp, pointed canines. "No, you most definitely are not." He tilted his head again, tasting the air. I looked around for a weapon to use against him, with a more permanent result. My foot kicked something solid and it skittered away from me, leaves rustling in its movement as I turned to face the vampire.

He wasn't there.

Blinking hard, as if that would return him to that spot, I looked around, wanting to see him, to know where he was, just as much as I didn't want to see him. A sudden movement in the shadows flickered out of the corner of my eyes. I turned, too late to escape him as he grabbed my shoulder. I fell to one knee, my breath short from the pain, my fingers searching for what my foot had kicked away.

"This is a cemetery," I gasped around his grip. "Consecrated ground. How did you get in?"

He leaned in close, his nose caressing my cheek as he held out a small pouch. "This is New Orleans. Magic of all kinds can be found here, *ma petite*." He shifted, backing me into Elias's crypt, the jutting corner biting into my back. I winced as pain shot up my spine, sharp and cold as the stone itself. "It shall be an enormous pleasure and a privilege to tell my cousins in the west about finding you when they could not."

The silver chain tightened around my fingers and I instinctively put my hand on his sternum to push him off. Instead, I watched as the silver chain wrapped around my hand burned into his chest over a heart that had stopped beating more than a century ago, thin wisps of smoke spiraling up from beneath my palm. There was a cold, sharp spark from my palm.

From deep within his chest cavity, there was an answering throb from his long dead heart.

We both gaped – first at my hand on his chest, where the long dormant heart began to beat once more, then at each other – me, shocked, him in disbelief. The smoke emanating from beneath my palm was growing thicker, curling into tight, black knots. Deep within his chest, I could feel his heart find its rhythmic, steady beat.

The vampire sought my gaze. This time I met it, understanding that something almost human was reflecting back at me from his eyes. "Ah, *petite chienne*, what have you done?"

There was a whisper from the stone, too low to be intelligible, but I recognized it almost at once – Elias Johnson. My fingers brushed against the rough stone work until they came upon a smooth, almost polished, stick and wrapped themselves around it tightly. It came away from the stone easily and I had just enough time to glance at it briefly before thrusting it point-forward at the vampire, cringing back, shutting my eyes tightly.

The stake's point struck home, sinking between the third and fourth ribs, stunning him as I pushed away. His grip on my shoulder had loosened and I fell back easily. He was looking down, mildly surprised, at the stake in his chest, then looked back at me.

"What…?" he began and he burst into cold, blue flames that, when they died away, left him as a statue of ash, which then collapsed in a heap at my feet. I stepped to the side gingerly, my stomach roiling, the smell of sulphur sour in my nostrils. My knees buckled and I sagged against Elias' crypt, feeling drained. Closing my eyes for a few minutes, I listened to the night creatures surrounding me.

Somewhere, a trumpet called out a single, long note, bringing me back to the present. I felt awkward standing in a cemetery in the middle of the night with a pile of ash at my feet. So I scattered the ashes with my feet, mixing it into the dirt and leaves. A small rectangle emerged from the pile and I bent to pick it up. The light was too dim to examine it properly, but it looked like a business card. I stuffed it into my back pocket, resuming the mixing of ash into the dirt.

Once I was satisfied the vampire's remains were properly mixed up, I placed one silver coin on Elias Johnson's crypt door, hesitated, then left another. Reticent and distant though he was, he'd given me aid when he could have chosen not to and I would have understood him. Then, the pressure behind my eyes now receding, I hurried out of the cemetery and headed to Elysian Fields Avenue.

The timing was perfect – I'd gotten to the avenue just as the next streetcar came along and I hopped aboard, paying my fare and taking a seat for the ride to the French Quarter. Once back in the heart of the city, I navigated the crowds that flowed through the streets as they laughed, drank or danced to the music that stirred in the humid air. At one point, I got caught up in a group of dancers going in the opposite direction than I wanted to go, but I finally managed to correct my course and soon, I was hurrying down the street to Louise's house.

The front porch light was on, indicating that she had a client, and I hesitated briefly in the shadows. The front room was where she conducted business and, on occasion like now, she had clients after hours. To avoid interrupting, I would have to go through the back door. As I headed for the alley that ran behind the row of homes, the front door opened and a woman stepped out, clearly dissatisfied with her reading. I lost sight of her as I rounded the corner and trotted up the back steps. What I encountered as I walked into the kitchen was Louise herself.

She was sitting at the kitchen table, drinking tea,

comfortably dressed in jeans and a Princeton T-shirt. Her dreadlocked hair was still wrapped in a bright blue scarf, which confirmed the client who had just left moments before I walked in. A quick glance at the clock above the sink told me that it was earlier in the evening than I'd originally thought.

"Was he there?" she asked.

I nodded, setting my pack on the floor under the table. "Like you said he'd be."

"Did he name you?"

I nodded again.

She pushed a plate of gingerbread cookies towards me. "How'd you get free of him?"

I placed the wooden stake onto the table and pushed it towards her, taking a cookie at the same time. "Elias Johnson and his family were helpful."

She took the stake, her long fingers holding it as if it were an ancient artifact of great religious import. Which, in a way, I suppose it was. Without looking up, she asked, "Was there something else you were gifted with?" Without a word, I pulled out the crucifix and held it out to her. She shook her head. "That's yours, honey. So is this." She pushed the stake across the table towards me. I took it, curling my fingers around the polished wood, feeling comforted by its weight. "Tell me more about the encounter."

I almost didn't tell her about the strange spark and the resulting beat of the vampire's long-dead heart. But, in the end, I told her everything the vampire said and what transpired, down to the glimmer of humanity in the Undead man's eyes before he turned to dust. Her response was, to say the least, not what I expected.

Louise stood, the chair scraping against the floor in her sudden movement. "You are at the center of many undead things, Cadence."

I sighed, slumping back into my chair, taking another cookie. "Oh, yay. More vampires to look forward to."

She snorted, pouring herself a glass of wine, then rejoined me at the table. "Vampires are not the only undead things in this world." She leaned forward, her eyes warm. "The resentment you feel towards your parents will drain you just as surely as a vampire drains a human of blood. You need to deal with whatever lies they told."

"They're my adoptive parents," I said, automatically, then looked away, ashamed. They had been my real parents, right up until they'd died last year and I found out we weren't biologically related. With no chance for me to understand their choices, I suppose that was why the lies hurt so much. "So, how do you do it? Bury the undead?"

"Lay them to rest," she corrected, lightly. "You acknowledge them, the hurts they caused and then you forgive them."

I frowned. "But, how do you bury them?"

Louise settled back into her chair, sipping her wine. "You release them."

"Easier said than done," I grumbled, fingering the crucifix's chain.

She patted my hand gently. "You'll manage." Gesturing to the stake and the crucifix, she added, "You'll need those for where you're going."

"Who says I'm going anywhere?" I countered.

"The train schedule hidden with your birth certificate," Louise said, briskly. She took one of the cookies and bit into it, savoring it. "Someone came to my door while you were out."

I thought of the woman who had just left. "She didn't like her reading."

Louise shook her head. "No, she did not. She was very intent on speaking with you." She narrowed her eyes, but I saw the humor sparkle. "What does she want with you?"

I shrugged. "I have no idea who she is or what she

wants. Did she leave a card?"

In answer, Louise pulled out a business card and handed it to me. I took it, feeling the world fall back as I looked at the name. *C.P. Naughton.* The author of the article I'd been reading at Deke's place while scoping out the vampire.

I looked up at my mentor, questioning.

"She'll be back, make no mistake," Louise said, nodding in answer. "She's well protected, too. I can't read her intentions towards you." She made a gesture. "Go, take a shower and get some sleep." She sipped her tea, chuckling. "I'll make sure she goes on a wild goose chase before she knows you've gone."

I nodded, took my pack and headed towards the hall. Just as I got to the kitchen door, I paused, turned. "I don't need to leave, you know. I can do everything from here."

She snorted, amused. "That knot you call your family history didn't start here and it didn't start in Massachusetts, either. California is where it started, so back to California you go."

There was an implacable note in her tone that advised me not to argue. I knew she was right, in any case, so I switched topics. "He called me an *impremere*, Louise. That's what you called me, isn't it?"

She nodded, a slow movement of her head. "It's what you are, child. You can pull magic to you, as all *impremeres* do in varying degrees. Deep into your bones, it's who you'll always be."

"And that's how his heart started beating again?" I asked, troubled by the implied power she referred to. "I pulled his life back into his body?"

She hesitated, said, "What an *impremere* pulls is unique to each one. There have been so few born in the last century alone that what I know would fill an index card." She gave herself a hard, brisk shake. "Now go. It's going to be an early and very long day tomorrow. If what you told me is true, that woman won't be the only one looking for you."

I studied her for a long moment, then headed upstairs to do exactly as she'd suggested, taking another cookie as I went. Packing didn't take long – including an old laptop, everything I owned fit into a student-sized back pack. Heading into the bathroom, I started a bath and stripped down, tossing my clothes into a corner. Something fluttered to the floor and, picking it up, I recognized it as the card I'd found among the vampire's ashes. It was from a law firm in Wickerman Falls, California – Moorehead, Montgomery and York.

The name of the attorney it belonged to was O. Raul Kendrick.

The vampire had mentioned cousins in the west. Wickerman Falls was in the same county I was born in, according to the travel article. Which meant that someone in California knew of my existence. How, though? I didn't know of my connection to California until very recently. Turning off the bath water, I sat on the bathroom floor, closed my eyes and focused on the name beneath the law firm, tuning out my surroundings. After a minute, my breath deepened and I felt connected to the card, as though it were another layer of skin on my hand. There was a warmth to it, kindness, and then nothing.

Perplexed, I opened my eyes and stared at it, wondering who the owner of this card was and if he was the one who had sent the vampire. There wasn't any reason to suspect he had, but there was also no evidence to suggest he hadn't. Timing was everything and nothing is a coincidence, as Louise is so fond of pointing out. Tucking the card back into my jeans pocket, I slipped into the tub and had a nice soak before taking myself off to bed.

The next morning, the sun not yet cracking the sky with light, I left Louise's home for the last time. The stake was wrapped in a towel and stowed in my pack, along with my few possessions that included a second-hand laptop. The pack was now slung over both of my shoulders. The crucifix and the Celtic knot hung around my neck, tucked under my shirt, warm between my breasts.

Louise Tremont drove me to the train station and, over my objections, paid for a sleeper car ticket to California. She only looked at me and I fell silent. I had no more words to offer her, not even in thanks. I hugged her fiercely, missing her already.

Then I was onboard and in my berth, watching the world go by.

Ahead of me was California, a state that was big and easy to get lost in, with the forests and the cities. More important, it was where I had started. That I couldn't have gotten my answers from my parents still irked me. What made it worrisome was that they either didn't want to say, they were unable to say or they were being prevented from speaking. And I wasn't sure which it was, or if it was a combination of all the above.

As the train rolled west along the tracks, the vampire's words about his cousins out west stirred restlessly in the back of my mind.

One

My train didn't arrive at Wickerman Falls directly – the nearest station was in San Francisco and from there, I took a bus north-west to the small city. I arrived in the wee hours of the morning, long before any businesses not a hotel or a restaurant would be open. So, I found a hotel, got a room, showered, and took a nap before venturing out to find the law firm. Its address on the card directed me to a street behind city hall and I soon found myself staring up at a late nineteenth century Victorian mansion, now converted into office space.

On my journey to California, I'd used the train's spotty internet service to look up O. Raul Kendrick, the attorney who may or may not have sent that vampire to Deke's place. Moorehead, Montgomery and York had been established as a firm in 1943 – most of their work consisted of property, wills and notarizing, but they also took on criminal cases, mostly pro bono. What I was here to find out concerned none of the above – just the ramifications of altering a birth certificate and possible reasons to hide someone's place of birth.

I also wanted to get a sense of this Raul Kendrick in person. The vibrations I'd picked up from his card didn't mesh with the intent behind the New Orleans vampire. While my instincts adamantly rejected that he was responsible for that vampire, I couldn't entirely rule him out as a threat to me until I'd actually interacted with him. Somehow, O. Raul Kendrick's business card had found its way into that vampire's possession. That same vampire had referred to cousins on the west coast, but hadn't specified California.

The business card, however, did and suggested even more – that whoever sent the vampire had some sort of connection within this office. Whether it was the card's owner or someone else would remain unknown until I went inside. Now, I took a deep breath and climbed the steps to the old Victorian's front door. Just inside and sitting at the front desk was a formidable-looking woman in business attire. This impression did not soften, even as she stood to greet me warmly.

"May I help you?" she asked, pen poised to take notes.

I held up the grave-smudged card. "I was wondering if I might have a minute to talk with Raul Kendrick. I don't have an appointment, though."

To her credit, she didn't flinch as she took the card, her gaze softening. "Raul's not shy about passing these out." She grew pink, clearly more than just an admirer of the lawyer. "He's such a champion of those who aren't able to speak."

That boded well for the man, but I still wanted to make my own assessment of him. "Is he available?"

"Let me check his schedule." She turned to the computer, her fingers moving swiftly over the keyboard. "He's free right now, but only for twenty minutes or so. He's got a case at the courthouse at one."

"That's perfect, I only need a minute," I said.

She gestured to the ornate staircase. "It's the second door on the left."

"Thank you." Taking back the card, I followed

her directions upstairs, hesitating briefly on the landing. The door to Raul Kendrick's office was only a few feet from where I stood, but my feet felt leaden. The minute I chose to knock on that door, I'd be inviting changes into my life I wasn't sure I was ready for. Were my adoptive parents criminals? Lying about where I was born wasn't illegal, but maybe the reasons for them to do so were.

A woman with her hair swept up in a Victory curl popular during World War II walked briskly in my direction. In her hands, she held a number of files, which she almost lost when the heel of her Oxford pumps caught on something and she stumbled. There was bruising around her neck, barely hidden by the strings of pearls she wore. "Do you have an appointment?"

"Sort of," I said, holding up the card. Unsure if she was aware of her spectral status, I asked, with caution, "Can I help you?"

She shook her head. "I'm fine, thank you. But those stairs are in need of repair. My heel keeps catching the runner." She glanced at her pumps, a slight frown crossing her face as she made a gesture to the staircase behind me. "Last week, I nearly broke my neck when I fell. The custodian is not very reliable."

"It happens," I agreed, then asked, "Are you aware of any place in the area in need of a part-time employee? Preferably one that wouldn't ask too many questions?"

She pursed her lips, thinking. "Try the Sandover Cemetery, down in Sleepy Eye Cove. It's almost impossible for them to keep good help there." She eyed me, thoughtful. "I believe that they may need a caretaker."

"Thank you," I said, grateful for her suggestion. The time I'd spent volunteering at St. Roch Cemetery No. 1 had been the best time, the best job. I could only hope that the Sandover would be just as rewarding. And if there was a caretaker's position, then maybe there'd be a place to stay, a home of sorts.

She spared me a smile, then walked through a door marked 'Supplies', her shoes clacking on what was now pale, wall to wall carpet. Turning back to my mission, I stared at the door bearing Raul Kendrick's name and took a deep breath, preparing to step forward.

The door opened, taking my decision from me, a man's irritated voice saying, "And kindly take my face off, while you're at it, Julian."

Take his face off...? Speechless, I watched, as yet unnoticed from my place on the stairs, as the two men stood just inside the office. Black hair, dark blue eyes, the two men could have been twins, if not for the color of their suits. The man holding the door open wore navy blue trousers and a button-down shirt with a pale blue tint. The second man wore a black three-piece suit, white button-down, holding a matching overcoat in one hand and a black briefcase in the other. Both men stood a little over six feet and had a definite presence that filled the landing.

The man in the black suit grinned. "Easily done, Raul. Sorry it disrupted your argument in court, though." His face shimmered in such a way that I felt the need to rub my eyes, like something had gotten in them. In the next second, I was looking at a man with ginger hair and dark gray eyes, his lips curved into an amused smile.

I didn't like him – he was too sure of himself, felt dark and cold despite his classic good looks.

"Good afternoon, Julian," the other man said, pointedly.

"See you in court." Julian smiled, brushing past me with barely a glance.

I watched him go, relieved. Louise had taught me to better recognize a sorcerer and I had the feeling I'd just met my first one. She would have had some choice words about him. Then I turned to find that I was being studied closely.

"Raul Kendrick," he said, standing aside and gesturing to his office. "I only have a few minutes….."

"Well, this won't take long, anyway," I said, accepting his invitation and, stepping past him, I caught a whiff of his scent – clean, masculine, warm. It reminded me of a summer night in New Orleans, just after I'd arrived, and how the air tasted of spice and languid movements. Then I shook my head and entered his office. I was acutely aware of him close behind me as he guided me to the chair in front of his desk.

Taking my seat, I fussed a bit with my pack as he crossed to his chair behind the desk. As I settled into my chair, I noticed the open files on his desk. The name *Galloway* leapt out at me and I instinctively leaned forward to get a better look. With a quick movement, he closed the files and put them aside, then leaned back slightly in his chair. We sat in silence for a few minutes, studying each other.

Thoughtful, he asked, "What can I help you with?"

"My name is Katie Gray," I said, acutely aware of the irony of my using a false name. There was no one in Wickerman Falls who knew I even existed and yet, I felt the need to keep my identity as private as possible. "I've got reason to believe I was born in this county and I've already turned in a form to get my birth certificate replaced, but…." I paused, searching for words. "From a legal standpoint, why would someone lie about a child's place of birth?"

His brows shot up in surprise. "This happened to you?"

I nodded. "Well, yes, and I can't think of any reason why."

"Did you ask your parents why they lied?"

Shaking my head, I explained, "They died in a car accident a little over a year ago. I didn't find out until after their funeral, when I was going through some papers."

He straightened in his chair, picking up a pen and tapping his notepad. "May I ask why you waited so long to start an inquiry?"

Hesitating, I said, slowly, "Can we just leave it at grieving and trying to just move forward?"

He smiled, the simple act warming his features. "Of course." Pausing, he glanced down at his notes. "Did you attempt to look into possible reasons for why they would lie?"

"Yes, but they didn't even have a parking ticket attached to them," I said, jumping on the new topic with relief. I thought of the hours I'd spent, both in the library and the court house, searching for answers that clearly didn't exist in Massachusetts. "It's like they just…..popped into existence or something."

He settled back into his chair once more, closing his eyes, thoughtful, his pen still tapping lightly. "And what brings you to Wickerman Falls?"

I shrugged. "I want to know the area, I guess. The altered birth certificate says I was born in Maurier County, but not much else. The new one won't be available for a few more days."

He made a noncommittal sound, eyes still closed. This gave me an opportunity to study him closely, so I did. His black hair was cropped short, with just enough to make me wonder what it would be like to ruffle. Shifting in my chair, I quelled the feelings that thought inspired and looked at the hand that held the pen. There were some callouses, formed over a period of years by how he held his pen and again that wondering thought of how it might feel against my skin stirred up images I didn't want to have.

At least, not right at that moment.

"The thing to do, then," he said at last, "is to wait until that birth certificate comes in, then come back to me and we'll go from there." He opened his eyes and shifted so that he was looking at me, his expression curious. "It does raise questions, though. Why would your parents raise you to believe you were born in one state when it would eventually come out that you were born in another?"

I shook my head. "I wish I knew."

And it bothered me that I hadn't seen their ghosts – had they crossed over? Were they happy to go? Didn't they have unfinished business? In point of fact, wasn't I their unfinished business, to be dealt with before crossing over? Or was it my own anger and resentment at their secrets that kept me from being able to make contact with them? That was something Louise would suggest, and I suppose it was possible. For now, though, it was just another example of the nature of our turbulent relationship, but it still stung.

Raul Kendrick leaned forward, his blue eyes dark with sympathy. "I am sorry to that your parents died. And that they left you with so many unanswered questions."

I averted my gaze, my cheeks warm. "Thank you." Clearing my throat, I asked, "So should I call to make an appointment?"

He handed me a new card. "Yes, as soon as you get it."

"Great." With some relief, I took the card, glanced at him hopefully. "Is there any way you could maybe call the courthouse and put a rush on my request?"

He laughed, a warm, rich sound. "Sorry, unless I have a court order, it's not possible."

"Kind of figured," I said, "but I wanted to ask."

Standing, we made our goodbyes and I soon found myself back on the sidewalk, his new card still in my hand. As with his card from the cemetery, I felt only Raul's sense of purpose – to assist, to guide, to aid. So who had given his card to that vampire? According to the New Orleans vampire, it was to find me, but to what end?

As far as I knew, no one in Maurier County even knew of my existence, so it was a mystery that the vampires were cognizant of that fact, both here and in New Orleans. And until the deaths of my parents, I hadn't even known I was missing. So who knew about my real identity?

Staring at Raul's card, I felt a cold chill run up my spine.

Whoever had given this card to the vampire down in New Orleans knew.

Two

The on-site caretaker's shack at the Sandover Cemetery wasn't much to look at, but it was tucked in the north side of the property, close to the stone wall marking where the cemetery ended and the forest began. The roof was solid, there was a gas-powered generator hidden in alcove outside by a trap door on the west side and a dormant vegetable garden by the front door. Inside, there was a small refrigerator to my immediate right and, just beyond it, the sink. The bed was pushed into the far corner on my left. It looked like it had seen better days, but I'd slept in worse. The head caretaker, Wesley Burke, had promised to get a new mattress, but it wouldn't get delivered and put in for at least a week.

"I can survive until then," I reassured him, then pointed to a hot-plate on the counter next to the sink, both of which were under one of the two windows. "Is that it for a stove?"

Wes nodded. "This isn't really set up for a full oven, plus the last guy didn't care much for cooking. Are you?"

"Am I what?"

"Particular to cooking?"

I shook my head. "No, not really. Never had much of

a call for it."

"Then this'll suit you just fine." He showed me the rest of the place – the tiny bathroom, with a claw-foot tub under a tiny window to my left and the toilet hiding behind the door. Back in the main room, he showed me the television – an old tube set hooked up to a DVD player. Most of the furniture in the shack appeared to have come from thrift shops or yard sales. "Cable is set to be installed, but not until next year. Or so the powers that be tell me." His eyes twinkled with merriment and we ended the short tour on the front porch, where he handed me a set of keys and a request to meet at the cemetery's office the next morning.

Then he set off across the lawn, leaving me to my new abode.

*****

My first night was eventful, to say the least.

After locking up, I sat in the middle of the main room and cast a spell designed to locate any vampires in the area. It was a simple casting, using a sheet of blank paper to mark the cemetery, the village down the road and Wickerman Falls. Then, using a pin, the card I'd found in New Orleans and a bit of thread, I chanted the spell, taught to me by Louise Tremont. The crude map I'd made glowed, then began to fade. I studied it closely – as the light faded, areas where there might be vampires would turn black.

Nothing of the sort happened. Relieved, I gathered everything up, stood and stowed it in the tiny trash can underneath the sink. Changing into my night clothes, I turned in, and was just about to drop off to sleep when I heard a loud, shrill chattering.

Sitting bolt-right up in bed, I snatched the flashlight I'd always kept close and switched it on, scanning the room slowly, lingering over the windows. I'd made sure to secure and lock them, but the place wasn't exactly Fort Knox. Switching on the bedside lamp, I swung out of bed

30

and stood in the middle of the space, listening.

The high-pitched chatter had stopped and there was a heavenly silence. Then, just as I was about to turn back in, it started up again, only it sounded like it was coming from underneath the floorboards. Frowning, I bent down and grabbed hold of the faded green rug, yanking it back to reveal a trap door. The chatter stopped, only to be replaced by a tentative scratching. Taking hold of the latch, I gave it a twist and then pulled. The trap door flew back easily and I skipped back just in time to keep my bare toes from getting flattened.

The raccoon shot out of that dark space and across the room, its chatter higher and more excited than before. Going to the door, I opened it wide and stepped away from it, giving the raccoon a wide berth. It looked at me, eyes shining from its furry masked face, then scampered out into the night. I stood in the doorway, watching the tiny shadow blend into the darkness and sighed heavily.

"Well, that's a relief," a voice piped up. "I was having the devil's own time trying to help that poor creature."

"Thanks for letting me know it was there in the first place," I said, shutting the door and locking it before facing my spectral companion. A girl of sixteen, she wore a plain, dark blue dress, a frilly white apron and the maid's cap on her head covered a coil of braids. On closer examination, I saw soot – it stained the edges of the apron and, though well-hidden by the color, it was all over her dress. The style of clothing suggested early twentieth century and that was as close as I wanted to commit to. "How long have you been attached to this place? You seem more suited to one of the old Victorian houses in Wickerman Falls."

She beamed. "I was with the old Rogers family. Their mausoleum isn't far from here."

"Same question," I said, arms crossed. "Why aren't you there? Or with your family's plot?"

She colored, glancing down at the floor. "I was

mistaken for one of the Rogers children after the fire in 1927 and buried with them by mistake. Old Mr. Rogers took exception to that." She tipped a curtsey. "I'm Dottie Perswalski, at your service."

"Cadence Galloway," I said, resisting the urge to curtsey back, "but don't be surprised if you hear the living call me 'Katie'. I'm keeping a low profile at the moment."

She perked up. "Are you here about the vampires, then? They are a nasty lot, quite rude of them to take it out on the church."

I laughed. "Yes, they are." Crossing to the trap door, I shone my flashlight into the darkness below, curious, only half-paying attention to my spectral roommate. "Tell me about the vampires, then. Are they causing any major problems?"

"They broke into the church down the road two nights ago," Dottie said and then went off into a very long explanation of what went down. As she spoke, I gave the space below the trap door a cursory look with the flashlight. It was small, square and it looked like there was a tunnel or something. Taking a step down, I flashed the light – yup, it was a tunnel and it looked like it led to the back side of my humble shack.

Then Dottie's voice caught my attention. "...and Father O'Mare is quite worried about the vandalism they wrought. But now that the congregation is up in Wickerman Falls, there doesn't seem to be much call to put things right." She added, confidentially, "No one seems to share Father O'Mare's conviction that it's vampires."

"Uh, huh," I said, slipping on my sweater. I wanted to check out the other end of the tunnel, which meant going outside. Stuffing my feet into my sneakers, I laced them up quickly and went to the door.

"It's because most are still among the living, I suppose," Dottie mused, following me out the door. "Father O'Mare passed on in 1979."

"And naturally, Father O'Mare can't share his concerns with anyone," I said, amused by the conundrum Dottie faced, then shivered, regretting that I had not pulled on my jeans.

"It puzzles me that they should destroy church property at night," she said, hovering to my right. "No sense in that, without being able to see."

I considered telling her that nighttime was usually the best time to commit vandalism, especially when it's known that the building is no longer in use, but refrained. I didn't think Dottie would understand my sense of humor, given that we just met. I liked hearing her chatter, much more than the raccoon. I guess it's like having a younger sister, but being an only child, that's all speculation on my part.

Dottie hovered next to me. "Cadence, might I ask you something?"

I ignored the cold spot she created, walking around the shack to where I figured the tunnel came out. She followed, her demeanor subdued. "Sure."

"It's very important, Cady," she said, serious.

"Okay. I'm listening."

"Do you think it could be vampires?" She floated closer to me.

I looked at her, surprised. "What makes you think it could be vampires? It could be teens taking on a dare or something?"

Dottie turned pink. "In the pictures, it was always something supernatural."

My spectral friend seemed to have quite the romantic imagination. "Well, sometimes the most obvious explanation is the right one."

She eyed my sneakers. "Is that why you've got your shoes on? Are you going to go look at the church? To put Father O'Mare's mind at ease?"

The question caught me off-guard and I took a minute to answer. "Well, one, he didn't ask for my help, so it's pretty much up to him if I do. Second, I don't know if

33

it's vampires or angry teens. There's no way to tell unless I go look at it."

Dottie looked at me, earnest. "But you will find out? And you will put a stop to it?"

I smiled at her, amused and touched by her concern. "Of course."

By this time, we'd come around to the side of the shack where I'd figured the tunnel came out to. A wood-framed door lay wide open, the tunnel exposed to the wilderness at large. Frowning, I managed to get it shut and throw the latch, searching the area for the padlock that surely had come loose. There was none to be found, so I grabbed a stick and broke it down, shoving it into place to hold the latch until I got a new lock.

Dottie sighed dramatically in my ear.

I glanced at her. "What?"

"When will you put a stop to it?"

I laughed. "You want me to start now?"

She drew herself up. "And why not? You're awake, they've been there and gone, and it needs resolving to Father O'Mare's satisfaction."

Dottie had a point. And, if they were the same ones that the New Orleans vampire had referred to, I had my own reasons to address them. I made a noncommittal noise, wondering how this nest of undead managed to get into the church. Vampires are unholy creatures of the night and hallowed ground is not easy for them to breach unless it had already been defiled by suicide or something and not consecrated again. The vampire in Louisiana had been able to get into that old cemetery with the use of a charm.

I had to see if the Sleepy Eye Cove church had been the scene of such an incident. And if it was indeed a vampire situation, then it would be reasonable to assume that they had access to a charm as well. And if they did, then someone had either made that charm themselves or had gotten one from a powerful witch and gave it to them.

Much like that charm the Louisiana vampire had possessed.

Since I was new to the area, the thing to do would be to ask the locals currently residing in the cemetery. Ghosts can get pretty chatty, probably because so few of the living can hear them, so it wouldn't be too hard to get some of them talking about the past. Plus, they wouldn't ask any of the awkward questions that the living seem so fond of.

Dottie floated over, anxious. "Do you suppose whoever vandalized the church was looking for something?" She poked at my shoulder, leaving a cold sensation behind. "What do you suppose they were looking for?"

"That's a good question," I said and then, because I couldn't resist teasing her, "What do you think they were looking for?"

"Pirates!" she exclaimed, clapping her hands together, excited. "Of course, that's who it must have been! They're looking for their gold!" Cold filtered through my shirt and I felt her breath on my cheek, raising goose bumps. "Don't you think so?"

I shivered. "I've heard crazier things."

Dottie sniffed. "It's not crazy. There were lots of pirates on the Pacific." The cold spot left and I felt myself begin to warm up again. "I wonder which pirate captain led his crew here? Did they all have to sign a pact to return? Or did the captain kill them, like in the movies?" She sighed, wistfully. "Father O'Mare would have made a fine pirate, had the notion taken him."

I stifled a groan. Clearly, Dottie had a romantic nature and it took very little to inspire her to natter on over any possibility while cheerfully throwing out random ideas about the vandalism at the church. As cautious as I was about the situation, I didn't like the idea of vampires roaming the area nor the fact that they had somehow found a way to walk on consecrated ground. Or that they had enough of an idea of who I was to have tracked me to

New Orleans.

Decision made, I stepped into my shack long enough to pull on a pair of jeans and grab the key ring Wes had given me earlier in the day. Then I shut the door behind me and set off across the cemetery grounds, intent on getting to the church.

Dottie finally noticed what I was doing and swooped close to hover next to me like a vaporous cloud of worry. "Where are you going?" she asked.

I shook the keys. "I'm going over to the church and look at the damage. Wanna come?"

Dottie clapped her hands together in childish glee. It was cute, for a ghost who had died more than ninety years ago. Chuckling, I touched the silver crucifix and Celtic knot that hung around my neck and we trekked through the cemetery grounds in companionable silence. The moon's pale light streamed through the trees, creating elongated shadows.

"Things are fine," I muttered under my breath, skirting past a marker over-grown with ivy and almost tripping over a misplaced stone at the same time. "No use worrying."

"No use worrying?" A man garbed in late nineteenth century clothing paced beside me, his over-combed mustache quivering. "My first wife is accusing me of murder and my second wife continually asks why I didn't love her and ten children who are demanding that I make good on my word. How can you say I've nothing to worry about?"

I stared at him, puzzled. "I'm sorry, who are you?"

He stared back, affronted. "I am William Ellis Sandover."

Ah, the founder of the cemetery. Wes had talked about him while giving me a grand tour of the area during the interview. I'd been studying a map of the cemetery's plot lay-out and had commented on the name, which prompted the conversation. Sandover had died of heart failure in 1905 and his funeral had quite the turnout to honor him, but it was clear that he did not rest in peace.

"I was talking to myself, Mr. Sandover," I said, stalling to recall the lay-out of the cemetery that Wes had shown me, "but if you want my opinion, get some help from a psychiatrist." I stopped, orienting myself, then pointed south-west. "Margery Carlson was practicing for forty years. She came over last year. I think she can help you."

Sandover scowled. "A woman psychiatrist? I think not. I could hardly trust my wives with our children. Why would I trust a woman with my psyche?"

"Suit yourself." I continued on.

"Aren't you going to help me?" he cried, panicked.

I kept walking. "Why? I'm a woman, after all. What help would I be?"

Dottie looked mortified at first, then giggled. After a minute, I joined in. We were both still snickering when we came upon the parking lot. Two hearses and a cemetery truck were parked close to the office building's main entrance. Fingering the ring of keys in my pocket, I went to the truck. The only living soul around to hear it start up would be me. "Come on, Dottie."

Dottie floated along beside me, cheerfully excited as she settled into the truck's cab next to me. This was easy to see, because she would occasionally wink out, then wink back in a minute later. She never noticed.

Three

"You'll be chatting with Father O'Mare," she was saying as we neared the church. "He's on duty every night."

I glanced at her. "He's your priest, right?"

Dottie beamed at me, pleased. "You *have* been paying attention, then! Yes, he gave the sermon at my funeral." She sighed. "He was much younger then, and quite handsome."

I shuddered. It's a little unnerving to hear Dottie refer to her funeral in the same way some people casually refer to their birthdays. The old church loomed suddenly out of the shadows to our left and a minute later, I found a deep enough shoulder to pull over. Cranking the steering wheel around, I made a u-turn and drove back towards the church, parking the truck just north of the old churchyard's stone wall. Tucking the truck keys in my pocket, I climbed over and made my way to the back door. Despite being a few miles outside of town and, therefore, not in a high traffic area, I wanted to avoid being visible from the road.

The church welcome sign's overhead light flickered as I approached and I paused to read the announcement posted. With the building's closure as of a month ago, the services would now be taking place in a new location in Wickerman Falls.

"I'll be right back." Dottie went right through the door. From inside, I heard her muffled voice call out, "Father O'Mare?"

She popped right back out a minute later. With her was an old man wearing a priest's collar and cross. This was the first time I'd seen the late priest up close. His hair was iron gray and receding a bit; he looked to be about ninety or so, his face was lined and bore the serious expression I'd come to expect from the clergy.

"Father O'Mare?" I asked.

He nodded, eyeing me with mild curiosity. "You are going to rid my church of vermin?"

"Well, I hope to." I hesitated, gestured to the door knob. "May I come inside and take a look around?"

He sniffed, disapproving. "With your grievances hanging on you, are you sure you'll be able to help?"

Stung, I retorted, "Well, if you want, I can just leave and let the vandals tear this church apart, board by board. Makes no difference to me."

He glowered at me, then nodded and slipped his hand inside the door knob. After a long minute, and, with some relief, I heard the tumblers roll over. The back door popped open a few inches, causing me to take a step back. Father O'Mare sighed. "I don't much enjoy expending my energy in this way." He glanced at me, made a gesture indicating that he was resigned. "I shall leave you to it." He vanished.

Dottie slipped through ahead of me. Pushing the door open wider, I followed. The back entry opened onto the church kitchen. Switching on the overhead light, I walked through to the main hall. Once I was in the nave, where the services were held, I made my way to the head of the pews, stopping abruptly when I saw the damage done to the pulpit.

The pulpit had been destroyed. Its wooden frame was

40

blackened, as if scorched by fire. The metal brackets, which held the cross and framed the podium, had been deformed and twisted out of shape. The cross itself was now a short stub of broken wood, the remaining piece charred, as if from a barbeque pit. I'd only seen things like this in one of Louise's books, recording an incident involving vampires in the late nineteenth century.

What I looked at now resembled the images in the book.

And whatever had touched the pulpit was clearly not of the holy spirit.

I circled the pulpit cautiously. "This happened two nights ago, Dottie?"

She nodded. "Yes. Why? What's wrong?"

Even from where I stood, I could catch a whiff of the sour scent of sulphur, a calling card of vampire presence. I studied the pulpit again, wondering again how the vampires even got in to do this kind of damage. They'd need a charm of some kind, to walk on hallowed ground, like my New Orleans vamp. He'd indicated there were more than one vampire, but how many? More important, where were they hiding? Even with the office, a small kitchen and main entrance, the church didn't seem to have that many places to hide one vampire, let alone a nest. Once I was done here, I'd check the outside area, but it seemed unlikely that there was any place in the building or on the property for them to hide out.

More to the point, if they had been able to access the church by way of charm, who made it for them?

From his place at the door, Father O'Mare observed me as I studied the pulpit.

"Is there a basement or coal cellar or something?" I asked him.

He considered me a moment. "There's a woodshed just outside the kitchen door, where the groundskeeper put the firewood. Is that what you mean?"

I nodded. "I want to check it out before I head back

to the cemetery."

While the damage had the definite mark of a vampire, it didn't answer the question of why it happened. Or who the vampires were working for. Or what either party was searching for. I took another look around the altar, then checked the windows and doors, searching for clues as to how the vampires got in. I couldn't find any, none that were visible to my eyes, anyway.

I turned to Dottie. "I'm ready to head back to the cemetery." To Father O'Mare, I said, "I'm going to look at that woodshed. You may lock up behind me, if you wish."

Both the spectral priest and my spectral roommate vanished, reappearing only when I was standing outside on the back steps. Dottie headed for the cemetery truck. Father O'Mare waited for me at the bottom of the stairs, expectant. "I trust your inspection was helpful?"

I trotted down to meet him. "It was."

I followed him to the back of the church, where the woodshed was kept. It was small and above ground, more of a shed that had been built next to the church's kitchen door. Still, I inspected the tiny space closely, observing the firewood that had been stacked neatly on a stone floor that had no trap door. Given that, until recently, the space had been in constant use, it seemed unlikely that vampires would be using the shed as a hiding place, particularly since it had no crawlspace underneath it. Closing the shed's door, I walked across the lawn back to the truck, my steps silent in the damp lawn, my thoughts churning.

The late father fell in beside me, matching my pace, his presence colder than the night air itself. Frowning, I said, "Dottie told me that the vandalism happened sometime after midnight a couple of nights ago. Did you see them come into the church?"

He considered me for a minute. "They were simply not there, and then they were."

I understood. "How many of them were there?"

"Three. A male and two females." Father O'Mare

considered a moment, then added, "One of the females appeared to be in charge."

I glanced back at the door I'd just exited. No scorch marks, no obvious signs of a break in, nothing to indicate how they got inside the building. "How did they get in?"

He shrugged, a slight move of his thin shoulders. "That is beyond my powers to explain. That is for you to uncover, is it not?"

Indeed, it was.

My task now clear in the case of the vandalized pulpit, I thanked him for his time and patience, then climbed over the rock wall and headed for the old truck waiting for me.

Dottie was in the passenger seat as I climbed in on the driver's seat. "Did you know that there was an oak tree near the front gate of this church? A large branch cracked and fell during a storm when I was twelve." She sighed. "I did like climbing that tree, Cady. I could see out over the shore and watch the ships travel north."

As we drove back to the cemetery, a shadow flickered at the corner of my eye. Putting my foot on the brake, I slowed the truck and cast a quick look to the right, where the shadows pooled into something even darker. Lit only by the sliver of moon that hung in the sky, shadows made by the surrounding trees dominated the road we idled on, reaching out like gnarled old, hands. I waited a few minutes for the flicker to repeat itself and when it didn't, I released the clutch and continued on my way.

We got back to the Sandover Cemetery a few minutes later. Dottie vanished as I pulled into the truck's space and killed the engine. I hurried back to my shack, wanting to do some research before I went back to bed. Once inside, I grabbed my laptop and fired it up, hoping to connect to the wi-fi signal from the cemetery's office building. No time like the present to find out if it was strong enough to reach the shack.

"C'mon, c'mon," I muttered, impatient with the

agonizing slowness as the laptop booted up to the main screen, then clicked on an icon to search for the cemetery's server and connect to the internet. It seemed an age before I was able to log on, but when I finally did, any page I tried to find went into a state of either freezing or continually loading, with no actual results. Clearly, the signal did reach the shack, but was too weak to maintain a solid connection.

Frustrated, I shut the laptop off and went back to bed, turning off the light.

As my eyes adjusted to the darkness, I thought about how to get access to the internet. There would be computers at the local library, of course, and since I was now a local, I could sign up for a card and be able to utilize their services. I added that to my list of things to do, after my first day on the job at the cemetery.

Four

As described in the travel magazine, the Sandover Cemetery had been established in the spring of 1863. It's located twenty minutes north-west of Sleepy Eye Cove, California, and has spectacular views of the ocean and several old redwoods.

What I had been hired to do is grunt work, which basically translated to repair and maintain anything that looks like it's about to fall over. Today, my boss, Wesley Burke, was taking me on the rounds, showing me what areas he would need my help in making repairs. There were some water pipes and a couple of spigots on the north-west side of the cemetery that were in need of replacing, so that's where we were headed.

Wes had shut off the water main located behind the main building before we met up. Then we marked off the areas that needed to be dug out in order to do the repairs. The spigots had started to calcify and rust through, which suggested that the pipes buried underground might also be in need of replacement. The local plumber, Archie Fisher of Fisher Cut Bait Plumbing, was waiting for us to arrive and took the lead. Wes and I acted as his helpers and for the rest of the morning, I succeeded in getting myself very dirty and sweaty, with soggy shoes.

Around four, as we trudged back to the main office, I told Wes I needed to take the truck for an errand.

"That's fine," he said. "While you're out, make sure the tank's full, will you? One of the part-timers took it out last week and neglected to re-fuel."

Which meant Wes had been stuck with an empty tank. "Sure thing."

He paused, added, "Also, if you can, stop by Wen-Some Plants and have Abby put in an order for some new rose trees. I'll have the list at the office for you."

I tried to remember where I'd seen that nursery and recalled that it had been on the way into Sleepy Eye Cove. Nodding, I said, "I can do that, too. Who's Abby?"

"She's the owner and helps keep the cemetery in bloom." Wes turned towards the office building. "Come on in, the list is on my desk."

I started to follow, then glanced down at myself. "I'm gonna need a shower first. Meet you at the office in twenty?"

He nodded, trotting up to the office building, and I cut across the lawns to my little shack for a quick (and freezing) shower. After pulling on a fresh shirt and jeans, I found my keys, stopped by the office for the list and headed for the truck. Soon, I was driving out of the cemetery towards town, stopping long enough at the tiny library to see that they had already closed for the day and would be open the next morning at eleven.

Back in the truck, I made a left and found myself on Route 5 towards Wickerman Falls. Even if Wes hadn't asked, I wanted to stop by the nursery. Louise had been teaching me about charms when I'd left New Orleans and the one I was working on right now needed a couple of items I couldn't find in the forest surrounding the cemetery.

It was about a twenty minute drive from Sleepy Eye Cove to the nursery on Route 5, redwoods lining the road on either side. A popular song came on over the radio and I hummed along, enjoying the late afternoon sun as it played with the shadows across the pavement.

The pulse of a strobing red light in the rearview mirror practically sent my heart through the cab roof and my mind froze. The rush of panic-induced adrenalin surged through me, my muscles tensing in response. Breathing deep, I slowly guided the truck to the side of the road, putting it in park, cutting the engine. Then I waited. I hadn't had so much as a jaywalking ticket since I was a teenager. My hands shaking, I rolled down the window.

An officer got out of the police car parked behind me. As he walked towards my window, I wracked my brain, trying to figure out what I had done to get pulled over. I'd been driving just at the speed limit, had obeyed all the traffic signs while in the city limits, and always came to a complete stop when at a stop sign.

I didn't think I broke any laws, but there was always that one.....

The name tag on his uniform read *E. Jimenez*. I stared at it, trying to ground myself, trying to conjure up a smile that hid my unease.

"Can I help you, Officer?" I asked, the high, cheerful note in my voice sounding false, even to me.

"Your right tail light isn't working," he said, removing his sunglasses. I noticed that he had light brown hair and grey eyes. It was just enough information for me to know that Dottie would have been sighing over him if she had known he existed. "You need to get that fixed soon or I'll have to ticket you."

My heart stopped slamming against my ribs at his words and I relaxed. "Sure, I'll let Wes know when I get back to the cemetery. Thanks."

He smiled absently as he scribbled something down on one of his tickets. Tearing it out of the book, he handed it to me. "You're new in town, aren't you?"

I nodded. "Just came in over the weekend."

He put on his sunglasses. "Thought that was you at Madame Sofia's coffee shop. Next time, it's my treat."

"Your treat for what?" I asked, mystified. "Coffee?"

His smile only deepened as he turned and walked away. The strobing light stopped and then he was turning the car around and driving back to Sleepy Eye Cove. It was a few minutes before my hands stopped shaking. Then I looked at what the ticket said. He had written his full name (Efrain Jimenez) and phone numbers down – all three. Home, work and cell.

Crap. He wanted me to call him. I shoved the ticket into a pocket, not sure what to think about his gesture. I drove on, inhaling the scent of pine, trying to relax. The nursery wasn't too far away now – I recognized the turn-out on my left. Nestled deep in a thicket of trees and backing into part of the forest that surrounded the area, the shop looked like something out of an old fairy tale, with wisteria climbing the porch pillars and spanning the roof.

Approaching the nursery's entrance, I studied the sign carefully, charmed by the name – Wen-Some Plants & Nursery. It lent a sense of fun and playfulness on behalf of the owner. Below the nursery's name was a Chinese symbol. If it meant what I thought it did, then the owner was a practicing witch. Below that was a name, written both in Mandarin Hanzi and English – Wen Guan Yin. It was very likely that what I needed would be here. Besides, whether or not my reading of that symbol on the sign was correct, I could at least hope to encounter some help regarding the herbs for my charm.

I parked the truck at the far end of the graveled lot, got out and pocketed my keys. Slamming the door shut behind me, I headed towards the porch steps. There was only one other car in the lot – a dark blue BMW with out of state plates and a rental sticker in the window.

Pushing the door open, I walked in, the bell above me jingling at the movement.

A young woman stood at the register, writing something on a note-pad. "Will that be all, Ms. Naughton?"

The customer nodded, her short reddish-blonde hair glinting in the light. "For now, yes. And if Abby could call me regarding that order of lavender….?"

"Sure." The young woman wrote that down, then glanced over at me. "Hi, I'll be with you in a minute."

The customer turned and gazed at me, curious.

"I'm here to see an Abby…?" I asked the clerk, giving the woman a brief nod.

The clerk brightened. "Oh, you must be from the cemetery." She pointed to a door just past the terra cotta flower pots. "Abby's out back, playing in the nursery or something."

She grinned and turned back to the note-pad. The woman gave me a curious look, as if trying to place where she'd seen me before. That look was just a little too long to be comfortable and I stared back at her until she looked away, her cheeks reddening a little.

I made a mental note of her appearance, then made my way through the shop to the pots and opened the back door. I could still feel her gaze on me and wondered briefly who she was. Then I was outside, in the magic of what was the shop's nursery. Stretching as far back as I could see, it appeared to go right up to the forest. To my right were rose trees and a variety of flowering plants, potted and ready to go. To my left were sapling trees, some in huge, slatted pots, probably placed there so that it would be easier to take out to the loading dock.

There was a small *chink*! of metal into dirt. I started forward, then paused, trying to pinpoint the sound. Upon hearing the noise once more, I followed it through a maze of plants and planters, coming to a halt when I found myself in the north-west part of what I'd been thinking of as the garden.

A Chinese woman about my age was busily churning

49

up the earth, singing in Mandarin under her breath as bits of dirt flew. My shoes crunched on the gravel as I walked towards her, inhaling the scent of jasmine. She didn't look up, just waved a dirt-stained hand in my direction. "Have a seat where you can find one and state your case. I can multi-task."

On the ground by her knees was a pair of gloves, clean and untouched.

Sitting on a nearby stump, I gestured to the gloves. "Won't you get your hands dirty?"

She glanced back at me, dark brown eyes laughing. "I like how alive the earth feels in my hands. Wearing gloves disconnects me." She started to hold out a hand, then hesitated on seeing the dirt covering it, and waved, instead. "I'm Abigail Wen. You can call me Abby."

I made a quick decision. "I'm Katie Gray."

"A pleasure," she said. "I'd shake hands, but my hands are dirty."

"No worries," I said. "That Chinese symbol on your shop sign, sorry, I'm gonna mangle it, my Mandarin is nonexistent." I pronounced it as carefully as I could, making a vague gesture towards the store. "Does it mean what I think it does?"

She sat back on her heels, eyes even merrier. "You pronounced that very well."

"Thanks, I had a very thorough teacher."

She studied me, curious. "What do you think it means?"

"That you're a witch. That you practice magic."

She laughed. "And you would be correct. Seventh generation on my mother's side."

"Who's Wen Guan Yin? Your grandmother?"

Abby shook her head, her mouth tightening into a thin line briefly when she answered, an edge in her voice, "That's my proper name, but only my grandmother calls me that when I go home. I prefer Abigail, though." Brushing off dirt from her hands, her tone light, she asked,

"What can I help you with?"

I held out Wes's list. "The cemetery has a need for rose bushes."

She took the list between forefinger and thumb, being careful to get as little dirt on it as possible, then handed it back to me. "I know the roses he's referring to. I'll call the cemetery when they're ready for pick up." She studied me closely. "And you? What are you here for?"

"I'm working on a charm," I said, and then listed a few of the items I needed. As I did so, she led me back the way I came, pausing every now and again to pick an herb or a flower and hand it over to me. By the time we got back to the shop's rear door, my hands were full. I stared at the bundle I held, astounded. "I think you gave me way more than I actually need."

Abby held out a paper sack and, with care, I put my bundle in it. "You'll need more than you think you do. That's been my experience."

I fumbled for my wallet. "How much do I owe you?"

She held up a hand. "This witch never charges another witch for herbs and other small items on their first visit to my nursery." Her eyes twinkled again as she pulled a small paper sack from a bucket by her sneakered foot. Holding it open, she grinned and added, "Owner's discretion, of course."

"Thank you," I said, feeling that the simple words were inadequate. Carefully, I placed the items she'd picked into the sack, then took it, liking the way the brown paper sounded as it crinkled in my grasp.

Her grin widened. "What are friends for?"

I had no ready answer for that, so I said nothing. Most of my friends growing up had been of the spectral sort, so I didn't have many among the living. In the few days since I moved to Sleepy Eye Cove, it seemed there were signs that it was changing.

She wiped away sweat from her forehead, leaving a streak of dirt. "So, what else is up?"

I took a breath and decided to trust her. "Do you know anything about the Sleepy Eye Cove church? The one on the north side of town?"

She considered the question for a minute, her brow crinkling in thought, then shook her head, apologetic. "Not really, no. I'm just a transplant, like you."

My jaw dropped a little, then I stammered, "I'm not a transplant, I'm a temporary. And how did you know?"

She laughed. "I saw you get off the bus by Madame Sofia's Brew." Apparently, the coffee shop was the place to be to know everything. "Besides, I only moved here five years ago, from San Francisco, so I don't know much about this town." She eyed me, curious. "What's going on, if you don't mind my asking?"

"Vampires," I blurted out. Abby gripped my arm so hard that I gasped. "Ouch!"

"Sorry," Abby said, not sounding apologetic at all, but she let go of my arm. "What about vampires? And what does it have to do with the church? You know that they stopped using it a month ago."

Rubbing my arm, I nodded and said, "I'm wondering if there had ever been any reports of vampires hanging around the area." I hesitated, then told her about my late-night visit to the church to investigate the vandalism that had the spectral Father O'Mare concerned. I did not mention his comments about my grievances. "About what they have to do with the church or how they might have gotten in, I'm not sure yet."

Abby frowned, muttering an oath. "I haven't heard anything about vampires in the area and my coven's pretty sharp on that." She looked at me, troubled. "Which means there's a ward shielding them."

That wasn't the only thing the vampires had going for them. "Then they're getting help."

Abby nodded. "That's what it sounds like."

"But from whom?"

Abby shrugged, studying the flower bed. "Anyone

who knew they existed and willing to deal with the trouble the undead bring to the table. Not easy to narrow that list down." She glanced over at me, dirt smudging her nose. "Dottie's been encouraging you to get involved to find out, hasn't she?"

I stared, unable to hide my surprise. "How'd you know about Dottie?"

Abby laughed. "I was riding my bike out past the cemetery my first week here." My new-found friend regarded me, amused. "She's a sweet girl, but boy, am I glad she's your roommate and not mine." Her expression turned serious as she considered my question about the vampires. "I suppose that's why you're interested in the church's history."

I nodded. "They're looking for something and I'm not entirely sure it has to do with the church itself."

Abby was silent for a moment, mulling over her thoughts. "Have you got a plan?"

"I've got some ideas," I said, thoughtful, "but nothing concrete. I need to do some research before I put anything in motion."

She gave me a look. "And will you be casting for some of your answers? Or are you going to be stubborn about it and pretend you don't know what I'm talking about?"

I gave up. "Are all witches and hoodoo priestesses gifted with Sight? Or is it just my luck that I've run into two?"

Abby quirked a brow at me. "Just your luck?"

I ignored that. "I'm gonna look up the cemetery records later, see if there are any locals that might help."

Abby frowned. "How many spirits are there that might help?"

I thought. "I just met the Sandovers, but they're caught up in marital issues. Dottie's still stuck at the movies. I spoke to Father O'Mare, but other than allowing me access to the church after hours, I didn't get much from him." I paused, thoughtful. "I got the feeling he wasn't being entirely forthcoming with me, though."

She shrugged. "I wouldn't know, I've not yet met him."

"The library in town was closed," I said, thoughtful. "Do you know how late the library in Wickerman Falls stays open?"

"The public one closes at 6, so your best bet is to go to the college," she said, after a minute's thought. "That library stays open until nine or ten. You're not a student, so you won't be able to check anything out, but you'll still be able to use their system."

Pulling out my cellphone, I checked the time. Quarter past five. Wickerman Falls was another forty minutes up the road. Depending on how fast I was able to get there, find parking and whatever information about the area, I'd be back in my humble shack by ten at the latest. The entire trip was hinging on a lot of 'ifs', I realized. For a more efficient use of my time, it was probably better to wait until my day off, which was most likely the coming Saturday.

In the meantime, I could utilize my connections with the cemetery's residents. Decision made, I started to leave, then paused, turning back. "Your clerk was helping a woman in the shop when I came in. Naughton, I think her name is, and she gave me a once over that wasn't exactly casual for my comfort." I described the woman to Abby as she continued to work the earth.

Abby frowned. "Yeah, that's Claire Naughton. Don't know if you saw it parked out front, but she's been driving a rental for the last couple of weeks."

"Why? What happened to her car?"

Abby waved at a fly buzzing close to her face, uttering a small oath in Mandarin. "These flies are going to be a menace this summer." She shook her head. "Oh, man, there's been some problems in that family."

My adoptive parents came to mind and I became

aware of the tension in my stomach as I recalled the lies they'd told that had come to light only with their deaths. I took a deep breath, exhaled sharply. "That's nothing new, Abby. All families have issues."

She raised a brow. "Not all of them have magic to back up their fights. Her parents died almost thirty years ago and no one's been able to figure out who did it. The official story is they happened on a break-in, but rumor has it that magic was involved."

Something else to look into when I got to the Wycliff library. "So, I'm guessing Claire Naughton was the target of vandalism or something?"

Abby frowned, thinking. "That, I'm not so sure. But her car did go into a ditch. According to coven gossip, a brake line was cut, but that's as far as I know."

That was serious. "Any idea of what the family fight was about?"

She shook her head. "No, just the usual sibling jealousies, I'd expect." She sighed. "My shop's too small scale for most of the magical community in the county, but Claire Naughton sometimes comes in for a few specialized items that I carry." She grimaced. "I'm planning to expand that side of my business, within the next year, but for the moment, I'm just a nursery with a sideline in magical herbology."

Confused, I glanced around her nursery. "How are you too small scale? The place seems huge to me."

Abby snorted. "Not that kind of small scale." She stood, wiping the dirt first from her hands and then her jeans.

I fell into step beside her as we started to make our way back into the shop. "By the way, do you know Efrain Jimenez?"

She fanned herself, executing a mock swoon. "Of course. Chief of police in Sleepy Eye Cove, erstwhile do-gooder. Also, very handsome and extremely eligible. Why?"

I pulled the ticket with Jimenez had given me out of my back pocket. His numbers, though a little smudged, were still legible. I handed the paper to her. "I think you might be interested in this, then."

Frowning, Abby took it, then looked at me. "Efrain Jimenez gave you his phone numbers and you're giving them to me?"

I nodded. "What am I going to do with them? I don't even know him."

"Well, calling him would be a good start," she said, then sighed, tucking the ticket into her back pocket. I didn't see the point in telling her that he had offered to buy me coffee. "I can't believe you're passing him up."

I didn't have anything to offer except, "I don't want him."

She snorted, disbelieving. "Why not? He's cute, he's smart and he obviously likes you."

"We don't have anything in common."

Abby rolled her eyes, exasperated. "How would you even know? You didn't spend more than five minutes talking to him." We stepped inside the shop. Her clerk was standing over an open box next to the cash register, busy pricing items and then restocking the shelves.

"I'm still not interested," I said, firmly. She sniffed.

"Paige, this is Katie Gray," Abby announced as we approached. "She's working over at the cemetery now, so she'll be doing a lot of pick-up orders." To me, she said, "That's my clerk and part-time apprentice to my craft, Paige Somers."

"Hi, Katie," Paige said, cheerful. "Welcome to Sleepy Eye Cove and Wen-Some Nursery."

"Good luck with your research," Abby said. "And let me know how your charm works out."

"I will," I promised.

Then Abby went to her office, Paige went back to re-stocking and I took my leave, climbing into the cemetery truck and putting it into gear. At the end of the shop's drive, I paused, watching for traffic and an inner city bus cruised by, heading towards Wickerman Falls.

I turned right and back to Sleepy Eye Cove, already working out a plan to carry out when I had the time to go to Wickerman Falls.

Five

As I half-expected, Wes gave me Friday afternoon off.

At noon, showered and in clean clothes, I drove the cemetery truck into Wickerman Falls, going past the town square towards the college. Once on campus, I stopped long enough at the security booth to get a day pass, found a parking spot between the bookstore and food court and slapped the pass onto the truck's dash. Grabbing up my pack and swinging it over my shoulder, I got out and locked up behind me.

I started walking, keeping my eyes open for a kiosk that had a campus map. I found one next to the campus bookstore, where I picked up a fresh notebook and a couple of pens. There was also a small electronics section, with newer laptops, flash drives and other useful items. Among these were wireless hotspots and I added one to my shopping basket.

Upon leaving the campus bookstore, I stopped at the kiosk and scanned the quad, using one hand to shade my eyes from the sun as I tried to orient myself in relation to the library. Using a finger, I traced a path on the Plexiglas from where I stood to the library, then turned my gaze to the surrounding area, frowning. The library was on the other side of the campus, but there was no direct pathway. I'd get lost without a map and, remembering that there was one in the list of classes, I turned to go back into the bookshop and walked into a solid mass of muscle.

"Sorry, excuse me," I stammered, then looked up into familiar dark blue eyes. Realizing who it was, I blinked, my face warm. "Aren't you a little far from your office?"

Raul Kendrick smiled down at me, dark blue eyes wrinkling with humor. He was wearing track shorts and a T-shirt emblazoned with a superhero logo of some kind – lots of red and white, but I couldn't immediately place it. "I teach a couple of classes on Friday afternoons, unless I'm in court." He glanced down at his attire, a half-grin softening his features. I was acutely aware of the scent of his sweat – warm, musky, and with that hint of spice. "And sometimes I make use of the gym." He paused, glanced at the notebook in my hand and gestured to the bookstore. "Thinking of attending?"

"Maybe," I said, figuring that was answer enough. "Thought I'd at least check the place out, so here I am." I faced the campus again. "Can you help me find the library?"

"Even better," he said, cheerful. "It's on my way to my campus office."

We crossed the well-kept lawns, falling silent soon after the exchange. My steps were muted and I automatically began noticing the patterns made by the mowers. It was almost one-thirty in the afternoon, so the campus was relatively quiet. It was as though we had the campus to ourselves, almost as if the place was deserted. The impression wouldn't last, I suspected, when classes let out and the student body swarmed the area in droves, either to get to the next lecture, the food court or head home.

As we walked, I made a note of specific landmarks, like the statue of a little girl reading to a small dog, so as to find my way back to the truck. The statue seemed incongruous to the campus and I eyed it, curious, as we walked past it.

Raul noticed. "There's a story attached to that statue. Rather sad."

I shook my head. "Sorry, I wouldn't know it. New to town and all."

His eyes twinkling, he said, "Then perhaps one day, I take you to coffee and give you my version of an historical tour."

My face warmed and I met his gaze, shy. "Why not start with the statue?"

He obliged by sharing the story. The statue was of Eleanor Wycliff, daughter of Milton and Samantha Wycliff, founders of the college. During the library's original construction, young Eleanor had somehow gotten trapped in the tower and fell to her death. After the library's completion in the spring of 1894, Samantha Wycliff, having never fully recovered, climbed the building's tallest spire and followed her daughter's path. Access to the spires, my companion finished, were then sealed shortly after.

"Wow," was all I could think to say in response.

The twinkle in his eyes deepened with merriment. "Rumor has it that Samantha Wycliff haunts the library, so beware."

Since running into her ghost was the least of my worries, I only grinned. "I'll be careful if I see her, thanks."

We paused at a concrete path that split in two directions. He gestured to the one going to the south end of campus. "My office is down this way, so this is as far as I go. Keep to the right and the library will find you."

I laughed. "You make it sound sentient."

He only smiled, the lines around his eyes softening. "Buildings can have long memories to share, if only you know how to listen to them." I looked at him, curious. Raul Kendrick sounded as though he'd had some experience with the specters haunting the library. It wasn't clear to me, yet, whether or not his encounters were pleasant. He turned and started to walk away, tossing over his shoulder, "Good luck on finding what you're looking for."

"Thanks." I watched him go, admiring his almost regal bearing as he left, the way his shorts hugged his hips as he walked. Then he rounded a corner, disappearing from view, and my reasons for being on campus came back to me. Shaking my head, I hurried along the path that Raul had shown me and soon found myself trotting along the pebbled path towards the college library.

The campus grounds sloped and curved, the earth dictating to the contractors of the past how structures were to be built. Downhill from me was the library, a Gothic-inspired building with six spires reaching up to claw at the sky, an ominous presence looming over the quad, separate from the other buildings and mature trees. A flutter of shadow danced at the bottom of the primary spire, then seemed to leap from the roof, catching my eye. I paused and stared up at the spire and roof, waiting for the flutter to repeat itself. It didn't, so after a minute, I began moving again.

As I drew closer, I saw that the weathered-gray brick façade was covered by ivy, but not over-grown with it, adding to its ominous appearance. I wondered what it felt like on days that were overcast and cold, maybe even rainy. Staring up at it, I was unnerved by the dark windows that seemed to absorb the sunlight and stare back at me.

Taking a deep breath, I headed for the main entrance, climbing the concrete slab steps. I hesitated briefly when I reached the doors, my heart pounding. I reminded myself fiercely that it was just a library, a place of books. Nothing more, nothing less. Chanting this under my breath, I pulled open the library door and stepped inside.

I saw students sitting around tables, or using the small computer stations. There was a coffee shop off the main lobby to my right and it was buzzing with activity as students bought snacks, drinks and chatted amongst themselves. Not something that I'd have expected to find in a library, but it made sense, especially for the long study sessions some courses seemed to require.

Six

What I needed was the archives, old newspapers that had any reports involving vandalism at the old church in Sleepy Eye Cove. Walking further into the main wing of the library, I discovered the front desk and two librarians. Both men were in uniform gray sweaters, helping one student at a time. There was a line of another ten students waiting patiently.

I took my place line, troubled by my spell's failure to locate the vampires that were clearly in the area. Its failure suggested that stronger magic was at work and, as much as I wished otherwise, it didn't seem likely that I'd be able to avoid another encounter with vampires. Obviously, given the vandalism, either my intent was not clear enough or the vampires had been well obscured or both. I wondered if a certain member of the Naughton coven had anything to with it.

Mentally, I went over the steps Louise Tremont had taught me, forcing me to memorize them without writing it out. As I thought, I hadn't missed any. By the time I'd cross-checked myself a fourth time, the student ahead of me moved to the left, talking to an older woman with glasses behind the desk. Then the girl to my right thanked the male librarian for helping her, took her slips of paper and disappeared into the labyrinth of books behind glass doors.

"Hi, I'm Keith," he said, gesturing for me to step closer. The overhead light glinted off his prematurely silver-gray hair. "How may I help you?"

I blinked. "Me? Oh, yes." I stepped up to the desk. "I'm looking for back issues of the local newspapers."

"Are you a student?"

I shook my head, smiling. "Thinking about it. I don't want to check anything out, just look at the archives."

"How far back did you want to go?" he asked, scribbling notes on paper with a pencil.

"About 1924 to 1926," I said, after a brief thought.

He handed me the slip of paper. "Take this to Grace Whalen. She's in charge of the archives downstairs. She'll set you up with what you need."

Thanking him, I made my way downstairs, where I immediately came upon a desk helmed by a dark-skinned woman who was illuminated by the computer's monitor. To go by the name plate on the edge of the desk, this was the Grace Whalen I was looking for. She had on wire-framed glasses and was reading a magazine, an unlit cigarette clamped firmly in the left corner of her mouth. An insulated travel mug sat next to the computer key board.

I ignored the female ghost standing to her right, her haunted eyes wet with grief.

I stopped at the desk, cleared my throat. "Are you Grace Whalen?"

She didn't look up. "I am. How can I help you?"

I stepped closer, handing over the slip Jim from upstairs had given me. "I need to look through the newspaper archives. I was directed down here."

Standing, Grace Whalen took the slip I held out to her, barely glancing at it. "The machines are in the back. I'll get the reels. Follow me."

Obeying, I skirted around the desk and hurried to keep up, trying not to let my eyes be drawn like magnets to the ghostly woman in the corner. Grace opened the door to a small room, pausing to wait for me, and soon had me in sitting in front of a computer that shared space with another type of machine, its large screen dark, its engine cold. This was the microfiche machine and, within minutes, she had it running, instructing me on how to use it.

"Some of the news archives are still on microfiche," she explained, powering on the computer next to the microfiche as well. "Most of what you'll find will be here, in the database, but it goes back only to the thirties. You requested earlier than that, however." She glanced over at me, curious. "Working on a paper of local history?"

"Something like that," I said, half-expecting a barrage of questions.

She offered none, just a few more instructions on how to handle the machines, and then left me with boxes of newspapers on reels, assuming that I was just another student on campus. This, in its own way, lent me a kind of anonymity. Then I turned to the boxes of reels, wanting to find out what had really happened to that church in 1925. Each reel held about four weeks' worth of Wickerman Falls Tribune. I needed to be thorough – things started happening before the vandalism in 1925 and the fire in 1926. There were thirty-six reels to sort through.

I threaded the first reel of 1924 in the machine, aware of the low hum it made as I cranked it forward until the first images appeared on the huge screen in front of me. Not a lot seemed to be going on, just births, life, marriages and death.

There was a brief notice about an attack that fall, a man named Marcus Pellington had been walking in the early morning when he was assaulted. A retired Navy captain, he had chosen to retire in the area after his stint in World War One. He had been taken to the doctor by a local man who had not been identified. Finishing up 1924, I reached for the first reel of 1925. Pretty much the same small town drama, just a different year. I sped through the reels without finding anything interesting.

It wasn't until I got into July that the church was mentioned for the first time.

If the July 7, 1925 issue was anything to go by, the most recent break-in and vandalism wasn't the first time it had happened. And I was beginning to suspect that the vampires were a tad bit more native to the area than I'd originally thought. Or one of them, anyway. I wrote down the pertinent information – dates, times, names of people involved – then fed a couple of quarters into the printer and made copies of the pages.

The pastor of the church was none other than Father O'Mare – he had been a young man at the time and actually looked more comfortable smiling than he did now. According to the article, he had reported vandalism in the church two days before the fire burned it down. I found the reel for that report and searched, a little more alert. There it was – he had filed a report about the pulpit being vandalized, that the cross that stood on it had been damaged.

I sat back, chewing on my lower lip, thinking. Fire had power – one only had to look at the forest fires that had devastated California over the last year alone. It's an element that consumed whatever lay in its path, taking on a life of its own until there was nothing left for it to burn or the firefighters had put it out. That we believe we can control it is an illusion at best and probably why it has often been regarded with as much awe as fear since man first discovered it.

Sinking deeper into my chair, I re-read the article about the church fire.

Awe and fear – that was the compulsion that drove Father O'Mare to burn his church to the ground. Awe for the power fire wielded and fear of what had soured the church he tended. Then it clicked – fire purified that which had been tainted by evil. With the original structure gone, it could be rebuilt fresh with no attachment to the past. I suspected that Father O'Mare had placed a special emphasis on blessing the ground before construction could begin.

Sitting in the basement of the Wycliff College library, I stared for a long time at the computer screen, the image of the church's skeletal remains post-fire etched into my mind. It had been a big fire, big enough to scorch a few of the trees that had surrounded it ninety years ago and have since been felled. The gazebo had not yet been built, but I could see the area where it would eventually go – a weeping willow tree stood in the gazebo's future spot. It had been badly damaged by the fire, to go by the picture, and I suspected that it didn't take long for the church leaders to have it removed.

The destroyed church dominated the poorly reproduced picture and I stared at it for a long time, my thoughts circling. Had Father O'Mare also been trying to purify his church from vampires during that long ago summer of 1925?

Seven

I went through the rest of the reels and the only other thing I learned was that the investigation had been left open and that any clues to the perpetrators were being followed up. The only other reference was on the rebuilding of the church and the dedication that would follow.

Glancing up at the clock on the wall above the backroom door, I saw that it was almost half past four. I'd been in the basement for almost two hours. I put the last reel of microfiche in its box, gathered up the others and left them on the counter for Grace Whalen to put away.

Then I asked for the reel for March the year I was born. The birth certificate in my pack said I had been born here that month, in Maurier County. If that was so, then there had to be some sort of announcement in the local papers. Spooling the reels in, I whipped through March, slowing down only when I got to my birthday, March 17. I knew nothing would be posted in that day's issue, but I wanted to know what the news had been, the day of my birth.

The usual national and local news, snippets of the international scene, sports scores, local politics, a St.

Patrick's Day party gone awry in – surprise – the local Irish pub, aptly named the Auld O'Malley's. I scrolled on, keeping a sharp eye out for birth announcements. There had been five babies, all girls, born on or around the 17th, but no listing for Galloway.

I came to the end of March, puzzled. That couldn't be right. Either the newspaper was wrong or my birth certificate was a fake. Now I was more curious than ever to get my hands on a new copy of my birth certificate. I wrote down the names listed in the announcements for reference, including one for Baby Girl Welles and her parents, Bennett and Callie Welles.

I studied the list of names, thoughtful. Glancing around to make sure the archive librarian wasn't around, I scooted closer to the computer she'd switched on for me. The server was already connected and, in a few seconds, I was online and pulling up the site for the *Wickerman Falls Daily*, searching each set of names. When I came to the Welles couple, I stopped, goosebumps rippling up my arms. According to the lead story, the couple had been found dead in the living room of their home. No murder weapon had been found and any description of how they were killed was kept vague. The only witnesses had been the babysitter, who had been tied up and shoved, unconscious, into the hall closet, and their third daughter, six year old Cecelia Naughton, who was found sleeping soundly in her own bed upstairs.

The other stories I clicked open told a variation of the same report and the more recent articles left me with the impression that the case itself was still unsolved. After several more minutes of searching with no further development, I accessed my email.

I have very few contacts in this world, so after deleting a number of spam emails, I found the one I was looking for. Clicking on the email with the subject *Birth Certificate Request*, I scrolled through the generic message, noting the name – *Patty Rhodes* – that was signed at the bottom. A jpeg file had been attached and I clicked on that as well, reading the print carefully on the image that opened. Frowning, I pulled out my copy from my pack and held it up to compare with what I was reading.

"That can't be right," I said aloud, trying to quell the growing sense of unease in my heart, then glanced around quickly, hoping I hadn't attracted any attention. Now I knew why I couldn't find my birth announcement – I'd been looking under the wrong name. If this birth certificate I'd just clicked on was accurate. The only way to find that out was to go to the courthouse and find this Patty Rhodes. Maybe she could help make sense of what I was looking at. Printing out a copy of my digital birth certificate, I logged out of my email account, shut everything down and headed out.

The weeping ghost of Samantha Wycliff was no longer mourning in the basement when I finally left. Grace Whalen wasn't at her desk, either, so I went back upstairs.

I stopped at the main desk. Keith was still behind the front counter, sitting at a desk and typing. "Do you have a city map?"

"Sure, one minute." He pulled open a drawer and went through some folders, pulling out a couple of folded pamphlets. I took them and thanked him, quickly opening the city map and spreading it out on the counter. The college was marked clearly and then I noted Turner Street and the court house. There was no direct way to get there from the college.

I looked at Keith. "May I keep this?"

"Sure." He glanced at the clock. "The courthouse closes at five today, so take the number 6 bus. That will drop you off right in front and you'll still have maybe half an hour. If not, it opens again tomorrow morning for limited hours." He looked at me, curious. "I hope your business isn't urgent."

I wrote down the information quickly. "Thanks, but I have a truck. No, not urgent, but pretty necessary." My stomach gurgled. Keith looked at me sharply, startled and I grinned, a little sheepish. "Sorry. I forgot to eat lunch."

He grinned back. "Do you like Indian curry?"

"I've never had it before," I said, "but I'm game to try it."

He told me about a little place on Rose Street, maybe ten minutes away, and wrote out the directions as I shoved my notebook and papers into my pack. I thanked him and he handed me a sheet of paper with directions on them. I walked away from the desk, any questions I may have had silenced under the need to get something to eat.

Soon, I was outside and breathing the cool air as the afternoon sun began to settle low in the sky. I felt unsettled, on edge, as I walked back to my truck. There had to be something that I was missing, something that hadn't been odd enough to report, but strange enough that it had to be remembered by an old timer. Maybe one of my resident ghosts would know about it. It would be late when I got back, but they didn't keep living hours and most of them liked to talk. The best time was when the cemetery was closed to the public.

It was a twenty minute drive to the courthouse and I found a parking spot easily, locking up before heading across the lawn to the building. At the building's entrance, I found the directory and searched for the records office – downstairs. Before I could get to the stairwell, however, I had to go through security, where my pack was put in a bucket and went through an X-ray, while I had to step through a scanner. The guards manning the station seemed bored, handing my pack back to me with an amiable greeting as I went on my way.

Heading downstairs, I approached the clerk's office with some anxiety. Now that I had my birth certificate, I had more questions than answers. I wasn't sure what I'd expected, other than confirmation of my having been born in Maurier County. Having another name entirely had not even been on the radar. If I could resolve that, maybe I could live with the fact that the people I'd thought of as my parents had lied to me.

There was only one person at the desk – reading her name tag with relief, I found myself standing across the counter from Patty Rhodes. She was on the phone, handling the caller's questions and checking the computer while writing out notes to herself on a pad of paper. She saw me, held up a hand to ask for my patience and went back to the call.

"Sir, I don't give out that kind of information over the phone," she finally said, impatience creeping into her voice. "You need to come here, fill out a form and then you can get the answers you need." She listened. "Well, those are the rules, sir. And I live by those rules. I'm sorry you feel that way. Have a nice day." She hung up, turned to me. "How can I help you?"

I took a deep breath. "I requested a copy of my birth certificate by mail a couple of weeks ago and just got an email with it attached." I put the print-out on the counter, then put the altered one that I'd found in my parents' papers last year next to it. "I'm a little confused about this. I'd always been told that I was born in Essex County, Massachusetts, but this" – I tapped the one I'd kept hidden in my pack, – "says I was born here, in Maurier County. And this one" – I tapped the one I'd printed out at the college library, – "lists different parents and different names. Can you help explain this?"

She took both certificates, frowning as she compared them. "Well, this is all wrong."

I felt relieved. "Yeah, I thought so, too."

Patty Rhodes shook her head. "No, the county's correct. See these numbers here?" She turned the certificates around so that I could see. She pointed at the top left corner. "That's the code for Maurier County. So both of these are correct, that you were born here, because the county code and name are right. But look at what's wrong with the parent names." She tapped the certificate

I'd always believed was true. "See how the names are smudged? Someone typed over the original names."

It was what I'd expected, considering the newer certificate. "So, why would someone alter my parents' names?"

Patty Rhodes scowled at both of my birth certificates. "Good question. It's a crime to commit fraud with someone's birth certificate."

I froze. "You mean, neither of them might not even be mine?"

She looked at me kindly, patting my arm gently. I felt comforted, if not less confused by the turn of events. "Someone altered your birth certificate. The whys of the matter are beyond both of us, but this one, the one that you requested, that's the correct birth certificate." She frowned, her brow furrowing in a manner that reminded me of Louise Tremont. "I am going to have to file a report on that altered one, however. It's a felony to falsify legal documents."

I pointed at the names of the people I'd grown up believing were my parents. "If they hadn't died a year and a half ago in a car accident, I'd start with them."

Patty Rhodes took down names of the Galloways, eying me curiously. "Why them?"

"Because everything they'd told me is a lie." I thanked her and took both birth certificates, stuffing them into the hidden pocket of my back pack, blood pounding in my ears as I left the records office. The court house was beginning to shut down for the day as I trotted across the main landing and few people other than the security guards were milling around. I headed for the main entrance and was outside in seconds, sitting on a concrete bench overlooking the lawn and town square.

Feeling lightheaded, I put my pack on my lap and leaned over it, taking in deep, slow breaths, trying calm the swell of grief, rage, and confusion suddenly rising up in a wave. Louise had been right – the Galloways did have a reason to lie and it was most likely connected to the murder of Calliope and Bennett Welles. If I didn't find a way to forgive them, then my own emotions would drain me the same way a vampire drains its victims of blood. I needed help, and fast.

Digging my cellphone out, I found Raul's card and called his office. His answering machine picked up and I stammered out my message. "Um, hey, hi, I don't know where your campus office is, but I'm wondering if it's possible to schedule a meeting with you as soon as possible? I have a lot of questions. Call me when you can." I left my number and hung up, feeling shaken by what I'd learned.

Getting into the truck, I rested my forehead on the steering wheel, still shaking. Not only had I been lied to about the whereabouts of my birth, but about my birth parents, as well. It was a lot to take in and I hoped that Raul would call me back soon. I needed to talk to him about it and, if what'd I'd seen on his desk was correct, then he was also looking for the Galloways.

My stomach rumbled, reminding me that I was hungry, and I recalled the restaurant Keith the library clerk had recommended to me. Until Raul returned my call, I had to take a step back and get my head together to process what I'd learned. I wasn't a Galloway, as the couple I'd known as my parents had led me to believe. And their reasons had gone with them to the grave, secrets only they could answer for and that I would never be able to understand.

Pulling my pack onto my lap, I pulled out and unfolded the correct birth certificate I'd found in my email's inbox an hour ago and stared at the names of my real parents.

In black and white was my full name – Cadence Rose Welles Naughton, daughter of Calliope Naughton and Bennett Welles. And it abruptly occurred to me to wonder why, in all of the various news reports of my biological parents' deaths, there had been no mention of a fourth child, an infant, in that house.

Eight

It was half-past five when I pulled off of Rose Street and into the parking lot for the Curry Elephant Restaurant. The place was quiet, so I must have arrived before the dinner crowd. This filled me with relief and, after I parked, I remained in the truck for a few minutes, taking in deep breaths to compose myself. The information on my genuine birth certificate was overwhelming and how I ended up with the Galloways was just another knot in the mystery of my life. Finally, I got out of the truck and crossed the short distance to the entrance.

Inside, I heard music playing from hidden speakers – strings and wind instruments creating a haunting sound. I liked it and said as much to the waiter who approached me.

He beamed, pleased. "This way, please. Only one?"

I nodded and followed him to a small table by the window. Taking my seat and the menu handed to me, I glanced outside and saw that it looked out at the building next door. Built out of stone and framed by weathered timber, it housed a bookstore. At least, that was according to the sign hanging on the corner.

"Naughton's Books and Antiquities," I said under my

breath and shivered. I didn't believe in coincidence much and I studied that store sign with anticipation. Crossing paths with someone by the name of Naughton, finding my real birth certificate and then sitting at a restaurant directly across the street with the same name was significant.

It would be worthwhile to go over after dinner, perhaps browse around the stacks of books and see if there were answers to be found. Whether they were about the vampires or about my family, or both, was up to chance. Picking up my menu, I shook my head, amused. I had no business wanting books I couldn't afford to buy. But looking couldn't hurt and I did want to have a closer look at the woman I'd encountered earlier in the week.

I wasn't quite ready for officially meeting my relatives, though. Still, I had the advantage – I knew them, but they wouldn't know me. I toyed with that thought until the waiter appeared at my table, poised to take my drink order. Since I had already decided on what I wanted to eat, I ordered one of the milder curries with rice and vegetables, along with hot chai. It was a creamy, spicy tea and it went down my throat like warm silk.

I asked for another one about five minutes after my first cup was served.

While I waited for my dinner to arrive, I studied my notebook, curious about the Pellingtons and wondering what that connection was about. I scribbled down a note to look them up once I was back in Sleepy Eye Cove. I ignored my birth certificate for the moment – I wasn't quite ready to look at that again, at least for a while.

My dinner arrived faster than I'd expected and I picked up my fork. In no time at all, my plate was empty, traces of the curry the only evidence that there had been any food. I was going to have to try this again. Although I'd clearly liked it, I had been so caught up in my thoughts that I hadn't really tasted my food. I gathered up my pack, stuffed my notebook back inside and paid cash, leaving a generous tip behind.

Once outside, I hesitated, then crossed the street and walked up the steps to Naughton's Books and Antiquity Shop. The bell above the door rang sharply as I stepped inside. The scent of books enveloped me in a warm embrace and I inhaled deeply, my eyes drifting closed. When I opened them again, I took in the soft lighting from the electric candelabras – they flickered in a pleasing way, like real candles, but without the potential fire hazard. Whoever had designed the interior of the shop had a real love for books and a flair for display.

The register stand to my right was empty, but I could hear voices coming from the hall to just the right of it – a male and a female. From the tone of her voice, the woman was not pleased. Her male companion, rather than being upset, sounded highly amused. Wanting to see who they were and what their argument was, I crept forward.

From where I stood at the start of the hall, I could see an open doorway into an office. The woman's back was to me, but I could see the man reflected in the antique mirror on the wall next to her. He was tall, just over six feet, with black hair and blue eyes and at first, I thought it was Raul, but some instinct stopped me and I simply watched. Although I would normally describe the features as handsome, something in those eyes suggested a dark nature, one that I didn't want to cross. He laughed again at something the woman had said, then shuddered.

His entire visage began shimmer, tremble and remake itself. It was so startling that I blinked hard, unable to believe what I was seeing. Except that I had, at Raul's office behind the courthouse, when I had first met him. And when he was done, a coldly handsome man with ginger hair and bright gray eyes stood before the woman, his lips curling in a thin smile.

I recognized Julian Webster immediately.

She swore. "Damn you, Julian, that's not funny! Imitating Raul like that almost lost him his case. Do you know how much work it took him to undo what you did?"

"So he explained to me," the ginger haired man said. "In greater detail, however."

Not wanting to be caught looking, I backed away from the hall slowly, then, when I turned to flee, I bumped into a small table and knocked over a small display of books. There was no time to get to the door and run out, so I picked up the books and tried to stack them neatly. I almost dropped them again when a voice spoke from my left.

"Can I help you?"

I turned to face the speaker, recognizing the woman from Abby's nursery earlier in the day as Claire Naughton. She was related to me, somehow, and it felt surreal to know this about her, whereas she was oblivious. Now that I had a more up-close view of her, I observed the fine worry lines around dark blue eyes behind dark-framed glasses.

The man beside her was something else altogether. Deeply tanned, the ginger haired man had a surfer's build under his navy three piece suit and the lithe movements to go with it. I didn't like the way he was looking at me – a dark predator sizing me up through cold blue eyes. It was not lost on me that Claire kept some distance between them. My own instinct was to step back and away from him.

"Is this your first visit to the shop?" Claire gestured to the book I was still holding. "Did you want to purchase that?"

I looked down and saw that I held a copy of *Oliver Twist*. It had been a favorite read of mine growing up. The spectral child that shared my bedroom had had me read it to her a chapter at a time more than once, in the hour or so before I went to bed.

"No, sorry," I said, handing the book to her. "Yes, first visit."

"That's okay," she said, gracious. It didn't quite erase the question in her eyes.

"How could you possibly not have been in here before?" Julian asked. He hadn't lifted his gaze from my face. He gestured to my pack. "You're a student, aren't you?"

I held my ground, not breaking his gaze. "I hope to be," I said, the lie coming easily.

He took a step closer, his blue eyes still cold, still calculating. I continued to hold my ground, not wanting to give him an inch of space. "What do you plan on studying?"

"Cultural anthropology, with an emphasis on death ceremonies," I said, suppressing the urge to back up.

He raised a brow. "Curious subject. Rather morbid."

I shrugged. "We all die. Someone has to process the bodies."

He snapped his fingers. "You were at Raul's office."

I nodded. "He was recommended."

He waited, but I didn't explain.

"It's time for you to leave now, Julian," Claire broke in, her voice cold. "I have a customer and you have work." She turned her back on him, placing herself between him and me. Her gaze flicked down to my hands. I looked at the book in my hands, then closed it and then set the book back in its place with the other Dickens titles. "And when you get back to the office, tell Raul to check his messages. I left him three today."

A brief memory of Raul in his shorts and superhero t-shirt teased me, his scent strong in my nostrils. Looking away from the two antagonists, I touched the spine of *Oliver Twist*, wishing I had my old copy to curl up with later on.

He laughed, holding up his hands. "I'm going, sister mine, I'm going."

Her glare bored a hole in his back as he slipped out the door, the little bell above ringing as he left. "Not even in your wildest dreams," she muttered, then turned to me, a tired smile on her face. "I'm sorry about that. He wouldn't be here, except that my sister usually works today, only she's decided not to come in." She stopped, uttering a nervous laugh. "I don't even know why I'm telling you that, either."

Until I had a better understanding of the family dynamics and how Julian Webster fit in, I decided to remain quiet about my birth certificate. It seemed to be the wiser choice. Still, I felt the sharp, melancholy pang of wanting to know what it must have been like growing up and arguing with siblings. "Sometimes, you tell things to a stranger that you can't tell to close friends."

She considered that, nodding. "True. I'm Claire Naughton, the manager. My family owns the shop."

I hesitated. "I'm Katie Gray." I glanced back at the door. "I'm sorry I came in at such a bad time. Is he really your brother, Ms. Naughton?"

She snorted back laughter, relaxing a little. "He only wishes he were." She held out her hand expectantly. "Please call me Claire."

I took her hand and felt a bright blue spark shiver up my arm. It was sharp and hot and painful and itched. I jerked back with a gasp, releasing her from my grasp. Claire must have felt it as well, for she looked down at her hand, startled, as if seeking answers or the cause of the spark. Her face even paler than before, she looked at me closely.

"I know I've seen you before, at the nursery," she said, curious. "But…..Do I know you?"

"I don't think so," I said, feeling apprehensive. I had a sudden urge to be out of the shop, old books be damned. "I only moved into the area recently."

Claire Naughton stepped forward, her eyes never leaving my face as she studied me. "You look like someone I know."

"I get that a lot," I said, with a grin that felt too tight. "Look, it's a great store and I'll come back soon when I have more time. I've really gotta go."

Claire reached out for me. "Wait! Stay for tea. We can talk…."

"No, thank you," I squeaked. I felt her fingers through the fabric of my sweater and I pulled away. I was neither graceful nor casual – I wanted to be away from her, just as clearly as she wanted to touch me again. Before she was able to get a strong grip, I pulled myself out of reach, turned and took flight.

I ran out of the shop, the tiny bell ringing loudly as I slammed open the door to escape, cold air greeting me. Behind me, I heard Claire call out and I risked a glance back. She was at the large bay window to the right of the door, her eyes on me, and she was on the phone, speaking intently, her free hand making sharp gestures in counterpoint to her words. I thought I heard her say a name – 'Raul' – and then the door shut and she was silenced.

I ran for the cemetery truck and was soon on my way back to Sleepy Eye Cove.

Abby had said that Claire was a witch.

She was extremely powerful, too, if that shock running up my arm was any indication. And now I wondered, for the first time since I discovered my altered birth certificate, if maybe the Galloways had had good reason in keeping their distance and the truth from me, after all.

*****

Back at the shack, Dottie fussed over me as I heated up some water for tea. Instead of feeling annoyed and snapping at her, I actually felt comforted. This was where I belonged and this was where I felt safe. The dead were familiar to me in ways that many among the living were not – it was one of the dead who had helped me escape from the detention center in the middle of the night, after all. And it was, technically, the dead who had helped me secure my current job and home situation. The living, so far as I was concerned, had a lot to measure up to.

Pulling out the notes and print-outs that I'd gathered at the library, I curled up on the couch, spreading out the sheets of paper on the floor in front of me. Father O'Mare had been holding out on me about the arson his church had suffered in 1925 and I wanted to know why he had kept it to himself. As I re-arranged my notes into chronological order, I found myself thinking more about the Naughton Bookshop, the woman who ran it and the spark confirming magic.

Claire Naughton had power that could make her dangerous to me or prove helpful and I wondered what kind of witch she was. My hand tingled where she had touched me and I rubbed it, before rummaging around my pack for my cellphone and hitting 'dial' on the icon next to Abby's name. Her voice mail came on. I left a brief message asking her to meet me at the cemetery's north wall, near where Wes and I would be working early the next morning.

As with Claire, I thought about my birth certificate, but felt reluctant to share my findings, so I didn't and hung up. And even though I knew I'd end up paying for it tomorrow by staying up late tonight, I curled back on the couch and read about the break-in that had left my biological parents dead, me with secretive adoptive parents and no indication that anyone living in Maurier County knew that I even existed. Although my bed was only a few feet away and much more comfortable than the couch, I felt warm and cozy where I was. Sleep came in the middle of a thought.

That night, I dreamed of Cat for the first time.

Nine

Cat had long, dark blonde hair, almost the shade of dark honey, that she kept tied back in a loose braid. On her forehead, just above dark blue eyes, there was a deep cut and drying blood, some of which had begun matting in her hair. There was a tiny dark freckle on her right cheek, just below her eye. She wore a white blouse and dark blue skirt.

She seemed familiar to me, somehow.

We were sitting at a table, but the room was dark and I couldn't see any details. She sat across from me, her tone urgent, trying to warn me about something, touching the same hand Claire had touched. In her other hand was a box, tied with a green bow. She kept pushing it towards me, urging me to take it. I listened, intent on her words, but dreams being what they are, her words came out hollow and garbled, as if she was speaking to me while underwater. The one word I was able to decipher was 'sissy'. I wasn't sure if she was calling me a sissy, or if she was referring to someone else.

That sense of urgency I felt did not dissipate when I woke up. I flung the blankets off and got out of bed. Dottie had clearly come in during the night, because I saw that she had neatly laid out my clothes on the nearby chair.

For some reason, she seemed to think that I was an incompetent dresser. I was both touched and amused. Touched that she cared, amused that most of what I own are t-shirts, sweaters and jeans.

Perfectly suitable for my roaming lifestyle and the jobs I take on.

Taking a quick turn under a cold shower, I quickly got dressed and slipped on sneakers, the dream not quite going away. Pulling out my notebook, I found a pen and began writing, trying to recall every detail. Once I'd finished, I went to my galley kitchen to make coffee and see if I had anything of interest to eat for breakfast or if I needed to go shopping. I usually had to do the latter, so I was surprised and pleased to find an apple in the tiny fridge. Slipping on an old sweater, I munched on the apple and walked out into the day, wondering who the woman in my dream was and what she was trying to tell me. My dreams weren't usually this vivid, nor this intense and they certainly didn't affect me this strongly.

Something was different.

My cellphone rang as I hurried along the path to the north wall. My breath was a fine mist as I checked it. The caller ID read Abby. I answered. "Hey, Abby, what's up?"

"I got your message and am on the north wall bordering the forest, about twenty yards from your humble abode," she replied, cheerful despite the early hour. "There's a cinnamon roll and a latte with your name on it."

My mouth watered at the mention of the pastry. "I'm almost there."

"Good. See ya in a bit." She hung up.

Spurred on in anticipation of the good stuff, I broke into a jog. I found her sitting on the wall, sipping her own coffee and watching squirrels argue over squatters' rights in a nearby tree. She was wearing a green scarf around her hair, much like Louise Tremont would as part of her costume for the tourists.

Abby turned her head as she approached and sighed

when she saw me. "Katie, you sure are a magnet for interesting things."

I hopped up on the wall to sit next to her, giving her a brief run-down of the previous day's events. "Don't you mean 'trouble'?"

Abby chuckled, handing me the second cup of coffee and a paper wrapper holding the cinnamon roll. I took both gratefully. "Yeah, that, too. But Claire Naughton's family is kind of a big deal up here in Wickerman Falls."

I thought of the spark. "I kind of got that. Who's the leader of their coven?"

She pondered that. "I suppose, given that their parents are dead, that Cat – Caitlyn – would be the leader, but she's usually off on assignment somewhere. So, I guess it's actually Claire who's in charge." She sipped her coffee, thoughtful. "You know that their parents' case is still an open one, right? They never found out who broke in or even how they died."

I did know this, but wasn't ready to openly acknowledge that with Abby. That would mean telling her who I really was and why I was here. Given what I'd seen so far, I also didn't think it was entirely safe for her to know, at least, not yet. "No, I didn't. Do any of them belong to your coven?"

Abby shook her head, licking the sugar of her own pastry off her fingers. "It would be quite the coup if they did, but no. They are a coven unto themselves and don't invite outsiders into the mix unless it's necessary. They're related to a couple of powerful families down in the Los Angeles area." She took another long sip of coffee, asked, "Why did you want to know?"

I told her about my trip to Wickerman Falls between bites of my cinnamon roll and coffee, including my encounter with Claire Naughton at the family bookshop. I also mentioned Julian Webster's deliberate provocation by taking on the face of someone else and the spark I'd felt when shaking hands with Claire.

Abby whistled, impressed. "Wow, you had a pretty intense day." She frowned, thoughtful, her brows drawn close. "Sparks like that aren't that common, Katie. That only happens between a relative or someone with equal power." She eyed me, curious. "How much power do you have, anyway? That's why you're blocked, isn't it? Or are you related somehow?"

She had inadvertently touched on what I wasn't ready to talk about and I shifted my position on the stone wall. "My folks were private, so I don't know much about any family. I've got some skill with magic and I talk to ghosts, which seems enough to me." I changed the subject. "I'm a little curious about Julian Webster. Do you know why he would be arguing with Claire?"

Abby was silent for so long that I wasn't sure she'd heard me. After a minute, she spoke, her words careful. "Katie, you need to be very careful. Julian Webster is a sorcerer. He has the ability to assume another person's face."

The memories of what I'd seen at Raul's office and at the bookshop rose, unbidden. "How can he do that?"

"It's called a *glamour*," Abby explained. "A person who can *glamour* can become someone else, but they have limitations."

If a person had the ability to make themselves look different, it didn't seem like they would have any limitations. "Such as?"

Abby considered her words, thoughtful. "Well, for example, a six foot tall man can't become a five foot tall woman. Someone with the ability to glamour has to stick within their own gender and physical frame, but within that, there's a lot of possibilities, of course."

That explained much of what I'd seen at the bookshop. "What does that have to do with this Julian guy?"

"He wants to be a part of their coven in a big way." Abby sounded even more troubled than before. "He's also partners with an attorney that works for the Naughtons. You really need to be careful, Katie. I mean it."

I was quiet. Claire had indicated the same thing. "What about Claire?"

"Typical middle sibling mediator. She's tough, but fair." Abby paused, eyeing me. "I have my spell book with me. Can you do a protection spell or am I going to have to do it?"

"I've already got one in place at the shack," I said, taking the book with extreme care, "but it couldn't hurt to reinforce it." I breathed in deep, exhaled. "I need to see if the vampires left behind any traces that the human eye can't pick up. Do you have a spell or charm that could help with that?"

"A visibility spell? Don't you know how to do that?"

"I've been practicing, but it's not very strong," I said, embarrassed. "I can't seem to get the balance of it right."

She snorted. "Sure. I'll work one up for you. It won't be ready until Friday, though," she added, finishing her tea. "I'll drop it off when it's ready, if you want."

I considered my schedule. "That'll work. I have some other things to check out before I go back, anyway."

Abby chuckled. "Well, that and for Father O'Mare's peace of mind, you don't want me to accidentally make things worse than they already are."

I laughed. "Well, when you put it that way….."

"Good." She glanced at her watch. "Damn it, I'm late! I've gotta go!" She jumped down from her perch, started to walk away, then stopped, turning to me to add, "I don't like this, Katie, you getting close to the Naughtons like that. It gives me the willies."

"You don't need to convince me to stay under the radar with the Naughtons," I said, trying to reassure her. She had no idea how close I really was to the Naughton family and their coven power plays. "I don't want the attention. I'll see you later."

She walked off. I remained seated, the stone I was

91

sitting on cold through my jeans, sipping the remains of my coffee. I felt more troubled than I was before we talked. Other than being in a cemetery at night, not much frightens Abby. The Naughtons scared the hell out of her for some reason. Not that I blamed Abby – power is intimidating, no matter who wielded it.

At the moment, it felt safer to avoid the Naughton bookshop in general until I could gather more information. Avoiding any of the Naughtons in particular seemed to be the wiser choice, given Abby's warning. I checked the time on my cellphone and hopped down, hurrying back to my shack. There were a few things I wanted to grab before heading down to the cemetery office and checking the plot layout. The route I took wasn't the same as the one I'd taken when heading out to meet with Abby – it wound closer to the cemetery's stone wall that bordered the woods and federal land.

As I turned down a seldom-used path, I glanced to my left and stopped. Peering through the hedges, I saw a man and a woman following a different path, heading towards the surrounding woods. They were on a gentle slope several feet below me, so unless they looked up, they wouldn't notice me at all. I couldn't see the man very well, but the woman had a long, blonde braid draped over one shoulder. Neither of them seemed to be enjoying themselves – then again, not many found a cemetery to be an enjoyable place to visit.

As I watched, wondering who they were here to pay respects to, they disappeared among the trees, their voices loud, indistinct and argumentative. Then, glancing over my shoulder at the way they'd gone, I continued down the path to my humble abode.

Dottie was nowhere to be seen when I got back, so I figured she was out with her spectral friends, doing whatever it is ghosts did for fun. I picked up one of the notebooks I'd bought at the college, thinking. Before I took the afternoon off yesterday, I'd been out with Wes in the south side of the cemetery, trimming the rose bushes. While we worked, I had asked if there were any charts that showed how the Sandover cemetery was laid out.

He had considered my question, thoughtful. "Any particular reason why you want to know?"

"I want to know the cemetery better," I had said, which was true.

Naughton's article was the reason I was in the area. Being able to work in the cemetery had been something of a risk, but the more time I spent walking the grounds with Dottie or tracing the carved lettering in the markers, the more at home I felt. It was quiet (as most cemeteries are), the trees created natural canopies and I was generally left alone to do my work. In the short time I'd been there, I'd gotten to know some of the late residents and, like any person curious about their home, I wanted to find out more.

Also, it would be helpful in pinpointing certain residents' final resting places.

"There's a filing cabinet in the back office," Wes had said, thoughtful. "It shows all the plots that the Sandover Cemetery has – those that are taken, those that aren't, including the mausoleums and the number of urns kept in them."

A closer look at those charts had been all I needed. "Great! I'll look at them this weekend."

He had glanced at me, amused. "Some sort of project you're working on, Katie?"

I shrugged. "Sort of."

He had laughed and said no more, except to instruct me on our tasks.

Now, as I headed to my tiny galley kitchen for something to eat, I wondered about who I might find on those charts.

There was a brief chill in the air as the temperature dropped abruptly, then Dottie was next to me, hovering anxiously. "You're back! Did you see them? They just left."

"Of course I'm back," I said. "See who?"

"The man with ginger hair," she said and frowned. "They were chasing after an orb."

"What kind of orb?" I asked. "Was it another ghost?"

Dottie shook her head emphatically. "No, not a ghost. I think it was a spell. They were looking for someone."

"Did you get a good look at them?"

My spectral roommate collected her thoughts. "A blonde woman and a man with ginger hair and dark eyes." I thought of the couple I'd seen on my way back to the shack. What had they been looking for here? Dottie shuddered. "That woman was not what my mistress would have called a lady, not with the language she used."

I suppressed a grin. Dottie hadn't lost her sensibilities. "What did you do?"

She tilted her chin up. "I told them to go away, but they didn't hear me."

I wasn't too surprised – being able to interact with ghosts seemed to be a rare skill, even among the magical community. "Did they find anything?"

"No, that's the odd thing. They were standing right next to the shack, but they couldn't see it at all," Dottie said, quivering. "The woman wasn't happy about it. She kept insisting that she had to be around here somewhere."

Good for me, too bad for them. "Well, it just shows that I was right to put that misdirection spell into place." Dottie sniffed – she had argued against it when I moved in. I was glad that I didn't listen to her. "Did they say who they were looking for?"

Dottie shook her head. "No, just that they couldn't find her." She huffed. "Seems rather rude, though, to chase after someone who didn't want to be found, don't you think?"

I did think so and said as much, adding, "I'm going back to the office to look something up a little later. Wanna go?"

She perked up. "What's at the office?"

"Charts," I said, making sure my keys were in my pocket, "and then we need to go back to the church. Father O'Mare left some things out."

Dottie beamed. "When are you planning to do this?"

I glanced at my phone. The digital face read a quarter past ten. "Now."

Ten

The cemetery office's lobby was dark with shadows, despite the morning sun streaming through the windows. It was also unsettlingly quiet without Wes at his desk in the office to my left or Mae, the part-time secretary, at the desk to my right.

Shutting the door behind me, I flipped the lights on, my eyes taking a few seconds to adjust to the sudden brightness. Then I was at the filing cabinet, trying all of the smaller keys on the ring Wes had given me on the day I was hired. Three slid in perfectly, but it was the fourth that turned the tumblers. The drawers were three inches deep, two feet wide and three feet long, more like a tray. And it was here that I found a map of the cemetery. Numbers dotted the map, but it came with a corresponding chart that identified the numbered plots to names. Pulling it out, I went to the photocopy machine, waiting impatiently for it to warm up.

Then I made my copies, put the cemetery charts back in the drawer and proceeded to turn off the lights before stepping outside and locking up the office. My plan was to make a list of viable contacts within the cemetery, who might be able to help shed some light on the church and what really went down in 1925. The best time to talk to them would be at night, since the psychic energy of the living tended to interfere during daylight hours. In the meantime, I wanted to stash the copies under my couch for later perusal.

Dottie flickered back into view as I approached my shack. "Have you found what you're looking for?"

I unlocked my door, pushed it open. "Not yet." Holding up the roll of papers, I knelt at the edge of my tattered couch and stuffed them inside the frame. "But I've got a copy of the cemetery's layout, so that'll be helpful." Standing, I swiped off dust and went to the sink to wash my hands and face. "Come on."

Glowing with excitement, Dottie followed. "What are we going to do now?"

I grinned, heading for the cemetery truck. "Church."

*****

The sky was clear as I drove towards the church, the thin wisps of fog trying to come in along the coast. Parking in the same place as I had before on the side of the road, I let the engine die before getting out of the truck. Even though there was no other car on the road driving up from the village, I still looked both ways before crossing over to the church. Dottie flickered out of the passenger side, then materialized by the church wall, waiting.

"Shall I fetch Father O'Mare?" she asked, helpfully, then paused, suddenly doubtful. "What if he's counseling one of his parishioners?"

Even as a ghost, Father O'Mare had to tend to his dearly departed flock, so I wasn't eager to interrupt him. But confirming what I'd found in the newspaper archives at the library was fairly important, at least, to me. I had the feeling there was more to the story than what was originally reported and I wanted the spectral priest to fill in the details.

"Well, if he's not busy, tell him it's urgent," I said, trying to be patient. "But if he's with one of his parishioners, let him know I'm here and have questions."

Dottie nodded and disappeared. I sat at the bottom of the stairs to wait. It wasn't a long wait, perhaps five minutes, when my spectral roommate came back.

"Father O'Mare is with a parishioner," she said, cheerful, "but he told me to inform you that he'll be with us as soon as possible and that the door is unlocked."

Climbing up the steps, I was soon standing at the back door where I'd met the late priest the day before. Before pushing the door open, I glanced back towards the road for a quick check to make sure that no one was around, then slipped inside to the church foyer. With the door behind me, I reached over and flipped on the wall light. The lights came on, full and strong, unlike the last time, when they had given off a soft flickering, but faint, glow.

The bulbs had been replaced, I thought, suspecting the village council had taken on some of the building's maintenance. Walking down the hall, I passed the kitchen to my right and took a quick peek. Standard space – sink under the window, an older refrigerator and a stove next to the pantry. I continued on towards the chapel and, just as I put my hand on the door, Dottie appeared next to me, her excitement palpable.

"He's almost finished," she said, cheerful. "Such a terrible thing, to jump to one's death and not have any memory of it." Dottie popped out again.

Clearly, gossip was as much of a past-time in the after-life as it is in mortal life. Shaking my head, I opened the door and walked into the presbytery, approaching the pulpit. Someone had covered it with a tarp since I'd been in last. Lifting it, I studied the damage hidden beneath. It was as bad as I'd remembered it being. The metal fixtures were still blackened and melted out of shape, the wooden cross itself was still a pile of ashes on the stand. I dropped the tarp.

Dottie reappeared, quivering with excitement. "He'll

be with us soon. He's been counseling the woman who can't accept that she died." She sighed, her shoulders drooping. "Poor Sarah. A fall from a cliff is fatal for anyone, not just her."

I've heard stranger things among the living. I nodded and went back to examining the pulpit more thoroughly. I went so far as to lie on my stomach and examine the boards. They were a little loose, but the building was almost a hundred years old. Not unusual. I tried to grip the edge of one board and pull it up, but although it gave a little, the nails had been hammered down deep. If there was something hidden under them, I would need a hammer to pull the nails out.

Ten minutes later, Father O'Mare materialized. I sat back on my heels and straightened, turning to face the spectral priest.

"You left some things out the last time I was here, Father," I said. He didn't reply, merely bowed his head in acquiescence. "What went on here, in the old church, in 1925? Why did you feel you had to burn it down?"

"What makes you think I had anything to do with it?" he asked, affronted, but he wouldn't meet my gaze. "I'm merely a humble servant of God."

"You reported the original vandalism," I pointed out. "The pulpit was destroyed in pretty much the same way as it has now, only the whole place was 'accidentally' burned down. You were the only one with any real access to the church, so it wouldn't have been difficult."

"Vampires," he said at last, choking over the word. "They were looking for someone. When they couldn't find who it was, they desecrated my church." He met my gaze, defiant. "I would burn this church down again, if I could."

I didn't doubt his sincerity on that. Vampires were not to be trifled with and definitely not easy to get rid of. "Who were these vampires looking for? Or what? What was so important to vampires, then and now, that they came into a church to look for it? And why did they think the answers would be found here?"

Father O'Mare shook his head, a slow, deliberate movement. "There was a man, I didn't know him, he never came by the church until that night. But the vampires called him an old one or some such thing, because he knew the old ways, their ways. And when he had thwarted their attempts to turn a man called Pellington, they tried to turn him instead. They failed, but it marked him and now he ages very little. Even then, they were soulless creatures to be destroyed and I fought them off as best I could." He met my gaze, appealing for my understanding. "But my church had been defiled, even after I had it re-consecrated. I had to burn it down and then salt the earth it stood on, to be absolutely sure." He shrugged, unashamed. "No one but that man knew it was me."

I pondered this. "How did he know? And why didn't he report you?"

Father O'Mare leaned close, his face alive for the first time with mirth. "Because he helped me burn it down."

I considered his words, my eyes on the pulpit. "What's his name? If that binding held, then he's still alive. Maybe I can call him up and ask him a few questions."

At this, the spectral priest burst out laughing. "Ah, child, you know him already."

"How…" I stopped, realization dawning. "Oh. It's Wesley Burke."

"It is," Father O'Mare confirmed.

There didn't seem to be much else to say, so I studied the pulpit again. As with any other break-in, clues were going to be left behind. I'm not sure what physical evidence, if any, a vampire could leave behind, but they are still physical creatures inhabiting a physical world. If they had left anything tangible behind, it could be found.

I turned to Father O'Mare. "Why did they came back? What were they looking for?"

He shook his head. "I did not realize they were awake

until this happened."

"Did they leave anything behind?" I asked. "Other than damaging the pulpit?"

He shook his head. "No. All that you see is what was left."

I shook my head. "No, I mean, back in 1925. Was there anything found around the church that they might have left behind? Like a talisman or a charm, that would allow them entry to begin with?"

He brightened at that, remembering. "Yes. The day after the fire was put out, I was in the yard, praying for enlightenment when I found a charred pouch. There were some bone fragments – animal, I think – human hair, a couple of teeth, a crystal and some twigs." I recognized the charm he was describing almost immediately – it was an undead passkey to the living. It was similar to the one the New Orleans vampire had used. "I put it in a jar, filled it with salt and holy water and threw it into the ocean."

The proper disposal of such dark items, though I suspected that Father O'Mare only went by what his Bible had taught him. It still didn't explain why the desecration of the church happened back in 1925. Or why the vandalism happened again. Or who the vampires were looking for. Or what.

This suggested only one thing and I brought out my theory with care. "The vampires who vandalized the church a couple of days ago are the same ones from 1925."

He laughed. It was a rich, deep sound and truly surprising to hear, because I didn't think he knew how. "Exactly! Vampires don't stray far from the site of their unnatural re-birth...."

"Unless they carry a bit of their grave with them," I finished for him. The idea of carrying my own grave dirt in one pocket was not a pleasant one.

Father O'Mare nodded, pleased. "Even that writer, Stoker, knew." The spectral priest tapped my shoulder. It felt like an icicle poking through my sweater and I shivered. "You need to put an end to them, Cadence Galloway. I will not stand for the desecration of my church for a second time, even if I am a ghost." He paused, drew closer, his expression strangely compassionate. "The undead are not always made from the people, as I'm sure you know."

The depth of his insight caused the already chilly room to drop a few degrees cooler and I shivered. It certainly wasn't because his words echoed what Louise Tremont had said the night I'd left New Orleans. "Yes, I'm aware." Clearing my throat, I added, "I'm going to do the best I can to get rid of them, sir."

"I would be grateful." He started to fade away, then paused. "Kindly remember to turn off the lights upon leaving. The new maintenance man from the city is rather fussy about unnecessary electricity charges."

With a sniff, Father O'Mare disappeared.

And that was my tip for the night.

Eleven

Sunday morning, I woke up early enough that the grey-light of dawn hadn't peeked through the windows quite yet, my mind churning busily over several thoughts.

One thought managed to surface.

According to Father O'Mare, Wesley Burke had been around the area since 1925. Which meant he had some explaining to do. An hour later, I was staring up at him as he stood on the roof of his front porch, an old broom and trash bag in his hands. Wes Burke lived alone in a tiny cabin just outside the village of Sleepy Eye Cove. He frowned down at me, irritated, as he leaned against the broom, considering my question.

"The old church up the road?" he repeated.

My hackles stirred and I frowned up at him, shading my eyes with my hand. "Funny, I didn't realize we were in a tunnel for it to echo. That's what I just said. You know that old church up the road. It was vandalized about a week ago. And it happened before, in 1925."

Wes removed his faded baseball cap, running a calloused hand over his bald and freckled pate. "Couldn't tell you, Katie. Sorry about that."

My frown deepened. "Quit shining me on and

changing the subject, Wes. Father O'Mare told me that you've lived here for more years than you let on. I also know that you were around when the church burned in '25."

He met my gaze, sighed. "All right, Katie. I was there when the fire happened."

I crossed to the ladder and climbed up. "Start talking."

He handed me his pair of work gloves and the large, black garbage bag. I took them and, once I was ready, Wes began scooping piles of rotten leaves into the bag I held open. Neither of us said much at first – the only noise came from the rustle of the plastic bag in my hands, the scrape of the shovel against the porch roof and the labor of our breathing. Then, as we got into the rhythm of the work, Wes broke the silence.

"Father O'Mare started the fire," he said, thoughtful, "but it was touch and go, when I came upon him. Whenever he got a flame going, it'd go out as soon as he moved."

"So you helped him." I shifted my weight, easing a sudden cramp.

Wes grinned. "Not at first, no. But when he explained the situation to me, I couldn't refuse him." He paused, added, "He was part of the reason I chose to stay."

I raised a brow. "How?"

He stopped, straightened, gazing out and around at the cemetery grounds. "O'Mare found a way for me to work here, no questions asked."

I didn't press him for details. It was too similar of how Wes had hired me on the spot to help work around the cemetery and offered me the old caretaker's shack as a place to live. Minus the additional years, obviously. "You've been here a long time."

He met my gaze, amused. "I have."

"How long?" I asked, then, clarifying, "I mean, well, yeah. How long have you been around, life-wise?"

His amusement dimmed a little. "Long enough to remember this continent before its secession from King George."

I blinked, startled by the information. Then, taking a deep breath, I decided to trust him. Just a little bit, anyway. "Then tell me about the vampires. Was that your only encounter with them, back in 1925?"

He focused on his porch roof, sweeping up stray debris. "I've seen them around more than once since then."

"Were they from around here, originally?" I asked, pressing for more details. "Or are there missing persons reports from other cities?"

"One of them is local, in the sense that she was far more familiar with the area than the other two," he said, pausing in his sweeping, thoughtful. "I tracked them for months, but was never able to find their nest after helping Father O'Mare." He rubbed his neck. "I've scouted a number of likely sites, but it never came to anything."

I watched him. "What was your first encounter with them like?"

"Unpleasant," Wes said, curt. "It's an experience I'd rather not repeat." He frowned, glancing at his watch, then pulled the gloves he loaned me off my hands. "It's getting late. Thank you for helping me out here, but I can get the rest by myself."

That dismissal clearly meant I touched a nerve he didn't want to look at, so I took the hint and climbed down the ladder. As I headed for the cemetery truck, I paused, turned and called out to him, "See you in the morning!"

He waved. "Meet me at the office and we'll go over what needs doing."

I nodded and waved back. Back in the truck, I headed into the village, planning to do some shopping at the market and explore the area a little more. My first impression of the village was mostly a blur of buildings as

I'd gotten off the bus a week ago, trying to orient myself. But the one thing that did stand out was the coffee shop and it became my first stop. It was there I went after I left Wes to finish cleaning up his roof.

Madame Sofia's Brew was the local coffee shop in town and I remembered rushing in to grab a cup before heading up to the cemetery. At the time, Sofia Thomas, the silver-gray proprietor and maker of the most perfect coffee, had convinced me to try her newest latte – salted caramel with a dash of cinnamon – and I'd been craving one ever since. Now I parked the truck up the street and headed over, needing that latte more than ever. Maybe I'd take a couple of the cinnamon rolls displayed in the case to go with it.

My stomach growled in anticipation.

Sofia Thomas, owner and proprietor, looked up from behind the pastry case, her silver-gray hair pulled back in a loose bun. Her green eyes sparkled out from behind a pair of diamond-studded glasses. "Katie, good to see you."

Warmed by her memory of me, I stepped up to the pastry display case, eyeing the other yummy treats, even though I knew exactly what I was going to get. "Hi, Sofia, it's good to see you again, too. May I get a salted caramel latte, please?" I gestured to the cinnamon rolls, although the chocolate croissants were silently calling my name to add them to my list. With some difficulty, I restrained myself. "And a couple of your biggest cinnamon rolls?"

She swooped in to take care of my order, snatching up tongs and a paper sack, opening up the case to select the biggest rolls. Then she handed the bulging sack to me, which I took eagerly. My mouth watered in anticipation of tasting the delectable pastry.

"You've been here a week now," Sofia said, cheerfully, going to the espresso machine. "What do you think of our little town so far?"

I paused mid-bite long enough to thoroughly chew the bit of roll before swallowing. "A little more than a week, actually. I like it so far, I just don't know it well enough to have a solid opinion."

Sofia laughed. "Trust me, this place will grow on you pretty quick and then it'll be like the home you never grew up in."

Unable to reply with the second bite of cinnamon roll in my mouth, I could only nod.

She continued, "You've come at one of the quieter times of the year. Come Fourth of July, you'll see a wilder side of town."

With the combination of fireworks and carnival-like festivities, I could only imagine. Then the conversation stalled while she steamed the milk. When the milk foamed over, she shut off the machine and set it aside, letting it cool for a minute while she prepped the large to-go cup. Taking the tiny canister of brewed espresso, she poured it into the cup. Then she added the milk, creating a little design with the milk's foam and the espresso. She handed it over to me, which I took with eager hands. "There you go. Where are you off to today?"

"A self-guided tour of the town, grocery shopping, stuff like that," I said, inhaling the latte's aroma as I paid. "Kind of a boring day, actually."

The door opened and more customers came in, speaking what sounded like French.

"Well, enjoy then," she said, and moved to help the newcomers.

I dropped my loose change in the tip jar by the register and left.

*****

Walking along the sidewalk from the coffee shop, I savored my rolls and latte and stopped at various shops, studying their window displays. Although the village seemed to be a ripe spot for tourism, the local economy seemed to be doing well for itself. There were few high end shops, but overall, it seemed that the village had found a way to keep their way of life from being overrun by out-of-towners.

The town square was a tree-filled park, complete with a gazebo and child's playground in the center. I found a bench near the gazebo and sat, enjoying the shade and listening to the birds chirp and flit about. At some point, a couple of squirrels got into a high-pitched argument over what only squirrels could argue over, chasing each other over the lawn in front of me and up the nearest tree. Laughing to myself, I got up, threw away the now empty cup and paper sack in the nearest trash bin and went back to the truck.

Prescott's Market was crowded when I pulled in to the parking lot. I found a space for the truck at the far end, parked and walked back, mentally sorting out what I'd learned over the last few days. Once inside the store, I grabbed a hand basket and went through the aisles, gathering an assortment of fruits, some sandwich fixings and juice. Most of what I picked up had a long shelf life, like peanut butter, some canned foods and salt. With a tiny refrigerator, I didn't have a lot of space to keep fresh produce, so that would have to be picked up as I went along.

I paid for my items and left, stopping long enough to drop some coins into a slot and get a local newspaper from the newsstand. It would help me get a better sense of the community I was now a part of, even peripherally. Back at the truck, I climbed in and headed back to the cemetery, ready for some down time to collect my thoughts and make a list of what I needed to do.

The drive back was peaceful and, with nothing other than the few perishables in my bags, I was in no hurry to get back. Passing by Wes's place, I saw that he had finished his roof work and had disappeared – either inside or around back of his home. Half a mile or so later, I passed the old church. And now that it was daylight and I was approaching from the right direction, I saw to my right what looked like an old road, no longer used and overgrown with weeds and surrounding shrubbery.

Something flickered – faint and slight – but it was brief and vanished when I slowed down enough to look directly down the lane. Frowning, I continued on to the cemetery. Whatever slept there had just begun to stir awake. Had I come across any information pertaining to that spot, while I'd been at the Wycliff library? I wasn't sure, but it wouldn't hurt to double check my notes and, now that I had a wireless hotspot, I could surf the internet for more information.

Back at my tiny shack, the cemetery truck safely parked in its spot, I fired up the laptop and set up the wireless connection, my notes spread out on the kitchen table before me. While I waited for both to connect, I scanned my notes, searching for any reference to the hidden lane. I found none, but the story about Marcus Pellington and his attack while walking along the main road outside town caught my eye again.

Re-reading that small report, I realized that where he'd been found several miles from town itself, which suggested many things. For one, the nearest house was Wes's, but it hadn't been built until the late forties. Pellington had to have been living close by, since he'd lived in the area since the early nineteen-twenties. But not even the report of his attack listed his address, which was now another note to check up on. It was entirely possible that he had lived at Black Rock Lane, although it seemed unusual that a haunted lane wasn't part of Sleepy Eye Cove's lore. Even Danvers, where I'd grown up, had all kinds of haunts, including the old asylum-turned-apartments.

Those kinds of tales are usually the first to be told, but not even Wes had mentioned the old forgotten lane. Whatever happened there must have been so horrific that the entire town conspired to forget about it. And I wondered if Marcus Pellington was at the center of it.

Signing onto the internet, I searched Pellington's

name in connection with the village and found that Black Rock Lane had been his private road. He'd bought it with severance pay after being honorably discharged from the service in 1917. Injuries sustained during the Great War had expedited his discharge and he was sent home.

Sitting back, I chewed my lower lip, thoughtful. Somehow, all of this was connected to the vampires, I just couldn't see it. Pulling out my notebook, I began making a list of things that needed to be checked out.

At the top, I put Black Rock Lane.

Twelve

I found Wes at his desk the next morning and sat down in the chair opposite. Mindful of how he had abruptly ended the conversation the day before, I decided to not bring it up.

"Okay, boss, what's on the agenda today?" I asked, cheerful.

He glanced up from his computer. "Well, for a start, the south-west patch needs mowing. The mower is gassed up, so all you need to do is cut the grass and collect the clippings." Leaning back in his chair, he added, "Also, the old hearse needs to go in to Olson's for maintenance. Key's on the hook. They're expecting it this afternoon and Olson'll work on it in the morning."

Standing, I snatched the hearse key from its hook and paused, debating. Then I turned, facing him. "There was a family named Pellington living in the area at the time of the fire."

He started, almost knocking over the round glass paperweight near his hand, catching it before it fell to the floor. "Where did you hear that name?"

I watched him, curious. "I was looking for articles on the church fire and found one about the attack on man named Pellington. There was also a birth announcement for a girl named Anna. The announcement listed the residence as Black Rock Lane."

Wes grew still, his eyes thoughtful, but he did not clarify. Instead, he gestured to the door, something of his old self warming through. "Better get going on that."

I frowned. "What don't you want to tell me?"

He raised a hand. "Let me get to this in my own way. There are…..complications."

"What kind of complications?" I asked, folding my arms. "I mean, this is a yes or no kind of question."

He grimaced, rubbed his eyes, sweat beading his brow. "I realize it's that simple. And for any other topic, it would be easy to respond. But I am bound."

I started to ask what he meant by that, but the look in his eyes stopped me. Father O'Mare's words about binding echoed in Wes's comment. So I nodded and let it go, then left the building and crossed the parking lot.

The Sandover Cemetery stores two hearses – the silver-gray 1957 Ford I was to take to Olson's and a black 2006 Chevrolet. The local mortuary owned them and since their parking lot was too small to keep the vehicles and for mourners to park, it had been arranged for them to be kept with us. The bonus was that the cemetery employees got to use them whenever it was deemed necessary, such as taking it to the mechanic. This wasn't as often as I'd have liked, since the '57 hearse had sleek, classic lines.

Climbing into the driver's seat, I fired it up. Herbie Nickerson, the ghost attached to it, wasn't currently present – presumably he was at the mortuary, his other favorite hangout. Pulling out of the parking lot, I settled in for the drive to the local mechanic.

Not long after I'd left the cemetery, I drove past Black Rock Lane. Once again, something fluttered out of the corner of my eye. Slowing the hearse, I shot a quick glance down the lane, but the flutter didn't repeat. Something – or someone – had wanted my attention and I wondered who it might be. The energy felt masculine, so it couldn't be Anna Pellington. Perhaps her father? Or some unfortunate neighbor?

Whoever it was, they would have to wait until later for me to help them. If that was what they needed, then I wanted to take my time with them.

*****

Pulling into Olson's Garage, I was directed by one of the mechanics to park the hearse close to the main bay. I was relieved that the lot was wide enough maneuver around. From where I sat, I could see one of the mechanics wave a hand for me to leave the hearse where it was. Nodding to show that I understood, I left the keys in the ignition, unbuckled my seat belt and opened the door.

"Stupid witch," a low voice growled in my ear.

I jumped, looking around. Only the mechanics were around, but none of them were close enough to have said what I'd heard. I looked in the vehicle's back section and my immediate surroundings carefully, confirming what I'd already known, that I was alone. Since Herbie was absent from the hearse, it couldn't be him. Also, I'd met him while cleaning out the hearse my second day on the job. We had struck up a conversation about books. He had a quiet voice, one that he'd cultivated to soothe the grieving.

This voice was dark with hate and I wondered to whom it belonged.

Climbing out of the hearse, I walked towards the shop's office to pick up keys for the loaner truck and got an estimated time to come back for it the next day. Then I headed across the street to Madame Sofia's Coffee Shop, wanting something to boost my energy before exploring Black Rock Lane and whatever haunted it.

Approaching the door, it swung out and I stopped dead in my tracks. Efrain Jimenez was standing in the breeze-way, his back to me. Stepping around him was Julian Webster. From the tension in Jimenez's shoulders and Webster's thinned mouth, it was clear a disagreement of some kind was in progress.

Neither man had seen me as yet and while I wanted to duck out of sight, there was no place for me to go. My only recourse was to just keep moving forward, despite feeling exposed. I wasn't sure if Julian Webster would recognize me as he had at the Naughton Bookshop, but I sincerely hoped he wouldn't.

And then they both saw me.

Their reactions when they saw me spoke volumes – Efrain Jimenez relaxed a little, his expression warming a little, although there was still some tension around his eyes and his mouth had a tight curve to it. Julian Webster's expression had settled into an inscrutable mask. There was no way to tell if he'd recognized me.

Efrain Jimenez made the introductions, glancing at the other man. "Katie, this is Julian Webster."

"Nice to meet you," I said, hoping my voice didn't betray my unease.

He held my gaze. "I've seen you before, at the bookshop."

Jimenez glanced at me. "What bookshop?"

I managed a casual shrug, answering, "I was in Wickerman Falls the other day and found this bookshop." To Webster, I said, "I guess you have business with the chief here, so I'll leave you two to get back to it."

"It's not pressing business," Julian Webster replied, still studying me. "Just a few questions regarding local property laws."

Efrain Jimenez never looked away from me. "Not sure why you needed to talk to me. Sounds like something an attorney that specializes in property law could answer."

The other man made a noncommittal noise. "Perhaps."

"Well, anyway, I'm on an errand," I said, moving to get passed both men. "Have a good afternoon, Mr....?"

He held out his hand. It felt like an eon before I took it, quickly pulling my hand back when he let go. "That's right, Claire did not properly introduce us. Julian Webster."

"Mr. Webster, then."

Jimenez cleared his throat. "I've got to be getting back the station. Busy day today."

He was lying, of course. From what I'd seen, it was never busy, even when the local tavern had three loud drunks instead of one. Or when the dive on the south side of the village had fights break out on a Friday night. There wasn't so much as a vandal or pickpocket to make an arrest for the weekly blotter. Sleepy Eye Cove did not get its name because of the night-life.

Julian Webster gave a brief nod, indicating that he understood his meeting with Jimenez was now over. "Thank you for your time, then. Have a good afternoon."

With a glance at me, the lawyer turned on his heel and walked towards a BMW that looked like it had just rolled off the lot. Then he was gone, dust rising from the car's wheels as he pulled a sharp U-turn and drove off.

I turned to Jimenez. "Is that what he really wanted to know?"

He shook his head. "No, he originally came by to follow up on a missing person report filed this morning." He faced me, quirking a smile. "His partner apparently went missing over the weekend, despite a case both are working on. Thus the property law questions." He glanced down the road, even though Julian Webster's car had long since disappeared. "Strange thing is, it felt like a fishing expedition, but I'm not sure why." Then, with a sigh, he said, "Nice to see you around, Katie. Watch out for him."

"I will," I promised, watching as Jimenez headed towards the tiny police station on the other side of the town square. On my way back to the garage, I realized there were a few things I needed from the grocery store and made a quick detour before picking up the truck.

Then I was driving out of town and back to the cemetery.

<u>Thirteen</u>

Henry Gray was dead when I met him shortly after I left town and had been for more years than I could account for. I'd been expecting him to show up since I saw that shadowy flutter as I'd driven past Black Rock Lane earlier. The loaner truck was a three-in-a-tree transmission and it was taking me some getting used to, pushing down on the clutch and shifting into the desired gear.

I drove past the brightly painted *You Are Now Leaving Sleepy Eye Cove, We'll Miss You* sign, following the two-lane road as it curved to the right, taking me away from the California coast and the sea. Then I was missing the heavenly, cool ocean breeze as the air grew warmer almost at once and I cranked my window back up, reaching for the air conditioner.

By the time I passed Wes's little cottage, I was getting the hang of the stick shift and clutch, although the truck did lurch once or twice. A deep, dull pressure was slowly building up behind my right eye socket, preceding a dull throbbing sensation. This indicated that I was being approached by a long-dormant male ghost. Female ghosts made themselves known with a similar pressure behind my left eye. No, it's not at all a pleasant feeling to have. It sometimes leaves me with a pounding headache.

Fortunately, long-dormant ghosts weren't a normal occurrence.

I had just driven past the local church on my right, still tasting the salty air, when the pressure behind my right eye abruptly stopped. I became aware of the presence to my right and I knew that I wasn't alone in the front seat of the old hearse. In rapid succession, he made me aware of his name, that he had died at someone else's hands and he wanted my help. I spared a quick glance at my spectral passenger. Henry's name certainly suited him – his clothes, his skin tone, even his hair were all various shades of gray. Even so, he must have been young when he died, because he didn't look much older than the kid who'd bagged my groceries.

He hadn't died recently, either, although that was difficult to tell for sure. His clothes were generic enough to be anywhere from the forties to present day – jeans and a plain T-shirt, the kind I favored. Even his shoes – converse high-tops – seemed modern. Still, I suspected that he had died years before I was born. Maybe a decade or two.

He didn't feel recently deceased, anyway.

"Spill it," I said. He wanted something from me or he would have moved on years ago. I am not in the habit of helping ghosts pass over into the light, but I have never been able to refuse them help, either. I'm nice that way. "What do you want?"

He said nothing, but out of the corner of my eye, I saw him turn his head to look at me. Not a second later, pain shot through my neck and I couldn't breathe.

The pain in his neck was unbearable, and yet, exquisite, almost as if he were in a perpetual state of orgasm without release. Her face filled his vision, the sharp lance of her teeth piercing his skin, the world going slowly dark around him.....

Both of my feet reflexively slammed down hard on the brakes. The tires screamed against the pavement as the car spun and for one heart-stopping moment, I thought it would roll. Instead, it spun around in a one-eighty and stopped, facing back towards town. The engine rattled once and died. I put the truck in park, my right hand shaking so badly that it took longer to shift the gear than it should have. My seatbelt cut so deeply into my left shoulder and across my chest that I knew I would have some major black bruises the next day, not to mention the stiff muscles that go along with them.

All of which were very small potatoes – I was just glad to be alive. I rested my head back against the seat, listening to my heart as it slowly calmed down.

When I felt able to speak again, I asked, not looking at him, "Your neck was broken?"

No, I don't think so, he said, a frown crossing his face.

"Did you do something to piss someone off?"

I got the sense of a smile. *I was twenty-one when I died. Of course I did.*

Great. A ghost with a sense of humor. Smart aleck. "I'm Katie Gray. It seems we share the same last name. Sort of."

He shook his head, reminding me that all ghosts know my real name. *I know who you are, Cadence Galloway. Why else do you think I'm here?*

He had me there. "How do you know who I am?"

He gave me a look. *We know who can listen and who can't.* Again, that slight frown crossed his face and he muttered, almost to himself, *Galloway. Why do I know that name?*

"I couldn't tell you, Henry," I said, starting the engine and drove on.

Henry Gray didn't speak again until we passed Black Rock Lane.

Here I died, he said and blinked out.

I hesitated, then pulled off the main road, parking the truck under a large tree. Fog was coming in off the ocean in thick wisps and seemed unusually heavy this late in the day. Looking out at the ocean through the trees, I shivered a little, pulling my sweater close.

Standing at the lane's shaded entrance, I looked past the over-growth and broken pavement that curved to the right, vanishing into the densely wood forest beyond. It was so seldom used that nature had pretty much taken over and obscured the lane from view. The only reason anyone would know it was there was if they'd been around when it had been in use. Not even the street sign on the corner was visible – ivy had drowned the post and sign, reaching for the tree next to it.

As before, something fluttered just out of the corner of my eye, only this time, it wasn't Henry – there was a second spirit attached to this lane. Although I suspected there could be more, these two were, so far, the only ones I could sense. Climbing over the ivy, I followed the lane as far as I dared. Then I stopped and knelt, opening myself to the second spirit, determined to locate the spot it was tied to. About ten yards ahead of me, I noticed the rock wall on either side that had been obscured from the main road. Clearly, Pellington had taken some pride in the appearance his residence had. The pressure behind my eye grew stronger, tugging a little to my right, and I crossed to the nearest crumbling section of wall. The pressure faded to a dull throb.

Pausing, I looked back at the loaner truck. It was maybe half a mile from where I stood, but it seemed further. Turning, I observed the fields on either side of me, blocked off by crumbling rock walls that lined the road I stood on. The field to my right tugged at my temple again and I turned, the pressure immediately relaxing, though not leaving completely.

There was more of that wild and tangled pile of ivy growing on the other side of the rock wall. It looked like the kind of ivy I'd seen growing on old buildings, like at Wycliff College, but never in nature and not like this. There was a plot with no marker hiding underneath it, an old grave that had not been touched since the ground had been broken and put back. And unless you knew where to look or had the knack of talking to ghosts like me, you'd walk right by and never see it, much like Black Rock Lane.

Clearly, no one wanted to tend to this one's grave, not even out of respect for the fact that he was dead.

There was a chill in the air, colder than the fog nipping at my sweater, and I shivered, studying the wildly grown ivy. It seemed to be a freakish force of nature, like it was hiding secrets about the dead from the living. I reached over and pulled at the green, leafy plant. After some resistance, it came away, easily. So I pulled, my breath coming in harsh grunts, until, finally, I came to the mound of earth.

The tall grass had grown over it like a thick blanket – the grass was a washed-out dirty yellow from lack of sunlight. I stared down at that patch, not liking it at all, the urge to wash off the unpleasant energy strong. The man who had been buried here hadn't been given last rights nor had he been fully human at the moment he'd died. A dull odor rose up from the over-grown patch, similar to the musty smell of an attic, but sour, like stale sweat. I placed my hand on the dirt, palm first, wanting to get a sense of who lay in this unmarked grave.

The man who lay here had a dark sickness in him that had demanded blood. He had given it freely and not just his own, which resulted in him dying violently. He had been buried facedown, his head pointed towards the ocean.

"Okay, buddy," I said in a low voice. "You want to talk? Let's talk."

I sat down with a hard thump on the grass, feeling the cold seeping into my jeans as I crossed my legs. I took a couple of deep breaths, inhaling and exhaling from my mouth. I didn't want to smell the foul air any more than I wanted to taste it, but there was no help for that since I needed to breath. I wanted to get this done as fast as possible and go. Even without calling him forth, I really didn't like the dead guy's vibe.

Taking a couple more deep breaths to settle my nerves, I said, "I'm ready when you are."

A cold spot enveloped me like a black fog. It tasted like foul earth as it manifested into a shadow in the shape of a man, bright spots where eyes should have been. What hovered before me wasn't a ghost but a shade, a shadow of its former self. This usually happened to a ghost if it's a malevolent spirit. It can also happen when the spirit has been earth-bound for several years, maybe decades. Like this one.

Then he spoke, fast and furious – too fast for me to understand what he was saying. If he'd been alive, he'd be spitting all over me.

"Slow down!" I said sharply. He flinched back, as if I'd slapped him. I stared back, more than a little astonished. It was almost as if I'd hurt his feelings. If so, I would need to tread a little more carefully. "You need to speak and I've got the time. But I have questions, too." He considered me for a long moment. I took the opportunity to study him back. I hoped that his desire to talk would outweigh his desire to pontificate. I would settle for a little of both. "Who are you? Why were you buried here and not in the cemetery?"

He loomed higher, as if taking in our surroundings. *My pets, my masters, they buried me here before our pact was complete.*

"Your pets?" I asked. "What pact?" A sudden thought, "Are you Marcus Pellington?"

His reaction was unexpectedly morose. *I have not heard my name spoken in seventy years, perhaps more.*

"Tell me about the pact," I said, my tone softer as I shifted into a more comfortable sitting position. "Who did you make it with?"

She came to me, not long after I married. It was a promise to ease my physical pain which drew me to her.

The news articles had referred to an attack on Marcus

Pellington. If it had been what he was now referring to, then I might actually get a lead on where to look for them. "Tell me more about her. Was she a doctor?"

He spoke as if in a dream, my question barely registering. *She promised that my pain would end, if I took her in. It was only a kiss, a prick of teeth, but it gave me such relief that I gladly gave her what she asked.*

The vampire, at least one of them. "She didn't give you anything in return?" In order for a vampire to maintain control over a human, blood had to be exchanged.

His next words chilled me. *Not at first, no. The second kiss, though, she cut a vein in her arm and offered me a taste of her sweet blood.*

Damn. He hadn't been turned, obviously, but he became her puppet. What had he said just a minute earlier? *"My pets, my masters."* His pets, in that he cared for and cossetted them, his masters in that he did their bidding. And there was more than the one he spoke of. Which would explain how his family had disappeared and under so much secrecy. But how did Henry factor into this?

"Tell me again about how she came into your house," I said, slowly. "What led her here and why? How many did she bring with her?"

He considered my question. *She claimed to be stranded and brought only two. Her children, she called them, though they appeared older than she was. We invited them in as our guests, my family and I. But I don't recall when they took their leave of us, however.*

Because they hadn't left. Wherever they had laid their nest, it was most likely still in use and under Pellington's invitation. Which meant it had to be close by and the only known building on this road was the Pellington house.

"Was Henry already here, or did he come later?" I asked.

The shade that had been Pellington tilted his head, studying me with the same intensity I'd subjected him to a few minutes earlier. *We lived a private life. My daughters did not understand the need for privacy. It was a cause for arguing on many occasions.*

There was a low beep from my back pocket, interrupting the shade, and I pulled out my cellphone, noting that it was a little after five. "Hi, Wes, I'm on my way."

"Good to hear," he said. "I'm going to need you at the south side of the cemetery when you get back. Someone's been tramping around and destroying my rose bushes. The boys helped with most of it, but they left at eleven and I still need another pair of hands."

"Great, I'll be there in a few." I hung up before he could say anything more. To Pellington's shade, I said, "I have to go. What else do you want to tell me?"

My last memory of her is of a kiss. Pellington frowned. *She was not alone, though. Why her brethren accompanied her, I cannot say. But I died and then found myself bound here, in this unmarked grave.* He looked at me, earnest. *When I lived, she called what was between us a blood-tie. And then I died and had no blood left to give her. But I could still sense her and her brethren as they roamed, could feel their prey's fear as they hunted.*

"It's called a soul-tie," I said, thoughtful. "It means you're still tied to them, even in death, and that she is a powerful vampire, to know how to create that." And that they were still causing problems. Like vandalizing a local church.

His tale now finished, the shade hovered before me, waiting. In all fairness, he had done what any normal person would have done, to escape the physical pain from injuries sustained in war. It wasn't my place to judge his choices, even though the ramifications of them were still being felt in the present. The tie to this world made sense now – his guilt kept him here. Guilt in accepting the vampire's bond, guilt at what it had cost his family and, ultimately, himself. Now, he'd served his purpose in giving me information and there was no need to keep him active.

The rest I could get on my own, especially when I found his house and gave it a thorough search.

"You've done me a good turn," I said, my tone kind. "Now you can let go and rest. When I stake the sire, there will be truly nothing left here to bind you." Taking a deep breath, unsure if this would work, I added, "I forgive you."

The shade that had been Marcus Pellington sighed, as if he had been waiting for those words to be spoken. The sound of his sigh was weighted with the past, then he faded from sight. The air around me lightened and I got to my feet, pushing the yellowed grass and ivy back into place as I moved. Standing back, I surveyed my work. Unless you knew where to look, you'd never know that the ivy was hiding an unmarked grave from more than half a century ago.

Climbing back over the rock wall, I cast a quick glance to my right. The Pellington home had to be further up.

And it would be there that I could find some answers.

Fourteen

The shade given off by the canopy of trees on either side of the lane was cold and I shivered, despite my sweater. As I walked, I pondered the encounter with Marcus Pellington, intrigued by his reaction when I offered him forgiveness. He would be tied to the earth until the vampire who bit him was staked, but forgiving him had definitely loosened its hold. The spot where he'd been buried had certainly felt lighter, more peaceful. Shaking my head, I kept an eye out as I searched for the Pellington house.

Henry didn't reappear by my side until I'd gone another half-mile up the lane. I glanced at him, thoughtful. Somehow, he was connected to the Pellingtons and what happened to them.

I gestured to the lane. "How far down?"

He looked around, as if to gather his bearings, though from his perspective, it would not have changed all that much. *Not far. Another half mile or so. Maybe less.*

Wonderful.

Glancing down, I noticed that at one time, the lane had been paved. Now it was cracked and crumbling from lack of maintenance and weeds had taken over. It had stopped being safe for even a heavy truck to drive over decades ago. Pulling my sweater tight, I kept walking and, soon I saw the rest of the stone wall. It was crumbling in places where some of the rocks had fallen off, peeking out from beneath the ivy that seemed to have a strangle-hold on the area.

A few minutes later, we stopped where the crumbling rock wall supported the weight of a fallen branch. Henry reached out to put a hand on my arm, but it passed through. Even though I was wearing a sweater, his touch sent cold chills up my arm and down my back. I forced myself not to shiver or move into the sun.

There. He was pointing to a place beyond the stone wall.

I stopped, shading my eyes with my left hand. At first, all I could see were the trees and the various plants and flowers that had grown wild. Then, as my eyes adjusted and began to take in more details, I could see that the flowers weren't the usual brightly colored poppies, but multi-colored roses. They had gone wild, like everything else growing around them, but they were still roses. They barely hid the faint marks of the dirt path winding its way deeper into the trees.

Henry stood maybe twenty yards beyond the stone wall, right next to the path, the over-grown grasses leaning away from his cold presence. He gestured for me to follow him and, after some hesitation, I clambered over the wall, almost falling when one stone shifted under my hand suddenly.

I followed Henry through the tall grass, bush fronds slapping at my jeans as I walked. Henry had no such problems, merely walking through as if they didn't exist. Which, if one thought about it, was probably the case with the ghost – when he died, the area was most likely in better shape and properly maintained.

Henry pulled his disappearing act again before I had set foot onto the partially obscured path, so I took my time, observing how the grasses seemed bent in some places. Crouching down, I studied the grass closely, wondering if someone else had come through recently. With that thought in my mind, I picked up an old tree branch that lay nearby, maybe three feet long. It was sturdy and heavy in my hands and I felt somewhat relieved to have it. Being alone in a forest where a ghost claimed he had died was not very conducive to feeling safe.

Gripping the branch tightly, I walked along the unkempt path, observing the rocks lining it on either side of me. As with the wall, I realized that the path had at one time been kept well-groomed and clear. What happened to the family that had once lived here was unclear, but its ruin was directly connected to them. I wondered if Henry's own demise was in some way at the hands of Marcus Pellington.

The density of the trees around me blocked out the sun just enough to make a false evening and the temperature drop another five degrees or so. I shivered, telling myself it was more from the sudden chill in the air than the nightmare forest from Grimms' fairy tales as I looked around, not wanting to lose track of the way I came in.

I almost missed it, the pointed peak of a rooftop. The low branches of the surrounding trees obscured most of it from view, but the straight, man-made lines among the curved limbs stood and caught my eye. This was the Pellington house, then. Searching for a clear way to get through, I had to retrace my steps back to the lane. About twenty feet up from where I came out was an opening to get through the foliage.

Touching the branches, I saw that someone had been here before me – some of the foliage had been cut back to create a path. Growing still, I touched the branches with care, wondering who had cut them back, and when, listening intently to the woods surrounding me for anything that didn't belong.

Henry suddenly appeared right beside me. *What are you listening for?*

"Anything that sounds like someone else is here," I said in a low voice.

There's no one here. They were here a day or so ago, carrying a rolled carpet. Henry thought for a minute. *She was worrying about her powers. He told her that he had everything under control and to trust him. I don't think they'll be back for a couple of days.*

I looked at him sharply. "'They'? Who else has been here?"

Henry shook his head. *I've never seen them before. He calls her 'sissy', sometimes, but I'm not sure why. She's anything but a sissy.*

The word 'sissy' reminded me of the dream I'd had. Was the woman Henry had mentioned was connected to Cat? "You said they wouldn't be back for a couple of days." Glancing in the direction of the lane, I wondered how they got a rolled carpet to the house without damaging their car and not disturb the over-growth at the lane's entrance. "How did they get in? I had to walk in from the main road and it's like a jungle."

Henry frowned, pointing at the lane, then gesturing vaguely north. *The lane doesn't end here, it continues on. They came the same way I tried to leave.*

"Which means, what?" I asked, puzzled. "There's another way in?"

He nodded. *I can't go that way. I've tried, but I can only go as far as the road to town, where I found you.*

That was interesting. What tied Henry here, other than his death? Thoughtful, I asked, "How often do they come out?"

He looked a little sheepish. *Once a week, maybe more?*

Huh. "Do you remember when they first started coming out?"

He shook his head. *My sense of time is skewed. I think they started coming out here after the last rain.*

It hadn't rained since late March. We were already ten

132

days into April. So, whoever it was, they'd been coming around the place for at least three weeks. I looked down the path the mystery couple had most likely made, suspecting that it ended somewhere near the house. Henry didn't think they'd be back out for another couple of days, but if his sense of time was skewed, then I didn't want to stay here longer than necessary.

Pulling my sweater close, I stepped carefully down the path, pausing every once in a while to listen. The people who had been here before me had done a good job of cutting back the growth and I was able to make my way easily to the small clearing facing a two-story old house.

I stared up at it. "How is it that no one in Sleepy Eye Cove knows about this place?"

Henry shrugged. *Old news and old timers often pass without mention.*

True.

So, the couple who had cut the fresh path must have a personal connection to the property, otherwise, how would they know about it? Both the porch and the stairs were fairly clear of debris, considering that the place was abandoned. My guess was that this minor maintenance was due to Henry's unwelcome guests.

Stepping forward, I touched the banister leading up to the front porch. The wood had been painted at one time, but it was now faded and peeling, revealing a natural grain. The railing had lost its polish and was now cracked. I jerked my hand back when a tiny splinter pierced my skin, hissing. Damn it, that hurt. Shaking my hand in reflex, I tested the bottom step with my weight. I didn't want to fall through the wood, even if the people Henry had mentioned had had no issue putting their weight on it.

The board creaked, but held steady. The next few steps were easy and soon, I was standing across from the door. With care, I made my way across the porch, trying to leave behind as little evidence as possible about my presence. At the window, I peered inside, shading my eyes in order to see through the disintegrating curtains. Lots of furniture, covered in sheets, cobwebs all over and dust coating everything.

Here was another confirmation about the presence of Henry's unwanted guests entering the house – fresh scuff marks in the dust covering the floor.

Whoever they were and whether or not they were coming back soon wasn't what bothered me, though. It was the very fact that Henry's unwanted guests knew of this abandoned house's existence, when no one else in the area, other than Wes, seemed to have a clue that it was here. An old, remote home with a tragedy attached to it was always local color to be shared among the people of any town. Though a part of me wanted to explore right now, I knew I'd feel better if I had someone else out here with me.

I wondered how Abby would feel about a little breaking and entering…..

Something big and dark, almost pitch black, skittered away from the window and I jumped back a foot, breathless. It held its position at the window, as if staring at me, then vanished into the shadows deep within the house.

A shadow person, I thought, intrigued despite my initial fear, and turned to Henry, who was waiting for me at the bottom of the porch stairs. "Are there any other spirits here besides you and that shadow person?"

Henry shook his head. *If there are, they haven't revealed themselves to me. We don't always share the same energy.*

Retracing my steps, I went down to join him, studying the house's foundation where it met the ground. I was hoping to find a window so that I could take a quick peek in the basement. None were visible from where I was standing at the front of the house, so I started to walk around to the back. Being closer to the house, it was easier to push the branches open enough where I could slip through, closing them back behind me.

Henry seemed to understand what I was about.

There's a door over here, next to the kitchen steps, Henry said, standing a few feet ahead of me. He pointed past a spot where a small tree had fallen after a heavy storm, the exposed roots still half-buried in the churned-up earth. I stood and stared, frustrated. The tree's limbs had fallen across the back porch and where the basement door would have been.

Well, I couldn't get in that way, not without chopping up the tree.

I kicked a nearby rock with force, frustrated. When it hit the ground, it scattered some loose gravel in a wide spray. I heard a soft *clink* as one connected with what sounded like glass. I dropped to my knees, carefully pulling at the ivy that had spent the last few decades crawling up the outer walls of the house. Scooting as close as I could on my hands and knees, I was able to get to the window, which reflected my dirt-stained face and the trees behind me. I peered inside, cupping my hands on either side of my face to cut down on any light.

After a few seconds, my eyes adjusted to the darkened space. It seemed like a normal basement – weathered steam trunks stacked against one wall, heavy wooden crates tucked in the darkest corners, untouched by the light, a coal bin that still had enough coal in it to keep the place warm for at least one more winter.....

My eyes stopped at the large, rectangular wooden crate stashed in the far corner across from me. I frowned, pressing closer to the glass for a better look, taking care not to smudge the undisturbed dust that coated it in a thin film. To my left and almost out of my line of vision were two more crates. All three were made of what looked like plywood, very simple in design and hastily put together. They were also of a size that could comfortably fit a human being, but why would someone stash three corpses in the basement? Unless....

I sat back so fast, I lost my balance and almost

sprained my wrist. Fumbling to my feet, I tried to mask my presence on the property as best I could, then hustled back to the lane. As rattled as I was, I tried to keep from making my presence obvious by retracing my steps on the path I'd taken, being extra careful to not break any new foliage, branches or grass in the process.

It probably took me ten minutes. It felt like ten years.

I had found the vampire nest.

Fifteen

"You know, you could have told me that there were vampires in the basement."

We were walking back down the lane towards the truck. When I finally emerged from the overgrown hedges, I discovered Henry waiting for me at the rock wall. I didn't speak to him as I climbed over it, breathing a sigh of relief when my feet touched the lane once more. There was a small wink of light and I saw the truck, waiting where I had parked it further down.

I started walking, my thoughts swirling. The vampire in New Orleans had mentioned cousins in the west. Were these the 'cousins' he was referring to?

Henry fell in beside me. *Why are you surprised? You knew they were close by.*

True. Still, my heart hadn't stopped pounding since the discovery. "Yes, I know, but I didn't know they were *that* close." This earned me a chuckle from the ghost. I scowled, irritated. "I'm serious, Henry. It would have been helpful information."

They're looking for answers, just like you.

Well, yeah, I got that. The question was, who would find it first, whatever *it* is? We reached the truck and I climbed in. Henry remained where he was.

"What answers do they think they'll find on consecrated ground?" I asked. "I mean, it can't possibly be the same thing now that it was way back in 1925. Too much time has passed."

I wish I knew. Henry looked upset, as if he'd failed. *I'm not sure about the church, but it always seemed strange to me that Captain Pellington kept the basement locked.* Henry shrugged his discomfort. *But it was his house, his rules.*

Yeah, I knew that phrase quite well. "Same vampires vandalize the same church twice in less than a hundred years. What's the connection?" I muttered, starting the truck up.

I can't go any further than this lane. Henry popped out of sight.

"Later, 'gator," I said under my breath, put the truck in gear and drove back to the cemetery, pulling in just in time to see Wes step out of the office. He paused, watching as I parked the truck and made my way over to him. "Sorry I'm late. Do you still need me to go out and work on the rose bushes?"

"Yes, that'd be just fine, Katie," he said. "What took you so long to get back?"

I took a deep breath, exhaled. "Long story. Can we talk about the abandoned house on Black Rock Lane?"

He grew still. "What about it?"

I took a breath. "Did you know the family that lived there?"

It might have been a trick of the growing shadows as the sun went down, but I thought I saw something flicker across his face. "I knew of them, can't say that I knew them particularly well."

"What were they like?" I asked.

Wes studied me for a moment. "Why do you need to know, Katie?"

"Because something's out there," I said, not ready to tell him my real reasons, "and it wants my attention."

He gestured for me to come inside and soon we were settled in his office once more as he considered my question. "Private. At least, he was. Captain Pellington, I mean. His daughters were either attending school or church or running errands into town. Friendly. Not sure of their mother, as she was even more private than he was."

That confirmed what Henry had said. "What exactly happened to them?"

He shrugged, clearly uncomfortable with the topic. "No one knows for sure. Just that their bodies were found after the fact. Anna was the last one."

I remembered his reaction when I'd mentioned her name the day before. He had blushed a little, his gaze never quite meeting mine during the conversation. I blinked, suddenly realizing why. "You knew her, didn't you? Not just in passing, but to talk to." He didn't deny it, but that tell-tale blush came back. "You *liked* her."

He nodded, the blush deepening. "Yes, I did, quite a lot. It's…..complicated, Katie."

"How is it complicated?" I asked. "You knew her, you were friends, you….oh." I stopped, feeling embarrassed. "It was like that, wasn't it?"

His face had gone bright red, but this time, he didn't drop his eyes. "Yes. But it was not reciprocated. And I was content to let it be what it was – a friendship. That was all she was asking from me."

Embarrassed to have touched on a sensitive spot for Wes, I sought to change the focus. "Did she tell you anything that was going on in that house? I mean, like having unknown guests stay with them or strange goings on?"

He was silent for a moment, thinking over the past. At last, he said, "No. I think she was bound in the same way I was." He tugged on his collar, pulling it down a little and I saw the scars – silver, jagged tears in his skin. "I couldn't be sure, but I couldn't ask, either."

"Then how are you able to talk to me now?" I asked.

"The one who made these scars is long dead, so my binding is weak." He grimaced, shifting in his seat, uncomfortable. "But it hurts when I try to talk around it and the binding won't break until the entire nest is gone."

I considered his words. "So, if the nest is destroyed, you'll be free?"

He nodded. "Yes."

I stood, headed for the door. "Then I guess that's what I have to do."

He stood as well, worry lining his face. "Where are you off to now?"

I turned to look at him, struck by the exhaustion in his face. "I'm making a list of some of the spirits that I want to talk to, who've lived here during that time period."

Wes followed me to the door, standing on the edge of the porch, watching as I made my way across the manicured lawns to my shack. "If one of them is Mabel Richards, be aware that she is a talker. Don't let her get off topic."

I nodded. "I won't."

*****

Dottie was in a state of hysterics when I finally walked into the shack an hour later. Since she can be something of a drama queen anyway, I let her get it out of her system, washed my hands clean of the dirt from working on the rose bushes and began to put the groceries away.

Finally, Dottie started to calm down. "I thought you would never come home!"

"Take it up with Wes," I said, waving a hand to the door. "He's the one who sent me out on an errand. Besides, I was talking to him about Black Rock Lane."

Dottie sniffed. "Oh, that place. It's not very interesting, Cady. They all committed suicide in 1947, after the old captain went insane." She drew out that last word in a sing-song voice, with an emphasis on the long 'a'. "That's why Sarah's having such a hard time coping with her death and why Father O'Mare is counseling her about it."

"Uh, huh." I paused in the middle of putting away my ice cream. "Wait, what?"

"Have you found out any more about the vampires?" Dottie could never keep on point.

"I think so, but I need to talk to Father O'Mare again." I wanted to find out more about this girl Dottie's late pastor was guiding in the afterlife. "What did you say about him counseling someone named Sarah about her suicide?"

Dottie sniffed, wiping at her eyes. "Poor Sarah's father went insane and killed her beloved and then he went off and killed himself." I gestured impatiently for her to continue. "Sarah committed suicide about six months later. She jumped off a cliff. She and her family are buried on their property." Dottie ruffled her apron, as neatly pressed now as it was before she died in the fall of 1927. "Suicides can't be buried in a churchyard."

"Would her last name be Pellington, by any chance?"

Dottie thought about it. "It could be. We were never formally introduced." She added, in a rather confidential tone, "Different times, you know."

I didn't, but refrained from asking for clarification. Pulling out my copy of the cemetery's plot charts, I found several ideal candidates. Then I cross-referenced them in my log book and matched the numbers with actual names. There were six plots that matched my need to a T – all were local citizens that had been born and raised in Sleepy Eye Cove. They had all been alive and kicking during the forties, when the Pellingtons met their fateful ends.

Grabbing a pen and paper, I wrote out their names and ages at the time of their deaths, noting that three of them had died in the last ten years: Mabel Richards, age ninety-five; Herbert Stillman, age one hundred and two; and Ethel Stillman, Herbert's wife, age one hundred and three. The other three had passed on in the last forty years: Clyde Freeman, age eighty-two; Pola Debuvoise, age eighty; and, last, but not least, Marvin Kessler, age ninety-two.

I studied the names, thoughtful. I wanted to confirm Henry's story and these six seemed like my best bet to get that done. Thanks to Wes' heads up about Mabel Richards, I was prepared to ask my questions. Folding the paper into squares, I slipped it in my jeans back pocket, then grabbed my pack, searching for loose quarters. Pocketing the change, I put on my sweater, tidied my place and left.

The afternoon sun was hovering low in the horizon, the bright orange and yellow and hot pinks streaking the sky and reflecting in the ocean. Shadows were starting to deepen, different shades of purple and black.

The sun wouldn't set for another hour, but the surrounding trees made it seem later than it actually was. As I quickened my pace, I found myself anticipating the stories these six spirits might share with me. They'd be shedding insight not only onto the forgotten lane, but of Sleepy Eye Cove itself.

History can be a fascinating subject.

*****

It didn't take long for the six spirits to show up.

The first one to appear was Mabel Richards and, true to Wes' warning, she immediately began to pelt questions at me. Before I could even answer the first one, she was onto another subject entirely. By the time the other spirits manifested, I had Mabel's complete family history and most of her pet peeves.

"Well, that's not why I'm here…." I tried to break into her monologue, but Mabel was on a roll about some stolen necklace and the niece who was accused of the theft. Then Pola Debuvoise broke in, her voice soft, but firm.

"I'm sure that she'll find it quite fascinating, Mabel," she said, "but oughtn't we to listen to her request? Perhaps after she acquires what she needs to know, she'll be willing to help you with your questions."

That stopped Mabel and she regarded me closely. "That's an idea. What say you?"

I didn't see any problem with that. "It would have to be at a later time, since I'm busy looking into the business at the church."

Mabel considered this, then nodded. "Fair enough. Don't forget."

I turned to the others. "I have questions about Black Rock Lane, the Pellington family and a young man named Henry Gray."

They all focused on me, curiosity lighting up their features.

"I saw him first, out of all of us!" Mabel cried, delighted, eyes bright with memory. "He came into my store," she told me in confidential tones. "It was a fierce storm that had come through that winter, the worst one to happen in 1946. And it was still raining when I saw him walking up the street that February, not long after my thirty-third birthday....."

Well, it was pretty clear who was going to start this.

Sitting cross-legged, I pulled out a notebook and began to record their words.

The Spectral Six Spin Tales

February 1946

Mabel Richards was the first to spot the boy.

The mercantile store ("Which became the Prescott supermarket in 1967," Mabel informed me, "after I sold it and retired.") had a bay window that overlooked Main Street and the village park's gazebo. From where she stood, it was easy to see customers walking up and down the newly paved streets of Sleepy Eye Cove at any given moment.

Right now, however, with rain threatening and a cold wind blowing in from the ocean, there was only that boy. Pulling her sweater close, Mabel checked on the pot-bellied stove she used to keep the store warm, throwing in small pieces of wood to feed the fire. Satisfied, she went back to her place by the window to observe the boy.

Tall, slender, dark, shaggy hair in need of a cut, the boy could hardly have been more than seventeen. His clothes weren't patched, but even from her post, Mabel could see that the fabric was beginning to thin a little. The canvas rucksack slung over his shoulder had seen better days, as well. In spite of the gloomy weather, the boy seemed unconcerned, his pace casual and easy, as if he was in no particular hurry to get along to where he was going.

As she watched, it began to rain, small drops smattering the window at first. Then the sky let loose and the rain fell in sheets. Startled, the boy looked up at the sky, disbelieving. Within minutes, he was drenched.

Mabel frowned. The boy'll catch pneumonia and die in a ditch, she thought and moved from behind the counter to the shop door. Opening it to call out to the boy to get inside, she saw at once that she hadn't been the only one to notice the traveler.

An old truck, perhaps a decade old, had parked in front of the barber shop across the street and former Navy Captain Marcus Pellington slipped out the driver's side. He called to the boy, who approached him with caution. Mabel approved – caution was best when dealing with the unknown. Soon, however, the captain had him inside the mercantile.

"Good morning, Mrs. Richards," the captain said, smiling. The smile didn't soften his thin, sallow face and neither did it reach his eyes. Despite Pellington being a resident of Sleepy Eye Cove since his retirement from service, Mabel found that she had become increasingly reluctant to assist him when he came into the store. The boy hung back a little, uncertain of his own reception.

"Good morning, Captain," she said, forcing a smile. "Your order hasn't come in yet. Might be another week or so."

He nodded. "No matter." He clapped a hand on the boy's shoulder. "This young fellow needs to warm up. May he stand by the stove?"

Mabel softened towards the captain a little. "Of course."

The boy glanced first at the captain, then to her. "Thank you, ma'am." Then he went and sat in front of the stove immediately. Now that she had a closer look at him, Mabel realized that the boy was hardly a boy, but a young man, at least five years older than her own crippled son,

Georgie, who had just turned fifteen.

She turned to the captain, about to ask if there was anything else he needed. The question died on her lips when she saw his expression. Naked hunger had brought color to his pale face, eyes glittering with anticipation. Instinctively, Mabel Richards stepped back from him, her hip bumping into the counter's edge. The action distracted the captain and he turned towards her, his movements surprisingly agile.

"Will there be anything else?" Mabel was glad that her voice sounded steady, calm. ("I felt anything but," she said firmly to me, several decades later.)

Pellington thought for a minute. "A fresh set of clothes for him."

The boy – young man, Mabel reminded herself – looked over, surprised. "You needn't do that, sir. I'll be fine."

The captain shook his head. "I insist. And I need a little help around my property. Consider it an advance in payment."

Still, the young man hesitated. Mabel willed the boy to turn the captain's offer down. Then he smiled. "I suppose I could stay on for a couple of weeks."

The captain turned to Mabel. "Put it on my account, will you, Mrs. Richards?"

She nodded. "Of course, Captain."

After helping find the right sizes in pants, boots and two shirts, she directed the young man to the back room. Pellington turned abruptly and went out to his truck. A few minutes later, in his new clothes, the young man emerged from the back, shouldering his knapsack.

Mabel stopped him. "You don't need to go with the captain."

He smiled at her, an engaging twist of his lips. "Oh, I know, but it'll be only for a couple of weeks. Or until I find her again."

Her? Mabel felt her heart sink, disappointed. Young

love was not always in company with good sense. "Perhaps. But you're not obligated to him beyond those clothes. And since it's my store, I could make it so that you're obligated to me."

Some of her worry seemed to be rubbing off on him and he frowned, glancing towards the truck just outside. "Is there something wrong?"

How could she answer that, when she wasn't entirely sure herself? She shook her head and smiled, patting his arm with more reassurance than she felt. "No, I'm sure things will turn out just fine for you. This weather makes me moody."

He smiled again. "Thank you. If I need to, I'll ask for help. I'm Henry Gray."

She took his proffered hand. "Mabel Richards. Be well."

He went out the door. Watching through the window, Mabel observed him climb into the passenger side of the truck. Within minutes, it had backed up and was rumbling down the rain-slicked streets, spraying up mud. Then it rounded a corner and was gone.

Henry Gray never came back to her mercantile, but he never left town, either. She saw him on occasion, running errands in town. Once, she saw him at the Fourth of July picnic, holding hands with a girl she recognized as Sarah Pellington. The love she saw there frightened her, even as it warmed her, and she could not explain to herself why. They exchanged 'hellos' and waves, but that was all.

And then, one day, he stopped coming into town at all.

Late June 1946
Pola Debuvoise was only half-listening to Sarah Pellington as the young woman recounted to her about how she had met her beau, Henry. Pola was busy securing a colorful banner to the top of her booth. The Fourth of July was

148

only five days away, but the village had turned it into a week-long celebration of bake-offs, quilting and foot races.

("I didn't care for the heat or the fuss," Pola was saying, when Mabel chimed in, "Your flower shop made more profit than any other store in town and you know it." I shushed her and encouraged Pola to continue.)

Fortunately, this year, she had gotten her booth set up under the old oak tree that stood near the freshly painted gazebo. The two hundred year old specimen's branches spread over the lawn and the booths, providing plenty of shade.

"It was very romantic." Sarah giggled over the bouquet of purple pansies and pink roses she had just put together. She looked over at the older woman. "Sort of like a fairy tale."

Pola smiled, remembering her own youthful fancies. "Was it? Hand me the purple sash, will you, dear?"

Sarah picked up the requested item and handed it over. "Oh, yes! I'd gone for a walk and found him camping. I couldn't understand why, it was such cold weather."

Pola tied the purple sash around a large ceramic vase. "Why was he camping?"

The younger woman didn't answer right away. When she did, her cheeks had turned a bright pink. "He's a wanderer."

"Ah." They didn't say anything for the next twenty minutes, both busy with setting up the bouquets and vases and fielding questions from passers-by.

"Will Mr. Debuvoise be coming out?" Sarah asked.

Pola shook her head. "No, he's not feeling well. Headache." It was a weak excuse, she knew, but better than revealing her husband's night terrors and grabbing for a leg that was no longer there.

Sarah dimmed. "Oh, I'm sorry. I forgot he was in the War." She glanced away, pink, but not before Pola caught the surreptitious glance towards the clock tower.

The older woman smiled and checked the watch pinned to her blouse. "It's almost eleven, Sarah. Go see your young man."

Sarah grinned, put down the ribbons she'd been holding and started off. As she passed the old oak tree, however, she paused and reached for its trunk for balance, her face pale. Then, in an awkward motion, she leaned over and heaved. Pola was at her side instantly, holding back the girl's hair, but nothing came up. After a minute, Sarah's breathing evened out and her color came back, though she was still pale around her eyes.

"I'm fine, thank you, Mrs. Debuvoise," she said, quickly drawing away. "I'll see you in an hour."

She was gone, disappearing into the crowds.

Pola Debuvoise watched her go, frowning. Then Mrs. Simms from the church social club came over to discuss flower arrangements and Pola soon forgot all about her young helper.

October 1946

Over at the lumber yard, Clyde Freeman sat in his office, glancing out the window while sorting through the previous day's receipts. Earlier in the week, Pellington had put in an order for wood planks, indicating that the Gray boy would come in to pick it up. Freeman had been waiting on the boy for over an hour.

"Porch repairs," the retired captain had said. "Need to get it done before the rains. Henry will be around to pick it up when it's ready."

Freeman had murmured in agreement, striving to keep the encounter short. Despite the fact that Pellington had been a good customer over the years, Freeman wanted as a little to do with him as possible. He didn't like the predatory look in Pellington's eyes. ("Glad to know I wasn't the only one spooked by that man," Mabel muttered. I shushed her once more. She scowled, but

150

refrained from further comment.)

Freeman looked up at the clock hanging over the door. Half-past twelve. He wondered if he should just pack up the planks and take them out to Black Rock Lane himself. Bill the captain for the delivery later, of course. Maybe help the boy put the planks down, make sure it was done properly. He liked that boy, Henry. The Stillmans had yet to stop praising his work on their fence, making it secure so that their damn pooch wouldn't escape again.

Maybe he could offer the boy a job at the lumber yard.

At one, Clyde Freeman decided to make the delivery to Black Rock Lane and informed his floor manager that he'd be back. He said nothing about the boy, Henry. It was more than likely that the boy had decided to move on, see what was on the other side of the horizon. Henry had admitted he was a drifter when making a pick up for the old captain earlier in the fall, so it didn't seem unlikely. Freeman would find out soon enough what was going on there. No need to make anyone else a part of it.

Half an hour later, he turned the lumber yard truck down the narrow lane, pulling into the circular driveway in front of the Pellington house. The captain was out on the porch before Freeman could put the truck in park.

"Hello!" he cried. "I thought Henry was picking up the wood?"

Freeman swung out of the cab. "Never showed. Grew concerned. Everything all right out here?"

Pellington's jovial smile came a fraction of second too slow. "Of course. That's odd, Henry not showing up." He shrugged. "But he is a wanderer. I did warn my daughters not to become overly fond of him."

"So he's gone, then."

The captain nodded. "I haven't seen him since early this morning. Naturally, I assumed he was on his way to pick up the wood."

Freeman considered this. "As you can see, he didn't."

He spotted the Pellington truck at the far side of the drive. "What time did the boy leave?"

The captain thought for a minute. "Around nine-thirty, ten."

Henry had been due to pick up the wood planks at eleven. A time arranged for by the captain. Now he was gone. These facts swirled around Freeman's mind in the space of ten seconds.

"He didn't leave a note?" he asked. "No explanation?"

Pellington shook his head. "No. He was just….gone."

"That's a pity, then," he said, moving to the flatbed. "I'll unload these then, maybe send out one of the boys if you need help laying them out."

The captain made no move to help, merely stood back and watched. Freeman took his time taking the boards from the back of his truck and stacking them neatly next to the porch steps. He was keenly aware of the cold, predatory gaze following his every move. As he moved the boards, Freeman became aware of the silence permeating the air.

No bird cries, no giggles from the three girls that lived in the house, no calls from the captain's wife. It was the quiet of the dead, with only his harsh breathing breaking it.

As soon as the last board had been stacked with the others, Clyde Freeman got back into his truck. Putting it in gear, he maneuvered it back onto the lane and towards town, risking a quick look back at the captain. That flat, dead predatory look was back, darkening Pellington's eyes, and Freeman almost crashed into the stone wall. Hitting the brakes, Freeman turned the wheel hard, straightening out the truck.

Heart pounding, he kept his eyes on the road, driving as fast as the truck would go.

All the way back to town, he told himself repeatedly

that of course he didn't see the captain hold his hand out into the sunlight. He didn't see the captain's hand start to emit thin wisps of smoke. And that dead look in the man's eyes – just a trick of light and shadow.

By the time he had pulled back into the lumber yard, Clyde Freeman had convinced himself that nothing unusual had happened. The boy, Henry Gray, had taken off, as boys that age on the road often did. And soon, the town's memory of Henry faded, as if he had never existed.

December 1946

Marvin Kessler remembered the death of Marcus Pellington easily.

("Not a thing one is likely to forget," he told me at the beginning of his story decades later, sitting next to his grave. "Especially when it happens right in front of you." Mabel sniffed her disbelief.)

Pellington and his family had become reclusive and the captain made rare trips alone into the village for necessities. Rumors circulated that they had caught a wasting disease of some kind, but the local doctor hadn't been able to determine such a diagnosis. This struck the gossip circle as odd, but not even Mabel Richards could get any real explanation as to why. And then the family stopped coming into town at all.

So it was with some surprise, when he stepped out of the warmth of the mercantile store, that Marvin Kessler saw the captain, alone, in the little park, next to the gazebo. The storm that had been brewing for the last few days was now threatening to unleash its wrath on the coast and he wanted to be safe and warm in his own home before it started. His wife's beef stew was the stuff of dreams and his stomach rumbled in anticipation.

He paused briefly on the store's covered porch, buttoning up his coat, then made his way down to his truck. The clouds had gone dark, almost purple, and he could smell the rain that was threatening. Given the predicted strength of the storm, Marvin suspected that the cemetery was going to be in rough shape. That Burke fella was going to need help to clean the place up and remove any fallen trees.

Marvin supposed it would fall to him to hire on an extra hands.

His hand was on the truck door when he froze, not quite understanding what he was seeing only a few yards away. Stepping away from his truck, Marvin made his way to the little park, his eyes straying to the giant oak, uneasy. The tree was overdue for a trim – he didn't want to have a heavy branch fall on the captain. Marvin's gaze went back to the other man, who had turned his face up towards the sky, mouth open, as if tasting the air.

Marvin frowned, moving closer, hardly aware of his surroundings. His attention was solely on the man wearing only trousers and a loose shirt, his feet bare. Discarded shoes and socks had been placed neatly on the gazebo step.

Despite having been pale and thin for as long as Marvin could remember, Pellington now looked like the picture of health, his face flushed and full. But it was the red can at Pellington's feet that confused Marvin. So did the captain's wet clothes. He frowned, holding out his hand and glancing up at the sky. It hadn't started raining in town yet, but had it been raining near Black Rock Lane?

Then he saw what Pellington had in his hands.

"No, wait!" he cried, sprinting forward.

"I have peace now," Pellington said, and struck a match against the rough side of the matchbox. "They will not be so lucky."

The match fell. Flames engulfed the retired captain almost immediately. Marvin fell back, too horrified even to cry out for the help that would come. Pellington met his gaze, held it until he collapsed. From the mercantile came shouts of horror and shock, but Marvin barely heard them, his gaze fixed with Pellington's – a mad man who had finally found sanity.

He would not speak of those moments, nor of the deadly, final gaze of Marcus Pellington, not even to his wife.

January 1947

"Do you see that?"

Herbert Stillman glanced at his wife. It was the last week of January and they had just celebrated their seventieth birthdays. The storms had broken up for a while, but more were due in the coming days. The Stillmans had taken the chance to get out of the house and go for a long walk. Ethel brought along her binoculars to observe the sea lions or birds that sometimes made themselves at home on the rocks.

Now Ethel Stillman was clutching it to her eyes now, knuckles white, peering down at the beach. She handed them over to him, not looking away from whatever it was that had her attention. "Take a look, Herb. What do you think it is?"

Herbert took the binoculars and looked in the direction his wife was pointing, adjusting the lenses. He frowned. A bunch of clothes had been tossed carelessly onto the rocks below. But there was something odd about how the clothes had landed, almost as if they'd been weighted down or carefully arranged. And was that a wig?

He stepped back abruptly.

Ethel stared at him. "What is it, Herb?"

"I think we need to go get the sheriff," he said. His voice sounded far away.

She grew concerned. "The sheriff?" Then, "It isn't trash, is it?"

He shook his head. "No. I think it's one of the Pellington girls."

Her gasp was lost in the wind as he hurried towards

town, his wife close behind him.

When the body had been fished out an hour later, it was almost immediately identified as Sarah Pellington. A deputy had been dispatched to the house on Black Rock Lane to report the tragedy. It was expected that the house would still be in mourning over the death of Marcus Pellington a month earlier.

What greeted the deputy as he pulled into the driveway was a dark house, the front door standing ajar. Apprehensive, he unholstered his gun and approached with caution, pushing the door open further onto a dark room. Although there appeared that no one was home, he did not feel like he was alone.

"Hello?" he called, his voice bouncing off the foyer walls. No response, as he put into his report later that day, so he took a quick look around the house. Nothing was out of place and there were no signs of a struggle. Even the dishes on the dining table seemed to have just been laid out, along with the fine crystal.

He scouted the area, hoping that perhaps he would find the at least one other family member to report his unhappy news. He found one, near a gnarled, old tree, but not as he had hoped. The woman crumpled under the tree was Helen Pellington, Sarah's older sister. She had been dead for at least a day, her neck bloodied and torn. The deputy stumbled back, hand over his mouth and nose, trying not to breathe in the coppery scent of blood. Catching himself, he headed back for his car, only to stumble over the second corpse, lying crumpled against the stone wall that surrounded the house and gardens.

Catherine Pellington, the captain's wife, was in a similar condition as her dead daughter.

The deputy managed to get back to his car before he vomited at the side of the lane. He radioed for assistance, his voice sounding far away, numb.

Anna, the eldest sister, was still missing.

"Mark my words, that girl Anna ran off to the city. San Francisco, maybe, or New York. She won't be found."

Ethel Stillman ignored Mabel Richards's remarks. Half the town was of the mind that Anna Pellington had had something to do with her family's death, but the other half believed she had seen something horrific and fled. Ethel wasn't sure what to think, so she offered nothing. The two women were hiking in the woods, a rare outing for free-style sketching to take to a monthly art workshop. The heavy walking stick Ethel used for balance had a pronged bottom, allowing it to dig into the earth. It could also serve as a weapon, if needed.

Despite their age difference, Ethel Stillman rather enjoyed Mabel's company. The Richards woman ran a tight store, always had it properly stocked and well-cleaned. ("Well, I should hope so," Mabel interrupted. "A clean store creates space for merchandise and that means sales." After a pause, she added, "Thank you, Ethel.") Mabel's son, Georgie, was in charge of delivery, despite the accident which resulted in his limp. There was a second boy who had helped with deliveries until Georgie had recovered. Now he kept the store clean.

"Where is this flower patch?" Mabel asked for the fifth time. She leaned up against a tree, wiping her brow with the back of her hand.

Ethel paused long enough to take stock of their surroundings. "Next rise over."

The two women hiked on. Mabel sneezed, the old, sickly sweet smell in the air tickling her nose relentlessly. "What is that smell?"

Ethel sniffed. "Dead animal, I suppose."

Mabel sniffed the air again. "It's coming from over there." She pointed to the rock formation twenty feet to their left. Ivy had pretty much conquered it, leaving only the top visible to the sun. She wrinkled her nose. "Stronger."

Ethel followed her friend, catching the overwhelmingly sweet odor as they drew closer to the ivy patch. A sudden premonition gripped her and, just as Mabel began to pull back at the ivy, Ethel cried, "No, don't!"

Too late. The corpse grinned at her, all skeleton and hair and rotted cloth.

Mabel covered her mouth, reaching blindly for her friend. For several minutes, the two women clung to each other, unable to speak.

The missing daughter, Anna Pellington, had been found.

Sixteen

Wes hadn't been exaggerating – Mabel Richards was a talker. To go by the expressions on her neighbors' faces, illuminated more by their own ectoplasm than by the white candles I'd lit for the occasion, I'd say that this was a habit with her in life that carried over into her afterlife. Now she was re-enacting the moment of discovering Anna Pellington. My hand cramped and I winced, shaking it out.

"But are you sure you've got that right?" Ethel asked her friend. She glanced at me, adding in a confidential tone, "They never found out how Anna Pellington died."

"Of course I'm sure I've got it right!" Mabel's jowls quivered in outrage as she turned to face Ethel. "You were there, remember?" She turned to me. "We had to hike back into town and tell the sheriff that we had found her."

"But what killed the family?" I asked, curious. A light breeze kicked up, making the candle flame flicker, then died. The flame continued to burn. "Did anyone strange go to visit them or come to town to make odd purchases in their names?"

Herbert Stillman shook his head. "Pellington and his family kept to themselves. They didn't even have electricity connected out to their place." He shook his head. "If they

159

had a visitor, they would be unlikely to advertise the fact. If you go back far enough, that lane connects to the main road over to Wickerman Falls. That's usually the route they would take, is my understanding."

I considered that, remembering what Henry had said about the lane, tapping the concrete slab I sat on with one foot. Mabel frowned at me pointedly. I muttered an apology and shifted into a different position. It still didn't address the vampires and I asked, "What really happened to the church in 1925?"

They all stopped nattering among themselves to look at me. It was Marvin Kessler who finally spoke. "What do you want to know about that bit of tomfoolery?"

I eyed him, suspicion prickling my neck. "You know something."

Marvin fussed a bit with his coat buttons. "What makes you say that?"

"You're frightened."

He glanced at the others; not even Herbert Stillman would look him in the eye.

"Look, I've already got most of this from Wes Burke and Father O'Mare, anyway," I said, patiently. "I'm just looking to confirm a few things because this all started out as a problem with vampires at that church and now I'm dealing with a dead and the ghost of a man no one really knew about. Help me out here."

The six senior citizen ghosts exchanged glances. Then, finally, Pola Debuvoise cleared her throat delicately. We all looked at her with various degrees of expectation.

"I remember when Captain Pellington moved to Sleepy Eye Cove," she said in soft, cultured tones. "He was a tall man, quite robust and handsome. It was a shame that he took ill shortly after he was attacked in 1924." Pola paused, looked at me. "He was gaunt after that, never regained his former weight."

I recalled what Pellington's shade had told me about his encounter. "You're saying that Pellington was attacked by the same vampires who vandalized the church?"

The spectral senior citizens glanced at each other, their expressions grave.

It was Herbert Stillman who answered. "It seems likely, yes."

There was an awkward silence.

I eyed them. "So you knew about the vampires."

Marvin Kessler looked a little embarrassed. "We didn't know until later."

"How much later?"

Herbert Stillman sniffed. "Such things aren't possible. Vampires, ghosts – all of that is not for reasonable folk."

"And yet, here we are, talking like it was just another Sunday," I said, unable to keep the sarcasm from my voice.

He gave me a withering look. "Smart alecks like you are a disturbance to my rest. Which I, for one, would like to get back to."

I took the hint. "My apologies, Mr. Stillman. Thank you, all of you, for your time."

Before long, I was the only one standing among the graves. Stepping carefully, I blew out the candles and gathered them up, shoving them into a back pocket. From another pocket, I pulled out some change, making sure I had the right amount.

As a more formal 'thank you', I left a silver coin each on their markers and headed back to my shack.

*****

Information was chasing itself around my brain as I approached my shack. As soon as I shut the door, I dropped my pack onto the table and went to fix myself a peanut butter sandwich. Then I sat at my tiny table and pulled out my notebook, going over everything that I'd written while listening to the six specters, still processing what I'd learned. Then, pulling out the notebook I'd used at the Wycliff College library, I began to compare notes.

What the Spectral Six had told me certainly fleshed out the dry reports I'd found down in the library's archives and verified what Father O'Mare and Wes had offered. But they also raised more questions – such as, what connects the vampires, the Pellington place and the Naughtons to the current vandalism at the church? And the deaths of my biological parents that led to my hidden adoption? And the Galloways' secrecy about all of it?

Realizing that I wasn't going to get any answers, no matter how much I stared at my notes, I pushed the notebook away and proceed to finish eating my sandwich. Taking a deep sip of water, I had just popped the last bite into my mouth and was savoring the taste of peanut butter and sourdough bread, when there was a knock on my door.

Dottie poked her head through the wall, looking agitated.

"It's the witch, the one who works at the nursery," she said in a loud whisper. "I think she wants to come in."

Stretching, my muscles stiff, I got to my feet and went to let Abby in.

Abby pushed past me, looking worried. "Before this last visit, Claire had come in about six weeks ago and paid cash for an entire stock of herbs used to make protection spells." She handed me a sheet of paper. I took it, noticing that it was an invoice. "That's why she was in the store when you came in, to order more."

So Claire Naughton wanted to keep her personal circle protected. If she was buying out and ordering more from a smaller shop, like Abby's, then she must have bought enough at the bigger shops that they had run out of stock, as well. Claire hadn't seemed like the flappable type when we'd met, but obviously she was flapped about something.

I looked at Abby. "What do you think is going on?"

Abby looked at me with such fear that I stiffened. I didn't know her very well, but she didn't seem the type to be shaken by much, but something had her scared. "You'd think one of the more powerful families wouldn't have so much bad luck following them around, but the Naughtons are that family."

"Like the deaths of Calliope Naughton and Bennett Welles?" I asked; at her curious look, I hastened to add, "I looked them up the other day."

She nodded, the fear still present, but not nearly as intense. "Then you'll be interested to know what happened to Caitlyn." Abby settled deeper into my couch, pulling out a magazine and opening it to a marked page, handing it to me. Taking it, I saw with a cold fascination that it was the same article I'd been reading in Deke's place. Abby continued. "She's a freelance photo-journalist, so she travels all over the world to cover events and write some travel pieces. Like prize-winning. I think she was up for an award for one story about a shady former hospital back East, but I don't remember the publication."

She fell silent. Although I already knew something of the story, I nudged her, prodding for more of the story. "So, what happened to her? Did she get killed covering a riot or a war or something?"

"No." Abby frowned, pausing to collect her thoughts. "Oh, no, nothing like that. Caitlyn was working on a couple of travel articles in Louisiana."

The hair on the back of my neck prickled hard, sending an icy shiver straight down my spine, and I remembered the blonde woman leaving Louise's place the night I'd taken care of Deke's vampire. "How long ago was she in Louisiana?"

Abby thought back. "I'm not sure, but she got home about a week or so ago," she said, slowly, counting back. "Right after Cat got back, she got into this huge argument with Cecelia about her powers." She shifted, leaning closer, intent, eyes bright. "I'd been in their shop up in Wickerman Falls, looking for a book to send to my grandmother for her birthday. They really got into it." Abby paused, thinking. "Claire shoved them into the back office, but I overheard Cat say something about a missing child. Then Cecelia slammed the office door and I paid for the book and left. Cat disappeared not long after that, around the same time Claire had her car accident."

I blinked, taking in Abby's words, repeating them back to be clear. "So, Cat went missing and Claire got run off the road." That seemed entirely too coincidental to me. "Do you think her disappearance and Claire's car going into a ditch are related?"

Abby shook her head, unsure. "I don't know. But what's creepy is that when Claire had her accident, Cat apparently just left the house. The door was left wide open and she had left case files on their parents' death and notes about a woman named Louise. Her suitcase hadn't even been unpacked."

"Were there any clues as to what happened?" I asked, re-directing Abby's focus. "I mean, she couldn't have just dropped off the face of the earth." I wanted to get the conversation away from Louisiana and Louise. There were thousands of women named Louise in Louisiana. It didn't mean that this Louise was *my* Louise.

But of course, it had to be. It was Cat that I had seen leaving Louise's shop on the night I encountered the vampire in the diner. She was the woman who had prompted my abrupt departure from New Orleans. And it was she who had written the article detailing the highlights of Maurier County and one of the reasons I'd come here.

Abby shook her head. "No, there was no forced entry, no stolen items, nothing. It was as if Cat had just gone for a walk and forgot to shut the door."

It didn't seem like a coincidence that Claire's car accident and Cat's disappearance occurred at around the same time. While there was no evidence to suggest it, the two incidents seemed to be connected to the internal strife of the Naughton coven. The threads were there, I could feel it, but I couldn't see the pattern. I chewed on my lip, thinking.

Abby watched me, curious. "What's wrong?"

I waved my hand. "Nothing. Just sorting out ideas." Switching topics a little, I asked, "Exactly what kind of power does Caitlyn have? Can she *glamour* like Julian or is she an *impremere*? And what is Claire's gift?"

Abby was shaking her head. "No, Cat's pretty powerful with spell work and mimicry, but she can't *glamour*." She grinned suddenly. "There's a story about how she used a powerful spell to teleport herself from one place to another. It's been going around for years."

Something Abby had said earlier nagged at me. "What were they were arguing about?"

"Who? Caitlyn and Cecelia? Or Claire and Cecelia?"

I shook my head, not really sure. "All of the above, I guess."

"Well, on the one hand, they're sisters, so a man, obviously." She laughed and I was glad to see her mood lighten a little. "Cat was not pleased when Cecelia started dating Julian Webster."

I could understand Cat's reservations about him. "Why? I mean, it's not like Cat has any say over who her sisters choose to date. It's not like she's their mother."

"Maybe not, but the deaths of her parents and, later, their guardian, sort of put her in that position," Abby said, thoughtful. A shadow crossed her face and I wondered if she was thinking of her own family dynamics. Then, "I think Cat's main objection to her sister dating Julian was their age difference." At my blank look, she added, "Julian's well over a decade older than Cecelia, so I see her point."

"So....you don't think it's his abilities in magic that bothered her?" I asked.

Abby shook her head. "No, I don't think she'd care if Cecelia dated a witch or a non-magical person. But it could be due to his interest in pushing magical boundaries that concerns her. It makes him dangerous and unpredictable. And then there's his taste for the dark arts." She shuddered, looked at me. "Handsome or not, he is not someone I'd want to do business with."

I recalled Julian arguing with Claire in the bookstore. "He referred to Claire as 'sister', but she dismissed him as wishing for what he can't have. So he and Cecelia haven't gotten married or something, otherwise she'd have taken him more seriously."

"I know that he's part of the law firm employed by the Naughton family." Abby's face grew pensive when she added, "And he really wants to be a part of their coven by any means possible, even using Cecelia to do it."

"Doesn't he love her? That seems rude."

"He probably does, but it wouldn't stop him from doing whatever it takes to get whatever he wants." She looked at me sternly, beginning to regain some healthy color back into her face. I felt relieved – the fear in her eyes had been disconcerting. "Julian may be a good-looking guy, but he's dark with a hard edge, Katie. Stay away from him."

"He's dark like Cecelia, then."

She shook her head. "No, worse." She paused, lowered her voice, "He *glamoured* himself to look like Raul Kendrick at court and it almost cost Raul his license."

Claire had said something to that effect during her argument with Julian at the bookshop, when I'd overheard their conversation. And I'd seen him do something similar to what Abby was describing, both at Raul's office and at the bookshop – his way, I suppose, of teasing both Raul and Claire. "Did he get away with it? How did it play out?"

Abby shrugged, her expression troubled. "Raul was able to convince the judge that it was a practical joke made in poor taste."

I felt my brow wrinkle in concern. "What exactly did Julian Webster do?"

"He made a pass at the judge. During court proceedings. While defending Raul's client."

That didn't seem so bad. "How do you know about it?"

Abby blushed pink. "One of the filing clerks in Raul's office was there and told me about Julian's trick on a date."

If he could pass as Raul as a joke, then would he use that ability to his own advantage? It was likely, given what I'd observed of him. Something to watch out for and an excellent reason to know those around me better. "Is that the worst that Julian can do?"

She shrugged, shaking her head. "Not that I've witnessed but there are stories. He plays hard and for keeps and, like I said, isn't above using dark magic."

That sounded like the man I'd encountered and was more than enough for me. "Okay, I don't need to hear any more. I want to keep my skin on, thanks, not get it flayed off, magically or otherwise."

Abby dropped the subject gratefully and pulled a dark burgundy pouch out from her satchel, handing it to me. It smelled like lavender and jasmine. "I had some time, so I made you this. It will help protect you against any dark magic and negative energy that comes your way. Keep it on at all times, so that it can absorb your energy. It'll work better."

I took it, slipped it around my neck and tied it off securely. "Thanks."

Satisfied, Abby rummaged through her satchel once more. "I've got the visibility spell in here, too. I started working on it after we talked the other day......Ha!" She pulled out a small wooden box, triumphant, then grinned. "I've used this spell before, to help find some of the best seedlings for my nursery." At my curious look, she added, "The visibility spell is adaptable to the specific task. Seedlings, lost or hidden objects – it reveals what your eyes can't see."

"Thanks for this," I said, examining the box with care. "I'll be using this soon. I'm sure Dottie will want to participate."

Dottie poked her head in through the wall. "Did you

call me? Or am I hearing things?"

"No, Dottie," I said. "Go haunt someone else for a while."

She sniffed and disappeared.

Abby looked around, mystified. "I'll never get used to you being able to see and interact with ghosts like that."

I blinked. "Then how did you know about Dottie in the first place?"

"I can sense them, their energies and what they might have been like in life," she explained, with a shrug, "but I don't have the gift that you do." Her expression darkened. "My mother can see the dead and reminds me of it."

There was a story behind her words and I wondered if it was the cause or the symptom of her obvious estrangement with her mother.

Standing, I offered her some tea. "It's not fancy, just the store brand mint, but it tastes pretty decent."

"Sure, then I have to go," she said, her head resting against the back of the couch. She looked around, taking the shack in with interest. "This place is actually kind of cozy. It doesn't look like much from the outside, but it's cute."

"It serves," I said, getting cups from the cupboard and putting a tea bag into each. Turning on the hot plate, I put the kettle on. "Do you mind if I ask what the argument with your mom is?"

She laughed, but there was no humor. "Mom is......a mom. She's smart and funny really cool and we can get along, and then....." She paused, shifted. "Then there's the side of her that is very traditional within Chinese culture. A lot of it I appreciate, some of it I don't. And that's where we lock horns." She sighed. "We haven't spoken in five years. Grandmother keeps trying to bridge the gap, but it's been an uphill battle."

"Sounds like most mothers and daughters," I remarked, the kettle whistling. Turning off the hot plate, I poured the hot water into the cups, watching the steam rise in curling whisps. I thought of my own mother – my adoptive mother – and the fights we'd had while I was growing up, even after I'd been sent away. The arguments ended when I turned eighteen and fled for parts unknown, my no-contact rule with them becoming slightly more permanent with their deaths last year. "Are you going to talk to her again?"

"Maybe." But she sounded doubtful.

Letting it go for the moment, I offered her a mug. She took it, grateful for the change in topics, and we chatted for a few minutes more. Then Abby left, wanting to get back to the nursery to work on some inventory. I remained seated, examining the box that contained the visibility spell. It was simple, about the size of a hardback book and made of mahogany wood, stained rich, dark color and polished smooth, like silk. I liked the feel of it in my hands – the weight of it was comforting, almost restful.

I picked up the magazine Abby had left behind and straightened out the cover, studying it, thoughtful. Caitlyn Naughton's byline was on the bottom left of the cover and I touched her name, circling it with a finger.

Abby had referred to Caitlyn Naughton as 'Cat'.

Was the Cat I'd been dreaming about Caitlyn Naughton?

Since any other explanation would have been too fantastic or outrageous to contemplate, I was inclined to believe so.

Seventeen

After Abby left, I planned out my evening.

Before I went to the church to examine the pulpit with the visibility spell, I wanted to stop at Black Rock Lane and have another chat with Henry Gray. There were a few things I needed to clear up and he was the logical source. Glancing at the cheap clock above the tiny refrigerator, I saw that it was almost six in the evening and began cleaning, searching for my keys.

Just as I reached for a sweater, there came a loud pounding on the shack door.

Dottie shrieked and disappeared. I jumped, my heart thumpity-thumping against my ribs as I stared at the door. No one ventured out to my shack on purpose at dusk. They rarely came to the cemetery when the sun was shining at high noon, unless there was a funeral.

"Abby, is that you?" I called, scanning my tiny home. If it was her, she must have forgotten something.

"I can take the door off its hinges without lifting a finger," a woman said in cold tones. Not Abby, then. "I suggest, if you'd rather I didn't, that you open it."

I hesitated, not moving from where I stood. I wasn't that inclined to open a door to someone who threatened to rip it off the frame. Dottie popped back in, her eyes bright, but not with fear and I had a really bad feeling about why.

"Oh, what a beautiful woman!" she sighed in breathy tones, drifting back through the wall, pink-hued. "She looks just like Veronica Lake in *I Married a Witch*." She blinked. "I wonder if she's playing hide and seek with the homeless woman that's been wandering about?"

A Veronica Lake wannabe at my front door? I was going to have to curtail Dottie's movie viewing. "Tell her to go away. Who's playing hide and seek?"

"I'm not leaving," a strong voice rang out. "You and I have business to discuss."

"I don't have business with you!" I called back, my voice sharp.

"You visited Claire Naughton on Tuesday at our shop," the woman retorted from the other side of the door. "I assure you, there is business to discuss."

I stood, frozen to the spot. "I went into the bookshop because I like books and met her for the first time that day. I don't know her well enough to visit. I'd rather not continue the acquaintance."

"She says she knows you." Her tone dared me to deny it.

My eyes narrowed. "Are you calling me a liar?"

She sounded amused. "Says the woman who lives in a caretaker's shack in a cemetery."

"What does that have to do with anything?" I asked, surprised. "I work here, too."

The woman laughed. "Such a simpleton." She pounded on the door again. "Let me in!"

Dottie fluttered about anxiously, looking at me, curious. "Aren't you going to let her in?"

I shook my head. "If she's as powerful as she claims, she can open the door herself."

My visitor pounded on the door again. "Open up!"

I shook my head again, realized she couldn't see me

172

and yelled, "I don't want to talk to you and I don't have to. Go away and leave me alone!"

"We have a lot to talk about," she snapped. "And if you won't open this door, I will."

"Just don't rip it off the hinges!" I shot back. "If you break my door, you fix it." If she broke my door, I had a lot more to worry about than getting it fixed.

There was a *click* and the groan of old metal and the shack door swung open.

The woman standing before me gripped the door frame tightly, her mouth tight in pain. Her hands twitched, as if she was shaking something off them, like cobwebs or dust. I couldn't be sure, the light where she stood wasn't great, but to my eyes, it looked like faint ribbons of color were binding themselves tightly around her. I'd never seen that before and wondered if it was magic-related, self-imposed or something someone else had imposed on her. I decided to keep an eye on it and see if it would react in any way during this encounter.

"I suspect you already know who I am," she said, stepping inside my humble abode. Now that she was in better light, I could see how pale she was. Even the expertly applied make-up did little to conceal the shadows under her eyes. Her attitude, however, spoke of steel wrapped in velvet. "But to make things abundantly clear, I am Cecelia Naughton."

I lifted my chin. "I'd say it's a pleasure, but we both know that wouldn't be true. How'd you know where to find me?"

The youngest Naughton sister smiled. "Magic. But I wasn't looking for you. I found you by accident." She winced as the thin ribbons of energy I'd seen earlier tightened around her. "Damn her."

"Nice trick," I said, gesturing to the door. "Thanks for not breaking it. Why are you here?"

She laughed. "I only came here because my sister insisted I not." She gave my tiny space a cursory glance, then turned her focus on me. "But I'm also here for her. Where is she?"

I stared at her, puzzled. "Where is whom?"

Cecelia scowled, ignoring my question as she surveyed my space. "I know she's around here somewhere, my locater spell keeps bringing me back to this cemetery, but then it goes haywire when I get to this place." She glared at me. "You can't possibly be re-directing it, so it must be her. I'll ask again – where is she?"

I planted myself in front of her. "I have no idea who you're talking about. There's no one here but me." As an afterthought, I added, "And you, for the time being."

Her eyes narrowed. "Who are you?"

I swallowed. "Nobody."

"Somehow, I doubt that." She stepped past me, ran a finger on my faux leather lounge chair and wrinkled her nose. Gingerly, she sat down on the edge of the seat, then crossed one leg over her knee. "Make us some tea. Peppermint, if you have it."

I crossed my arms. "I think we can talk without the tea."

Cecelia Naughton looked at me. "I want tea."

We stared at each other for a minute. Then, wanting her out of my home, I sat down at my tiny kitchen table, my expression firm. This was my other sister, if my birth certificate and what I'd found at the library was accurate. I had no interest in making her aware of that connection, however. "So, what do you want to talk about?"

She regarded me, her blue eyes cool, disdainful, underneath the wave of blonde hair that fell past her shoulders. Although her expression was calm, I had the sense that she was sizing me up more than I wanted her to. "My sister, Claire, thinks you're a witch. But what kind of witch?" Her tone became mocking. "Are you a good witch or a bad witch? One for us or against us?"

I shrugged, feigning a casualness that I didn't feel. "What if I am? Why is it her business or yours? And why would I be for or against you? I don't know any of you."

Cecelia leaned forward, her gaze intent on me. "Are you a witch?"

I didn't look away. "No. I talk to ghosts and work in a graveyard."

She didn't believe me, which was obvious. I didn't care.

At last, Cecelia spoke. "She's convinced that you're a witch. You say you're not."

"That seems to be the long and the short of it," I said. "Why does it matter, anyway?"

"I prefer Ce Ce, thank you." She held out her hand. I stared at it. She sighed, impatient. "Let me see your hands, Katie."

I frowned. "Why?"

She narrowed her eyes at me. "It's why Claire thinks you're a witch."

I glanced at my hands, then back at her. "How can looking at my hands tell you why she thinks I'm a witch?"

Cecelia's gaze didn't waver from mine. "I could compel you to let me see your hands, but it would affect my reading of you." She flexed her fingers, then shook out her hands. The slivers of light binding her glowed briefly, then dimmed. "Also, it would be a waste of energy and I'd really rather not."

If the light I saw wrapped around her was what I thought it was, she couldn't work a lot of magic and was bluffing. Whoever bound her magic was pretty strong and it made her furious, to not have her magic readily available. I sighed inwardly – there were a lot of people in this town holding onto grievances, real or imagined, that were better left in the past. I was beginning to see what Louise meant, about burying my undead.

After a long moment, I gave her both of my hands.

She took them, turning both palms so that they were facing up. "Hold them still for a minute, please."

She pulled a penlight from her coat pocket. Turning it

on, she flashed the beam of light on my hands, studying the lines, taking each hand on its own, studying my palms, tracing a line on one palm with a finger. Her touch was light, but cold and the skin of my palm recoiled away from her. A thoughtful frown crossed her face and I wondered what, exactly, she was reading there that I couldn't.

Interestingly, the ribbons of energy pulsed a dark red as she studied my palms, tightening just a fraction around her. This was clearly uncomfortable for her, because she shifted in an effort to relieve whatever she was feeling. She did not have much success.

Finally I tugged at my hand, impatient. "Tell me how you're going to get information from my palms."

She gave me an exasperated look, pointed to the line curving around the base of my thumb to just below my forefinger. "See this line?" I nodded. "That's your life line. But there's this line," she touched the line creasing off the curved one, "and this one." She pointed to the line connecting my life line to another. "That's your heart line."

I frowned. "That sounds fascinating, but what does it all mean?"

Cecelia didn't answer right away, studying both of my palms a little more, then let go. "It means that your past is tangled up, Katie." Her tone was thoughtful as she considered me. "Why is that?"

I shrugged, not wanting to tell her anything about my past or that I may in some way be related to her. It was none of her damn business. "You're not the first to observe that."

Cecelia – Ce Ce – leaned back into the chair, crossing her arms, her eyes never leaving mine, her posture almost regal. "And you went into Wickerman Falls, why?"

I scowled. "I ask again, what business is it of yours? Or Claire Naughton's? Or anyone's, for that matter?"

She considered me for another long moment, then nodded, as if coming to a conclusion that she'd suspected was inevitable, but not wanted. "Claire told me about that spark when you two shook hands. It's how witches are able to recognize family members."

Pretty much what Abby had said. I shook my head, even more reluctant to share what I knew with her. "Or witches with equal power," I pointed out. "Sorry, Ce Ce, I just moved here. Besides, you read my palms and there was no spark."

Anger flashed in her eyes, darkening them. "My sister made sure to interfere with things that didn't concern her." She huffed. "She bound my powers."

Ah, so that's what a binding looked like. "Claire did that to you? How?"

Cecelia snorted. "Claire is too…..nice to try underhanded tricks like that. My other sister did it, claiming it would corrupt me." She flexed her fingers and the binding glowed, tightening once again. "I hate Cat for doing it." She studied me once more. "Why were you in Wickerman Falls, cemetery girl?"

Reluctant, I said, "I was there for research about the church." And I clamped my mouth shut, biting my tongue so hard it bled.

Her look sharpened. "What about the church?"

"I'm curious about the area," I said, shortly. "I like history and old buildings. Also, I work in a cemetery, so knowing about the history of places kind of goes in line with that."

She looked at me, disbelieving. "History."

I nodded, forcing myself to keep it short. "Yup, history."

Ce Ce was quiet, processing my words. "Why are you so interested in the history of an area that has no connection to you?"

"You're the witch. Why don't you go find out for yourself?" I headed for the door, opened it and turned to glare at her, my arms folded under my breasts, gesturing with my chin to the outside, shivering a little in the cool air. By this time, it was dark, the stars twinkling faintly through the mist coming in from the coast. "I think it's time for you to go."

She regarded me for a long moment from the chair, then stood and crossed the short distance to the door. "Not everyone can talk to ghosts as easily as you do. It takes magic for me to be able to do that. It is incredibly draining." She fell silent again, studying the evening shadows. "Do you know who Caitlyn Naughton is?"

I didn't trust her and liked it even less that she had intruded on my space. I didn't want to her to know how much I knew, so I shook my head. "Sorry, I didn't even know there were Naughtons until I walked into the bookshop. Why?"

She was debating with herself – even in the dim light of dusk, I could see that. Ce Ce met my gaze. "Cat's gone missing."

"And?" I prodded.

She searched my face. I stifled the urge to draw back. "She was searching for something, but we don't know what." That wasn't true, if what Abby had told me was correct. Cecelia was lying, the question was, why. "Cat was always tenacious when she had the scent of a story. It was impossible to get her to let it go. What do you know of it?"

I laughed. "Why would I know what she's looking for? I don't even know who she is."

Ce Ce Naughton did not look amused. "She had gone to Louisiana twice for this new story of hers." She sniffed delicately. "You smell of the bayou. Was it Baton Rouge or New Orleans or Lafayette?"

"Does it matter? I never met her and I have no idea what she was looking for." I made a gesture for her to leave. "Goodbye, Cecelia Naughton. I hope you find what it is you think you want."

"We're not done talking," she said, hand on the door.

"Yes, thank you, Ce Ce. I'm done." I stepped into her space. She fell back at my unexpected motion and her hand fell away from the door as she stepped outside.

"Have a good night."

I pulled the door shut and pressed up against it. The hinges groaned in a satisfying and rather creepy way and I threw the bolt, holding my breath, listening for her to leave. After a long minute, Cecelia Naughton did, the sound of leaves crunching beneath her feet as she walked off, muttering under her breath. I sighed, relaxing a little, then went to make myself another cup of tea. Given what little Abby had told me, that woman unnerved me. If I'd had anything of the whiskey persuasion, I'd add a dollop or two to the tea.

Dottie popped in through the far wall, waxing dreamy and romantic as usual. "I think you'll be seeing more of her."

Okay, I bit. "Why do you say that?"

A small, off-white square-ish bit of paper fluttered to the floor, landing at my feet. I stooped to pick it up, noting that it was expensive card stock. The lettering embossed on one side was spare and in a simple font. It appeared plain and non-descript, but clearly screamed quality and substance. The name 'Cecelia Naughton' was emblazoned on it, along with her job title at the book shop in Wickerman Falls, her number and email address.

From over my left shoulder, Dottie said, "She left that on the door. I think she wanted to make sure you got it." She floated back to my shack's only entrance. "I'm going off to see if the hide and seek game has picked up."

Waving a hand, I said, "Have fun. Be careful."

She vanished. I turned my gaze back to the card Cecelia had left for a long moment. Then I went to the kitchen sink, opening the cutlery drawer to pull out an old box of matches. Striking one, I lit the card on fire, dropping it with a hiss into the metal sink basin when the flame burned my fingers. Turning on the tap, I watched as the water dissolved the blackened paper into a soggy lump. Then, with an empty jar, I scooped the mess into it, poured in salt, a little holy water and screwed the top back on.

The jar felt solid in my hand, cool and weighted with what I'd put in. The water was now a murky grey, caused by the ash of the card, and broken up by the grains of salt. It looked like it had come from an old pipe that hadn't had running water in decades. It was entirely possible that I was over-reacting and had just destroyed a perfectly good and harmless business card.

It still felt good to see it reduced to basic pulp.

Then I took a deep breath and set the jar on the counter and went to get ready for my visit to the forgotten lane and then to the church.

Eighteen

About forty minutes later, I was staring down the over-grown entrance of Black Rock Lane, the old flashlight I'd found in the glove compartment a comforting weight in my hand. The truck was parked across the main road, locked, keys in my back pocket. There was still light, but the sun had long since disappeared from view, thanks to the surrounding forest. It would be dark soon, the better to cover my visit to the church a little later.

The lane itself seemed shadowed by something other than the trees and I quashed my over-active imagination. I was reluctant to go back down this road, but I thought I understood why Cat put me here, at this spot, in my dream. Whatever it was she'd been working on at the time of her disappearance, it was connected to the Pellington place. How it related to her New Orleans trip was also unclear. But she wanted me here, that much I was certain.

And the answer to my curiosity was at the house at the end of this lane. Pausing long enough to grab up the stick I'd thrown aside on my last visit, I found a comfortable grip and took a deep breath, exhaling slowly. Then, switching on my flashlight, I made my way down the lane, my steps coming slowly and with care around the broken pavement.

I wondered if you'd come back.

I jumped, heart racing. Henry Gray stood on my left, his expression curious and amused.

"Do you really need to do that?" I asked, taking a deep breath and exhaling slowly. "It's hard to want to help you when you keep scaring me."

Henry seemed amused. *Sorry, Cadence. I'll be more considerate in the future.*

"That's all I ask," I said, slightly mollified. "And why wouldn't I come back?"

You would be the first to come back since I died. But then, you can hear me, so maybe that's the difference.

He sounded lonely and it surprised me to realize that. Thoughtful, I started walking again, my ghostly companion close behind. Now that I knew where I was going, it didn't take long to find the old lot. I spotted the roof of the mostly-obscured-by-trees house and climbed over the rock wall. Once on the other side, I began to push back on the over-grown pushes. I found the path I'd made before and began to retrace it.

"Except for what some of the locals told me, there's no mention of you anywhere," I told him as we walked. I spoke, partly to get some answers and partly to break the unnerving silence. Even the cicadas were silent. "You're not even in the papers. How do I know you're buried here? And that one of the Pellingtons murdered you? The locals think you took off of your own free will, not that you were killed."

I was a drifter, he said. *Of course there's no mention of me.*

Of course. "Were you an orphan, or did you have a family?"

He gave me a look. *I had a family, but I ran away.*

"Why?" I asked. "Did they hurt you, treat you like you were crazy or something?"

No. I was one of seven siblings. I wanted to see the world, make my own way. They wanted me to go into the family business.

Ah. "Were they, you know, mafia types?"

No. Teachers. He paused, a frown crossing his face as he added, *My sister cut herself off from our family because her husband believed that the supernatural world was evil.*

"And obviously, you didn't think that way," I guessed.

He shook his head, grinning. *Obviously.*

I stopped, taking in my surroundings, recognized that I was standing in the same spot as on my last visit to the house, and turned to him, curious. "How did they even know about the supernatural world? It's not open to everyone. Unless she had magic, your brother-in-law couldn't know or see anything."

Henry frowned, searching my face. *Ruth had a talent for making plants grow just by her touch. Even potted ones. She brought back her favorite rose tree after a bad freeze killed it.*

So? "That doesn't sound like a big deal."

It was a big deal for Stanley. When he found out how that plant came back, he forced her to rip it out of the ground and had the gardener shred it.

I poked at the bushes in front of me with my stick. "That was a little extreme."

Henry shrugged. *She convinced him to move back to the east coast after that. She felt safer being closer to the rest of us. Their son stayed behind for college.*

"How long before you died did that happen?" I asked.

I left the month after they moved back, he said. *So, perhaps six months.* He brightened. *I'm remembering.*

"Good for you," I said. "Anything else?"

Henry shook his head. *No. This clarity comes and goes.*

I studied him, curious. There was color in his features now, warming up the grayness I'd seen when he first came to me in the hearse. His hair was a pale brown, which I suspected would grow darker the longer he interacted with me. It was a phenomena that I'd seen before, but hadn't seen any reference to it in books. I suspected that it was because few could actually see ghosts, in the way the I do, and even fewer would be open to the concept of ghosts to begin with. My theory is that the energy of the living somehow nourishes the energy of the dead and can sometimes contribute to what become reported hauntings.

It seemed that my energy was feeding Henry, which allowed him to become grounded in my presence. In some way, it was similar to vampires and their consumption of blood. Or, as Louise Tremont pointed out often, unresolved feelings. Glancing at my spectral companion, I wondered if he would eventually be able to speak in the same manner as the Spectral Six at some point. It would be something to watch out for, I reasoned. And his slow grounding around me meant that people rarely traveled along this lane.

Or did the unwanted visitors he'd mentioned also contribute their energy? I asked him about it as I stepped through the path I'd found on my last visit.

He considered that. *You're the only one who's visited, besides them. It's possible.*

Using the stick, I wiped out cobwebs that had almost taken over several shrubs, not wanting to get caught in them, picking my way through the over-grown yard. Ahead, I could see the peaked roof of the house, more shadow than substance, from where I was standing. It wasn't until I got to the row of badly neglected rose bushes that I realized I'd come at the house from the long-hidden driveway. The bushes stood taller than my five-foot-nine frame and ivy had masked them, easily disguising the roses and thorns. All of this growth had taken over the drive and, after more than sixty years, that was hardly surprising.

Starting from a familiar point seemed like a good idea, so I made my way to the front porch and around the steps to the far edge of the house. The fallen tree was still lying across the path to the kitchen door. Hesitating, I surveyed the area, acutely aware of the silence. The lack of cricket noises, squirrels squabbling over tree rights and birds chirping made me feel loud and awkward, a trespasser not just of the property itself, but of nature at large.

Henry stood at the far end, watching.

I gestured to the bushes. "Is this a good place to start?"

He nodded, frowned. *Hurry. I'm remembering......*

In his agitation, Henry Gray faded out, leaving me alone in the weighted silence. Taking a deep breath, I looked up at the house, studying the forgotten house more closely. It was a Victorian-style house and I could see how, at one time, it must have been an elegant home. With no one to take shelter within its walls and care for it, the house had wilted in on itself, becoming a shell of what it used to be. The paint had long since been peeled away by the weather, so there was no indication of what color it had been prior to its abandonment. Most of the windows were broken, the panes' sharp edges still in the caulking. Some of the roofing had rotted away and a drain pipe hung precariously over the porch roof.

Still, I heard no sound other than my own breathing. Even the birds had gone quiet. Tracing the rough bark of the fallen tree, I looked around for a way to get around it, following the trunk until I came to its roots. Climbing around it, I found my way back to the house and the kitchen back door. Just under the door knob was a latch and padlock. Although worn from the elements, it was clearly new and had been put there recently. Touching it, I frowned, wondering why this door had a padlock and not the front.

Possibly, I reasoned, it was to limit the number of ways to get into the house. Since no padlock in the world could keep vampires in or out of a building, then it was there to keep the living from poking around.

Like me.

Turning, I made my way back to the front porch,

wanting to take a quick peek through the window. Once there, I re-traced my path up steps, remembering from my last visit which boards could hold my weight and which couldn't. The wood creaked, as it had the last time, but it felt sturdy, so I put more weight onto the step. Making my way over to the nearest window, testing each board carefully, I put my hand on the sill and looked in, using the flashlight to see in the dimly lit room.

There was a slight tingling sensation against my palm, a deep warmth that felt.....welcoming and I lifted my hand, studying it. Then, curious, I placed my palm on the exterior wall, flattening it so that it was fully engaged. There was a rushing sensation as the house welcomed me, glad for my human touch as it enveloped me with its own energy. Bemused, I turned my attention back to the window and the room on the other side of the glass. The light bobbed over the cob-webbed and dust-covered furniture that met my gaze. Nothing moved in that grayed out world, forgotten by the living. Even the large carpets – Oriental rugs, by the look of the design and cut – had gone gray through neglect.

Cadence, what are you doing? Henry Gray stood on the porch next to me, worry exuding from him, chilling the air.

"What does it look like?" I asked, glancing at him. "I want to find a way in."

Are you sure that's wise? He was starting to fade in and out. *People have been here, they may be back soon.*

"No one is here right now, except us," I pointed out, although I appreciated his concern. "And I'm not going to take long, I promise." The house had no concept of time, so without taking my attention away from it, I asked Henry, "When were they here, those other people?"

The day before you found it. I think they hid something upstairs.

"You couldn't have told me this before I climbed up the porch," I grumbled, stepping back from the wall and rubbing my hands against my jeans. Now that I was no longer touching the house, I suddenly grew aware of how drained I felt, that kind of exhaustion one gets from walking too long in the sun. Sinking to the porch floor to catch my breath, I looked out at the forest surrounding me and listened. Silence.

"I think we'll be okay," I said, keeping my voice low in any case. "But if anyone's coming, warn me."

Henry looked doubtful, but didn't say anything.

Acutely aware of the anxiety tingling in my stomach, I peered through the window again, wondering about the family that had once lived here. Then, with dust tickling my nose, I stepped away, pausing long enough to sneeze twice. Henry muttered something – it sounded rude, so I didn't ask him to repeat it. Kneeling in front of the door, I studied the lock, then reached out to trace the lock, my hand brushing against the door knob. There was a shock, a sharp bolt of energy that raced up my arm, tingling. I jerked my hand back, shaking it out as I stared at the knob, perplexed.

The shock was similar to the one I'd experienced when I shook hands with Claire Naughton at the bookshop. Abby had mentioned that shocks like that were of recognition, either of family or power or both. With my original birth certificate clarifying matters, I knew that I was somehow related to Claire, which explained that shock. What our familial relationship actually was would be determined when I finally worked up the courage to talk to her.

But this house was another matter entirely. Somehow it was connected to the Naughtons. Did the retired captain know the family? As I pondered the question, I heard the tumblers turn and the door popped out of the frame, swinging open a few inches.

I sat back on my heels, my heart racing. The house was letting me in. Peering in through the crack, I could see the foyer, grey with dust, and the archway into the living area. Gently, I nudged the door open with my foot.

Something else caught my eye – two sets of footprints in the dust, some stepping on top of the other. Frowning, I knelt down to get a better look, but the lighting was poor – it was impossible to see if they were made by a man or a woman. Or both.

Gesturing to Henry, I said, "Well, lead the way."

I really don't think this is such a good idea, Henry grumbled, but he slipped through the wall and met me in the foyer. I shut the door behind me.

"You're a ghost. Stop worrying."

You should be worried, too.

His quiet certainty was unsettling and only underscored the silent remoteness of the house itself. No one would know to find me here if I fell and broke something. Turning, I surveyed the immediate area. It hadn't been the window's smudged state that had made the interior look grey – it really was grey. More than sixty years' worth of cobwebs and dust covered every inch of the place in a thick veil.

Henry's report of people being here before I discovered the house was evident everywhere I looked. Footprints were visible in the dust covering the hardwood floor leading to the stairs. On the banister, where hands had been, I could see the contrast between the coat of dust and the polished wood. The carpet runner on the stairs had once been white and the dust only grayed it out, but even from where I stood at the front door, I could see where it had been disturbed. More footprints veered off towards the right, presumably towards the dining room or the kitchen.

Whoever it was that had been here, they'd clearly examined the house and then gone upstairs and with a purpose. I didn't want to expose my presence to them, so I stepped with care onto the already-disturbed areas, approaching the staircase. The peaked roofline I'd observed outside suggested that there was an attic above the second floor.

I wondered what, if anything, had been hidden there.

Mindful of my surroundings, I kept my hands to myself and ascended the stairs, alert to every sound, including the heft of my own breath, flashing my light ahead to see where to put my foot next. Henry appeared on the landing above me, still worried, but calm. When I reached him, I saw that the landing curved into a short hall. At the far end and facing north, there was a window. The curtains, which used to hang on the now-broken rod, lay in a puddled heap on the floor, allowing the fading sunlight in.

Pausing long enough to find areas where the dust had been disturbed, I used it as my path and slipped down the hall. In much the same way Dottie did, Henry hovered close, flickering in and out, clearly uneasy.

What are you doing?

"I want to know why they came down this way," I said and stopped, reassessing my path and flashing my light around, curious. "This is weird."

What?

I frowned, pointed at the carpet. "The footprints end here." Flashing my light around, my curiosity grew. "They didn't go into any of the bedrooms. So where did they go?"

Nineteen

Flashing my light to the gray carpet beneath my feet, I studied the dust patterns. Except for where it had been disturbed, the dust just ahead of and to either side of me remained untouched. The closed doors on either side of me indicated bedrooms, but it was clear that no one had gone into either one. Then, just as I turned to retrace my steps, I noticed the strange, thin, rectangular marks in the dust, almost obscured by the footprints themselves.

Turning the flashlight to the ceiling, I looked up, a soft gasp of recognition escaping me when I saw the trap door going into the attic. Despite the dim light, I could see that someone had installed a heavy padlock there, as well. If they were practitioners of magic, then there would be wards, to keep out any unwanted guests. I thought of the front door and wondered again why they hadn't put a padlock there, too.

Certainly, that spark from the door knob could have been a ward of some kind, but given the familiarity of it, I didn't think so. Still, if there *had* been a ward there, why didn't it stop me from coming in? Did it recognize me, too, in the same way the house seemed to? Whatever it was, it meant that those who had come before me had known about this place and were using it for their own purposes.

They were awful busy with that trap door, Henry commented. *She was very angry with him for taking so long to install that lock.*

I glanced at him. "Who are they?"

He looked back at me, thoughtful. *She's a witch, always casting locator spells. But she's not finding what she wants. He's helping her, because her powers are blocked in some way. They're not happy.*

That sounded like Cecelia Naughton and the man with her had to be Julian Webster. How they knew about this house and what their reasons were for being here were unknown to me, but they had to know about the crates in the basement. They had to know about the vampires and they had to have some kind of understanding with them.

And mostly, I was curious about that padlock on the attic door. "What's up there?"

Henry shrugged. *Just a bunch of junk. They shoved an old, rolled carpet up there a few days ago.* He gestured to the space above us. *It's more of a crawlspace than an attic.*

I studied the trap door. It was too high for me to reach and I wasn't sure how much time I had if and when Cecelia and Julian came back. "Why would they put a padlock on the trap door if it's just full of junk and a discarded carpet?"

Henry started to speak, stopped. A thoughtful expression crossed his face. *I'm not sure. A lock suggests that they don't want people poking around. Hold on.* He vanished, reappearing a few minutes later, a curious expression on his face. *There's nothing up there beyond what I'd just told you. But it looks like they threw some old clothes up there, too.*

I frowned. That was an odd assortment of things to put in an attic. Most of it sounded like stuff one would throw in the garbage. And yet, there was a padlock on the door. "Henry, that rolled carpet. Is it still up there?"

I'll check. He disappeared again, coming back a minute

later. *The carpet is still there, but it's not rolled up.*

Food wrappers, old clothes, soda cans, a padlock, an unrolled carpet. "That lock could be there to keep people out. But it could also be keeping someone in." I glanced at Henry. "Are you sure that's all you saw?"

Henry bristled. *Of course! I would have said if there was someone up there.*

"If whoever was up there is gone, how'd they get out past the lock?" I mused, my thought racing. "Is that what Cecelia and Julian were arguing about?"

It could be, but it sounded more like she was trying to find something or someone. Henry perked up, a little color blooming. *She was not happy about it.*

Still thinking, I glanced around at my surroundings. One of the bedroom doors was open and I saw a chair knocked on its side. Flashing my light on the carpet, I tiptoed as carefully as possible to retrieve the chair, retracing my steps with equal care to put it under the attic door. Standing on it, I touched the lock, tracing it lightly. Then I cupped it, feeling the cold metal grow warm against my palm. Closing my eyes, I focused on it, *reaching* for the tumblers within.

There was a low *pop!* and the lock fell loose in my hand. Opening my eyes, I unhooked the lock and stuck it in my pocket before stepping down from the chair. Reaching up, I pulled the attic door open and unfolded the stairs.

"Henry, take a look around, let me know what you see?"

He nodded, drifting up. The seconds dragged by, but soon he was hovering beside me. *There doesn't seem to be anything out of place, it looks much like it did before.*

"Okay, then I'm going to climb up," I said, with more bravado than I actually felt. "Go back up there and guard the entrance." Henry nodded and acquiesced, disappearing. Then, using my flashlight to illuminate the space, I climbed my way up, cautious, poking my head into the attic like a bunny peering out of its warren.

Scanning the space, I noted the trash Henry had mentioned, the old clothes tossed to one side and the large carpet, now unfurled in a haphazard fashion. Curious now, I climbed the ladder until I could hoist myself up and into a sitting position, my legs dangling over the edge. Flashing the light around, I saw that it was more like a crawlspace than an actual attic, convenient for storing items not in use, but little else. It ran the width and length of the house, with windows too small for anything but light and ventilation. The eaves slanted sharply into the floor, making it a small and cramped space. Dust and cobwebs coated everything, heavier and thicker than the rooms below – so thick, I could almost taste it in the air.

Some of it went up my nose and I managed to stifle a sneeze. The board I sat on gave a little and I shifted over, shining my light, curious as I tested the board again. It was loose enough that I was able to lift it up part-way. Aiming the flashlight, I saw what looked like a bundle of envelopes tied together with ribbon. Pulling the bundle out, I stuffed them in my pocket, intent on reading them later back at the shack.

Henry drifted over. *Are you all right?*

I nodded, wiping at my nose. "Just a little dust." I flashed my light around, letting it settle on the unfurled carpet directly ahead of me. "Is that what they brought here?"

Henry nodded. *Yes, they had the devil's own time getting it up here.*

Curious, I crawled over to it, wanting to get a closer look. Tugging at one corner, I managed to pull it towards me. The carpet was maybe six feet wide and about the same, if not a couple feet more, in length. It was an area rug of some quality, I realized, but from where? And why stash it up here?

Out of the corner of my eye, a shadow moved.

At the same time, Henry cried out, *Watch out, Cadence!*

With Henry's warning ringing in my ears, I turned and swung my flashlight around like a baton, feeling it strike hard. There was a howl of pain and then I was tackled, falling forward and hitting the attic floor hard, air rushing from my lungs in a *whoosh*, followed by intense sneezing when I inhaled dust.

"Now I'll know for certain who you are," a familiar deep, masculine voice growled, taking me by my shoulders and turning me around. Pushing hard, I almost got free of his grasp. Then his hands tightened and I winced. "Stop that, you're not going anywhere." My own flashlight was shone in my face as he asked, "Are you one of the people who put me here?"

"No, I didn't even know you were here," I choked out. Squinting into the light, I realized I did know him and saw that he was beginning to recognize me. "Raul Kendrick? You were declared missing a couple of days ago."

He stared at me for a moment, bewildered – then slowly, recognition set in. "You came to my office that day…..and you were at Wycliff College, as well."

I nodded, taking him in. Blood was drying in trickles along his cheek from a wound on his temple as he stared back at me. It didn't look fresh, like maybe a day or two old, but I wondered how long he'd been hidden here, in this house, if not necessarily the attic. "You look pretty beaten up. Did Julian do that to you?"

Raul shook his head, winced. "No, I didn't see who it was. Right after I left you, I went to my campus office to change for class. As soon as I opened the door, I realized there was a spell waiting to be triggered. The next thing I knew, I'd been wrapped in a carpet and dragged here."

This led to my next question. "What'd you do to piss them off?"

He laughed, winced, then took a deep breath, studying me long and carefully. "I'm not quite sure yet." He released his grip on my shoulders and leaned back hard against the attic's eaves, wincing. One hand went to his temple, his posture suggesting exhaustion. "How did you find this place?"

I sat next to him, eyeing him curiously. "Can I trust you?"

"I'm a lawyer, of course, you can….oh, I see." He chuckled softly. "Yes, Miss Gray, you can trust me." He studied me as closely as one could in the shadows.

I took a deep breath. "I wasn't exactly honest with you that day, in your office."

He nodded, a smile teasing his lips. "Yes, I had the feeling you were holding back."

In a rush, I explained to him how I came to be in his office – how I'd found his card on the vampire in New Orleans; that it had referred to its west coast cousins; that both his card and my own reasons had brought me to Wickerman Falls in the first place; how the resident ghosts led me to discover this old house we now sat in.

"There are some other things I should tell you, but I think I'd rather wait until we were out of this house," I finished, skirting the issue of my birth certificate and touched his arm. He winced, pulled back a little. "We should find another place to lay low, so that we can get a better look at your wounds."

"Agreed," he said and gestured for me to lead the way, wincing a little.

We crawled the short distance to the trap door and sat on the edge, legs dangling. My left foot caught the first step and I started down, gripping the railings. Once I reached the floor, I looked up to spot him as he came down. Once on the landing, he tried to walk, but his face went ashen and he staggered hard to the left. Gripping the ladder railing with one hand tightly, he massaged his temple, eyes closed, lips pressed together in pain.

I eyed him, concerned. "Are you going to be able to walk? 'Cause I can't carry you."

"Yes, give me a minute. I feel like I got slipped one

hell of a magical mickey. Food and sleep will go a long way to help undo it." He sat down hard in the chair I'd pulled out, leaning back, taking in slow, steady breaths, using his fingers to brace his head. I kept an eye on him as I pushed the collapsible step-ladder back in place. It folded neatly and, with a gentle push, the trap door shut easily, hiding the attic space. He'd have to stand for me to use the chair so that I could put the padlock back on, but he needed to get his strength back in order to walk back to the truck, so I waited. Eventually, I saw some of his color return and when he looked up, he seemed more centered. "Your flashlight's going to die soon."

I glanced down at it. Sure enough, the beam had begun to fade, so I turned it off. We were immediately bathed in darkness, broken only by the pale light coming in through the windows at the end of the hall. "There's a hotel on Route 5. I'll get a room under my name and let you in through the back entrance. No one will ever think to look for you there."

He shifted, winced, and stood. "Sounds agreeable."

Grabbing the chair, I fished the padlock out of my pocket and slipped it into place. Done, I put the chair back where I'd found it and started for the stairs. When I realized he wasn't behind me, I hesitated and turned. "What happened to you?"

Raul Kendrick watched me. Even in the shadows, he felt guarded, unlike the humorous and charming man I'd encountered on the college campus. "What do you mean?"

Gesturing around, I asked, "How did you get here from the college? Sleepy Eye Cove's police chief said you went missing."

He considered my words, thoughtful. "The last thing I remember is unlocking my office to get ready for my class." He frowned. "I.....heard my name, turned and woke up breathing in dust from that carpet in the attic."

I had a pretty good idea of who it might have been, but felt that conversation could wait until we got him to the Blue Rose Inn.

Twenty

By the time we got back to the cemetery truck, it was pretty obvious to me that whatever magical cocktail he'd been served was still causing him a lot of pain, even after a few days. Raul needed to stop and rest to catch his breath several times, which only fueled my worry that his captors might be close by. Anxious to get him to the hotel, I drove a little faster than I should have, but we passed through the village easily.

I didn't know much about the Blue Rose Inn, other than it was close, it was always busy and it was located across the road from a mini-mart gas station. It was a five-story affair, with parking in front and a pool in the back. As I pulled in to the hotel lot and parked, I wondered if there was also a little diner inside to grab some dinner for my companion.

Glancing at him, I was a little alarmed by how pale he was. "Are you going to be okay, while I go get a room for you?"

He nodded. "I'll be fine."

I left him in the truck and hurried to the lobby, taking the steps two at a time, feeling for my wallet. If I got the least expensive room, Raul could hide out here for at least two days to start, with an option to stay on longer, if necessary. Upon entering the lobby, I paused, waiting for my eyes to adjust to the dim light. I noted the restaurant, but it was closed for renovating. Rats, then it was a trip to the mini-mart, instead.

The clerk at the front desk had a name tag that read *Nick*. He quoted me eighty bucks for two nights, plus tax. I handed him cash and, not even bothering to look up from his book, Nick handed over a key and registration card. I signed the card in a mad scribble and pocketed the key.

"Is there another way up to the room?" I asked, having noted that the room was on the second floor.

Nick the clerk gestured down a hall. "You can use the way in from the pool, probably closer, anyway."

I thanked him and left.

Back at the truck, I brought Raul up to date. "After I get you into that room, I'm gonna head across the street to the mini-mart and get some food." I eyed him critically. "Maybe some juice, too. You look like death."

He smiled, despite his exhaustion. "Thanks. To all three."

That gave me unexpected grin, knowing he had a macabre sense of humor. Shifting into gear, I drove the truck around back, parking once more as close to the pool as possible. Then, with his arm around my shoulders for balance, we walked slowly to the back entrance of the hotel, looking for the elevator. I was highly aware of his distinctive male scent and of the muscle flexing across my shoulders as we walked. Briefly, I wondered what it would feel like to be held close enough to feel his breath tickle my ear, then shoved that thought aside when I saw the elevator. Pushing the Up button, we got on and landed at the second floor. From there, it was only a few steps to the room I'd paid for and soon, he was leaning back across the bed, his eyes closed.

I eyed him, tempted to stretch out next to him, but

then I saw how pale he was underneath the exhaustion. It occurred to me that he was also dehydrated. Going into the bathroom with a glass, I got him some water and set the glass on the nightstand next to him. "Drink this, but not too fast, you don't want to get sick. I'll be back in a few with some snacks."

He gulped the water anyway, setting the glass down with a grunt as he slipped under the covers. "Not sure what my appetite will be like, but......" His voice slurred into a snore and he was fast asleep.

I shut the door behind me quietly.

*****

The mini-mart clerk barely looked up from her magazine at me as I walked in. Muttering a 'hello', I went to the refrigerators, pulling out two sandwiches, an iced tea and a large bottle of orange juice. I paused by the T-shirt and ball cap racks, thinking that Raul would probably like a clean shirt to put on when I left him, so I grabbed a couple of men's extra-large black. *Wickerman Falls High* was printed on the front in light blue and team numbers on the back. Then I headed to the counter, pausing long enough to add a small bottle of aspirin, some rubbing alcohol and a large package of chocolate chip cookies along the way.

Less than a hundred dollars later, I had my purchases neatly packed in a paper bag. Stepping out of the mini-mart, I paused to check for traffic, then walked the short distance across the road back to the hotel and was soon climbing the stairs back to my room. Raul was fast asleep on the bed, snoring softly, as I let myself in. After setting the bag of goodies on the table, I pulled the drapes shut as carefully as possible, so as not to disturb him. With the room now in shadows, I went to the closet and found an extra blanket, unfolding it as I crossed back to the bed. Tucking it around him, I was acutely aware of how sleep softened his features.

Stepping back from the bed, I turned to the bag of perishables and put them in the tiny fridge next to the dresser. Then I set the aspirin on the nightstand with his water, put the new shirts on top of the dresser so that he would see them, and left the room key on top of them. I wrote a short note, asking him to keep his whereabouts under wraps until I got back, adding my cellphone number at the bottom.

Once outside, my hand on the door, I whispered a protection spell, similar to the one I used on my shack. Done, I hesitated, then left. He would be fine, I reasoned as I walked back to the cemetery truck. No one would ever think to look for him here, even if they did realize he'd escaped from the Pellington place. There were too many places for him to hide out in and he could easily mask his whereabouts, if necessary. And even if by some chance they did find him (whoever 'they' were, though I had my suspicions), I had no doubt whatsoever that he'd handle it with ease. He was a big boy.

I told myself that more than once as I drove back to the old church in Sleepy Eye Cove. My unease would not be convinced.

*****

Parking the truck in the same spot I'd used before, I went searching for Father O'Mare. It didn't take long for me to find the spectral priest who watched over the place – he was out in the churchyard, singing a hymn to a small group of ghosts. They promptly vanished at my presence, but Father O'Mare didn't seem too perturbed.

"What can I do for you, Cadence?" he asked.

"Listen, Father, it's very important that I talk to Sarah Pellington," I said, feeling urgent and hoping it came out at the very least sincere. "She might know something that might help explain why the vampires targeted your church. And if she does, I can make sure more vampires won't come back to do the same thing."

Father O'Mare and I sat on the steps leading up to the church door. Dusk had fallen early as I walked from the cemetery to the church. My hands were dirty, despite my wiping them off on my jeans repeatedly. After obtaining Father O'Mare's permission, I had buried the jar in a corner of the churchyard next to the stone wall. The moon had just begun to rise at that point – now, it was peeking out over the trees, casting soft shadows.

At last, Father O'Mare stirred. "She may not want to speak to you, however."

"I understand," I said, patiently. "Tell her that it's related to the events that led to her fiancé's death."

He nodded and slipped into the shadows. I mean that in the literal sense, of course. A few minutes later, he materialized on the walk at the foot of the steps. A young woman with blonde hair done in a single braid was with him. She was dressed in a green skirt that fell just past her knees and a white blouse.

She regarded me with pointed curiosity. "You look familiar."

"I've been getting that a lot lately," I said, rising to my feet. I stepped down to the walk, the gravel crunching underfoot. "I'm Cadence Galloway."

Her gaze sharpened. "You're the one Dottie lives with."

I nodded, Dottie's own words about Sarah coming back to me. "Well, that makes things easier. The living know me as Katie Gray."

Memory colored her, bringing her subdued demeanor into sharp relief. "Is Henry Gray of your family?"

I shook my head. "No, we're not related. He's still over at Black Rock Lane. He showed me where the vampires are. He wants to know why he died."

Sarah Pellington turned as white as a ghost could get. "You were in the basement?"

"No, I was able to look in through the windows from outside," I said and described my experiences. "They'd been there for a while, it looked like."

Sarah grew pensive. "They were his pets and his keepers."

I repeated her words, puzzled. Pellington's shade had said much the same thing. "In what world do vampires cultivate that kind of a relationship with humans?"

"Papa didn't talk much about them," she said at last, her voice low. "But one of the females, the one who called herself Cassiopeia, talked to us late at night. My sisters and I would gather round the basement window and listen to her. It was like ghost stories around a campfire. She only did it when Papa wasn't around. He did not want us associating with her. But we had so few friends...."

She stopped abruptly, her words hanging in the cold night air. Father O'Mare touched her arm with a comforting hand. I cleared my throat. "I know you guys were isolated in that house, with minimal contact to the village. Did he do that on purpose, to hide the vampires? Or was there another reason?"

She shuddered, her eyes not quite meeting mine. "He did it to hide the vampires, to keep us close and to conceal his changing nature."

"They intended to make him one of their own?" I asked. It didn't sound like they'd been feeding on his daughters, which was a relief to me. However, I suspected that if the family hadn't died when they had, it would not have been long before the vampires started feasting on all of them, not just Pellington himself.

Sarah glanced at me. "I suppose so. Why is this important?"

I met her gaze. "Because someone gave those vampires charms to specifically access this church. I'm sure you saw the damage to the pulpit."

That caught her attention and she looked at Father O'Mare, frightened. Then she was racing across the churchyard, her ghostly skirt fluttering out behind her. "I have to go back! I have to know if it's still there!"

I stood, following after her. "Sarah, wait! I'm not finished talking to you!"

But she had vanished into a wisp of mist.

I glared at Father O'Mare. "Will you please tell your congregation to stop doing that? It's really hard when I'm trying to help them."

He sighed. "I do apologize, Miss Galloway. She's a bit flighty, more so lately than I've seen before."

I stared in the direction that Sarah had vanished. She was headed in the direction of where her old home stood. "How is she able to travel between her home on Black Rock Lane and the church?"

Father O'Mare frowned. "I'm not quite sure what you mean."

"Well, there's a ghost attached to the property on Black Rock Lane," I explained as he led the way to the church's back door. "More than one, actually. The one I'm speaking of died and was buried there, but seems unable to leave the grounds. It seems odd that she can, if she was buried on that same property, along with her family."

He considered this, thoughtful. "It's possible that there is something that frees her from being tied to one place. Such as a direct family member that still lives." He eyed me, curious, his presence like ice in the cool air. He gestured to the box I carried. "Would you like to come in and use that now?"

I checked the box that held my visibility spell, then followed him up the steps. I stopped and paused long enough to take another look back in the direction where Sarah had run off to. Then I went inside, the door closing behind me.

Twenty-One

The pulpit was as I had last seen it – charred beyond recognition and more suited for a barbecue pit than a church. I settled down on the floor behind it and facing the pews, placing the box before me. Opening it, I surveyed the variety of items packed inside the velvet-lined box, feeling the powerful energy they emanated.

There were five large white quartz crystals and I lifted each one out with care, setting them around me on the five points of an invisible pentagram for protection. The candles were next and I set them before me, a black candle for protection, a blue one for communication and a white one for clarity. I lit them, then took Abby's spell out of my pocket and unfolded it, breathing in deep, trying to clear my mind. This was a new spell for me and I wanted to focus my attention.

I sat there, cross-legged, my gaze on the flickering flame. I invoked the spell, my voice low, the words falling from my lips, rippling through the air like pebbles in a pond. I felt the energy I sent out come back, enveloping me in an undulating wave invisible to the naked eye. The hairs on my arms and neck prickled and goose bumps covered my skin in a quick shiver.

I felt Father O'Mare hovering close by and I risked a quick look at him. And I blinked once, then twice. Hard. He had changed, or the spell had changed how I saw him. No longer was he a faded version of himself, a ghost or apparition that would spook the semi-sensitive. He appeared quite solid, vibrant, as he would have been in life.

"Miss Galloway?" he queried, concerned.

I held up a hand, trying not to be distracted by the waves of pale blue energy that I saw emanating from it, and said, "I'm fine. It….things just look a little different, that's all."

He frowned, but accepted my explanation. I took a minute to adjust to my new sight, then cautiously rose to my feet. The church itself had changed now – I was seeing the energy from the wood and stone and metal throughout the room. Even the threads in the rug I stood on shimmered in a bright myriad of colors.

I looked up at the pulpit and I recoiled sharply, my lips pulling back in a tight grimace.

Under the spell, the pulpit looked worse than it did with my normal vision. What hung over it resembled a small cloud, but it was thick, black, and heavy, dripping over the surface of the damaged pulpit like spilled ink. I didn't want to touch it, let alone go near it. The dark energy attached to what I was seeing was repulsive and yet, I felt the curious impulse to touch it, to gain a better sense of what it was.

Shifting so that I was on my knees, I examined the pulpit as closely as I could, avoiding being in a position to touch it unless I absolutely had to. There were several little cubbies, each of them empty, even the very bottom ones. These I examined with my head on the floor, my cheek resting on the rough threads of the carpet. Stale dust barely covered the beginning scent of rotted wood, courtesy of the damage done.

Not even a hymnal occupied one of the cubbies.

Still, I kept looking for anything out of the ordinary –

a relic of some kind, or residue from a protective charm. Nothing, which seemed odd. There didn't seem to be anything of interest that would warrant the pulpit's destruction, which was odder still. Disappointed, I moved to get to my feet when I noticed the faint flash of blue from a crack in the floorboards. I froze, caught in that rather awkward position of half-kneeling, half-standing.

It pulsated in soft waves and I realized that whatever it was lay beneath the boards that I'd earlier observed was loose. Could it be what the vampires had been looking for? There was only one way to find out. I examined the old floorboard, now loosened by my kneeling on it. The board had popped up by a fraction, the nails no longer flush with the wood. The pale blue energy was stronger underneath it and when I reached for the board, the energy zapped me, a sharp sensation that felt like a thousand nettles stinging my hand all at once. I jerked back and examined my hand closely, but there were no marks. It was a purely psychic attack and I suspected that if the vampires had found it, it may have had a similar effect on them.

Cautious now, I gripped the board as best I could.

The wood was rough against my fingers, the nail heads sharp and cold against my skin. Unlike the Pellington's porch, the church's floor boards were not only in better condition, due to consistent maintenance, but harder to pull up. The nails wouldn't give and I sat back on my heels, frowning, my fingers tingling with energy now that the stinging had subsided.

"Is there a tool box around somewhere?" I asked.

Father O'Mare gave me a withering look. "Of course. In the kitchen pantry."

I made a face at him, climbed to my feet and headed for the kitchen. In the daytime, the space was probably very cheery and welcoming. Now, as I watched dusk quickly turn into night through the windows, it presented a very different atmosphere. The energy I was seeing through Abby's spell made the kitchen seem like an overlay of what it actually looked like. It was not the cozy feeling one would associate with kitchens, especially one in a church. I certainly didn't want to have a meal in this room.

Father O'Mare stood by the pantry. "Here, on the top shelf, near the back."

I crossed the kitchen and opened the pantry door, reaching for the string attached to the overhead light bulb. Then I realized that the glow from my hands was providing enough light for me to see the tool box on the top shelf. Reaching up, I pulled it down, crouching as I set it on the floor. Opening the tool box, I found and pulled out a small hammer, hefting it for its weight in my right hand. Satisfied, I headed back to the nave.

Father O'Mare followed, muttering.

Back at the pulpit, I knelt down, using the hammer's claws to pry at the nails, working them out with care. I had pulled out five of them when the board made a sudden movement. Setting the hammer on the floor next to me, I lifted the board and felt around underneath it. At first, all I came up with was a bunch of dust bunnies, bent nails from a previous carpentry job, a nickel and a splinter in my thumb. Then, just as I was about to give up, my fingers touched something smooth, like plastic. There was another sting of energy, but not like before and I pinched the object by its corner and pulled.

I sat back on my heels again, staring at the object, perplexed. It was a small book, about the size of a large paperback. Turning it over in my hands, I saw that it wasn't a work of fiction or even a hymnal, but a records book, wrapped in plastic. It looked old, with the plastic starting to fall apart in my hands, and the dust that was caked all over it. It pulsated a soft blue, the stinging sensation fading now that I had pulled it free.

The book must be what the vampires had been looking for, or at least been sent by the person who suspected that it was hidden in the pulpit. And the stinging sensation in my hands had to be from a protection spell that had been placed on it prior to its being shoved under the floor boards and nailed over. Glancing from the book to the hole in the floor, I wondered who had hidden it originally and who was looking for it now.

With care, I placed the book on the floor next to me, then took the nails and the hammer and carefully pounded the board back into place, making sure it was flush with the rest. Once that was done, I gathered up Abby's spell work and put it back in the box, setting the records book on top of it. Then, tucking both under my arm, I hurried back down the hall and into the kitchen, going straight to the pantry. I put the hammer back in the tool box and lifted it back to its shelf, pushing it back in place. It was a little after ten, according to the church kitchen clock. Taking a quick look around the kitchen to make sure that nothing was out of place, I made my exit.

Ten minutes later, Abby's wooden box and the book in hand, I was outside, sitting on the back stoop. I breathed in the crisp night air, relieved that the job was done. The moon had climbed higher in the night sky, still illuminating my surroundings. I stared at my hands, curious about the blue energy still emanating from them, wondering when it would wear off. Or if it would wear off. Abby hadn't mentioned that when she explained the spell to me. Calling her when I got back to the shack was first on my list of things to do.

Father O'Mare materialized beside me. "That book belongs to the church."

I glanced down at the dusty object. "I think this is what the vampires were looking for."

"How can you be so sure? They missed it." He peered for a closer look. "It's only a records book, after all."

"I'm not sure why or how they missed it," I said, "but it's what I found. And there may have been a spell that hid it from them." I described the stinging I'd experienced.

"Or maybe they missed it because it is so mundane to very human concerns. Considering that there's more supernatural in Maurier County than mundane, they were probably looking for a talisman or a cursed relic or something."

The spectral priest considered this. "Perhaps," he admitted grudgingly.

I held up the book. "On the other hand, if this really is what they were looking for, they aren't the only ones." Standing, I moved towards the door. "If you want the church to remain a target, then by all means, let me put this back."

He relented, albeit reluctantly. "Very well. You may take it."

"Good." I glanced around the tiny church yard. It was now half past eight and I was tired, both from a long day at the cemetery and from the magic I'd worked to find the book. Hiding a yawn, I turned back to the spectral priest. "I need to speak to Sarah again. Can you ask her to come out, please?"

He sniffed, shook his head. "She will not appear again tonight, but I'll convey your message to Miss Pellington."

"That would be helpful, thank you." Dropping a few silver coins into the donation box by the door, I bade him good-bye. Then I set off back to the cemetery and the tiny shack I call home, the full moon high in the sky and lighting my way.

*****

My hands still had that blue glow when I got back to the shack.

Even Dottie noticed. "Have you been dabbling in the occult?"

I nodded, placing both Abby's wooden box and the dusty book on my dining table with care, placing my ash stake next to it. "Kind of had to, Dottie. Abby would take offense at you calling it the occult, though." I gestured to the records book. "And I found this."

Dottie floated over to the table, exclaiming in soft 'ohs' and 'ahs' over the book. "Is this what the vampires were looking for?"

"I think so," I said. "It was hidden beneath the pulpit, so odds are that it is."

She looked at me, hopeful. "You'll be able to get rid of them soon? Father O'Mare will have nothing more to worry about?"

"Yep. Nope." She was pleased, I could tell. It made me feel good, in a big sisterly sort of way, like I'd solved a huge problem and now her life, er, after-life would be fine. "Soon you'll be able to help him as much as you want and not worry."

She twinkled. "I might at that." She gestured to the second packet I'd set on the table. "What's that? Did you find that at the church, too?"

I shook my head, touching the smaller packet with gentle fingers. "No, I found this at the Pellington place." Picking it up, I took a pair of scissors and slit the plastic open, taking care not to damage the contents it held. Tied in a black ribbon was a packet of letters, perhaps a dozen or more.

"Oooo, letters!" Dottie exclaimed. "Are they love letters?"

Thinking of Sarah, I thought it was entirely possible. "Want to read them with me?"

She materialized onto the couch. "Yes, please!"

Joining her, I undid the ribbon and let it fall onto my lap. Unfolding the first letter, I saw that the correspondence was from the early 1940s and between two women – Hallie Welles and Elizabeth 'Eliza' Pellington. From the warm nature of the greetings, it seemed that they were very close, either good friends or relatives.

I began to read out-loud.

Wisdom Between Witches

10 December 1940

My dear Hallie,

Such a delight to have you visit the Cove at long last! The girls were especially thrilled at your visit, though I must apologize once more for Marcus' short temper. I can't imagine what it is he has been keeping in the basement all these years that would incur such sharpness. I've only been in it once, shortly after we married. It's dark and rather dank and certainly not a place I would consider spending much time in.

He says he's working on some old furniture that needed repair, but really, I think it's just an excuse to lock himself away from the world. Not that we have any neighbors to speak of – as you saw, the closest is the village itself, which is only four miles or so from here. In that way, we're also locked away from the world and I sometimes wonder if that's good for the girls or if they ought to be more involved with other young people their age in the village. It didn't seem to matter so much when they were so young, but now, they get so restless.

Especially Anne, since she's the eldest and has a desire to go to college. She's developed an interest in botany and spends much of her time in the woods, identifying and classifying as many plants as possible.

Thank you for understanding my reluctance to discuss the family 'gift'. Marcus has not always been keen to know of it, though he is quick to accept its benefit, particularly when it comes to the vegetables I've been able to grow in my garden here. If it has been passed onto the girls, they have shown no signs of it.

I sometimes catch myself watching the girls, to see if they have any flash of talent in that regard and I must say there is some guilt that follows the relief I feel when I find nothing. Anne, most especially. She is so much like Marcus in temperament that it would be disastrous if her skill was of the telekinetic sort.

Yours in light,
Eliza

15 December 1940

Eliza, darling,
The Cove is absolutely gorgeous and the village too quaint for words!! Why did I wait so long to visit? Why have you not chastised me more when I've turned down all those invitations? Ah, well, it is now my destination as the occasion arises.

Patience with your girls, love, time enough to see how that develops. How has Marcus gone all these years, not knowing of the family gift? It's something that ought to be addressed, just in case one of the girls starts to exhibit signs of her gift, though it seems rather late, given that Sarah is now thirteen. It wouldn't do for him to discover this by surprise.

If I recall right, you didn't come into your gift until late – you're an impremere, *correct? Let me see if I've got this right and you can correct what I've misunderstood. An* impremere *is empathic by nature, capable of taking on the magic, elements or skills of those around them, correct? The book I read while researching the topic was rather archaic and the language was quite high-brow, but I believe that I understand the gist of it.*

All men need a space to hide away from the women-folk, my uncle Silas once told me. A rather antiquated view, I've always felt, but there are days when I would very much like to shut myself away in a quiet room and work on my herb lore (it's shocking how little I know!), so I do see the sense behind it.

Perhaps you and the girls should turn the tables on Marcus and claim a space for women!

Oh, before I forget, I simply must have that cookie recipe from you. I have not stopped thinking about that treat since I stepped into my car for the drive home. And I shall cook a fine Italian meal for the lot of you, on my next visit.

I do hope you like garlic?

Yours in light,
Hallie

19 December 1940

Merry Christmas, lovely Hallie!

A few days early, at any rate. It's cold enough here that it feels like it may snow, which would delight the girls to no end. Had we lived in a higher altitude, it would have been a seasonal treat to enjoy, though Marcus would grumble at having to shovel the drive and lane on his trips to the village. I, of course, would tell him it's good for his circulation. He would only snort.

It's been raining quite hard for the last couple of days and I am sitting in the front parlor, watching as the rain pelts the earth. I love this weather – the cold air is bracing and the smell of damp earth is so rich and warm and I know the gardens are going to bloom bright and wild this year.

On the other hand, this has kept the girls are cooped up in their rooms to amuse themselves and it's only a matter of time before one of them starts a fight. Marcus is currently in the basement and I've been working on a needlepoint while keeping an eye on the ham I've got roasting in the oven.

Yes, I'm an impremere, *though my skills are rather limited.* Impremeres *can also enhance the power of those around them. But it's their ability to pull elements apart and absorb it into their own*

217

magic that makes impremeres *quite unique. Some would say valuable, but those people would use anything and everything for their own gain.*

As I've mentioned previously, I've found that it's been most useful in the garden, so that's where I put my focus. Thus the abundance of vegetables the girls dislike eating so much during meals and the rose gardens they so enjoy playing hide and seek in.

Marcus hardly pays attention to what I set in front of him – it all gets eaten, though I do worry about the weight he seems to be losing. I've had to take in his trousers at the waist six times in the last year alone, since he refuses to purchase anything new until what he wears has fallen apart around him.

Hallie, it's perhaps my imagination, but what with raising the girls and the general housework, I hadn't noticed how much time Marcus has spent in the basement until this current storm. And perhaps it's a trick of the light when he comes into the kitchen from downstairs, but he seems quiet. Pale. Almost a ghost.

See how this weather affects me! I have become fanciful and poetic!

Yours in light,
Eliza

P.S. I love garlic, but unfortunately, Marcus is highly allergic to it, as I discovered during the first night of our honeymoon. Apparently, the secret ingredient in the soup had garlic oil in it – he spent the rest of the week in our rooms.

23 December 1940

Happy Christmas, my dear Eliza!
A little early as I write this, and certainly a day or so past when you receive it!
You were always inclined to be artistic, my dear – I still have some of your poetry from when we were in school. You see so much and give yourself so little credit for it.
Has Marcus produced any masterpieces in his basement workshop?

Or is it just tinkering, as men are so often wont to do? Perhaps surprise him with a light snack and take a peek at what he's working on? And most definitely something garlic-free – that is an extreme reaction to it, so sorry to hear that!

My dear, you seem uneasy over something, whether it's about Marcus and his health or the girls or something else altogether, I am not quite sure. But it comes through your letters, dear, and so I have to ask if all is well with you?

I must extend an invitation to you and your daughters to come down the coast for a visit.

Yours in light,
Hallie

31 December 1940

Happy New Year's Eve!
By the time you get this, it will be a few days into 1941.
And yes, I am worried, Hallie, deeply so, as you ascertained. And yes, it's about Marcus.
Not just his weight loss or his obsession with the basement and his insistence that the girls and I are never to go down there, but it's his general behavior that has me worried. I hadn't wanted to say anything, as it's all just shadows and fancy, but there are secrets in this house.

His secrets.
Some years ago, he had put a padlock on the basement door and keeps the key on a chain around his neck. I don't recall when he had done it, it was just there one day, and I commented on it, but his reply was so short to the point of surliness, that I let it drop. I wanted no argument with him and have not mentioned it since.
However, once, while preparing dinner, I thought I heard him conversing with more than one person. I couldn't hear what was said, just a low murmur of voices. When he came upstairs to sit down, I asked if his guests wanted to join us for dinner, though I had not seen another soul approach the house.

Marcus stared at me with such a blank expression that I grew frightened. Then he said he'd the radio on and hadn't realized it was so loud. He apologized and promised to keep it at a more moderate level in future.

I accepted his explanation, as I had no evidence to suggest otherwise. But I have kept watch. And it is a strange thing to be doing, watching my husband and in my own home.

Our home.

So strange, that in telling you all of this, I am finally facing this truth. This house is not ours, in the way it was in the beginning, when Marcus and I were first married. It has become his house, my house, the girls' house.

We keep to the spaces where we feel comfortable.......or safe.

And the only times we are together is for meals. Sometimes.

It is nebulous, this feeling of mine.

And it is also very late and I am jumping at shadows that are not even there and scratches against the walls that sound like nails, but are only tree branches in the wind.

And there is that poetic side, seeking expression once more! Perhaps in the morning, things will seem aright.

The girls are very excited at the kind invitation and we will accept, perhaps sometime over the summer, when the weather is not so dampening to the spirit.

Yours in light,
Eliza

February 7, 1941

Darling Eliza,
Happy much belated New Year!
I am sorry to be so long in my response, but your last letter brought to mind my uncle Silas, whom I hadn't thought about since his death years ago. He had often told me about the strange noises out at his farm in Arizona, shortly after the Great War ended in 1918. Being a child at the time, I gobbled up his stories as if they were candy. As

I grew older, of course, I discounted them as the exaggerations of an old man, since he was surrounded by equipment and animals that could easily explain what he heard.

The scratching noises and shadowed voices you describe are very similar to what old Silas had regaled to me, and I went back through his letters, re-reading his later ones. All of them were the same as he had told me when I was younger, only he finally named what had been tormenting him – vampires.

Yes, it strikes me as fanciful now as it did when I decided that I was too old for fairy tales and folklore, but we both know better than that. As I write this, I'm going through all of his surviving papers – he managed to eliminate an entire nest somehow and he wrote me the details about it the year before he died.

Do you still have your mother's silver crucifix? Would you put my mind at ease and wear it, and perhaps find something for your daughters, as well? Your Father O'Mare ought to be able to provide some items for you.

It may very well be that I am seeing things that aren't there, and I certainly would be delighted to laugh at this later, when it is proven that I am the one jumping at shadows, but taking these precautions would make certainly put my mind at ease.

Many blessings!
Yours,
Hallie

February 13, 1941

Darling Hallie,
Curious that your mind went to vampires, whereas mine went to poetry, but I did as you asked and, while it may be fanciful thinking in the end, it has put my mind at ease, as well. The girls grumble on occasion and I've had to reprimand Sarah a number of times, but they wear their crucifixes without too much trouble.

Marcus hardly noticed, but has retreated even further into his basement. On the rare days when I am alone in the house, I have tried to find a way into the basement, but he has the only key to the padlock. The windows are too small to crawl through, even if I could open them, but they are sealed shut with age and weathering.

Last week, I sent him on an errand into town with the girls. It was to be a family affair, only I begged off with a headache and when they were gone in the car, I had gone outside to look into the basement through its windows. They were dirty, mostly from grit on the outside and dust on the inside, and some were near impossible to peer through, but I was able to see what he has kept down there – three plain wooden crates. If stood on end, they would be only a few inches taller than me. Though they did not seem out of the ordinary, in my mind, they were crude coffins, made for a reason that only Marcus could give.

That I was able to prepare dinner with a smile upon their return bodes well for my courage, I suppose, but it was not an easy thing. I don't recall when that thought occurred to me, but it took root not long after and it disturbs me for many reasons.

Who would strike a deal with a vampire and for what purpose?

If they are seeking longevity, it comes with a price, and not a worthy one.

Many blessings,
Eliza

March 2, 1941

Darling Eliza,
It took some doing, but I've found the letter in which my uncle managed to deal with his vampire problem. I've not tried it, not having the need for it, but I've enclosed it with this letter.

Please continue to wear that crucifix and be careful. Get some holy water to sprinkle about the house, particularly around the girls' rooms. As for Marcus, have a care around him – his secrets are clearly becoming less so. He may not like your interference.

Send the girls down to visit with me. Make up any reason, if you need to. Come with them, if you are able.

Warmest,
Hallie

March 13, 1961

Hallie,
I've gone over your uncle's method carefully. It is unusual, but if it worked for him, then I am eager to try. I shall keep you posted on how it works for me and hide your uncle's method in a safe place.
I'm mailing the family book to my sister in Wickerman Falls — it's her turn to carry on that little tradition of ours.
I'll return Silas's letter to you as quickly as I can.

Blessings,
Eliza

Twenty-Two

As I finished reading the last letter, Dottie let out a soft sigh and shivered.

"Such a sad family," she said, wistful.

I was inclined to agree, folding the letters up again and putting them to one side. Uncle Silas's letter containing his solution to his own vampire problem was missing. Either Elizabeth had needed to destroy it (likely) or she had sent it back to Hallie (probably). In any case, that missing letter held the key to dealing with the vampires in the here and now.

Picking up the plastic-wrapped book, I cut slits into the plastic using a pair of scissors with care, not wanting to damage it. Dottie peered over my shoulder as I worked, equally curious as to what the book contained within its pages. Whoever wanted this book thought it contained something important enough to work with a nest of vampires to vandalize the church. It also raised the question of what led the vampires to vandalize the church in 1924. The book hadn't been hidden there yet, but something had drawn them to the place.

Tossing the plastic wrapping to one side, I discovered that, despite the covering, dust had accumulated on the book. Going to the sink, I dampened a paper towel and carefully wiped as much dust off as I could. Grimacing at the unpleasant touch as I cleaned the old book, I thought about the pulpit and its destruction. Was it because the vampires couldn't access the book? Or was it because they couldn't 'see' it, even knowing it had to be somewhere in the pulpit? In which case, the person who hid the book in the floorboards underneath it had to have placed a protection spell over it.

Finished, I threw out the paper towel and wiped off my hands, wanting them to be as dry as possible before I opened the book. When I did, a musty odor wafted up from the yellowed and stained pages, tickling my nose. I sneezed into my upper arm, then opened the book with care. The first few pages were blank, but at the top of the fifth page, I saw that someone had written *Births* in a neat script.

Beneath it, in a cramped script, lists of dates, names and genders filled the page and every one after. Noting that the first birth recorded had been a boy in 1893, I flipped ahead, being careful of the thin pages. It became clear to me that this was the Naughton family book and it didn't take long to find Catherine Naughton's name and, just below it, Marcus Pellington. There was a mark that indicated marriage and then three more names – Anna, Helen and Sarah. There were other names, next to Elizabeth's – Cassiopeia, Francis and Margaret. Sisters, it looked like.

Turning another few pages, I found Calliope Naughton's birthdate, but no mention of her parents. Next to her name was Bennett Welles and the same mark indicating marriage. Below both of them were three names that I also recognized – Caitlyn, Claire and Cecelia. All three of them were older than me, Caitlyn the eldest by ten years. I kept rifling through the pages, reading names, feeling the weight of their untold stories within the scratches of ink.

There were a dozen other entries marking a birth in the years following Cecelia, but only one caught my eye. There was an entry with no name attached, either to the child or the family it belonged to. The date itself was smudged, as if written in a hurry and the writer couldn't be bothered to take care. Was this my entry?

Pulling out my unaltered birth certificate, I compared the names of my parents listed on the document with the names I'd found in the book. My parents – my biological parents – were listed, showing that they were the parents of Caitlyn, Claire, and Cecelia. Well, I thought, here was the absolute confirmation I needed that I was not only related to them, I was their baby sister. It also seemed that we were related to Hallie Welles. I exhaled abruptly, just now realizing that I'd been holding my breath. It still didn't offer any explanations for why I had been kept a secret, or why the Galloways whisked me away. I suspected that those answers would only come from talking with the women I now knew were my sisters.

Of the three, Claire was the logical choice. She was around, unlike Cat, and she had a more grounded personality, unlike Cecelia. If anyone could explain why the Galloways had adopted me and lied about it, then Claire could. And it seemed that the best approach was to gather more information, to back up what I was telling her.

Raul Kendrick could help with that, I thought, warming at the thought of him. He would need to see both of my birth certificates, in addition to the book, now lying open on the table.

The book of births.

I paged through the rest of the book, searching. The notation of the nameless child's birth had been the last entry written. I closed the book carefully and pushed it away, staring at it, but not really seeing it, my thoughts churning. According to the letters, Elizabeth Pellington had charge of this book and had indicated that it would be sent to her sister, who was the most likely person to have taken the pains to hide it under the pulpit.

The question was, why? Was she hiding it from Pellington? Or was it from the vampires he kept hidden in the basement? Or was there some other reason? And which sister?

My head was beginning to pound and I rubbed my eyes, tired. Everything was leading back to that family – the book, the abandoned house, Cat Naughton's visit to New Orleans, my trip to Wickerman Falls. The book was important – not just to the person who hid it and not just to the vampires, either. It was important to whomever wanted it found.

My fingers brushed against the interior binding and I froze. There was something not quite right about the back cover. It felt thicker, somehow, not quite as well-bound as the front and I flipped it open, feeling the inside binding with care. Although smoothed over, something was clearly hidden under the paper that held the pages to the backboard.

Quickly, I found a sharp knife and, inserting it between the paper and the board, I slit it open in slow strokes. My hands trembling, I pealed the paper back to reveal a folded sheet, yellowed with age. Setting the knife down, I removed and unfolded the sheet, unfamiliar script greeting my eyes. Silas Welles had written, in extreme detail to his niece, Hallie, about the small nest of vampires. He had found their burrow in which they slept during daylight hours while out tracking coyote. Though there were only five and sleeping, he was well aware that he would be dead before the first one fell.

I skimmed the rest of Silas' letter, noting how he'd monitored the nest; the spells and charms he'd made to both protect himself and weaken the vampires; that the way to completely destroy the nest for good was to take out the sire. He did not dare involve anyone else in his small town – the fewer who knew about the vampires, the less likely it would be that they themselves became targets.

Silas wrote about the night he went out to destroy the vampire nest – the full moon in the sky glinting off the silver crucifix he carried as he approached, shadows looming in sharp relief in the pale light.

But it was one specific paragraph that caught my eye.

How Silas had managed to avoid confrontation with the nest, he did not say. How he dealt with their sire stood out, as if written in thick, bold strokes.

"The only weapon I had was my grandmother's crucifix, which I boldly brandished before me while reciting the incantation," Silas wrote. *"The vampire froze where it stood, only inches from me, and I was able to place my free hand on its cold, dead chest. I kept chanting, my focus narrowing on that hollow husk where a heart once beat. Though it must have been seconds, it seemed an eternity before the cold skin beneath my palm warmed and another few before I felt a faint* thump *as the vampire's heart regained its original purpose. I risked a look into the Undead thing's eyes and saw a glimmer of the human it once was. With very little time left, I plunged my stake into its heart and pressed my grandmother's crucifix against its skull, where it burned into the thin flesh. There is not much more to write about it – the vampire uttered an inhuman shriek and, as it became dust at my feet and mixed in with the dirt I stood on, I could hear its nest die with it, their shrieks blending with the howls of coyote."*

Silas went on a bit more, but I read and re-read that bit several times, the memory of my own encounter with the Louisiana vampire strong. The similarities between my experience and Silas's were close, which meant that my first vampire had been a sire, or at the very least, a lone vampire who had yet to create a nest. What really mattered to me was that Silas and I had managed to pull the soul of a vampire back into its body.

But where Silas had to use charms and incantations, I had done it through instinct. Folding Silas's letter, I slipped it back into the pocket I'd made in the book's cover, then shut the book a little harder than necessary. Then I folded the letters and tied them with the black ribbon. Kneeling in front of the couch, I felt underneath for the protective cloth that hid the metal springs and gave it a hard yank. The thin material fell away easily and I stashed the book and letters carefully among the springs, the metal cold against my fingers.

Satisfied that it was secure, I sat back on my heels with a sigh. The blue glow had faded completely and my hands had regained their normal hue. The book itself wasn't magic, but the reasons for the vampires' vandalism had become clearer — Silas Welles's method for dealing with the Undead. The vampires may not have known what the book hid, but whomever set them on the church did.

I didn't feel much like sleeping after that.

*****

Of course, I did fall asleep.

And I knew I was dreaming, that I was in my actual bed in my humble little shack. I could feel the weight of my blankets wrapped around me as I dreamed and I snuggled even deeper in them, seeking more of their warmth and comfort. Perhaps I was also trying to change the nature of my dream.

Because I was also at the end of Black Rock Lane. The sun was beating down on me in hot waves, broken only by the ocean breeze. I knew it was a dream because the lane was well-kept and clearly in use, unlike the over-grown and shaggy-from-disuse look it currently maintained. I became aware that I was not alone and I looked to my right.

Cat stood next to me, still wearing the white blouse and blue skirt. Her hands were empty of any gift wrapped in ribbon this time. The wound on her left temple was still there, but the dried blood was gone, as if she had washed it off.

She looked at me, touched my temple. "You have the gift."

I looked down at my hands and realized I was holding the box with green ribbon. In the previous dream, she had tried to give it to me, but I hadn't taken it. "How did I get this? I didn't take it from you."

She chuckled. "You've always had it. Now you must own it." Then, she pointed down the lane. "It started here."

I looked back at her. For some reason, I had very little interest in looking at the lane – I knew where it led. "What started?"

Cat smiled. "We did." Then she grew pensive, biting her lower lip, not looking at me. Her silence bothered me. She wanted to say something and I wasn't sure I wanted to hear it.

She looked at me and I was struck again by that strong sense of familiarity. I shrugged the feeling off, impatient with myself – of course, she looked familiar to me. She looked almost exactly like Claire and Cecelia.

Her sisters. *My* sisters.

Even in my dream, that bit of knowledge about our relationship felt surreal. I found myself wishing Cat would speak up, say what she wanted to say, instead of looking at me in that pensive, speculative way. It was starting to give me the shivers.

"The six is where it comes," she said at last.

I blinked. "Come again?"

She paused to consider her words, then spoke again. "From behind, it will strike. Someone of the blood will seek to bind you."

Well, that didn't sound good. "Can you be a little more specific?"

Cat gave me a look – *are you kidding?* – but sighed and gathered herself. I could feel the energy she was pulling, how difficult it was for her to shape the words. "She comes. She is close. She will find you."

I was struck cold. This was a warning, then, not just an idle spear of words to throw out and see how they landed. There was the feeling of someone interfering where they had no business to and that didn't sit well with me.

"What do I do?" I asked Cat.

She smiled. "Family is the key, Cady."

"I have no family," I said, automatically, then bit my lip, ashamed of the lie that had fallen so readily. It didn't matter I hadn't known about my family until a year ago, it mattered that I knew about them now. Lying only hurt that connection. Cat only watched me, her expression one of understanding and patience. She touched my cheek in a sisterly gesture.

"You will find clarity," she said. "And you will trust her."

Then Cat leaned forward, touching my forehead with a gentle kiss.

Twenty-Three

I woke up with a cramp in my neck from sleeping on the couch. Shifting onto my back, yawning, I studied the ceiling above me, still hidden in shadow. My dreams about Cat were unusual in quality, similar to ones I'd had as a teenager. Then, I would receive cryptic messages from people I didn't even know. I was never sure if they were even actual people, since I'd never seen them in my waking state. Most of the time, the cryptic messengers were dead — they felt flat and static, like most ghosts I encounter.

Cat was the opposite — her energy was bold and vibrant, vivid in a way that could only belong to someone still alive and breathing and active. Cecelia had been tracking someone the other day, she'd said as much, and I wondered if it was her oldest sister. If so, she was having very little success, since Cat was clearly making things difficult for her in a way that only the living could, by staying one step ahead of her.

Stretching, I glanced over at my alarm clock. It was almost eight in the morning, so I got up and quickly put on some fresh clothes. As I laced up my shoes, Dottie popped in, singing a cheerful song from her childhood. "Morning, Dottie. I'm going back to the church tonight and update

Father O'Mare on a few things. Wanna go?"

Dottie was tempted. I could see it written all over her. Ghosts are not able to hide their true feelings. "As long as I'm back by midnight."

"That's fine, we'll be home long before then."

She clapped her hands. "Excellent!"

"I'm gonna leave at dusk, so be ready."

"I will!" She slipped through the stone wall, then back in. "By the way, there's some whispers going on. You should watch out for friendly faces. They don't always mean well."

Then she was gone. I was really going to have to curtail her viewing habits. Instead of cereal for breakfast, I decided to make a quick trip into town for pastries and coffee to share with Mae in the office and then I set to work. As I made my rounds, I thought about the old Pellington place. I was going to need back-up when I went back to tackle the vampires.

They had answers, about who sent them to the church and what they were looking for. The trick was figuring out what the questions were. After reading Silas's letter, I was more convinced than ever that more than one person was involved with the vampires. And that it would take more than one person to go out and question them. No way was I going to question those vampires alone, even in broad daylight.

*****

The nursery's parking lot was empty when I pulled in, except for the pink moped parked at the far corner. I parked the truck next to it and climbed out, heading to the entrance. The tiny bell above the door jingled and Paige looked up from watering the small bonsai tree behind the counter as I walked in.

She brightened, the book lying open in front of her now forgotten. "Hey, Katie! How's the research going?"

I shrugged. "It's going all right. Is that your moped out front?"

"Yeah." Her grin faded a little. "I had to leave it at the mechanic's for a month while they waited on a part and I felt so lost without it." She made a face. "Public transit around here is not the greatest."

"But public transit gets you around when you need it," I pointed out.

Paige shrugged. "Yeah, true. It's inconvenient, but useful."

I glanced around. "Is Abby here?"

Paige nodded. "Out back as usual, digging in the dirt."

Of course. I looked around the empty shop, curious. Normally, it was hopping with people and it didn't matter what day of the week. "Slow day?"

She grimaced. "Yeah, but that's fine. I just got finished stocking the shelves and now I'm catching up on some studying."

I nodded and headed out back.

Abby was busy planting bulbs next to the stairwell, her gloves on the ground beside her, as usual. I couldn't tell what type of flowers they would be, but I was sure Abby would tell me, how long it took for them to grow and bloom and if they were perennials or annuals. Unlike last time, she had on headphones and was singing along to a classic hit from the seventies. Every once in a while, she emitted a low howl, singing the refrain under her breath. Warren Zevon, if I understood the lyrics correctly. A song to howl by.

Which Abby did again, this time putting her full energy into it by turning her face up to the sky and gave a long, loud howl. She almost choked when she saw me, turning bright red as she pulled out her ear buds.

"Hey, Abby," I said, sitting on the bottom step.

She went back to her planting, grumpy. "Jeez, Katie, you have the stealth skills of a ninja!"

I gave her a look, gesturing to her ear buds, now lying on top of her gloves. "You're kidding me, right? With those on, you'd never hear Godzilla tearing the place apart, let alone a bear."

She looked at them and laughed. "True. What's up?"

"I'm going out to Black Rock Lane," I said, and described the Pellington house. She sat back on her heels, the planting forgotten as I spoke. "There are a couple of things I need to do out there and I'd rather not do it alone. I was wondering if you'd like to come along and help."

Her eyes narrowed. "What are you really up to?"

I took a breath. "Well, I found the nest belonging to the vampires that vandalized Father O'Mare's pulpit. In the basement of the Pellington place."

Abby's spade dropped with a sharp *thunk*. "That's where the vampires are nesting?"

"According to what I'd found," I said, slowly, thinking of Sarah Pellington and her mother's letters, "Marcus Pellington hid them there after they attacked him back in 1924. And either they just stayed on after everyone died or they move around and use it as their main hiding spot. Since the house is remote and hasn't been used for decades, that makes sense."

That got her attention. "You're kidding."

I shook my head. "Nope. Afraid not."

She stood abruptly and trotted up the steps, wiping the dirt from her hands. The trowel lay in the flower bed, forgotten. "We're gonna need stakes, I've got the salt and some mason jars, oh, and silver pieces…."

I hurried after her. "Abby, I need to know why they've been going after that church."

Abby stopped, her hand on the door to the shop, and turned to face me. "You need to dust them immediately, Katie."

"I know that," I said, patient. "But I need to know why they destroyed the pulpit and who sent them." And if I could find that out, then perhaps I'd find out why the book was hidden in the church in the first place. At her look, I added, "Staking the vampires is also part of the plan."

Paige popped her head out the door, almost hitting Abby in the arm, her eyes sparkling with excitement. "Oh, sorry, Abby, didn't know you were there. Mrs. Whitcomb is on the phone for you. I think it's about that order you had to place for her, to help get her rose bushes to grow more than a foot high. Also, I was wondering if I could leave early, since it's dead and I've got a major exam this evening."

"Sure, go ahead," Abby said. "Tell Mrs. Whitcomb I'll be there in a minute."

"Will do." Paige disappeared.

Abby turned to me, scuffing the ground with her foot, thinking. Small pebbles sprayed in an arc away from her. "Fine. I'll help you with the vampires." She pointed a finger at me, trembling a little. "These questions had better be important."

"They are, I promise."

"And promise me that you'll dust them as soon as you're done." Abby's face was inscrutable, but I could sense her worry. "They'd kill you just as soon as turn you. You of all people should remember that."

I held up a hand to beg pardon. "I'm going to dust them as soon as I get my answers."

She looked at me a moment longer. "Good." Then she turned and went into the shop.

I followed her, catching the door as I called out, "The stakes need to be ash!"

Abby waved a hand, disappearing into her office. "I know."

By the time I reached the front counter, Paige was already gone and a quick glance at the main door showed that she had thoughtfully turned the sign from *Open* to *Closed*. Abby had shut the door to her office, but I could hear her voice as she took care of business over the phone, the conversation broken by laughter at one point. Exploring Abby's shop while I waited, I fingered the silver crucifix hanging around my neck. It was cool to the touch, despite being nestled between my breasts.

Planters pots of various sizes and styles were stacked neatly against the far wall to my right and I took a moment to admire them. Most of the glazed pots had been made a local potter and I traced their logo with one finger. Bags of seed, small potted plants, garden fixtures and statuary also lined the walls. Hanging plant holders, bird houses and bird feeders hung from the ceiling, with good measure for head clearance. The nursery shop had a nice, comfortable vibe to it and I suspected that she maintained the space with positivity spells.

The door to the office swung open abruptly and I headed over to meet her. Abby stepped out and locked it behind her, pulling on a blue and green sweater over her head. From the hook just behind the counter, she grabbed an old leather satchel and began to fill it with items she'd need for spell-casting. The last to go in were a couple of wooden stakes.

"Sorry, that took longer than I expected," she said. "I thought it was something simple."

"It usually isn't," I said. "You set to go?"

"Yup."

She locked up the store and then we headed to my truck, both of us silent. The task ahead of us was daunting – I had a list, a very short list, of questions that I wanted to ask the vampires before dusting them. I wasn't sure what Abby was thinking. Her cellphone rand as we approached the truck and she pulled it out, scowling at the name on the screen. I caught a brief glimpse – *Mom* – before she silenced it and tucked it in her pocket.

She caught my look. "What?"

I shrugged. "I don't know what went down with you and your mom, but I wouldn't let it drag out for much longer."

She huffed. "What are you, psychic?"

Shaking my head, I said, "No, I've just been coming

to the conclusion that holding onto a grudge isn't the best thing in the world."

"Like you?"

Choosing my words with care, I said, "I didn't know what lies were told until after it was too late to ask questions." She started to object, but I didn't let her finish. "I haven't been able to talk to their spirits, mostly because my own anger was blocking my ability. But your mom is still here, so I'd make peace over whatever it is that caused the rift."

She was silent as she climbed into the passenger side of the truck, slamming the door shut hard. "I swear, Katie, this is not my idea of fun." She gave me a hard look. "And I'm talking about the vampires."

I glanced at her. "And you think it's mine?"

Her only reply was to give me a dark look.

We pulled back out onto the road and headed south, back towards Sleepy Eye Cove and on to the forgotten and hidden lane. On the way, I told her about finding Silas's letter, how he'd pulled a vampire's soul back into its body before destroying it and, by association, its nest. I also told her that I had managed to do the same thing back in New Orleans, minus the aids Silas used.

If I hadn't been driving, I think she would have hit me.

Twenty-Four

I parked the truck in the same spot as last time, under a tree and facing the main road. Abby got out first, taking in the forgotten lane, intrigued. Getting out and walking around towards the truck's flatbed, I watched her as she pulled her sweater tight, the satchel of items she'd brought with her shifting on her shoulder with every movement. The shade provided by the trees where they converged added an extra bite to the chill and I wished I had a sweater in the truck.

Abby turned as I walked up to her. "This is the only road in, right?"

I took the lead. "And the only way out to Sleepy Eye Cove. But if you keep going past the house, it comes out on Route 5, which made it easier for them to get over to Wickerman Falls, I guess." I frowned. "I don't recall seeing the lane from Route 5, though."

She shook her head, muttering in Mandarin again as she fell into step beside me, casting glances to the crumbling rock walls on either side of us. It sounded rather unflattering about Marcus Pellington and his predilection for isolated areas. Keeping my eyes open for Henry, I said nothing.

Cadence, you came back.

Henry Gray stood just ahead of Abby, almost directly in her path. He looked absurdly grateful at my presence. I felt a little embarrassed. "Hello, Henry."

Abby stopped, turned, shivering a little. "Your friend is here?"

I nodded. "You almost walked through him, but that's his fault."

"That explains the chill, then." She shivered again. "Glad I stopped when I did."

I kept Henry's gaze. "What made you think I wouldn't come back?"

You seemed pretty spooked about the vampires. He shrugged, a movement that didn't quite mask his joy at my presence. *It didn't seem too far-fetched to think that you'd stay away. I would have understood.*

The poor kid. I shook my head. It's easy to forget that even the dead can get lonely and that not everyone can see them, to help alleviate that loneliness. Henry was a good sort, I liked him, and it felt good to know that I'd cheered him up simply by coming back. We walked, Henry disappearing and reappearing at odd intervals. Abby kept close, jumping when I stepped on a twig, its sharp snap loud in our ears.

As we walked, I studied Henry's appearance a little more closely. He was beginning to look as he did in life. Color was seeping into him, enough so that I could see the color of his eyes – hazel green. Even his hair color was coming through – a light brown mixed with red. It seemed that the longer he was in the presence of the living, the more defined he got.

"Are we almost to the house yet?" Abby grumbled, rubbing her arms. In spite of the sweater she wore, she seemed cold.

Another twenty feet, Henry said, gesturing. *You're almost there, come on!*

"Just a few more minutes of walking," I told her.

242

"We're almost there, it's kind of hard to see from the road." To Henry, I said, "Relax, all right?"

Abby gave me a look. "What's he saying?"

I glanced over at Henry. "He's impatient."

"I don't know why he should be," Abby grumbled. "He's dead. It's not like he can't wait awhile longer."

I was inclined to agree.

Dead or not, I still deserve to know why she killed me. Henry scowled at both of us.

I relayed his words to Abby. "Henry wants to know why she, whoever she is, killed him." I turned back to him. "Who is 'she'? Was she in the house?"

Henry nodded. *I remember that it was dark, though. She moved easily and caught me by surprise. Beyond that, it's fuzzy.*

I considered Henry's words, thoughtful. If he was speaking of the living, then it had been one of the three other women in that house, other than Sarah – Catherine Pellington and her two eldest daughters. That didn't fit the woman who had written to her friend with family concerns and, later, supernatural ones. And if they had a servant that acted as maid and cook, that would put at least two more women in the house.

But the Spectral Six hadn't mentioned any such person in their recounting, nor was one listed in any of the newspaper accounts. Which left only one other option. Recalling the brief vision of a woman upon my meeting Henry Gray, I suspected that she was the one he was referring to.

"Was she a member of the household? Like a maid or a cook?" I asked, wanting to rule out that possibility right up front.

He shook his head. *No, I don't know what her role was in that house. The first time I saw her was the last time I breathed. I really need your help, Cadence.*

That would be an unsettling last memory to have and I relayed his words to Abby. "He has a point, you know."

Abby rolled her eyes in exasperation. "I'm not saying

we won't help him, I'm just pointing out that it won't hurt if a few more minutes passed."

Henry frowned. *When it's her time and she has questions from this side of the veil, I'm sure she'll be just as patient.* He vanished.

I chose not to share that with Abby. Instead, I offered a brief smile and said, "Patience is not something he has to worry about."

As we approached the stone wall, I looked out over at the clearing to our right. An old oak tree loomed over it, its massive trunk partially obscured by the over-growth and saplings that had begun to take over. There was a tranquility around that old tree that appealed to me, the kind of feeling you'd get when having a nice sandwich or a nap. If there was time after the vampires, I wanted to take a quick look over at that clearing and the oak tree.

In the meantime, Abby had stopped and was staring at the stone wall. Then she handed me her satchel. "I'm going over first and you can hand this over."

In minutes, we were both on the other side of the wall. Abby hung back to my left as she shouldered her bag once more. I stood further in from the stone wall, listening to the faint sounds of the woods around us. There was an occasional cry of a hawk and the anguished squeal of prey being caught, but otherwise the area was quiet.

Henry reappeared, hovering to my right.

"Has there been anyone here since my last visit?" I asked.

Abby stopped just beside me. "Wait, I thought you were the only one who knew about this place?"

And now she's going to be the fifth, Henry said, irritated.

"No, actually, I'm not," I said, taking the lead once more. "At least two people have been here off and on over the last few weeks, according to Henry." I glanced at him. He was ahead of me, winking in and out in turns on the path. "How long ago were they here?"

He considered. *Last night, after you had left.*

I relayed the information to Abby, who sniffed. "Great. Hopefully they won't be back any time soon."

I shook my head. "They're pretty spotty on visits, according to Henry."

She scowled. "That doesn't mean anything. They could come back in twenty minutes."

"Then we'll deal with it."

They won't be back, Henry said. *After they took the crate, the woman said she wanted to keep looking for her.......whoever 'her' is.*

"So, we'll be fine," I said to Abby, after relaying Henry's words.

"Famous last words," she grumbled.

I gestured to her satchel. "I'm sure you've got enough power in that bag to set up some kind of an alarm system to let us know if anyone's coming back. They'll know we're here, because of the truck, but it could give us time to get out before they found us."

She nodded. "Good plan."

The one who killed me is here, Henry said, looking towards the house.

I followed his gaze. "Who killed you? Was it one of the Pellington women or someone else?"

Henry raised his hands in a shrug. *I don't remember.*

"Then we'll find out." I turned to Abby. "Come on, this is the best way to the house."

With a quick glance back towards the stone wall, I led the way. There was a sharp tingling, a feeling I recognized as a gathering of pure, focused energy. I opened my mouth to ask Abby if she felt it when Henry grabbed my arm.

I stopped abruptly, staring down at the ghostly hand that gripped me, Henry looking just as stunned as I felt. Even ghosts that could manifest enough energy to move solid objects had never tried to touch or grab me. It was never clear to me if they could or couldn't or if they knew they could or couldn't.

Henry had not only tried, he had actually done it.

He looked at me, his eyes urgent. *She killed me. She's here.*

I met his gaze. "I know. But who is she? You just said you didn't know."

He shook his head, as if to clear his thoughts. *I don't know who killed me. But she never left.*

Abby tugged at my elbow. "What did he say?"

I stared through the shrubbery to the house beyond. "The woman who killed him is here."

Henry nodded. *She's in the basement.*

"He says in the basement," I said automatically, then stiffened, my thoughts galloping ahead of my comprehension. "Wait a minute. The woman who killed you is in the basement?"

Henry nodded, dropping his hand. *Yes. Captain Pellington caught me peeking through the windows into the basement. My last memory is of her standing over me.*

I started walking for the house. The spot on my arm where Henry had grabbed it itched and I scratched absently. "Come on, Abby."

Abby hurried to catch up. "What's going on?"

"What killed Henry is one of the vampires in the basement," I said over my shoulder as we walked. Nothing had changed out here, nothing physical, anyway, but I didn't like the feeling that nagged at me – as though we were being watched. "You're gonna get your wish, Abs. Dusting and answers."

Twenty-Five

Silently, we approached the house, the front porch gradually coming into view. Pausing at the foot of the steps, I stared up at the front door. Behind me, Abby stopped to catch her breath, exhaling in a long sigh of awe.

"Wow, in the five years that I've lived around here, I never knew this place existed." She stared up at the house, wonder on her face. "How'd you find it?"

I gave her an abbreviated account of my discovering the lane, leaving out Pellington's shade and his guilt. "I had a little help from Henry, too."

She looked around. "Did he live here?"

"As a kind of handyman, I think."

Henry popped into view in front of me. *Why are you just standing here?*

I gestured to Abby. "She needs to catch her breath."

Then you'll get rid of them? The vampires?

"Yes, relax, that's why we're here." Among other things.

Abby looked around, apprehensive. "Are you and your…friend debating on how to get into the house by nefarious means?"

"Sort of," I said. "Come on."

I trotted up the steps. Abby remained at the bottom, staring up at the house, her expression one of awe and curiosity. Kneeling in front of the door, I touched the knob with cautious fingers, remembering the spark I'd received the last time. There was a faint, but definite, metallic clink as the tumblers turned. I stared at the knob, still unable to believe what I was hearing. The knob turned a little and the door popped open and swung inwards of its own accord, the hinges groaning a little, then stopped. A cold breath of air leaked out.

Hearing the door creak open, Abby sighed as she climbed up the porch steps. "Finally."

She climbed up carefully to meet me; then, taking a deep breath, she stepped past me, giving the door a gentle push. It swung wider and she went in, standing in the foyer with a slight shiver that caused her to pull her sweater tight. The shiver was courtesy of Henry, whom she had just walked through.

Following Abby inside, I looked around, frowning. The rooms and furniture seemed a lot tidier than I remembered from my last visit, as if someone had come in and done a light cleaning, more of a promise to do better at a later time. It didn't seem likely that Cecelia or Julian were of a tidy nature, but there didn't seem to be any other way to explain the house's less cluttered and dusty appearance.

Vampires didn't exactly have any need to impress with their housekeeping skills.

And though I didn't have to worry about leaving behind footprints in the dust, that very fact made me nervous. Tapping Abby on the shoulder, I led the way further into the house, my stake in hand, liking the solid, almost polished feel of it against my palm. I felt reassured by its presence, its very weight a comfort. The sharp point at one end, the better to do damage with, probably had a lot to do with it.

I glanced over to my left, then stopped, my eyes

glued to the room in front of me.

Abby looked at me, puzzled. "What is it?"

I didn't answer right away, just stood in the middle of what had been the former parlor, my skin tingling. Shadows crawled across the walls and something fluttered out of the corner of my eye. I jumped back, expecting a spider, but it was only a shadow person, just as startled by my presence as I was by it. Despite the fact that there were no discernable features, I knew it was staring at me.

Unnerved, my breath came in a short, harsh gasp.

"Katie, what's wrong?" Abby asked. "You're shaking."

The shadow jerked at her voice and melted away. I turned, unwilling to look away from the spot where it had been. "I'm fine. Just a shadow person."

"Shadow person?" She glanced around, uneasy. "Is it good or evil?"

"I'm not sure." I finally met her gaze, took in her discomfort. "There are a lot of memories here. That's probably what that shadow is made of." I frowned. "Haven't you ever encountered one before?"

She shook her head, her expression now curious. "What I know about them is strictly from books. This is my first encounter. Sort of."

My fingers touched the silver crucifix as we headed across the hall to the kitchen. The Undead were waiting for us in the basement. It wasn't going to be easy, using any kind of method to get them to talk. Holy water and a silver crucifix aside, having the element of surprise was probably our best chance.

Henry was waiting for us, standing next to a door.

I gestured. "Is this the door to the basement?"

He nodded. *They're still sleeping. Better hurry, though. The shadows help them to move around.*

The padlock was still bolted to the door. Curious to see if what had worked for the front door would work here, I touched the lock, tracing the key hole lightly.

Nothing. Not so much as a spark to shack my fingers. Taking my lock-picks, I made quick work of it and opened the door, peering down the stairs. I could see the afternoon light stream in from the basement windows, bathing the bottom steps. "Okay, Abby. Get ready to stake first and ask questions later."

Abby held up her stake in one hand and a bottle of holy water in the other. She brightened a little when she looked at my neck. "What's that?"

I glanced down, saw that the silver crucifix was now hanging outside my shirt. Touching it with some pride, I said, "I found this when I met my first vampire."

"Good." Her face grim, she uttered a short spell, tracing lines in the air that I couldn't see until she had finished. Then her air tracing burst into existence with a bright yellow pop before fading from sight. She caught my look. "Protection spell."

With our weapons in hand and great trepidation, we cautiously made our way down into the basement.

Twenty-Six

The basement was much cooler than the upstairs and I shivered. Except for the difference in perspective, the space didn't look much different since I peered through the window from the outside on my last visit. The vampires' crates were still where I'd last seen them, in the most viable spots to avoid the sun's rays, even with the dirt-crusted windows. I held my stake in one hand, leading the way downstairs, Abby close behind.

I went to the crate that was directly across from the basement window, the one I had seen first, and placed my hands on the lid, the wood smooth against my palms. Any one of the crates could contain the primary vampire and, from what I'd gathered, it was one of the two females that hunted in this area. Despite the passage of time, the crate had not yet begun to crack or splinter with age. I took a deep breath and glanced over at Abby, then gestured for her to come closer. She went to the other side of the crate, hesitating.

I held Abby's gaze. "One of the females is the primary and she's the one who one needs taking care of. Then we'll either have solved the problem altogether or have de-fanged vampires to deal with."

She nodded, her expression set. "How do we interrogate it without getting bit?"

I removed the silver crucifix from around my neck, holding it up for her to see, the metal glinting in the pale light. "With this. Help me push this off. Be ready."

Abby nodded, her face pale and pinched around her mouth. Together, we pushed the crate lid off, unconcerned with the noise as it clattered onto the floor. Except for a bit of grave dirt and a yellowed scrap of lace, the third crate was empty. I reached in, frowning, holding up the bit of lace, shaking loose some of the dirt clinging to it.

"There should be a vampire here," I said, "Three crates, three vampires."

"Then where is it?" Abby asked.

I shook my head, dropping the scrap of lace back into the crate and wiping my fingers free of its dirt on my jeans. "Out hunting, maybe, but let's make it hard for it to come back to this place."

"Great idea," she agreed, fervently. Uncorking a bottle, Abby sprinkled holy water over the interior, soaking the scrap of lace and dirt for good measure. After, she helped me replace the lid, since I didn't want Cecelia or Julian to catch on that we'd been here right away.

Then I went to the next crate, Abby close behind.

"When we get this lid off," I said, my voice low, "do not look at its eyes. That's part of how they catch their prey, by hypnotizing them."

Abby gripped the bottle of holy water tightly, her knuckles white, and nodded. "Okay."

Together, we lifted the lid off, leaning it against the wall nearby, taking care to not make a sound. Poised to strike with my stake, I leaned forward, peering into the open crate. Abby was close behind me, the bottle of holy water uncorked and ready. Almost too quickly, the female vampire crouched upright, her fangs exposed as she hissed at us. Her hand shot out, gripping my wrist before I could strike. With a yelp, Abby splashed the holy water at the vampire, jumping back at the same time.

Some of the holy water missed, but a good deal of it landed on the vampire.

There was an inhuman shriek and the Undead female lurched back, blisters forming where the holy water had made contact. Before it could strike back, I draped my silver crucifix around its neck, knotting it in its hair.

Then I leapt back, heart pounding.

Despite the pock marks made from the holy water, she looked young, like a Norman Rockwell sweetheart. The clothes dated her as being from the early nineteen hundreds and I wondered if it had been the mad vampire of Wolf's Head Bay who had turned both her and the Gilded Age male from human to immortal. She was white lace and blue bows, golden curls and bright pink lips and reeked of innocence, except for her eyes.

I risked a quick glance at the vampire, being careful not to catch her gaze. Her eyes were black and feral and I looked away fast, uncomfortable. Behind me, Abby hissed and there was a low *thunk* as a metal object being dropped onto a wooden surface. Then I heard it – a light, hollow scratching of nails against wood.

Without taking my eyes from the female vampire, I asked, "Abby, what's going on?"

Her voice shaking a little, she said, "The other vampire in the crate by the stairs just woke up. I've got my crucifix on the lid. That should keep it down."

"Keep the holy water ready."

"Always."

"Good."

The female vampire glanced at my stake, her rosy lips thinning as they curled back over her pointed teeth. "How kind of you to bring a pick to clean my teeth with."

My hands trembled a little and I forced myself to be calm, to be focused, to avoid looking at her eyes. "Exactly what am I supposed to be?"

Her lips drew back even further. "Supper. We've

been waiting."

"Katie, look at this." Abby was back at the empty crate, holding up a black leather pouch by the strings, disgust crossing her face. "It's a charm." She dropped it back in the crate with a shudder, wiping her fingers on her jeans with some force. "It feels like dark magic. Someone powerful made it."

I didn't want to touch it and was glad Abby had dropped it. "Can you trace the maker?"

Abby scooped it into a jar, sprinkling a little salt and holy water in with it. "I think so. Most of what I need is back at the nursery." She held up the jar. "This will nullify its power."

"Let her take it, bleeder," the female vampire hissed. "There will be another."

"Who made it?" I asked, not meeting the vampire's gaze. My fingers ached with tension as I gripped my stake. There was a scraping sound and I risked a quick glance at the other crate, glad that Abby had thought to put her crucifix on top of it.

I risked a quick glance at the female vampire's face. She gripped the sides of her crate, panting, her eyes glazed. I could see from where I stood that they were blue. Her skin had gone pasty and burn marks were starting to pockmark her skin in reaction to the crucifix.

I repeated my question, putting steel in my tone. "Who made that charm?"

Her eyes became slits, her lips curved in a deadly grin. "Don't you know?"

Abby stood next to me, cautious, tightening the lid of the jar containing the charm. She took a closer look at the vampire's neck. "Um, Katie, is her skin supposed to burn like that?"

I flicked a glance at the vampire's neck. Thin wisps of smoke had begun to curl around the chain. "It's just the silver."

We both looked at the vampire. The way her gaze

had settled on me didn't exactly make me feel any better.

"There's a shroud over you." The vampire spoke, her voice low, rough. I could see that it took some effort for her to speak. "Even I can see it."

Captain Pellington said the same thing to me, Henry said, staring at the vampire.

The vampire hissed at Henry, recoiling. Interesting. She could see ghosts. And she did not seem to like them very much. Henry didn't seem to like her very much, either, if his expression of utter loathing was anything to go by.

"How can you see ghosts?" I asked, taking care to avoid her eyes.

The black gaze felt like a dead weight as it settled on me. "In the time before, I could see the spirits. What you possess in life stays with you when you turn."

"You're Cassiopeia." I made it a statement.

Her eyes narrowed, calculating. "Who I am matters not. We called. You're here."

"Where did you get those pouches?" I asked again. "Who made them for you?"

The vampire glared at us. "Remove this vile thing from me and I'll tell you."

Abby popped out the bottle of holy water and sprinkled a few drops onto the vampire. The vampire leapt back with a loud screech, the force of her movement causing the crate to rock back a little. She hissed, fangs bared.

"Talk and we'll think about taking the crucifix off," Abby said.

I held up the jar holding the black leather pouch. "What's this for?"

The vampire's cold gaze slid towards me. Avoiding her eyes, I sensed something dark and crafty hidden behind her expression, a dead weight feeling, oppressive and suffocating. I wished she would look elsewhere, anywhere, except at me. "Ask me how it feels, knowing that every year, you pass the day of your death, bleeder?"

I shook the jar a little, drawing her attention to it. "Once again, vampire. What's this charm for? What kind of magic is it made to do? And who made it for you?"

She curled her lips, her eyes never leaving mine. "It unlocks doors."

I studied the leather pouch inside the jar. It had an ugly feel to it, like rotted flesh. My skin began to crawl. "What kind of doors?"

She laughed. It was the most unnerving sound I'd ever heard – low-pitched and grating, like stones being crushed. "None that you know about."

Snatching the bottle of holy water from Abby, I uncorked it. "Tell us, or I pour."

The vampire stared up at me through her blonde hair, her mouth open in a snarl of fury, but still she laughed. The crucifix had buried itself into her skin, sending thin wisps of smoke into her face.

I glared at her. "What's so funny?"

"You, bleeder," she said. Her mouth twisted into a smile. I shuddered. "I was wondering when you would get here. We waited such a long time for you."

I froze. "What do you mean?"

Abby touched my arm, her face grim. "Don't listen to her, Katie. She's lying and trying to manipulate you. It's what they do. Stake her. Right now."

The vampire hissed, her eyes never leaving me, her holy water pock-marked face dark with glee. My silver crucifix, now sinking into the fresh scars around her neck, was beginning to turn black. "She won't. She can't. I know her."

"You don't know me," I said, my lips numb. "And I've staked a vampire before."

"We called you." The smile she favored me with now was soft, human, genuine. It was more frightening to see than her snarl. I shivered. She gestured to the small blue pouch Abby held in her left hand. "We called you with that."

I glanced at the charm Abby held, who held it up for better viewing. Dangling from a black cord, the blue pouch had been stitched together with red thread. During my stay in New Orleans, Mama Louise taught me about charms and their meanings. The use of color was for dramatic presentation only, since color choice wasn't always an option for the person casting.

The person's intent in creating the charms, however, was important.

"You didn't make this charm," I said, "so who did?"

She hissed, her lips curving in a shark's smile. "Take this cursed thing off and I'll whisper the name in your ear."

Abby stepped forward, bottle in hand. "Don't listen to it, Katie."

I put out a hand, stopping her. According to Hallie Welles' letter, I had to pull the primary vampire's soul back into its body in order to eliminate the nest. Just as I had done with the New Orleans vampire, whether or not it had a nest. "How can I trust you to not take advantage to try and turn me?"

The blonde curls shifted over one shoulder as the vampire slid its glance over Abby. "Your friend is armed."

"Don't do it," Abby said again.

What I planned to do needed to be done fast – whether or not I was successful in pulling the soul back into the vampire's body, it still had to be staked. Taking the holy water from Abby, I splashed over my neck, head and arms, being careful to not get any on my hands as I handed it back. I needed them to be free of it. "I know what I'm doing, Abby."

"Send her away, so that we can talk freely," the vampire said.

"Tell me why the captain invited you in," I countered and stepped closer, careful to avoid her eyes. "Who made these charms?"

Her smile widened. It reminded me of the National Geographic special that I'd watched on TV the other night. It had been about great white sharks. "Those who hunt."

"What are they hunting?"

That gravelly laugh came again. "You."

Ask why she killed me. Henry was at my shoulder, staring at the vampire with curiosity and anger. *Why she felt she needed to. It wasn't for blood.*

"No, not for any blood," the vampire hissed, her gaze on Henry. "For your blood."

That stopped me. "The captain asked you to kill Henry?"

The vampire only laughed. Abby shivered at the sound, shrinking back. I remained where I was, pretending a courage that I didn't feel. The faint hiss of the crucifix as it burned into the vampire's skin was barely audible. The vampire turned her gaze back onto me.

I didn't like that look she was giving me, resisted the urge to step back.

She seemed fully aware of that and was enjoying my discomfort. "Tell the ghost he was never meant to leave this house alive from the moment he set foot in it."

I risked a glance at Henry. He looked shocked. If he hadn't been a ghost, I'd have thought he'd seen one.

He met my gaze. *I don't understand, Cadence. Why did I die?*

The vampire touched the burned skin on her neck, eyes narrowing, never leaving me. "He knew too much and his blood was so bright. The oldest tried to warn him away, but the youngest had his heart." Her lips curved in a hideous smile. "His heart's blood was sweet, pure. I have not tasted the like before, or since. But he would not let me taste the child."

The vampire was enjoying the situation entirely too much and I wasn't sure if its words had any truth in them.

Kill it, Cadence, Henry said. His fury drained what little heat there was in the basement and I shuddered, seeing my breath and Abby's hang in the air like mist. *This monster deserves more than staking.*

"You don't have the heart of a killer, bleeder," the vampire taunted, laughter thrumming under her words. "A witch, a runner, a ghost talker, but killing takes a certain kind of nerve."

"You can't kill what's already dead," I said and slammed my palm onto the vampire's sternum, pulling at any residue of its previous life, seeking its soul.

Twenty-Seven

I only had a brief window of time to do this. Despite the holy water I'd splashed on myself, the crucifix around its neck and Abby as back up, I was all too aware of the vampire's superior speed and strength.

Focusing on the dried out husk that once pumped blood, I pulled energy into the heart, wanting it to strike its first beat in nearly a century. Teeth bared, the vampire lunged at me, one claw-like hand gripping my wrist tightly, yanking me close with such force, that I almost lost my grip on my stake. In one swift movement, I plunged the sharp end through its ribs and pushed up, gratified at the shocked expression in its eyes before it became dust.

Pushing myself away from the crate, I sat down hard on the floor, barely aware of Abby as she took care of the female vampire's ashes. Adding a mixture of salt and holy water, she twisted the lid back on securely and stashed the jar in her satchel. Then we turned to the crate in the corner, where the scratching sounds never quite stopped.

I frowned, puzzled. Staking the primary vampire should have turned its nest to dust. Unless, the vampire I'd staked wasn't the primary. Wordlessly, Abby and I stood next to the second crate and, on a silent count of three, we toppled the lid off. In the time it clattered to the floor, I had my stake ready and Abby had a fresh bottle of holy water open. This vampire, a male with a handle-bar mustache that called back to an era of stagecoaches and horse rustlers, zeroed in on me and rose up so quickly that I almost didn't have time to step back.

Then there was a quick arc of water in the air and it shrieked, pulling back. This gave me the chance to bury my stake into its chest. Within seconds, there was another pile of dust and Abby was quick to scoop it up. I watched as she secured the lid of second jar. "What are we going to do with them?"

"Throw them into the ocean," she said, fervently.

"Best way to bury them," I said, thinking of Father O'Mare. He had done the same thing with the charm he'd found at the church. "No one can use their dust after that."

Going to the first crate where I'd expected to find a vampire, I examined it more closely, uneasy over it being empty. My earlier thought had been that it was out hunting. If so, it had to go to earth when the sun came out, since it would only able to return at nightfall. But why not take its nest along for the hunt?

Abby came up behind me. "Where do you think this vampire is?"

I shook my head. "Either out hunting or out permanently."

She regarded the empty crate. "If somebody staked that one, why not the others? It doesn't make sense."

"Maybe it's easier to control these two without it." But I was having thoughts and I didn't like a single one of them. It was unlikely that the third vampire had been staked or simply moved to a location closer to its — captors? Caretakers? Neither term seemed appropriate and yet, there were no others that felt right. I didn't think even Julian would have the kind of power to control a vampire, let alone one who had sired its nest.

So where was the third vampire?

Abby shuddered. "Let's get out of here."

"Can you cast a spell that wipes out our scent?" I asked, suddenly, thinking of the people Henry had mentioned. "Make it non-detectable. I don't want anyone tracing us."

She considered my question, then nodded. "It's not the easiest spell in the world to work and the Latin's a little tricky, but not impossible." She gave me a wry smile. "Also, in order for this to work properly, we have to exit the way we came in. Backwards. Since you're familiar with the place, you're leading us out."

Alert to any sudden noises, I stood at the basement stairs, waiting, my hand on the railing, one foot on the bottom step. I felt the energy Abby was pulling around her, to her, as she worked her spell. When she began to speak, I didn't understand what she was saying. Then I did – she was casting her spell, speaking in Mandarin, only in reverse. She reached behind her, her hand grasping for me. I took it and, taking the stairs backwards, guided her up to the kitchen. She matched me step for step, her back to me, her pace careful.

It took several long and agonizing moments to retrace our steps through the house to the foyer in this manner. We paused long enough only for me to bolt the basement door shut before making our way to the front door. Retracing our steps backwards through the main part of the house was trickier, but once in the foyer, we both relaxed and stepped the front door and onto the porch. Abby navigated her way backwards down the porch stairs as I stood in the doorway.

The third vampire would come back, I knew, and find its nest disturbed, as well as its sired children gone. If I revoked the invitation Pellington had granted so many decades ago, I would be making it impossible for the vampire to enter the old house. Whether it had another nesting place to go to, I wasn't sure, but allowing it continued access to the Pellington place was no longer an option.

Standing in that in-between space of inside and out, I said, "I revoke the invitation that was given to you by Marcus Pellington."

On the overgrown lawn below, Abby looked puzzled, then understanding dawned. I spoke twice more, repeating the revocation before stepping out onto the porch. Shutting the door behind me, I caressed the ornate knob plate, feeling the tumblers turn over and locking under my tingling fingers. There were memories here, almost-ghosts weighted by emotion and kept in place, as if pinned to a map.

Staring at my hand, I gave it a quick shake, then, grabbing the banister for balance, I met Abby at the bottom of the porch steps. Henry stood next to her, beside himself with alternating moods of rage and confusion. Even in the sun, he was sucking the warmth out of the air. Abby was picking up on it, rubbing her arms, trying to generate warmth.

"Could you tell him to relax?" she asked. "I'm freezing."

What did she mean, Cady? What happened to me? And to Sarah?

"I don't know, but I'm going to find out," I told him. He muttered something not very nice and disappeared, reappearing again to help guide us back to the stone wall. Abby and I trekked backwards through the overgrowth towards the lane, taking care over the uneven terrain. Abby was still chanting her spell, but even with Henry calling out warnings of stones or branches before we tripped over them, the pace was slower. Climbing over the rock wall was a little trickier, but we managed and soon, we were heading down the lane towards the truck.

Without saying anything, I unlocked the truck and we both climbed in, Abby falling silent for the first time since we left the house. I pulled my crucifix out to stare at it.

The silver had turned black, like tarnish, and I rubbed it against my jeans, hoping to clean some of it off.

She watched me, grimacing. "I hope that crucifix still holds power because I am going to be really pissed off that you ruined it on a vampire."

I hoped so, as well. "I'll clean it up and soak it in holy water."

"Make sure you put it with some quartz, too. That should help charge it." She sighed, slumping back in her seat, then eyed me. "The ghost I couldn't see. Who is he?"

Turning the truck towards Sleepy Eye Cove, I gave her a brief run-down on Henry.

She shook her head, intent on her thoughts. "There's got to be more to it than that, Katie. He didn't just come here to fall in love and then die. And when it comes to the Naughtons, there's always a reason, a purpose." Abby looked at me then, her gaze steady. "You made that connection, I'm pretty sure."

Still wanting to keep what I knew to myself, I only nodded. "Yeah, but Catherine could be a cousin or something."

"It's still a connection, no matter how faint," she pointed out and sighed.

We drove back to her nursery in silence. I wasn't sure what Abby was thinking, but my own thoughts were consumed by the biological family I'd now discovered. If the Naughton coven was as powerful as Abby had mentioned, then who had killed my biological parents? Why and how had I ended up being adopted by the Galloways? And what was behind Cecelia's power grab as leader of her family coven?

I took some comfort in that I'd decided to keep my Naughton connection to myself. Since no one seemed to know that I existed, it was easier to hide. And whatever conflict was going on within the coven had nothing to do with me. So far, anyway. Whatever magic I may have, at the moment, all I wanted was to fade into the background and forget about it. My adoptive family hadn't prepared me for the dynamics of siblings, let alone aunts, uncles or even cousins.

The added bonus of magical infighting was overwhelming.

*****

We made it back to Abby's shop with no further incident. Henry never reappeared after his last comment, but his color had begun fading just prior to his disappearance and it occurred to me that he was regenerating from using up whatever energy he had pulled from us. I wondered if Dottie did the same thing, if ghosts disappeared in order to regenerate and resolved to ask her.

As we approached the nursery, I finally broke the silence. "Thanks for your help, Abby."

She glanced at me. "Well, it was interesting, to say the least. Just don't ask me to do it again for awhile." She frowned. "That vampire. She said that Henry's blood was the purest she'd ever tasted, but the captain wouldn't let her taste the child's." She met my gaze. "What child was the vampire talking about?"

I opened my mouth to reply, then shut it again without speaking as Abby's words began to sink in. The captain and his wife had three daughters, the youngest, Sarah, being nineteen. Henry was twenty-one when he died. There had been no reports of any young children living with the Pellingtons, let alone infants. Unless.....

"Unless it was Henry and Sarah's," I said, slowly. "That would be one reason for Pellington to use the vampire to kill Henry."

Abby didn't say anything and we were quiet for the rest of the drive. It wasn't until we were pulling into the nursery parking lot that she asked, "What happened to that child? Is it alive or dead?"

Parking the truck close to the shop's main porch, I shook my head. "I don't know. I haven't seen any mention of a child, but that doesn't mean it never existed." Once again, I thought of my birth certificate and my blood connection to the Naughtons. I very much wanted to confide in her, but I wanted to keep her safe, as well. The fewer who knew about my origins, the better. "What are you thinking?"

She mulled it over, considering her words carefully. "I was thinking of doing a search for it, but given the amount of time that's passed, I'm not sure it would be useful."

"Do what you feel is right," I said, encouragingly. "You'll know if it's a good path or not. I have faith in you."

She smiled, climbing out of the truck, her feet crunching on the gravel. "I'll let you know what I find." Then she handed me the satchel holding the jars. "Take care of these right away."

I placed the satchel on the floor of the truck with care. "I will."

Abby trotted up to the entrance, then disappeared inside. From where I sat, I could see Paige helping several customers at once. Then I pulled back onto the road towards Sleepy Eye Cove, my stomach rumbling. I made a quick stop at Madame Sofia's Coffee Shop, then drove through town towards the cemetery. About a mile or so after passing Black Rock Lane, I pulled over and walked the short distance to the bluff's edge. I hurled the jars containing the vampires' ashes into the ocean first, watching them disappear into the pounding surf.

Reaching into the satchel once more, I pulled out the last jar. This one needed to follow the others, so that it could not be used to create more harm. But first, I had some questions to ask about that charm. Unscrewing the lid, I removed the charm, shaking it free of the salt, and placed it on the grass at my feet. Taking my cellphone, I snapped several pictures and sent them to Mama Louise via text.

Then I secured the charm back inside the jar, giving it a good shake to stir up the salt, and hurled it into the ocean after its mates. Climbing back into the truck, I drove back to the cemetery, anxious for my mentor's return call. Half an hour later, after I'd parked the truck by the cemetery office and was making my way back to my tiny shack, my phone began to ring. Pulling it out of my pocket, I saw that the caller was Mama Louise.

Glancing around, I strayed off the path and sat on a nearby bench, almost obscured by the surrounding rose bushes and a young tree. Sitting, I breathed in the strong scent of pine as I answered my phone, cutting it off mid-ring.

Louise didn't wait on pleasantries. "Cadence, it took you long enough."

I flushed down to my toes, ashamed of my own misgivings about her. The warmth in her voice told me all I needed to know – she cared. "Hi, Louise. How's the shop?"

She snorted, the thick patois reserved for tourists dropping away as she spoke, which meant that she had just sent a client away. "Don't talk to me about the shop. Or the weather. It's not why I'm calling you back and we both know that."

"Yes, Louise," I said, chastised. "I need your expertise on the charm I texted you about a few minutes ago. Were you able to look up what kind of charm or talisman it is? And am I right in thinking that it allows vampires free rein over sacred ground?"

She snorted, a comfortable sound that suddenly made me miss being in her presence, and in the background I could hear pages being flipped through as she searched. The sound of her voice as she muttered, warm and low in its soft Louisiana drawl, came over the phone like a security blanket.

Her tone sharpened. "Cadence, who've you got giving charms like this to vampires?"

"I don't know," I said, nervous. "That's what I'm trying to find out."

"They're dangerous, little girl, very dangerous. But you know that." She clucked once and I heard more pages being turned. I didn't like that she was frightened — it made me feel even more afraid of who I was dealing with. "Your little witch friend, the one that likes to garden. Has she made you a protection charm?"

"She's made one for me, Louise," I said, with some relief. I didn't ask how she knew about Abby. She wouldn't have answered, anyway. "Magic doesn't like me that much, anyway, and I've got that block thing. You know that."

"Those who have power recognize it, Cadence. You'd do well to remember that." Louise was silent. I thought briefly of Cecelia Naughton and wondered if Louise had been thinking of her with that warning. Then she was talking again. "Cadence, these vampires aren't like the one you took care of for Deke. They are bound to someone with dark power and it's not the one who turned them, either. And neither party will take kindly to someone sticking her nose in where it doesn't belong."

"I don't imagine that anyone does." To lighten the mood, I added, "I dusted two vampires this afternoon, about an hour before I texted you."

Louise sniffed. "They're not the only ones you need to look out for, but you already know that, too." She paused, added, her tone soft, "You be careful, little girl. I don't want to make a trip to bury you."

I didn't want her to do that, either. I liked living. "I'll be careful, Louise."

And we simply hung up.

Louise was not all that fond of good-byes.

I've discovered that I'm not, either.

Twenty-Eight

The sun was low in the sky on the way to the church, its rays bathing the sky in vivid oranges and pinks. Dottie was waiting for me at the church gate, waving a hand, then popping into the truck's cab for the rest of the ride. As I parked the truck in its usual spot on the side of the road, I gave her a brief rundown of what happened at the Pellington place. "There's still a third one out there, but I think she's being used."

Dottie absorbed this, perplexed. "How is that possible?"

"I'm not sure, maybe by a charm or talisman of some kind." I described the charms Abby and I had found. "One of those could be like a passkey."

That stopped her. "Oh, I see. For trespassing into the church?"

I nodded, adding, "Among other things. Whoever created those charms works dark magic."

"Do you know who made them?"

"I can't prove it, but I think I know," I said, slowly. "The woman who came by a couple of days ago. She might have made them, or had help."

"Oh, dear." Dottie flickered in the seat beside me,

troubled. "It's getting a wee bit more complicated than I thought."

I glanced at her. "It's not your fault. All you wanted to do was help your priest get rid of a problem. How could you know it spin out like this?"

She brightened and by the time we got to the church door, she was holding steady. The church was dark when I got there, but a light tap on the door sufficed to bring Father O'Mare to me.

"She's here," he said without preamble. "I've no doubt she'll leave when she wants, but you may get some answers from her, in any case." He glanced at Dottie. "Miss Perswalski, your help is appreciated."

She dimpled. "Of course, Father O'Mare. It's my pleasure."

"Where can we find her?" I asked.

Father O'Mare indicated the main gardens. "Around back, at the gazebo."

He led the way around to the gazebo, a small and rather plain structure that had been built just outside the small churchyard. A root system had twined itself around the pillars holding up the roof. I supposed, in daylight hours, the flowers would open up and bloom like wildfire, giving off a natural perfume and adding beauty to an already somber site.

Sarah Pellington was staring hungrily into the forest, her gaze fixed in the direction of her old home. Father O'Mare muttered something that I couldn't quite hear.

I turned to him. "I'm sorry, what was that?"

He frowned. "She's not tied to this churchyard, she can move freely, if she so chooses, but she insists that she needs to repent."

"Repent for what? Her suicide?"

The late priest shook his head. "She doesn't remember committing suicide. It's not unusual to forget how you die, but her case is different." He eyed me. "I shall leave you now."

And he vanished, muttering about another parishioner, who wanted to play tricks at the new church's bingo night.

Dottie turned to me. "What does she need to repent for?"

I shrugged, making my way down the path to the gazebo. "Maybe she's wanting to repent for not taking action when she could have."

"We all have regrets, Cadence," Dottie said, thoughtfully. "What action does she regret not taking?"

"We'll have to ask," I said, acutely aware of my own regrets as my shoes crunched the gravel as I walked. "And we could encourage her to let go, in order for her to move on." I took a deep breath of the cool night air. "But she might not answer. It may be something that not even Father O'Mare could help with."

And then Dottie and I were at the gazebo, looking up at Sarah. She still had her back to us, but her posture suggested that she was very much aware of our presence.

"How long do you think this will take?" my spectral roommate whispered.

I shrugged. "Depends on what Sarah knows. And how willing she is to talk to us." Clearing my throat, I said, "Sarah, I need to ask you some questions."

"I have no answers," she said, resolutely keeping her gaze on the forest.

"Well, I don't believe you," I said, climbing the steps. "I found two vampires, a male and a female. The female said a lot of interesting things."

She finally looked at me, curious. "There were only two in the basement?"

I blinked. "Yes. How did you know they were down there?" Then I understood. "You knew they were there in life, didn't you?"

Sarah smiled. "I did." She gestured for me to sit and I did so. "What were you told?"

I gave her a brief summary of what the female

vampire had said, adding, "She told me that I had been called here, but not by whom."

Sarah mulled that over, thoughtful. "They would have been bound to not say, unless you named the one who called you." She met my gaze, offered a half-shrug. "My father had been bound in a similar manner."

Which meant he couldn't volunteer his knowledge of the vampires, it had to be known within his family for him to speak of them. This also suggested that the binding had some sort of physical object – not just blood drawn and drunk, but fashioned into a charm or something. Except for what Abby and I had found, hidden the crates, there had been no other object that seemed to tie itself to the vampires. If there had been no object still hidden there, then it had to be in the possession of those who were now using the Pellington place as their personal hide-out or dumping ground or something.

Turning to Sarah, I asked, "Did you see your father carry anything unusual? Something that he ordinarily wouldn't have?"

Sarah shook her head. "No, unless he wore it under his shirt." She paused, thinking, then shook her head. "I don't recall seeing anything." She shrugged, helpless. "I'm sorry."

"It's okay," I said, reassuring. "It's been a long time." Then I touched on the third crate. "I'm not sure why it was empty. Either the third one had gone hunting, was hiding out in a second nest or it had been staked."

Sarah was silent. "No, she would not have been staked. As the primary, she would be too valuable to eliminate."

I shut my mouth, barely aware that it had dropped open in surprise. "Who is the primary?"

"Cassiopeia."

I thought of the female vampire, with her blonde curls and pink bows. I'd assumed she was Cassiopeia, but she had never confirmed it. "What makes you think that the female vampire I'd staked wasn't Cassiopeia?"

Sarah laughed, but there was no humor. "You wouldn't be standing here."

That was pretty final. Which made it all the more intriguing – if Cassiopeia was as powerful as Sarah suggested, then who had enough power to control her? It? And how did they manage to do it? That led me back to the theory of a charm or talisman – it seemed the only way one could manage to control such an unpredictable creature like a vampire.

But how?

Something to brainstorm about with Abby, then. And possibly talk to Henry about, on my next visit out to the Pellington place.

Which reminded me. "Where's the child?"

Sarah jumped, as if bitten. "What?"

I persisted, sensing that she knew what I was talking about. "The female vampire mentioned something about a child. No one had reported finding a dead baby on the property when they found and buried you and your family. So it must still be alive. Where is it?"

Sarah studied me for a long moment, her expression blank. "My sisters made sure it was safe after it was born. That's all you need to know, Cadence Galloway."

"But was it a boy or a girl?" I asked, impatient with her non-answer. "I think there's more going on here than just vampires looking for a child born more than half a century ago."

"You told Father O'Mare that you had dusted the vampires," she pointed out. "How could it be in danger, even now?"

"Because if what you said is true, Cassiopeia is still out there," I said, furious. "And then there's the very real chance that your child is still in danger, if it's still alive." Sarah watched me, silent. I took a deep breath, continued. "Another child was born here thirty years ago. No one seems to know about this one, either. Is this normal here, in Maurier County? Babies who are born to no families or disappear with no name? Is it in danger, too? Help me out."

Sarah was standing in front of me before I'd finished speaking. The air around me, already cool, dropped a few more degrees as she searched my face. Energy crackled between us, sharp and ice cold. My first instinct was to step back, but I held my ground, aware that Sarah was studying me closely. I didn't want to distract her.

"You began here," she marveled, looking at me with new interest. "How strange."

"I was born here," I agreed. "I'm looking into why I was told otherwise."

Sarah continued to study my face. "Some secrets are meant to be kept and some are meant to be exposed. I didn't understand that, not until I died."

"It's not easy figuring out which ones are which," I said, sympathizing with her. "Where's your child, Sarah? How can I find him? Or her?"

"She's gone," Sarah said at last.

"Gone as in dead?" I asked. "Or gone as in missing?"

Dottie began to fidget. "Cady, I need to get back to the cemetery."

I hushed her. "We'll go as soon as Sarah answers my question."

Sarah watched us, her expression a mixture of amusement and sorrow. "She's been gone for many years, now."

"So you had a daughter?" I asked, relieved to have a little information. It was now possible to try and trace her, dead or alive. "How long has she been gone?"

Sarah reached out, as if to touch my face. "Almost thirty years."

As if that explained everything, Sarah Pellington vanished.

My cellphone chirped and I pulled it out of my pocket. "Hello?"

A familiar masculine baritone voice answered. "Miss Gray, I'm humbly in your debt at the humble repast you'd left me."

My face warmed. "You're welcome. Um, I've got some things I need to show you. Are you feeling up to a visitor?"

"As long as said visitor brings nourishment," Raul replied, humor coloring his voice.

"Okay, I've got a couple of things to do, but I'll bring pizza," I said, thinking out loud. "What toppings do you like?"

"Black olive and pepperoni," he said.

"All right, I'll see you in an hour," I said and, with that settled, we hung up.

I stood there, staring at my phone for a long while, bemused.

Twenty-Nine

We were back at the cemetery, truck parked in its usual spot half an hour later. After hanging up with Raul, I put in a call to the pizza place in Sleepy Eye Cove, placing the order. I had them add a side of cheese sticks. If pizza was on the menu, then cheese sticks had to go along. Besides, I had the feeling he needed to load up on his carbs. Then we got into the truck, with Dottie quiet most of the ride home. I was silent, as well, wrapped up in my own thoughts, troubled.

"I'll see you back at the shack," she said as I climbed out of the truck.

"Okay," I said, giving her a half-wave, and set off across the cemetery grounds back to my tiny home. Much of my thoughts on that walk was about power.

The only one craving power enough to have involved vampires was Cecelia Naughton and, if my suspicions were right, she'd had Julian Webster make the charms that Abby and I had found and thrown in the ocean. Why she needed the vampires to break into the church, I still was not entirely clear on. She didn't know about the book, so she was looking for something else and at some point had concluded that the old church's pulpit was the hiding place.

As for Julian Webster's involvement, it was simple –
one, he was Cecelia's lover; two, she needed his powers
because she couldn't access hers; and three, when she
gained whatever it was she wanted, Julian would benefit as
well. That they seemed to be using each other for their
own means wasn't surprising to me. They also knew about
and were familiar enough with the Pellington property, a
place that no one else seemed to be aware of, to be out
there and use it.

And then there was me.

If they knew about me, then it was purely in the
theoretical sense, since my birth had been documented and
was a matter of public record. They had no way of
knowing that the child they were looking for was, in fact,
me. And if Cecelia had found Cat's notes surrounding my
birth, then that may have added more fuel to the coven's
and the family's in-fighting. It wouldn't be much of a
stretch for her to share them with Julian and why not?
They may not have connected me as being the missing
Naughton baby, but they were clearly on the lookout for
me.

I liked that thought even less than the one about
having possibly overlooked a talisman that held the
vampires under one's control. Approaching my shack, I
climbed up the steps and entered, pausing to stare at the
ratty old couch, whose innards concealed the book and
letters that I'd found in the last twenty-four hours. That
couch held secrets that others clearly wanted and were
willing to do whatever it took to get them.

Getting on my knees, I reached under the couch and
worked the book and letters free. Putting the letters to one
side, I paged through the book until I came to the entries I
wanted, studying the Naughton names carefully. I stopped
when I came to Bennett Welles' name, tracing the ink with
my finger. Was he related to Hallie Welles of Long Beach,
a cousin maybe? This would make the Naughtons related

to the Welles family by marriage.

I touched my biological mother's name, tracing the faded ink with my fingers.

Why had I been given up as a baby?

That was an answer I'd been seeking for over a year and I wasn't sure I was any closer to getting it now than I was then. Taking the book and letters, I found a paper sack and stuffed them inside it, stowing it all inside my pack, pausing to finger the hidden pocket containing my birth certificates. A few minutes later, I was back in the truck and heading back to the hotel, stopping long enough in Sleepy Eye Cove to pick up my order from the pizza place.

Raul must have been listening for the elevator, because he was standing in the hall when I stepped out. He was wearing one of the T-shirts I'd left him – it was the black shirt and it fit him snug across the chest, tapering just past his hips. I wasn't at all prepared for the effect this had on me – I stopped in my tracks and blushed, unable to form a coherent thought as I took him in, seeing the raw sensuality of him that hadn't been there under the suit and tie a few weeks earlier.

But Raul clearly had only pizza on his mind. He lit up, delighted, taking the pizza box and bag of cheese sticks from me and carrying them into his room. "Ah, perfect!"

And then I was able to move, finding my breath as I held up the paper sack containing the letters and book I'd found. "You're going to want to look at these."

Setting the food down on the table, he took the paper sack, turning it over, curious. "What is it?"

I pushed the stack new notebooks and box of pens aside to set up paper towels as plates. Raul must have gone to the mini-mart for those, I thought, making the pizza box the center piece. My pack slid down my arm to the floor. "You'll see. Also, there's something else I think you'll want to see. But that can wait while you read those."

He started to open the sack, paused, then shut the

room door, absently securing the lock as he hefted it. "What's in here? Another mystery?"

"You have no idea."

We both sat down around the table, the pizza box open, eating in silence while he read the book and the letters. At one point, he took one of the notepads and pen he'd bought and began making notes. I was halfway through my third slice of pizza when he set everything aside neatly and leaned back.

"That's....an unusual find," he said at last. "Where did you find them?"

"The book I found in the old church by Sleepy Eye Cove," I said. "The letters I found in the attic right before I found you." At his pointed look, I clarified, "Before you found me."

He harrumphed. "Claire needs to be told."

"Claire Naughton?"

He nodded. "You know her?"

"Only in passing, I met her at the bookshop." I started to say more, then stopped, unsure of exactly what it was I wanted to say.

He watched me, curious. "What is it?"

"That day in your office," I said, slowly. "The folder was open and I caught a name, my name, on a document." Reaching into my pack, I pulled out my birth certificates, staring down at them and tracing the edges. Taking a deep breath, I told him the truth. "My name isn't really Katie Gray, I've been using that name because someone's been looking for me and I don't think their intentions are on the up and up." I held out the birth certificates to him. "My name is Cadence Galloway, only that's not my real name, either. It's Naughton."

He took the certificates, perplexed. "Does Claire know?"

I shook my head. "None of them do, except from what I've learned about Cat, I think she was on to finding me." I searched his eyes, anxious. "You're the only person besides me and city hall to know about those birth certificates. My parents – my adoptive parents – never told me about it before they died last year. I think they were afraid of something, to keep it a secret like this. Or someone."

His eyes crinkled with humor, despite the seriousness of his expression. "Are you invoking client/attorney privilege?"

I nodded, ignoring the warmth in my cheeks. "Yes, I am."

"Good, that's settled then. I'm representing you from now on." He paused, settled back once more in his chair to study the certificates. "What you saw was indeed about the Galloways, or, more specifically, about you. Cat hired me for that work." He closed his eyes and I could see how exhausted he still was from whatever it was that he'd endured at the hands of his partner. "When we get through this, I'll ask Cat to hand you the file to read. In a nutshell, though, it seems that the Galloways took you in to protect you from whoever killed your parents."

I exhaled a breath that I hadn't realized I'd been holding. Despite how they'd handled it, I felt a little better about my adoptive parents. Their intentions in wanting to protect a child were pure, even though I could only see it that way now. A weight seemed to lift from me and I thought that maybe I'd be able to see my past a little differently now. "I kind of gathered that. But I'm not even sure how they got me to begin with. There's no mention of me in the news clippings about my biological parents' deaths."

He muttered an oath. "Well, that's where it gets sketchy. The original call put to the police department shows that it was made by an anonymous male. There was crying in the background and a woman murmuring. After the caller requested help at the Naughton address, he hung up before they could get his name." Raul met my gaze. "I believe it was your aunt, Cindy Naughton, who made sure that your presence wasn't mentioned in the papers. Whatever happened at that house, she feared for your safety."

"Kind of makes me wonder what did happen that night," I said, my throat tight. Gesturing to the papers and book, I added, "I do want to get the book and letters to Claire at some point. I think she deserves to have them. And I also want to be the one to tell her who I am."

Raul nodded in agreement. "I second that." He leaned forward, eyes holding mine. "What brought you to my office in the first place?"

Reaching into my pack, I pulled out the ash-smudged card. "I found your card after staking a vampire in New Orleans." I gave him a quick rundown of that encounter. "The person who gave it to him was most likely following Cat, but the vampire found me instead."

He took the card, studying it, thoughtful. "You don't think I gave it to the vampire."

I shook my head, emphatic. "No, I don't. That vampire was sent to kill. Whoever gave that card to him had that same purpose, only they obviously failed. And I think that's why Cat is still missing. Besides, your card had your energy still attached to it." I paused, looked away, adding, shyly, "I liked it."

The smile he gave me warmed his eyes, making them a deep, dark blue. "Thank you." Then, to lighten the moment, he switched subjects, growing thoughtful as he pondered out loud, "So, who gave the vampire my card?"

"It seems likely that Julian Webster did," I said, measuring my thoughts. "As your business partner and office mate, he had ready access to your desk, cards, pens, whatever he wanted."

Raul nodded, accepting that theory as plausible. "Now, what are our ideas regarding who put me in the attic? It couldn't have been Cecelia, not with her magic being bound."

"I'm pretty sure I know who's behind that," I said,

thoughtful, "and I think you do, as well."

He nodded again. "My ne'er-do-well partner in law. Again."

"Yes," I said, relieved that it wasn't such a surprise to him. "And for now, it seems the best thing is to keep you under the radar. Especially since Cat's still missing." Shifting in my seat, I added, "Can you tell me about her ability to teleport? Or is that just a wild rumor going around in Wickerman Falls that my friend misunderstood?"

Raul leaned back in his chair, eyes closed in thought, hands folded across his stomach. I stole more than a few glances at him, observing the curve of his lower lip with curiosity. "Cat is….an unusual witch, to start with," he began, opening his eyes and catching me.

I looked down hastily, becoming absorbed in my pizza, aware of his gaze. "Unusual, how?"

Humor warmed his voice as he spoke. "When we were in the fourth grade, a bunch of us played hide and seek in the schoolyard. I was up in a tree, high enough to see Cat not even trying to hide behind one of those metal trash cans. One of the fifth graders, Adam Davies, was just about to find her when she….." Raul paused, searching for words. "Cat faded out, I suppose you could say. She blended in with her surroundings and Adam….well, he just walked right by her." He shifted in his chair, continued. "She can't teleport, not in the way the rumors would have it, but her talent will make you think she did."

I considered his words. "So, it's like misdirection?"

He nodded, sitting straighter, his eyes bright with recognition. "Yes, exactly like that." Taking another bite of his pizza, he added, "I don't think she's missing so much as she's hiding out."

"What about her stuff, just thrown around at her house?" I asked. "According to the article I read, it looked like there'd been a struggle."

He considered that, thoughtful. "If Cat had been

abducted, then why is Cecelia skulking about in your cemetery?" He shook his head. "No, she's in hiding."

"If that's the case, then they're looking for her," I said, meeting his gaze. "And we can both be sure they'll be looking for you, too."

Raul was silent for a moment, his eyes never leaving mine. "So I'm not to leave here under any circumstances?"

I shook my head. "No, that would be a very bad idea."

He grinned, a playful look in his eyes. "Then here I shall stay."

Restless, I stood, aware of my warming cheeks and the laughter in his eyes. Grabbing up my pack, I prepared to leave, pausing at the door to ask, "Is there anything else you need?"

He thought for a moment, scratching his jaw. "Not that I can think of, at the moment. Mostly rest, I suspect." He gestured to the letters, my birth certificates and the book. "I've got enough reading material to keep me entertained for a while."

"Then I'll leave you to it." And did so.

Thirty

The next morning found me up early and going over the notes I'd taken on my visit to Wycliff College. The deaths of Bennett Welles and Calliope Naughton had never been resolved and the cause had not been determined. Not homicide, not suicide, possibly accidental? And who made the call that brought the police? Whatever had happened to my biological parents resulted in my being taken in by the Galloways when I was an infant.

And their silence had become as much a part of the puzzle as the Naughtons.

I was purposefully avoiding any thoughts about Raul Kendrick.

After a quick breakfast and pulling on some clothes, I grabbed the wooden box containing the visibility spell's tools and headed for the cemetery truck. Forty minutes later, I pulled into Abby's nursery lot, parking as close to the entrance as I could. As I walked up to the shop's entrance, I glanced at the other cars parked in the lot. My steps faltered when I recognized one of them, the same one I'd seen parked at the Naughton bookshop a few days earlier.

Claire Naughton's car.

I hesitated at the car, glancing back at the truck, anxiety tickling my throat. Parked at the loading dock at the far end of the lot, my truck was obscured by a couple more trucks. Retracing my steps, I headed towards the loading dock. I wasn't ready to face Claire – she had questions and I wasn't sure I had the answers to any of them. Likewise, I had questions that she may not be able to answer. Best thing to do is to avoid her for as long as possible. Hoisting myself up on the dock, I slipped through the double-doors and made my way to the nursery.

Blinking for my eyes to adjust after the brief darkness, I scanned the area. I didn't see Abby or anyone else, but I heard voices – Abby's and a man's. I couldn't be sure about who he was, but he sounded familiar. Taking the stairs to my left, I stepped down and threaded my way through the patches of various plants and flowers. I came around a corner and stopped abruptly, then ducked behind the potted trees that had been lined up for me, ready to be taken out for loading on Monday.

I caught sight of Abby, who had her back to me while talking to the man. Even from where I was, I could see she was enjoying his attention. Then he moved and I saw his face. Efrain Jimenez was flirting with Abby, clearly enjoying her company. The wistful longing I felt while watching their interplay was unexpected, as was the thought of engaging in similar banter with Raul. Was it the simple connection building into something more I envied or was it the act of making any kind of connection? I pushed that thought away for the moment, turning away so that I wouldn't intrude any further.

A door opened and shut somewhere, then someone coming down the wooden staircase to the gravel walk. A few minutes later, a woman appeared, dressed in casual tan slacks and a plain blue blouse. I recognized Claire.

Abby greeted Claire as she approached. "Good morning, Ms. Naughton. How can I help you today? Oh, and may I introduce Officer Efrain Jimenez?"

Efrain turned to Claire and smiled, holding out his hand. "A pleasure."

Even from where I was behind the planters, I could see the tension in Claire's posture. She regarded him coolly, which struck me as odd. "We know each other."

His smile faded quickly. "Now, Ms. Naughton, that's no way to speak to anyone, especially an officer of the law."

Claire didn't back down, holding his gaze. "I have some important business with Ms. Wen, Officer. I think it's time you left."

I found that pause more than a little interesting and her attitude towards Efrain Jimenez even more so. Clearly, whatever that past encounter had been, Claire did not have good feelings about it or him. The officer regarded her, thoughtful. The tension in their respective stances was palpable, even from where I was hiding. With minimal movement, I shifted, trying to get a better view of the interactions.

Abby looked a little embarrassed. "Um, it's all right. I can wait while you two....discuss what you need to." She started to edge away, clearly uncomfortable at being caught in the middle of whatever dispute it was they had between them.

He glanced down at her, breaking eye contact with Claire. "My apologies, Abigail. I'll be back at a more....convenient time."

I frowned, trying to get a better look without revealing myself. Efrain was speaking a little more formally than was his habit. Or was it because of the animosity that clearly existed between him and Claire? After a quick nod at Abby, he gave Claire a cold look and took his leave.

She stayed behind with Abby and the two of them watched as Efrain disappeared into the store. Then Claire asked, "I stopped by because you mentioned you had some lavender plants on my last visit. Are they still available?"

Abby relaxed into a grin. "Of course. I've got three big potted ones and a dozen smaller ones, so whichever you choose, we can deliver."

They moved to a different part of the nursery, leaving my range of hearing. A few minutes later, Claire left, her hair catching the light as she hurried back up the steps and disappeared into the shop. She seemed determined, but brighter as well. Abby followed her a short distance, then stopped, not moving until Claire was gone.

I was about to stand and make myself known when Abby spoke. "Come on out. I knew you were there the whole time."

I got to my feet, grumbling and swiping at the dirt on my knees, then moving out from behind my hiding place into view. "Baloney you knew I was here. You had your back to me. What was Jimenez doing here?"

Abby frowned, glanced towards the shop itself, then turned her attention to the far end of her nursery that backed up against the forest. "I had a break-in this morning."

I froze. "Are you okay? Was anything stolen?"

She grimaced. "No, nothing's stolen. I'm fine." She headed for the shop. "Let's go to my office and talk."

Following, I asked, "Any idea of who it was?"

She looked back at me. "One of your interested parties, I presume." We passed the register stand, where Paige was ringing up a customer. Then we were in Abby's office, the door shut tight behind us. "They must have used a tracking spell, looking for something that isn't here."

"The jars of ash and the charm are in the ocean as we speak," I said and filled her in on what I'd learned from Mama Louise.

Abby whistled. "So you think Julian is behind the charms."

I nodded. "It makes sense. Cecelia has no magic to

work with, because she's bound."

Abby shuddered. "Bound witches are not fun to deal with. Especially the ones who hold grudges."

I was inclined to agree. "How did you bump into Julian Webster, anyway?"

"It was here at my shop," she said.

I stared. "He came into your shop? When?"

"Yup." She thought back. "Maybe after your first visit? He didn't stay long."

I scratched my arm, perplexed. "For what? He's loaded with power. What would he want from you?"

She gave me a look. "Thanks a lot."

"Sorry."

She waved me off. "Besides, why else would someone come to my shop? To buy a plant or two, some herbs, pots and soil and, in his case, a few spell pointers."

"A few pointers?" I said, sarcastic. "Again, why?"

She laughed. "Because he wanted to. And he was flirting with me."

"I'm guessing you flirted back," I said, recalling the *tete-a-tete* outside with Efrain.

Abby tilted her chin up, pleased. "I did, indeed."

I quirked a brow. "In spite of the fact that you're afraid of him?"

She grinned, mischief in her eyes. "Sometimes you just have to stop being afraid. Besides, I'm no threat to him and I know where his interests lie."

"And what did you get from him?"

She pondered my question, thoughtful. "Not a lot. He wanted something, that was obvious, but he never said what it was. So I gave him the herbs he asked about, avoided his questions and sent him on his merry way."

"Did he try to compel the answers from you?" I asked, curious. "I mean, you said that he's powerful."

Abby nodded to show she understood my meaning. "I've got the nursery protected by ancestral wards that prevents outside practitioners from using their magic. It's a variation on the wards that protect the safe." She made a face. "It's the one thing Mother and Dad insisted on that seems to actually be working."

I slumped against the high-backed chair. "Well, you know he's not exactly one of Claire Naughton's favorite people. I think she's a little afraid of him."

"And you should be, too," Abby said, serious. "He's a handsome man and it's hard to resist that charm, but I'm not stupid, either, Katie." She shuddered, her eyes dark with worry. "He knows more than I do and he knows that I know that. He didn't need anything from me and we both knew it."

Claire Naughton, on the other hand, was a different story.

"What was going on with Claire Naughton and Efrain?" I asked, bring Abby back to the present. "Did he give her a ticket over something minor?"

Abby shook her head. "I'm not sure. I didn't even know they knew each other, but whatever that was about, it's deep."

I nudged the wooden box I'd put on her desk. "Your visibility spell worked, by the way. I found something at the church."

Abby leaned forward. "What did you find?"

"It's a ledger, with a list of names," I said and described the book itself, leaving out the letter I'd found in it. "I think it's the Naughton family records book, since it seems to list their names only, but there were some that didn't seem related."

Abby looked intrigued. "Can I take a look at it?"

"I don't have it with me," I said, slowly. "I've got it hidden, at the moment."

She nodded, then handed me the list of add-ons to Wes's original order. "Can you have Wes double check that?"

I took the list, standing. "Sure thing."

Then I was back in the truck, heading home, the new

list in my pocket.

Thirty-One

The next morning, Monday, Wes okayed much of what Abby had added to his original list and called in to confirm. Once Abby's workers arrived, I helped Wes unload the potted plants around the folly. It took us most of the day to get them out of the truck and into the marked spaces, where we planted and watered them. After, I planted the seedlings in between the plants, making sure that each one had enough space.

Wes and I climbed into the truck to drive back to the office. We didn't say anything, though I felt that words lay heavy between us. The silence grew thick, even after I'd parked the truck in its spot and turned it off.

Neither of us made a move to get out. That alone was enough to make me uneasy and I fiddled with my key ring, the clanking noise soothing.

At last, I cleared my throat. "I have to tell you something about Black Rock Lane."

He glanced over at me. "I know."

"How do you know?"

He chose his words carefully. "Because I know about the secrets the captain had kept."

I pressed on. "You knew about the vampires in the

basement, didn't you? Why didn't you stake them? Why let them wander? More important, why didn't you tell me?"

Wesley Burke took a deep breath and looked at me. I pressed up against my door so hard, I could feel the handle bite into my back, my heart pounding in heavy thuds. Staring into my eyes was a man haunted by memories of people long dead, but they burned in him like fire. "I had no power to do more than watch them."

"You could do nothing but watch them," I repeated, skeptical. "I suppose you couldn't talk about them, either."

He reached up and unbuttoned his collar, pulling it down far enough so that the cotton fabric was stretching below his collar bone. The two sets of pin pricks were still there, silver in color and shiny with age. "Their sire bound me, so I couldn't speak."

"Tell me about that scar," I said, feeling out of breath. "Did you help Father O'Mare start the fire at that church in 1924? And was that how you got that scar?"

He shrugged his shirt back into place. "It happened when I tried to save Pellington from becoming a vampire." He paused, added, "Not that it saved him from tragedy later on."

"How did you manage to survive?" I asked. "You're not a vampire, not even with that mark that binds you. What are you?"

"The intent was to make me a pet, much like Pellington became," Wes replied, buttoning up his collar. "Father O'Mare's arrival prevented that, of course."

"How did you end up here, in Sleepy Eye Cove?" I asked.

He answered slowly. "My arrival here is a story unto itself." He met my gaze. "It's how I met Father O'Mare and encountered the vampires nesting here."

"And because their sire bound you, you couldn't dust them," I said, trying to hear out my thoughts. They didn't sound any more logical out loud. "But why couldn't you stake her when you had the chance? Wouldn't that have solved your problem?"

"Not with her nest still around," he said. "My binding prevented me from raising a hand against them. Thank you for taking care of them."

"Well, Abby and I only dusted two." I frowned. "But the third one is missing. According to Sarah Pellington, Cassiopeia is still out there."

Wes froze, leaning halfway out of the truck. Then he settled back into his seat, the door hanging open. "I think it would be wise for you to leave well enough alone, Katie."

"Well, it's too late for that and you know it," I said. "Who is Henry Gray?"

He grew still, spoke without looking at me. "Who?"

"The ghost who haunts the Pellington place," I said. "His name is Henry Gray. He died at that house, thanks to Pellington and his vampire pets."

He glanced back at me, his expression curious, thoughtful. "So that's the pattern."

"Why are you being so cryptic? What patterns? For whom?"

Wes was silent, his hand on the door, not moving. "You said his name was Henry Gray."

I nodded. "Yes. But I don't think he's ready to move on and go into the light, if you know what I mean."

"I do." Wes finally looked at me, his expression grave. "His business isn't finished. He has more to resolve from this life than knowing who killed him. Or why."

"And I suppose you have no idea what it is?" I asked.

He shook his head. "I can only speculate. It wouldn't be an answer."

I considered his words. "The female vampire I dusted said that she had called me," I said, then corrected myself immediately. "No, that *they* had called me here." I thought of the blue pouch, the one the female vampire had said was used, and of my altered birth certificate. Whoever called me here had a purpose that coincided with the circumstances surrounding my adoption.

Wes considered my words. "Did this vampire name you specifically?"

"No, but this is beginning to feel like premeditation," I said, angry. "Like someone had set a trap for me to fall into. I don't like it."

"Are you sure you haven't any connections to this place?" he asked, finally putting into words what I was afraid to answer. "No family or other relatives?"

I hesitated, my birth certificate coming to mind. Should I tell him what I knew, or wait a while longer? I settled on, "That's what I'm trying to find out." At his questioning look, I added, "I'd remember if I had any cousins." This was true – I don't remember having cousins or any other relatives in this area. I changed the subject. "I want to know about your encounter with the vampire who left those silver scars on your neck."

Wes studied me, thoughtful, then nodded. "All right." He gestured to the office. "Let's go inside and sit. It's a long story and I'd like to be comfortable when telling it."

The Moonlight Melody of 1924

Wesley Burke first came upon the vampire who would mark him a full year before he aided a local priest in burning down the church.

He had been aware of her presence shortly after his arrival to Sleepy Eye Cove only two months before and took his name from two separate graves at the Sandover cemetery. A shadow out of the corner of his eye while he worked around the graves on one occasion, a figure stepping behind a tree and vanishing into thin air on another. Following her was like trying to catch a feather on windy day but he tried, wanting to find the primary spot she rested in.

As yet, he had been unable to locate it during daylight hours. This had disappointed him, primarily because hunting a vampire at night was dangerous and more often than not fatal, even for experienced hunters. And he was sorely lacking in the skills needed in tracking vampires down and staking them. He'd encountered a vampire only once, when he was ten. It was an experience he swore never to repeat and, until he found himself in the small coastal California village, he had been either blessed or lucky to have kept that oath.

And always he wore the silver crucifix around his neck.

Wesley Burke glanced up at the star-studded sky, partially obscured by the trees. His stake rested comfortably in one hand, while he flashed his light along the road. The moon was full, but while its pale light was an added bonus to his flashlight, it wasn't completely visible. The road to the village by day was an enjoyable walk – ten miles of a narrow road with only the sounds of nature as his companions. At night, however, the shadows stretched ominously around him, almost reaching to pull him into the darkness.

He was approaching the private lane to his left when he heard the low cry. Gripping the stake and touching his crucifix, he hurried forward, alert. The rock walls lining the lane on either side of him were still in progress and he paused, listening to the sounds around him. The sound came again, a low, guttural male voice crying out. It was coming from the field to his left.

He quickly went around the unfinished wall, mindful of the rocks that had yet to be put into place, and hurried in the direction of the cry.

What greeted Wesley Burke was both expected, and yet, at the same time, unexpected. He had fully anticipated a confrontation with the vampire he suspected still roamed the hills. What he had not foreseen was the man clearly accepting the vampire's attentions on his neck. He understood at once – the cries he had heard were not of pain or despair, but of ecstasy. Disgust filled him, but he couldn't turn away – the sight was mesmerizing.

He must have made a sound of some kind, for the vampire fixed her gaze upon him, her lips curling back into a sneer, teeth bared and bloody. The man slumped to the ground, trembling, his neck bleeding from two small puncture wounds. Wesley Burke dropped his flashlight, pulling the bottle of holy water from his back pocket. The beam of light flickered in the tall grass, then grew steady, throwing enough light up for him to see.

"Stand away from him!" he commanded, holding out his crucifix.

The vampire crouched beside a nearby fallen tree and hissed. "I will find him. You cannot stop me."

This caught him off-guard. "Who are you looking for?"

The vampire hesitated, looking, in that brief instant, like the haunted, confused and unhappy human woman it must have been in life. Then the cold expression of the inhuman killer it had become returned. It leapt forward – the next thing he knew, he was on the ground, stones biting into his back and the vampire crouching over him. Its hands felt like claws – strong and thin as they gripped his shoulders, pinning him down.

He felt it tug at his collar, ripping the shirt back and its teeth plunging into his skin, drinking his blood greedily. He raised his fist, dimly aware that he still had the stake, and brought it down, point first. It struck, but not home – the stake went in only a few inches into the vampire's upper arm. At the same moment, its lips must have touched the silver chain around his neck, for the vampire recoiled, falling backward onto the grass, hissing. Thin wisps of smoke curled up from between its fingers as it covered its mouth.

Seizing the moment, Wesley scrambled to his knees, stake and bottle of holy water ready to be used. To his left, the injured man finally fell silent. He sent up a silent prayer that the man still lived, would live long enough to receive the help he needed. The vampire shifted slightly, its attention now back on the unconscious man. Aided by the moonlight, he could see the burn marks on its mouth.

Baring its teeth, the elongated canines glinting in the pale light of the moon, the vampire knelt to taste the unconscious man's blood once more. He drew his hand back and threw the bottle containing the holy water with such force that it shattered on impact when it hit the vampire's head.

It shrieked, an inhuman sound that rang in his ears, and vanished into the evening mist.

Going back to the unconscious man, Wesley examined him quickly. Despite the bleeding from his neck, the man appeared otherwise unharmed, but needed medical attention. Scanning their surroundings, he pulled the man into a sitting position, urging him awake. The man seemed slow to come to, but he finally became aware of his surroundings and of his rescuer.

"Who are you?" the man slurred, blinking owlishly. "What happened to that woman? She needs our help."

"She's fled into the woods," Wesley said, flatly, pulling the man to his feet. "Come, you've got to see a doctor. You'll have to walk."

It seemed doubtful, at first, but by the time they gotten around the unfinished rock wall, the injured man had regained some balance and was no longer leaning so heavily on Wesley. Joseph Greene, the local doctor, lived further down the main road, perhaps three miles from where the private lane began, and two miles outside of the village.

Stumbling along the gravel road, Wesley fervently hoped they would arrive with no further interference from the vampire.

When they reached the doctor's house, Wesley settled the injured man on the top porch step and went to the door, knocking several times. In moments, Joseph Greene appeared and took over for Wesley, who felt reluctant to leave until he heard that the man would be fine.

"Pellington!" the doctor exclaimed. "What the hell happened to him?"

Wesley gave a brief description, adding, "You know him?"

"Not well, only as a patient. And what have you got on your neck?" Greene asked, fixing a look on Wesley. "Is that blood, as well?"

Wesley touched his neck. "Only a scratch. Nothing serious."

Greene didn't quite believe him. "If you're sure….."

"I'll be fine." Wesley turned to Pellington. "How is he?"

"He's lost some blood, but he should recover overnight."

Wesley felt for the chain around his neck and unhooked it, handing the crucifix and chain to Green. "Make sure he wears this as part of his recovery. Insist on it."

Greene raised a brow, but said nothing, merely accepted the silver items. Wesley took his leave, satisfied that Pellington would be all right. Back at his caretaker's apartment at the cemetery, he went to the bathroom and examined the wounds on his neck carefully. Although the vampire had broken the skin and taken some of his blood, the bite was not deep. He suspected it had been the crucifix he'd left with Pellington that had saved his own life.

He went to his closet, pulled out a small iron box and opened it. Inside were three more silver chains and crucifixes. He pulled one out, replaced the box and fastened the new chain around his neck. There was a brief burning sensation, then it faded.

Thirty-Two

We sat in silence in the office for several long minutes after Wes had finished his story.

"When did you realize you couldn't move against the vampires?" I asked.

"Not long after," he said. "I'd found the nest and was able to trap them with silver, but when it came time to strike them down, I found I could not." He licked his lips, laughing self-consciously when he realized he had no spit. He got up and went to the water cooler, taking his coffee mug with him. As he poured water into it, he said, "The female I'd encountered previously stayed my hand and, in fact, convinced me to move the silver just enough to allow them to escape."

"What did you do then?"

"I destroyed that nesting spot," he said, his voice flat. "After that, I was unable to find them again, mostly, I suppose, because of this scar." He leaned close, eyes like flint. "Find that third one and make sure she's a pile of dust."

I nodded. "I will."

Then I took my leave of him and headed back to my tiny shack, digesting what he'd told me as I walked. I thought of the book of births and packet of letters that I'd left with Raul. I had the feeling that either Claire or Cecelia could answer those questions. Of the two, I was more inclined to talk to Claire. She, at least, had a level temper and might listen without jumping to conclusions or attempting a curse.

Standing on the front stoop of my shack, I turned and surveyed the cemetery as the sun began to settle into the late afternoon, its fading light streaming through the trees and glinting off some of the grave markers. My hand resting on the door, I stood, motionless, in the shade of the trees surrounding me, hardly aware of my breath, only of the pounding in my ears as my heart thudded heavily. Time stretched out, making me feel small and more than a little insignificant. Silence permeated my being – even the sounds of crickets and frogs and birds had stilled, as if waiting for something to make the first move. Or someone.

This was my home, by birth and, now, by choice. Taking a deep breath, I held it for a second, then exhaled and made the decision to go to Claire. I wanted answers about why the Galloways adopted me. The relief I felt was immense, as if a weight that had been sitting on my heart had lifted. There was an option to consider, regardless of what came next. Whether I'd be welcomed into the family or not, this was still home.

Then Dottie was surrounding me, her spectral form raising goosebumps on my skin. "Oh, Cadence, I tried to scare her off, but she couldn't hear me. She made a horrible mess and broke your table!"

"Who are you talking about?" I asked, pulling out my door key.

She flickered. Not a good sign. "I just didn't want you to think it was my fault, Cady."

"What's not your fault…," I began, when the door shifted open a few inches. I stepped back abruptly, shoving my key back into my pocket. "Check and see if she's still here."

"But it's awful!" she cried, wringing her hands.

"I believe you" I said, "Just check."

Dottie took only seconds to do as I asked. "There's no one inside, but it's such a mess. I'm so sorry, Cadence."

Pushing the door open further, I braced myself.

Everything had a film of moisture on it, as if it had been dragged outside and left to soak in the heavy morning mist. The mattress and box springs had been shoved off my bed frame, the sheets strewn about like drapes. Someone had taken a knife and ripped both open, pulling the stuffing out of the mattress and exposing the thick metal coils on the box springs.

On the far wall, next to my now-dismantled bed, someone had written Cat's words from my dream. *She comes. She is close. She will find you.*

Whatever they had used to deface my wall had begun to drip, making the already ominous warning even creepier. Then I was at the wall, touching it with cautious fingers. My hand was wet, not with paint, but water. The concrete crumbled a little at my touch and I stepped away, rubbing my hand dry on my jeans.

How could someone pull water out of the concrete and stain the wall with it while having it remain wet? And who could control water like that? Cecelia was an *impremere*, but if her powers were bound, how was this possible?

Numb, I surveyed the rest of my living area. The couch was on its back, some of its springs exposed. Sofa cushions had been torn apart, stuffing everywhere. The TV had been knocked to the ground, the screen cracked. My meager collection of videos had been scattered and at least one of them had been stepped on, the black case caved in between the reels.

There was only one person who knew I lived here, outside of Wes and Abby. Cecelia must have come here looking, either for the book of births or the letters, or both. Which meant she and Julian suspected or magically picked up on my presence at the Pellington place. With them safely in Raul's possession, Cecelia would never find them.

From where I stood, I looked over at Dottie. "You said you tried to scare her off, but she couldn't see you. Was it the same woman who came by the other night?"

Dottie nodded, miserable. "It was. She had no trouble unlocking your door and whatever binding her sister put on her, it's weakening."

Cecelia's power was coming back, strong enough to unlock my door with her magic, but not strong enough to locate and find the book. Still, she knew I'd hidden something here, otherwise she wouldn't have come out and dirtied her hands. Time to have that heart to heart conversation with Claire.

Pulling out my cellphone, I called the Blue Rose Hotel and had them connect me to Raul's room.

He answered on the first ring. "Kendrick."

"It's Katie," I said, "Cadence, I mean." His soft chuckle sent a delicious thrill through me and I forced myself to focus, telling him about the ransacking of my shack.

When I'd finished, he was silent. Then he asked, "Do you know who did it?"

"I'm sure that it was Cecelia," I said and gave him a brief rundown of her visit a few nights ago. "I have the feeling that her binding is starting to weaken."

"Julian may be behind that," Raul said, thoughtful.

That would not surprise me. "I'm going to head to Wickerman Falls. I'll have to stop by and pick up the book and letters. I think it's time to have a chat with Claire."

"Shall I call ahead and let her know you're coming?" he offered. "And would you like me to come with you?"

I hesitated, touched. "Um, no, I think she'll be receptive to me."

His disappointment was palpable. "Very well. Call and let me know how it went."

"I will." I hung up.

Standing, I surveyed the place. It was a shambles – even though it still hid the trap door accessing my small crawlspace, the heavy rug I'd laid out with care was a little askew.

Dottie hovered close by. "Are you leaving?"

I nodded, shouldering my pack. "Yes, and I'm not sure when I'll be back."

She beamed. "I'll keep an eye on things until you do."

Dottie is a good kid.

With a quick last look around, I left the shack for the second time that day. I didn't bother to lock the door behind me. There didn't seem to be much point.

Dottie appeared next to me, following as I walked back the way I came. "What are you going to do about your shack, Cady?"

I shrugged. "Not a darn thing, at the moment."

"Did they find what they were looking for?"

I shook my head. "No, but it's time to go see someone who can answer my questions."

And to unravel the secrets surrounding my adoption and why neither Claire nor Cecelia knew about me. I suspected that Cat had uncovered something, but without her around to ask, it would only remain speculation.

Dottie floated on ahead, then dropped back to my side, curious. "Where are we going? Is it an adventure?"

I shook my head. "Not today, I'm afraid. You need to stay here and keep an eye on things, though. That witch who did this might be back."

She flickered, anxious. "I was derelict in my duty. I'm sorry, Cadence."

I paused long enough to meet her gaze. "It's not your fault, Dottie. You did fine." Pausing in my path, I said, "Stay here and keep watch for strangers."

She beamed. "I'll make sure no one trespasses on the shack again." As I started to walk across the cemetery, she called out, "Who are you going to see?"

"My sister," I said, grim, speaking the relationship out loud for the first time. I didn't mention the missing third vampire to Dottie. There wasn't anything she could do about it except worry and she was already stressing herself out enough as it was.

As I walked across the cemetery lawn, my pack bouncing in time with my steps, I considered how to approach Claire. There was no real easy way to do it, no soft build-up to the statement "I'm your sister", so I'd have to let my birth certificates and the book of births do the explaining. Pulling out my keys, I climbed back into the cemetery truck, my destination Wickerman Falls. It was past closing time at the bookstore, but Claire was a businesswoman – she'd be there until the day's receipts were all accounted for and stock was replenished for the next day.

If I was going to find her anywhere, it would be at the Naughton Bookshop. Maybe then we could figure out where the third vampire was hiding and deal with her, as well as confront Cecelia and Julian. I wasn't looking forward to either scenario – both would end badly for one side of the conflict, of that, I was sure. I just hoped I was on the side that came out on top.

The truck's high beams cut across the shadows as dusk turned to night and, when I passed Black Rock Lane, there was a brief glitter light reflecting back at me, like the eyes of a night creature. I hit the brakes, the truck screeching to a halt. Then, shifting into reverse, I backed up slowly, looking down the forgotten lane, curious.

Parked underneath the first tree to my left was a rental car.

Claire was here.

Thirty-Three

After a minute, I pulled over and parked the truck on the side of the road, shoving my pack under the seat. At the same, I pulled out the ash stake I'd stashed there after my last visit to the Pellington house. Locking up the truck and keys in my pocket, I stayed close to the shadows, creeping up Black Rock Lane. Pausing long enough to check the rental car, I noticed that all four doors were locked. There weren't any personal items in the back.

I turned and stared down the lane, apprehensive. Something or someone had drawn Claire to the old Pellington place. Whether it was by her own choice or not was open to debate. In either case, no matter how powerful she was, she wouldn't be able to handle the situation on her own, especially if Julian Webster was involved.

I didn't think Cecelia would back her up, either.

Pulling out my cellphone once more, I called Raul again.

Again, he answered on the second ring. "Kendrick."

"It's me," I said, my voice low. "Something's up at Black Rock Lane. Claire's rental is here and I don't think she's alone."

His voice grew alert. "Stay away from that house, Cadence. I'll find a way to get over there."

In spite of myself, I laughed. "It'll take at least forty-five minutes for you to get here. By that time, Claire could be dead."

"So could you," he reminded me, then sighed. "You're right, of course. I'll stay put for the moment, since I'm not at full capacity, myself. But if I don't hear from you in those same forty-five minutes, I'm calling the police. And then I'll find a way to get there."

"Fair enough," I said, relieved. "Don't try to call back to change my mind, I'm putting my phone on silent."

He laughed, a low pitched sound that sent warmth through me. "All right. I'll await your call with bated breath."

We hung up and I tucked my phone into my pocket. Then I turned my attention to the lane ahead of me. Keeping to the shadows, I made my way to the Pellington place at the end of Black Rock Lane. It was full dark by this time, the moon just beginning its climb. Pausing briefly to catch my breath, I clambered over the rock wall, pulling out my small flashlight once I was on the other side. Scanning the area, I was glad that either Julian or Cecelia had chopped back the foliage on their visits. Dealing with it in the dark would have been a definite way to get injured and any noise interacting with it would have alerted others to my presence.

As quickly and silently as I could, I made my way to the house, covering the flashlight's beam with my fingers, muting it without plunging myself into darkness. I didn't think Claire was out here alone and if she had company, the less they knew about my presence, the better. Just as I stepped into the clearing near the front porch, I doused my light. As my eyes adjusted to the sudden darkness, I noticed a dim glow from the parlor window.

Using the moon's pale light to guide me the rest of the way, I crept carefully up the porch steps, fingering my crucifix. Reaching for the door knob, I paused before my hand even touched its cold metal.

The door was ajar and from inside, I heard movement and something else.

Voices.

Pressing close to the wall, I listened, recognizing Claire's voice immediately. "You kidnapped me from the store, Julian. What the hell are you and Cecelia up to? Why have you dragged me out here?"

"Restoring her powers, first of all," came the languid reply. "And for that, we require your esteemed presence. Taking control of the coven is next, correct?"

"Absolutely." Cecelia's voice was close, maybe less than ten feet on the other side of the front door from where I was. "And then we'll find out why Cat was so interested in that old family tree she found and how it ties to the church down the road."

"Where is she?" Claire demanded.

"Excellent question," Julian said. "Perhaps the resident ghost can answer that for us."

"If not him, then that vagabond working at the cemetery," Cecelia muttered, her tone short and growing close as she paced. "Perhaps she knows, Julian. That tracking spell you made kept leading me back to her."

Peering through the crack made by the open door, I tried to see the speakers, but my view was limited to portions of the foyer and the entrance to the parlor. The battery-operated lantern on the floor adjacent to the entry threw enough light to see shadows as they moved around, but I was still out of their sightline.

"All of this is over binding your powers?" Claire sounded bewildered. "Ce Ce, your powers were bound to protect you."

"Was that before or after our parents died?" the younger woman taunted.

Claire persisted. "Why does it matter?"

A man spoke from outside of my sight line. "The

timing matters, Claire. You know this. You were there."

Claire's puzzlement only grew. "I was a child then, I barely even remember that night."

A man shifted around the room, his shadow flung up the staircase as he walked by the lantern, illuminating his face. I blinked. The man looked like Efrain Jimenez, but the voice didn't match the face of the man I knew. Instinctively, I almost called out his name, just to hear him speak again, to know if I really did hear the wrong voice. But I kept my mouth shut, clamping my hand over it and watching closely. Something in his body language was unfamiliar to me, not quite like the officer I had run into over the last few weeks.

He was more......predatory, almost feline in his movements, like he'd been while at Abby's nursery and antagonizing Claire. The casual, easy movements I'd seen at Madame Sofia's coffee shop were absent. I frowned, studying him as closely as I could from where I was sitting. It had been after his encounter with Julian Webster that he'd become…different. There were a lot of little things wrong with him – how he twitched his hand, the curl of his lip that could slide easily into a sneer rather than a grin.

And now, he was here, helping Julian and Cecelia. He was so unlike the man I'd begun to know that I wondered how I could have missed it. Scowling, Efrain Jimenez stepped out of sight and back into the parlor, his voice too low for me to understand his words. Cecelia responded in kind and I suspected that they didn't want Claire to overhear.

The evening air's temperature dropped a few degrees and Henry Gray appeared. *What are you doing, Cadence?*

I made a gesture to indicate silence, then carefully crept away from the front door and back down the stairs, ducking to the side. There were enough shadows to mask my presence for the moment and I sank to the ground, relieved that so far, I hadn't been noticed. Henry appeared beside me, repeating his question.

314

In low tones, I said, "Hiding from the people inside."

They're not doing much, he said, *just trying to get the woman Claire to tell them about a secret.* He cast a worried look up at the porch. *They mean business, Cadence. And* she's *back.*

"Who, Sarah?" I murmured.

Henry shook his head. *No, the vampire. Cassiopeia. And she's angry, she wants to get back inside, but she can't.*

I stared at him. The vampire must have been out hunting, as I'd suggested to Abby when we staked the other two. And if there was a second nesting place where it needed to sleep, then it could have been Father O'Mare's church. The charm had given them access and, with it now desecrated, it was a readily available hiding place. Now it was back at the original nesting place and my choice to revoke Pellington's invitation kept it from getting inside the house.

From inside, there was a meaty slap and Claire cried out in pain.

I made a gesture for him to scope things out and he vanished. Crawling to the window, I sat underneath it, grateful for the thin panes of glass. Although muffled, I could hear voices and an occasional word. Wincing at a low creak in the boards, I risked a quick glance through the glass, grateful for the gauzy thin curtains and heavy drapes over them that obscured the window. What I saw was mostly shadows thrown in sharp relief by the placement of two lanterns as the people inside moved around.

Then one voice spoke clearly enough for me to hear. Julian's voice, but it sounded off, somehow. "I want to know how this Galloway family fits into all of this."

My blood turned cold. How did they know my name?

"The Galloways were a part of my family's coven decades ago," Cecelia said, scornful. She sounded close, maybe a couple of feet from the window. I ducked down, not wanting to be seen, grateful for the shadows and curtains. "Weak-willed and cowardly, from what I can gather. Aunt Sandy was right to throw them out years ago."

"Aunt Maggie didn't throw them out of the coven." Claire sounded muffled and then I heard her spit. When she spoke again, her voice was clear, stronger. "She sent them away, for their own protection, and for ours." She took a deep breath, coughed, spat and added, "What I never did understand was why."

"Cat would know. We ought to have asked her, before she disappeared," Julian said, humor in his voice. Once again I was struck by how odd he sounded. "If she had stayed put, like she was supposed to, she'd be sitting here, next to poor Claire, and answering all of our questions." The floor boards in the parlor squeaked as he shifted his weight. "Are both of your sisters inclined to such stubborn behavior, my love?"

"It would seem so," Cecelia said, disgusted. "Scry for that vagabond again. Maybe she can lead us to Cat."

There was silence as he presumably did as she asked. I hoped Henry was watching closely, in case something went wrong. Inside, Julian was muttering under his breath – it sounded more in vexation rather than conjuring. In seconds, Henry was hovering next to me.

He can't get a lock on you. Henry sounded amused. *He's not happy about it.*

Julian spoke, his voice closer to the window than I had expected. "She's been here, but whatever magic she's using is messing with my ability to ascertain how recently."

I silently thanked Abby's erasure spell.

"She's just like me," Cecelia snapped. "An *impremere* is weak and pathetic and has very little magic. She couldn't have cast magic strong enough to hide her presence."

"If she's an *impremere* like you, then she can, at the very least, pull her presence out of the space," Julian snapped back. "She's certainly got more juice than you do, skilled or not."

"Unlike me, she's not bound," Cecelia snapped back. "Even so, she wouldn't be able to do what you suggest,

316

more likely, she'd pull the house down around her."
Sounds of papers being shuffled reached my ears and then,
"Scry for anyone else. At the very least, she couldn't have
staked the two vampires in the basement by herself."

He grunted something, then fell silent, following her
wishes.

At my gesture, Henry slipped through the walls like
vapor. He was soon back. *The officer is acting strangely,
Cadence.*

How could Efrain Jimenez be inside the house and
not be taking an active role in either stopping what was
going on or participating? Why hadn't he spoken up to
question Cecelia's actions or Julian's, or even Claire?
Catching Henry's attention, I shook my head, indicating
that I didn't understand through a little bit of mime and
hand gestures.

He caught on. *That police officer. He's twitching like he's
got a fever.*

Was there a way for me to see? The gauzy curtains in
the window didn't help and neither did the heavy drapes
framing them. A porch board creaked under me, the wood
popping free a large splinter in the process, and I froze
where I crouched, my heart pounding as the voices inside
stopped.

In a flash, I was over the porch railing and hiding in
the bushes below when the front door opened. Heavy
footsteps crossed the porch and stopped at the top of the
stairs. I held my breath, pressing myself as close to the
rotted lattice work as I could. The bushes I hid behind
seemed a lot thinner than I liked, but there wasn't much I
could do about it.

"Most likely a branch falling," Julian said, answering a
question I hadn't heard.

"It could be her," Cecelia said from the doorway.
"She's been here before, she might be around." A beam of
light bounced across the wild garden, then splashed up
against the house in a sudden movement. "Are you all

right?"

Julian made a rude noise. "I'm fine. The spells on this place are affecting my magic."

"How much longer can you hold the glamour?"

"Not long. Maybe another twenty minutes." He added, "It can't be held indefinitely, Sissy, especially if the person I'm copying isn't under control."

"Well, we couldn't exactly kidnap the local police chief without anyone noticing," she said, tartly. "You almost got caught out twice as it is."

"What makes you think this vagabond, as you call her, is an *impremere*, like you?" Julian asked, genuinely curious. "You've only spoken to her that one time, in the old caretaker shack at the cemetery."

Cecelia didn't answer right away. "When I was reading her palms, I felt a pull that's similar to how I was able to use my power. You know, like calling to like."

Julian grunted, what sounded like him biting back pain. Through gritted teeth, he said, "You told me that *impremeres* can absorb magic or call it to them."

"Some of them can, if they're lucky," Cecelia agreed, her voice dripping anger. "I used to be able to call water from any source around me – rocks, concrete, trees. I would form puddles in the garden at home as a child. Now, thanks to that binding spell of Cat's, I can't even pull it from concrete." She paused, added grudgingly, "That was a nice touch, at the vagabond's shack, by the way."

"Your magic isn't gone, just blocked." There was a sharp crack as he slapped his thigh. At first, I thought he'd been stung by a bee. Then he said, "Either she's here or it's the house's spells, but I'm being drained as we speak." He groaned through a spasm of pain. "I'm losing control over this form. I can't hold it for much longer."

"You're the damn sorcerer, Julian," Cecelia said urgently. "Find a way to keep it!"

There was a thud, then he was stumbling down the porch steps, landing in the tall grass just within my line of vision. Cecelia was at his side, her back to me. I pulled back further into the shadows as carefully as possible, watching as he writhed in agony. He convulsed violently, unable to cry out in pain with the stick she had wedged between his teeth. It came out as a deep, guttural moan and spittle drooled from his mouth.

Then, as he relaxed, he looked up at Cecelia, holding one hand out to block the light from his eyes. I clamped a hand over my mouth to keep from crying out.

Lit by Cecelia's cellphone, I watched as Efrain Jimenez's face shimmered back into Julian Webster.

Thirty-Four

Watching the man who had been impersonating an officer closely, I focused all my energy into remaining still and silent, hidden against the tree and its shadows. There was a rush of cold air and Henry was flickering in and out beside me. He took in the man and woman at the bottom of the porch steps, understanding at once.

They're the ones who have been here before. Henry looked at me, determined. *I'll see if I can distract them.*

I nodded my head with care, to show that I understood.

Henry vanished.

Julian Webster was now sitting up, leaning heavily against Cecelia. The stick he'd bitten down on during the glamour change was lying next to her and she picked it up, giving it a hard toss over her shoulder. It landed only a few feet away from me. With some effort, I kept still, my breath coming in a shallow rhythm.

"Can you stand?" Cecelia was asking. She grunted sharply when Julian gripped her arm and shifted his weight. "We have got to make Claire undo this binding on me. And then we need to find Cassiopeia."

It was slow going, but Julian finally got to his feet.

"Hand me my phone."

She gave it to him and he turned on the flashlight app, turning to survey the area beyond the house, his attention fixed on one point. "Something's out there."

Henry? Or was it something else? I took in a deep breath, then exhaled slowly, being careful to make as little noise as possible.

"Cassiopeia?" Cecelia sounded calm, but there was an undercurrent of worry, as well. If Sarah was right, this particular vampire was even more unpleasant to deal with than the others.

"No, but it's not an animal either." He shone his light around, but it didn't throw as focused a beam as regular flashlight would have. From a distance, I heard what sounded like someone running through the shrubbery. He swore under his breath, his voice low and strained. "What the hell is that?"

Cecelia spoke, her voice low. "What is it, Julian?"

"There's someone running away from the house," he said, tense. "It could be her. It could be Cat, too."

"Fine, you go around to the left and I'll go right," Cecelia said, "We'll meet back here." She muttered an oath, her patience clearly at an end. "Working this curse while being magically bound is painful and difficult."

Julian touched her cheek in a gentle caress. "Don't worry, my love. We'll get you sorted out soon."

She nuzzled his hand, then sighed. "Damn Cat and her control freak ways, I wish we'd gotten rid of her before she re-set the binding on me."

"Speaking of Cat," Julian said, dipping his head low to kiss her, "I think I have a way to make that tracking spell work better."

Cecelia's response was muffled, but clear. She was happy with his idea and even happier with his kisses. With some reluctance, they parted and then went their chosen routes, to hunt down Henry's decoy. This left me with a few minutes to get inside the house undetected and get

Claire out. I waited a minute before moving from my spot, my limbs stiff and trembling from the adrenalin, not quite trusting myself to move just yet. When I did, my legs crumpled out from under me and I almost fell, but I managed to keep on my feet.

Once I felt steady, I hurried up the porch steps, pausing briefly at the door to take a quick look behind me. Nothing but darkness. Then I went inside, flashing my own cellphone's light app to guide me. Claire was tied to a wooden chair – even from where I stood, I could see how the ropes cut into her skin. Her face had more bruises than not and a cut on her forehead had opened up, but she otherwise seemed unharmed.

She looked up when I entered the house, her eyes widening in surprise. "You?"

I shushed her, moving quickly to untie the ropes that bound her. "Speak quietly. They're outside looking around for what they think is me, but it's a ghost. They'll be back soon."

"How did you know about this place?" she whispered, rubbing her wrists once I'd freed them.

"The resident ghosts showed me," I whispered back. "Come on, I don't know how long we have."

Claire tried to stand, but must have sprained her ankle at some point along the way, because she winced, biting her lip hard to keep from crying out. She gripped my arm, sinking back into the chair. "Go get help."

"I can't leave you here alone," I objected. "Besides, they'll know someone was here, with the ropes untied."

She smiled, but there was no humor in it. "I've magic of my own that they haven't even begun to touch. I'll be fine."

"Not with that third vampire is still around," I said, even more urgently at the thought. "You won't stand a chance."

Henry materialized behind Claire. *They're coming back. Whatever you plan to do, you've got to do it quick.*

323

There wasn't time to explain Henry to Claire, so I said, "I'll tell you how I know later, but we don't have much time. Julian and Cecelia are on their way back."

Claire shook her head. "I'll only hinder you. Go, now!"

Reluctantly, I left her and moved to the front door, only to stop when I heard voices outside getting closer. I couldn't get out that way, so I hurried up the stairs, being careful to step where the dust had already been disturbed. At the top of the stairs, I hesitated, unsure of the decision to leave Claire behind. Even at full strength, she was no match for Julian. There had to be a way to deal with Julian and Cecelia, get Claire out and take care of the missing vampire all in one fell swoop, but I felt distinctly out-numbered. Even if she could muster up any strength, combined with my skills, it would be dicey.

From below, the front door slammed open, startling me. In the parlor, I heard Claire stir and mutter something. I shrank back, keeping to the shadows. From my position, I could see her where she lay, rubbing her wrists as if she'd just snapped the ropes.

Cecelia walked in and stood over her sister, foot tapping in sharp staccato beats. Then she leaned down and grabbed her sister by the hair, pulling back hard. "Who is that vagabond from the cemetery? What did she want from you?"

Claire gasped in pain. "She didn't want anything."

"Of course she wanted something," the younger woman snapped. "Everyone is always out for something."

Claire's chin firmed. "And Cat? Is that on her? Or is it on you?"

"On Julian, actually." Cecelia smirked, letting Claire go. "She wasn't expecting him."

Claire sounded horrified. "So you killed her? Why, Ce Ce?"

"Power, dear. And she's not dead, not yet."

Claire watched her younger sister. "Where is she,

then?"

There was a pause. Then, reluctant, "I don't know. Not even Julian can trace her."

"Where is he now? On the way back to Wickerman Falls?"

"No, he's still looking around for what or whoever is out there." Cecelia moved out of my view, then back again. She held something in her hands. It looked like a bit of yellowed parchment paper. "Cat bound me from my magic. Help me use this to break it and perhaps you'll walk away from this."

Claire watched Cecelia, her posture tense, ready. Despite having been tied to a chair for who knows how long and bruised from physical roughness, Claire held her power easily. "Cat didn't want to bind you, Sissy. That was my idea."

"Then you can unbind me." The sisters squared off, the younger one challenging boundaries with her body language.

"I could," Claire agreed, "but I won't." She spoke over Cecelia's protest. "In order for it to be effective, Cat would need to be here as well."

"Where is she?"

"I don't know and I wouldn't tell you if I did." There was a quality to her voice that I'd not heard before, like a growl underneath the calm. It sent shivers up my spine and I recognized some of her power. "Whose face was Julian wearing this time?"

Cecelia shrugged. "A cop from Sleepy Eye Cove. I think his name is Efrain Jimenez." She leaned into Claire, her expression cold and blank. "Unbind my powers, Claire. I'll even read Cat's part. I won't ask again."

"Tell me where Efrain Jimenez is, and I'll consider it," Claire said, not flinching.

"Unbind me and I'll lead you to him," Cecelia taunted.

"Show me proof of life and you'll get the reversal

spell."

Cecelia was silent for a moment, then said, grudgingly, "He's alive and well in his office, none the wiser for Julian's trick."

Heavy footsteps echoed along the porch and soon, Julian Webster crossed the room. Claire suddenly jerked back, hitting the wall behind her. I heard the snapping of wood as the chair she was sat on hit the door frame and Claire's low groan as she slid to the floor. Then, as he came into view, I ducked back into the shadows, my heart thudding.

Cecelia, hands clenched, mouth drawn in a thin line, glared down at her sister. "I don't have time for this, Claire, and I really don't want to hurt you. Give me the damn spell."

Julian Webster, still in the police uniform, stood over Claire and yawned. "Please don't kill her, Sissy. We need her."

I frowned. That wasn't the first time I'd heard that word 'sissy', nor was this the first place I'd heard it, either. Cat had used that word in my dreams and at the time, I had thought she was calling me a coward. But both Julian and Claire had used it as a nickname to address Cecelia. Cat had been trying to warn me of who to watch out for.

From her position on the floor, Claire directed her rage at her sister's boyfriend. "Get the hell away from me, Julian." The fury in her voice was deep. "You can go, too, Sissy."

Julian Webster yawned again. "Claire, please. You're only making this harder."

"Am I, Julian?" Claire staggered to her feet, using the wall to keep her balance. I could see the top of her head and, just beyond, the shadows of the two she faced. "I thought I was merely protecting my family."

She made a sudden gesture – from my angle, I couldn't see what. Cecelia was knocked back hard, landing so hard against the door frame that it rattled the parlor's chandelier crystal. But Julian brought up his arm in a casual reflex, bouncing Claire's spell off of him and hit her hard, knocking her back into the wall. She sank down to the floor with a soft moan.

Cecelia crouched down, checking on her sister. "Well, you didn't kill her."

"I thought that's what you wanted." Julian sounded surprised.

"I said I wanted power," she snapped. "I didn't say I wanted them dead."

He frowned. "You have power, Sissy. *Impremeres*......"

"Are powerless," she interrupted, scowling. "Except for that one, back in the forties. She pulled elements from everything around her, magic included. All I can do is cast for water and pull it from a stone. What kind of power is that? I can't even do that now, thanks to Cat." She stood, scowled at her prone sister and turned. "Let's go find that vampire. She's got to be around here somewhere."

Julian gestured to Claire. "What about your sister?"

Cecelia shrugged. "If the vampire returns before we get back, it will take care of her, of course. It's hungry."

"I thought you didn't want your sister to die?"

She dismissed his question with a wave of her hand. "I want my powers back and I need her and Cat to undo the binding. Since she's refusing to help, death may be the only answer."

He laughed. "You are a woman after my heart."

She kissed him. "If you had one."

"Touche."

There was the sound of footsteps on the hardwood floors – then I saw Julian walk out the front door, closely followed by Cecelia. Taking the stairs one by one, I was able to keep them in sight until they disappeared into the woods. When I could no longer see them, I paused, hand on the banister, listening. Other than the sound of Claire's labored breathing, I heard nothing out of the ordinary.

Only the random chirping of crickets reached my ears, dusk falling outside their cue to emerge.

It would be dark soon. And, unless I figured out a way to get back to my truck, those outside this house, searching, would be back even sooner, trapping Claire and myself inside.

Thirty-Five

From my place on the upstairs landing, I debated my next move, my eyes never leaving the still form of Claire. It was clear that I needed to get her out of the house and back to the cemetery truck, so that I could get her to safety. How I would do this without being caught was another matter entirely. Now seemed like a great time to call Raul and have him come to the rescue, but I couldn't risk Julian or Cecelia hearing.

Stepping down the remaining stairs, I kept an eye on the front door and the porch beyond. I'd at least hear them before they got back, though I didn't expect them to find the third vampire close by. If Henry was right, then my revocation of Pellington's invitation prevented any vampire from crossing the threshold and entering the house, so we were safe from that danger, as well.

Especially from the one called Cassiopeia.

In moments, I was kneeling beside Claire, who was beginning to stir.

I helped her into a sitting position, slipping an arm under her. "Come on, we need to get you to a doctor." I glanced at the window above. "Can you stand up?"

She smiled faintly, wincing when she finally got to a

sitting position. "I guess so, give me a second."

Probably not, then.

"My truck's at the end of the lane," I said, "so I'm going to go for help. Will you be all right here?"

She frowned at me. "I'm coming with you."

"You can't even stand up," I pointed out.

She gave me a look, then braced herself against the wall. It took some effort, but I had the feeling the Naughton family was made of very stern stuff. Soon, Claire was standing, not quite steady, but definitely upright. "If you give me your arm, I think I can manage until my legs aren't so shaky."

With Claire using me for balance, we started for the door. As an *impremere*, I wondered if, instead of pulling energy from Claire, I could actually give her some of my strength, in order to help get her out of the old house. So I sent focused energy to her. She steadied almost at once, her steps a little more sure. This was good, since it would help get her to the truck. Once there, my plan was to get her to a doctor or, if that wasn't possible, the emergency room up in Wickerman Falls. I didn't think her injuries were life-threatening, but as far as I was concerned, the sooner I got her to help, the better.

Stepping out onto the porch, I stopped abruptly and my companion inhaled breath sharply.

Henry hovered beside me, miserable. *I'm sorry, Cadence, they figured it out.*

Julian Webster was leaning casually against the bannister, gazing up at us, curious. "Well, well, well. If it isn't the vagabond, attempting to be the hero."

Claire found her voice. "Let us pass, Julian."

From the corner of the house to my left, I could hear the rustling of bushes as Cecelia stepped into view. "Did you really think we wouldn't notice your presence?"

There wasn't anything to say to that, so I remained silent. So did Claire.

"I thought you were just some runaway trying to

weasel money or something out of my sister," she continued, casually. Something glinted in her hand and I saw that it was a very short, very sharp, knife. "But you're something more, aren't you? Who are you, cemetery girl? What do you really want with my family?"

I was very aware of the knife and kept my eyes on it. "I don't want anything from you."

She frowned. "I don't believe you."

In spite of things, I couldn't resist laughing. "I don't care."

Claire spoke up at once, her voice loud and clear. "It's true, Sissy. She never asked me for anything." She paused, glanced at me and squeezed my arm, added, "Though I'm certainly glad for her presence now." Then, taking the energy I gave her, she took a deep breath and spoke firmly, her voice clear. *"Ego conteram vobis magicae!!"*

There was a shriek, but it didn't come from Cecelia. Julian Webster had fallen to his knees in the dead grass, his hair slowly turning silver and thinning, his skin becoming liver-spotted and leathery. He was fading from a youthful appearance to an old man and he reached out to Cecelia with an almost skeletal hand.

She recoiled from him, disgust on her face. "Don't you *dare* touch me!" she screamed, the knife falling to the ground as she shoved him away.

"What's happening to him?" I asked, watching him in fascinated horror.

Claire didn't look away. "I'm breaking his magic. What you're seeing is every spell he used come back to him before it leaves his body."

From the ground, Cecelia shrieked at her sister. *"Do* something!"

"She is doing something," I said and *pulled* for her binding, visualizing it as a series of ropes looped around her body. Cecelia jerked, stiffened, then collapsed to the ground, her arms trapped at her side. As hard as she tried, she couldn't move.

She glared up at me, hate in her eyes. "What did you do to me?"

I exhaled the breath I'd been holding, feeling shaky. "I'm an *impremere*, like you. I pulled your bindings tighter."

Cecelia growled deep in her throat and tried to lunge at me, but her bindings and my *pulling* them tighter held. She moved only a few inches in the tall grass. Beyond her, in the shadows, Julian was still changing, a process that was clearly painful, if the hoarse, guttural cries were anything to go by. The words Claire had spoken continued to undo the magic he had invoked – now, it was undoing the *glamours* he'd used to transform himself into whoever he wanted. It looked like every face he'd used in his lifetime was being released.

I watched, fascinated and repelled, as Julian's features morphed, melted and solidified into one face before moving onto the next face. Not even in New Orleans had I seen such a profound rejection of one's own magic. Louise Tremont had once described it as being cut off from the source of your own power. The reaction was like going through detox – the stronger the magic, the harder the withdrawal.

From the way Julian looked, he was in for a long recovery. Cecelia, in the meantime, was muttering under her breath, blood spitting out as she spoke. The words she used sounded similar to what Claire had said, but nothing was happening, a fact not lost on her and which only fueled her fury.

There was a heavy sigh behind me and I turned to see Claire sink to the top porch step as she leaned into the railing. She looked exhausted and drained – if that spell could have such a strong impact on Julian, then the one casting it used as much as, if not more, energy. She caught my worried look and smiled wanly. "It takes a lot out of me, uttering that spell. And I had to wait until Julian was tired enough from holding his *glamour* in order for it to work."

"How about you?" I asked, concerned. "You look terrible."

"A couple days' worth of sleep and I'll be fine." She glanced over at the two writhing and cursing figures on the grass, then looked back at me. "How did you know to find me, us, here?"

I sat down next to her. "I didn't. I was actually heading into Wickerman Falls to find you, but I saw your rental car parked in the lane."

"And you got curious to see who was poking around," she guessed.

I nodded. "In part. Then Henry showed up and told me what was going on."

She stared at me, puzzled. "Who's Henry?"

Before I could explain, the ghost in question appeared to my left, agitated to the point where even Claire was feeling a marked chill in the air. She shivered, rubbing her arms to generate heat, her breath hanging in front of her like a fine mist. She glanced at me, curious. "It's him, isn't it, your friend the ghost?"

I nodded. "Henry, what's wrong?"

She's here and she's hungry, he said. *And whatever you did last time, it's holding because she can't get inside the house.* He glanced over to the left of the porch, towards the far corner of the house. Thanks to the trees and over-grown rosebushes, the shadows had grown darker and longer, taking on a sinister shape. *She wants to go home.*

"Get in the house, Claire," I said, turning to help her up. "The invitation's been revoked and you'll be safe until your powers come back."

"What is it?" she asked.

"Cassiopeia's home," I said tersely, trotting down the steps to fetch my stake. It had fallen by the lattice when I had ducked back into the shadows when Julian stepped out the front door and dropped Efrain Jimenez's face earlier. Kneeling, I felt around the grass, giving a small exclamation of joy when my fingers brushed against the

333

smooth surface of the ash stake. Plucking it off the ground, I stood and made my way out of the shadows.

Cassiopeia was waiting for me at the edge of the woods.

Thirty-Six

The vampire smiled.

Once again, I was reminded of a great white shark. "Your blood smells so sweet, even from a distance, that I would like sip of it to slake my thirst." The vampire glanced at Cecelia and Julian, both of whom had grown still at her presence. "Sweeter than hers, truth be told. Or the one inside my old home." Her lip curled contemptuously when she looked at Julian. "His, not so much." She turned back to me. "Might I have a taste of that sweet blood in your veins?"

"No, Cassiopeia," I said.

Her smile widened. "So, you know who I am."

"It wasn't that hard to figure out," I said, avoiding her eyes. "There are three crates in the basement here and one was empty."

She straightened, alert and tense. "So it was you that destroyed my children. Was it also you that has made it so I cannot enter my home?"

No point in lying to a vampire. "Yes."

Fury flashed briefly across her face, then she was considering me, thoughtful. "That one on the ground, the one with bound powers. She thinks you're some sort of

335

vagabond, a person of no real importance." She licked her lips. "But we know better, do we not?"

"That's not for me to say," I said, fingering the crucifix around my neck. The stake in my hand was a comforting weight, but useless at the moment. If I went for it now, she'd be on me before I could draw it. I had to bide my time.

Still, Cassiopeia was at my side before I could blink. What gave her pause was the silver chain around my neck and the crucifix attached to it. She hissed, shrinking back a little. "That smells of bayou dirt."

"It's from New Orleans," I corrected. "And it was a gift." We regarded each other for a long moment. It seemed as though the vampire was seeing me, not through her Undead eyes, but with her humanity. Her curiosity as she studied me was alive in her every movement.

"A Naughton so far from home," she murmured. "How did that occur, you not knowing who you truly are?"

"That's what I came back to find out," I said.

Her fingers gripped my left wrist before I had done more than flex it. "Let me taste the power in your blood." She licked her lips, leaning in close enough to fill my vision. The tiny hairs on my skin prickled at her proximity – it reminded me, eerily, of Henry's memory. "I've not found that spark and I want it. Now."

I avoided meeting her eyes, aware of her efforts to catch mine. "I'd rather you didn't."

Her gaze felt like a dead weight. "Your blood will taste so sweet," she purred, pulling my wrist up to her mouth. She opened her mouth, traced a vein in my wrist with her tongue. "I've tasted the blood of your family. I will enjoy tasting yours." The vampire leaned in, her grip on my wrist a vise that I couldn't free myself from.

"I said, 'no'," I growled, putting my right hand on her chest, repeating what I'd done back in New Orleans – I found and *pulled* her soul back into her body. Unlike the New Orleans vampire, whose soul was barely an ember of warmth after nearly two centuries of walking the earth as an Undead, I could *feel* hers, a sharp *spark*, faint and pulsing, but it still there. There was a brief pause – then, decades after it had beat its last, her heart throbbed.

She howled, a rough, coarse sound on dead vocal cords, and pushed me away, her hands frantically scrabbling at her chest, a keening wail issuing forth from her lips. Landing hard at the bottom of the porch steps, I sucked in breath and rolled to my knees, stake in hand, ignoring the pain that ripped up my back. The expression on the vampire's face was startling – shock, disbelief and fear. It had never occurred to me before that a vampire could feel fear, or even a close facsimile to it, but it was naked on her face just the same.

"Watch out!" Claire shouted from the door.

Pain from the porch steps digging into my back once more registered seconds before I even realized I'd been tackled. Cassiopeia pinned me down, her nostrils quivering as she inhaled my scent, her face so close to mine that that her lips curled over very sharp teeth blotted out everything else in sight. I tried to lunge to my right, hoping to at least loosen her grip, but it only tightened painfully. Still, I was able to twist my hand around, the stake's sharp point only inches from the vampire's body.

"So sweet," she purred, licking her lips in anticipation. "Your magic will purge that which you have done to me, bleeder."

"I said, *no!*" And I pushed the stake into her chest, feeling it strike deep.

Cassiopeia froze. Time seemed to stand still and, for a brief second, I thought I saw a flicker of relief and horror in the vampire's eyes. Then she disintegrated, leaving only a dull gray pile of dust as the only evidence of her existence. For several minutes, the only sounds were my harsh breathing mixed with the growing cacophony of crickets. Then, I slowly pushed myself up into a sitting position, wincing. I was going to be sore tomorrow and bruises were probably forming. On the porch above me, I heard Claire shuffle over to the railing.

"You okay?" she asked.

"Sore, but alive," I said, "so I guess that's a 'yes'."

From the over-grown lawn, Julian's moans had subsided, but Cecelia was still seething, her words too hard to decipher as she uttered spell after spell under her breath. With a sharp flick of her hand and a few choice words of her own, Claire silenced her sister. We were quiet for a few minutes – Claire was catching her second wind and I was staring down at the pile of dust that had once been Cassiopeia. With a shudder, I scattered the ashes with my foot, wishing I had some holy water to mix it with.

"Why doesn't anyone live here?" I asked, breaking the silence. "It seems like a waste of a home, for one man to have built it and then let it go to rot after the family died."

Claire considered her words. "When Cat disappeared, she was looking into a lot of family history, most of which started when she found the deed to this place." She glanced around, her eyes lost in the shadows that grew darker with every passing minute, then turned to me. "What do you know of the Pellington family?"

"I'll tell you, but we need to get you to a doctor," I said, eyeing her, worried. "Those wounds look deep and you might need stiches. Can you walk? My truck is at the end of the road." She nodded and, with her arm over my shoulders for support, we started to walk towards the stone wall. I glanced down at Cecelia and Julian. "What about them? They won't get away or anything, will they?"

Claire snorted. "No, their magic is done. Let's get out of here."

We got to the truck a few minutes later, me helping her into the passenger side. Her foot scuffed against my pack and she pulled it out, curious. "What's this?"

"My stuff." I was about to put the truck in gear when my phone buzzed in my pocket. Pulling it out, I recognized the hotel's number and answered. "Hey, I told you not to call."

"It's been an hour," came the terse reply. "The police should be on their way out. Where are you?"

"In my truck with Claire," I said, maneuvering back on the road. "Get a cab and meet us at the emergency room in Wickerman Falls. Bring the book and the letters with you."

"Will do." Raul hung up.

"Who was that?" Claire asked. "What book? What letters?"

"That was Raul Kendrick," I said, shifting into third.

Claire studied me. "What is my family's attorney talking with you about?"

I glanced at her. "He's my attorney, your sister kidnapped him and I found him. And I'll try to explain as best I can what I know."

As I maneuvered the truck towards Sleepy Eye Cove and Route 5, I told her what I'd found out about the Pellington place, about how the captain had somehow struck a deal with Cassiopeia and her nest. About Henry Gray, his relationship with Sarah, and how the townspeople barely knew that he was here, let alone that he at some point had gone missing. They certainly didn't know that he had been killed.

I had just finished describing how the Pellington family met their end when we pulled up in front of the emergency room in Wickerman Falls. True to his word, Raul Kendrick was there, waiting for us at the nurses' station. The nurse on call took one look at Claire and had her on a bed in seconds, armed with a tray of needles, sutures, and cotton swabs to get her cleaned up.

While an intern stitched up Claire's forehead, I opened my pack and pulled out both of my birth certificates. Raul handed me Hallie's letters to Madison and the book of births. In turn, I gave Claire all three items. "These letters were hidden in the Pellington's attic. I think they belong to you, or at least, to your family." Touching the book, I added, "This is a records book."

Claire took the items I handed her with care and placed them on her lap, studying me closely, then smiled. "You know, your hair color put me off at first, but I finally figured out who you remind me of."

I blinked, surprised. "Who?"

"My aunt, Hallie Welles. Great-Aunt, actually."

Raul eyed me more closely. "I think you're right, Claire. Now that you've pointed it out, I do see it."

I gave him a look. He only smiled back.

Grinning, Claire picked up the book of births and thumbed through it, stopping on the page where she and her sisters had been recorded. I thought about mentioning that we were sisters, but she would be looking at the birth certificates soon enough.

"Cat's been on a mission to find this," Claire said, handing it back to me. "She wouldn't tell me why, at first." She paused, asked, "Where did you find it?"

"At the church in Sleepy Eye Cove," I said, putting it on the table next to her. "Under the pulpit, to be more specific."

Claire laughed, delighted. "I told Cat that it couldn't be in Massachusetts. But she had to do things her own way."

"Why was she looking for it?" I asked, curious.

"She's been working on our family tree for years," Claire explained. "It was an interest that started shortly after our parents died, when she was ten. She felt that we needed to have our baptismal records." She gestured to the book. "Although, I don't think that's a traditional way to record such things."

"It is unusual," Raul admitted.

I agreed. "Have the police found any signs of where she disappeared to?"

Claire shook her head. "I thought that Cecelia was behind it, given her threats at the old house, but now I'm wondering if even she knows where Cat is now."

I looked from her to Raul. "Maybe Julian knows? I mean, Claire and I were lucky to get the drop on him, but only because his *glamour* drained him. If he's as powerful as I've heard, then he either had something to do with Cat's disappearance or he knows who does." Addressing Raul, I added, "You work with him, so maybe you can take a look at his files or something?"

"That is a possibility," he said, slowly. "But I'll need some time to undo his wards." I started to object and he held up a hand. "He may have protected his office and files in a way that would destroy any information if the wrong ward is triggered. It'll take time."

"And since you're in charge of that, I'll rest easy." Claire reached for the packet of letters, paging through them with care. "Oh, Aunt Hallie's letters! What a treasure these are! How did you get them?"

I shifted in my chair. "I found them hidden in the attic at the Pellington house." I glanced at Raul. "Right before I found him, actually."

"I believe it was I who found you," he murmured, his eyes never leaving mine.

My face grew warm as I became aware of Claire's curious gaze. Changing the subject seemed like the wisest course. I gestured to the letters. "I'm guessing your aunt, er, great-aunt, had been writing to Elizabeth Pellington for awhile."

Claire frowned at me. "Elizabeth was another aunt. I'm glad to finally know the end of her story." She tucked the letters into the fold of her sweater, then took up my birth certificates, looking first at the altered one, then at the original. "What are these?"

Neither I nor Raul answered, letting her absorb the information that I'd gotten only a few days before, the pages whispering as she turned from one to the other. She looked at me, confusion on her face, her eyes bright.

Her voice trembling, she said, "I don't understand.

You're my sister?"

I nodded. "It seems that way."

Claire studied me, still stunned by my birth certificate. "You're my sister. *Our* sister. How could you have been hidden from us for so long? Or why?" She held out her hand. After a minute, I took it. "Cat had to have known since childhood, which would explain her obsession about our genealogy, but....Why don't I remember you?"

I wasn't quite sure how to answer her. "I don't know. All I wanted was to get an accurate birth certificate and find out why my adoptive parents lied about where I'd been born."

Claire turned to Raul, asking again, "How could this have happened?"

He shrugged. "That was something I was trying to put together, with Cat's help. But she has the missing pieces and then she went missing, too."

"The Galloways." Claire frowned, thinking. "They'd been a part of the coven for decades, but left town not long after Mom and Dad died. Adopting you and leaving as they did must be connected in some way." She touched the book of births, thoughtful. "You said it was at the church in Sleepy Eye Cove. Where?"

"Hidden underneath the pulpit." I filled her in on how I found it, what had brought me to that church in the first place. How I suspected that Julian had supplied the vampires with charms that had allowed them to access the church.

Her eyes widened. "Damn Julian for that. Damn Marcus for keeping them."

I remained silent. Raul took a nearby chair, sinking into it with a sigh. He looked much better than when I'd left him earlier this afternoon, but I could see that he was still a far cry from the man I'd met only a week and a half earlier. Whatever magical mickey Julian had slipped him, it was a doozey and would probably take longer for him to recover than it did to knock him out.

342

Claire had begun reading the letters again, exclaiming over the old recipes and spells, but even I could see that the day's events were beginning to take a toll on her. "These are incredibly valuable, Cadence. The insights into *impremeres* are fascinating." She held up Silas's letter. "This one, though, is important. Where did he find the knowledge to pull a vampire's soul back into its body?"

"I know that *impremeres* can absorb or pull things to them," I said, studying my hands, thoughtful. Gesturing to Silas's letter, I continued, "I think that's what I am. And I've been told that I'm an *impremere*, but the source was a vampire, so I didn't take him too seriously." I paused, added, "Even though I pulled his soul back into his body before staking him."

Thirty-Seven

There was a silence so deep that I looked up to find Claire and Raul gaping at me, their faces in identical expressions of shock.

I shifted uncomfortably in my chair, not sure what to make of them or their silence. "What?"

"What you did was highly unusual," Claire said after a long moment. She held up the letters, her eyes holding mine. "Even Silas Welles had to use spells to create the magic to pull his vampire's soul back."

"Well, yeah, I didn't think it was easy," I said, uncomfortable with her gaze. "I mean, it's making the Undead not, um, the Undead. Sort of."

"When you pulled the vampire's soul back into his body, did you use a spell or tools or any other sort of magical item?" Raul asked, his eyes never leaving mine.

I shook my head. "No, I just placed my hand on his chest and......*pulled.*"

Raul and Claire exchanged glances.

"That's.....unusual," Claire said at last.

"I don't think I've ever heard of anyone being able to do that," Raul agreed. "I've read a lot on vampires and methods of slaying them. That is certainly not mentioned."

"Well, I did it again tonight, with Cassiopeia." I looked at Claire, then at Raul, hoping to find answers in their faces. "But if Silas needed charms and a spell, then how I was able to just......*pull* it back? Is that my *impremere* gift?"

Claire leaned her head back against the pillows, thinking. I studied the shadows under her eyes, acutely aware that she was exhausted. A glance at Raul told me that he was thinking the same thing. At last, she said, "*Impremeres* are incredibly rare individuals. Because of that, their ability to pull things – energy, magic, whatever – has never been documented properly." She looked at me. "Cecelia has the ability to pull water out of trees, the ground, even rocks, just by touch and focus." Claire sighed, her face pale. "She didn't feel that it was a very powerful gift." She looked at me. "What other gifts do you have, if you don't mind me asking?"

I exhaled the breath I wasn't aware that I'd been holding. "I can talk to ghosts, which is how I was able to work out most of what went on at Black Rock Lane. Lately, I've been able to unlock doors just by touching the knob and focusing on the tumblers. Spells and charms are a little more difficult for me, but I can work them." At their amused expressions, I added, "I've not been open to exploring this magical side of me, if you want to know."

She smiled. "I'm not surprised, given what you've told me."

"It's a story, that's for sure." I watched as she stifled a yawn. "I think I'd better go. You need to get some rest."

"Where are you staying?" she asked, worried.

"I've got a place," I reassured her. Going back to the shack was not real high on my list of things to do, but since the hotel room was still in my name, I could stay there. "I'll be okay. I just need to go back to Sleepy Eye Cove and straighten a few things out."

Claire settled back into her pillows, then took my hand, squeezing it gently. "I'm so glad to know you. To know about you."

I smiled, not sure what to say, and squeezed her hand in response. "We can talk some more tomorrow, maybe in the afternoon." She nodded, stifling a yawn. Collecting the letters, I put them on the table next to the book of births. Taking both copies of my birth certificate, I folded and put them in my pack, then slipped out of her room, walking quickly, overwhelmed by the day.

Raul followed, matching my pace as we walked down the hall.

"Are you all right?" he asked, glancing down at me.

"I will be," I said and then we were out in the parking lot, standing next to my truck. Unwilling to meet his gaze, I asked, "Do you feel safe enough to go back to your own home?"

He looked around, momentarily surprised, as if he'd forgotten he was in Wickerman Falls and no longer being sought by my other sister and her lover. "I guess I can make it back to my place from here." He turned to me. "And you? Where will you go?"

"Well, I paid for that hotel room for two nights, so that's a possibility," I said, voicing my thoughts aloud. "Or I can go back to my caretaker's shack at the cemetery." Which, given its current state, was the least attractive option.

"Cadence," Raul said, gently taking my hand, "you are a Naughton. You can stay at the family home, too. I'm sure Claire would be pleased if you did."

I was silent for a moment, both savoring the way my name sounded through his voice and taking in the warm, heady sensation of my hand in his. "I'm sure she would be, but this is all very new to me, so I can't accept that invitation. At least, not yet, anyway."

"Fair enough." He studied me, thoughtful. "Let me come back with you, to the cemetery. I'll help you gather whatever it is you need."

I shook my head, regretful. "I'll be fine, thanks."

He held my gaze for a moment longer, then nodded, acquiescing. "All right. Then, since you have my cellphone number, call in case you need anything."

I nodded. "I will."

We stood by the truck for several minutes, not speaking, unwilling to break the eye contact that held us to the spot. Then, giving my hand a firm, yet gentle, squeeze, he let go and walked away, rounding a corner and disappearing from my view. With a long exhale, my face warm, I got into my truck and pulled out my cellphone, scrolling down until I found Abby's number. Then, typing quickly, I sent her a quick text – *Forgive your mother.* Her response came back quickly – *Where are you???* – but I shut off my phone, climbed into the truck and headed back to Sleepy Eye Cove, where I made a quick stop at the market to pick up some dinner.

Driving past Black Rock Lane a few minutes later, I saw that everything was dark and wondered how things were resolved.

Henry Gray popped into the seat beside me, his color now as though he was among the living. *Where did you go?*

I managed to keep the truck from swerving into a ditch. "I had to get Claire, that woman I rescued, to the hospital." He was intrigued, as evidenced by the dropping temperature. So I gave him a rundown of what happened after I'd left him at the Pellington place. Then it was my turn to ask questions. "A friend called to let me know he'd called the police. Did they show up? Was there a cop named Jimenez?"

Henry Gray told me everything he'd witnessed.

Julian Webster and Cecelia Naughton had been duly arrested and taken away. All evidence of Claire's spell work had vanished and neither of them had had the strength to protest their arrests, let alone argue their case. One of the officers attending the arrest had indeed been Efrain Jimenez, a fact that I was relieved to learn from my spectral companion. Whatever tricks Julian had pulled to use his face, Efrain hadn't been hurt and, so far, seemed unaware of the charade.

I think I can rest now, Cadence, Henry said with a sigh, upon finishing. *That would be really nice, after so long.*

"Go rest, then," I said. "You deserve it."

He smiled, then vanished. I drove on.

*****

I sat on the ground in front of my tiny little caretaker's shack not much later, the cold dampness seeping through my jeans, thinking about the Galloways. What I'd learned since arriving in Maurier County certainly gave me a better understanding for some of their choices, but it did not absolve them of the lies they told me. That the truth came out after their deaths had only hastened the severing of a relationship that had begun to unravel years earlier. And still, I had unanswered questions about how they came to adopt me. Cat's visits in my dreams hadn't clarified much, of either the Galloways or her whereabouts.

I thought about Cecelia, her need for power and, behind that, control over her own life. That was something I felt that I understood in some way. Decisions had been made that took control away from us, either by magic or by adoption. We had had no choice in the matter, no say. But we did have a choice in how to handle it and, while I don't think I handled it in the best way that I could have, I didn't have that same resentment that Cecelia had. And I wondered if, in some way, this was also due to the Galloways. I did have a lot of anger towards them, justifiably so, but my choice had been to cut them out of my life when I turned eighteen. And until the day they died, there had been no communication between us.

My inability to see them after they'd died had a lot to do with my anger towards them and I wondered now if that would change. If I forgave them, let go of that hurt, lay it to rest – bury my undead, so to speak – would that open the lines of communication? It was entirely possible. There was only one way to find out.

Taking a deep breath, I exhaled and spoke. "I spent my life believing you were my mom and dad, only to find out it's not true. There were reasons, I'm aware of that now, but being honest with me from the beginning might have made a difference." I paused, listening to the wind rustling through the trees. "But for what it's worth, I understand that sometimes decisions are made that seem like the best ones at the time. It's part of being human, I guess, to make mistakes, to make choices that blow up in your face. I guess what I'm trying to say is…..it's okay. I'm okay. And that's in large part because of you. And if you really need it said, I forgive you and I release this burden."

Silence fell when I stopped speaking, broken only by my breath and the sounds of birds and insects chirping. Peace stole over me and I sat with this new warmth, embracing it as I thought about what I needed to do next. This naturally led to my little ransacked shack and I studied it, uncomfortably aware that I was reluctant to walk into the space that had been mine for such a short time. The destruction had made it a strange place that no longer felt like home and I was glad about the room at the Blue Rose Hotel.

As I'd indicated to Raul while at the hospital, I still had that room for at least two nights. My only purpose being at the shack right now was to get the rest of my clothes and see if there was anything left to salvage before getting a good night's sleep. Now that Claire knew who I was, I had the feeling that tomorrow was going to be the start of a long process of getting me sorted into the family tree.

I sighed, then gave the melancholy a firm shake and climbed to my feet. I was lucky – I had found most of the answers I'd been looking for, people who cared about me and family. I needed to remember that.

The spot next to my left grew colder and I looked at Dottie, who was blushing. "Oh, Cady, it's good to see you! And Father O'Mare says that his church feels much lighter.

Are the vampires gone now?"

I nodded. "Yes, they're gone. Have you seen Sarah?"

Dottie shook her head. "No, not for a couple of days."

I gestured to the shack. "Has anyone been here since I left?"

"Just that homeless woman," Dottie said, ever cheerful. "She seems a bit batty, if you know what I mean. Will you be moving back in? Because you're going to have to move her out."

Chuckling, I said, "I don't think so, Dottie."

She sighed. "That's a shame, Cady. I did so enjoy being your companion."

I stared at the shack door, then crossed the short distance to it, pushing it open. The damage was the same as I'd left it and as bad, but it wasn't any worse than it could have been. It felt cramped, smaller than I remembered, too. Everything was as I'd last seen it – the couch was overturned, the table I'd picked up at a thrift store was still in a corner, missing a leg. My carpet was still jacked back, revealing the trap door into the tunnel. The padlock was where I'd left it tossed onto the old leather chair, after gathering what I needed from the tunnel.

Dottie hovered close by and I turned to my former roommate, curious. "Are you going to clean the place up? Mr. Burke would appreciate it, I'm sure."

"Well, I guess I could, but I don't think I can undo Cecelia's damage." As she supervised, I packed up my few belongings, then began to clean up the mess as best I could. As I did so, I marveled at how, in just a few days, this humble place had become a real home to me. It was with some surprise that I realized I'd miss living here. Putting the furniture right, I found the meager set of tools and hammered the table's leg back into place. Then I swept up and threw away the broken tapes and DVDs and any broken glass before dumping it in the trash. With a damp cloth, I wiped down the kitchenette, checked the fridge for any leftover food (it was empty) and unplugged anything that required electricity to function.

After setting the mattresses right and straightening the sheets, I found myself at the door one last time, my rucksack of belongings at my feet. Casting a long look around, I knew that this was the last time I would be in this shack. In the days to come, I'd help Wes do a proper clean up and refurbishment of the place, to get it ready for its next tenant. In the meantime, as I surveyed the place, I decided it was clean enough to hand the keys back to Wes.

Dottie appeared beside me, nodding her approval. "The place looks cleaner than when you arrived."

"That's because it is." I hesitated, reluctant to leave. "Dottie, where did you see that woman last? And when?"

"Oh!" Dottie thought for a minute, brightened. "When Veronica Lake came to visit you that evening."

"Veronica Lake...?" I began, then remembered that was how she described Cecelia. "And where was she, when you saw her? The homeless woman?"

She made a vague gesture to the far side of the shack. "Over by the alcove, where you keep the generator." She shook her head, puzzled. "I don't understand how Veronica Lake walked right by her."

My gaze fell to the rug, covering the trap door that opened onto the tunnel that I'd used as a storage place. It connected to the trapdoor next to the alcove. Kneeling, I grabbed hold of the carpet and yanked it aside. Then, gripping the brass ring, I pulled hard, bracing my feet against the floor for leverage. Reaching for my pack, I pulled my small flashlight out and turned it, aiming the beam into the dark tunnel that yawned before me. Nothing seemed out of place, so I went down a couple of steps, using my flashlight to push back the dark. "Where? I don't see anyone."

Dottie rolled her eyes and made a face at me, annoyed. "She's right there. Just look." And vanished.

I took another step down, flashed my light around

again, then stopped and stared, stunned.

Where only the empty passageway to the outside had met my gaze, I was now seeing a woman curled up a few feet from me. She was wrapped in a blanket that didn't hide her injuries and she held up a hand, shielding her eyes from my light. A cut on her forehead had been hidden by a band-aid and was now partially covered with blonde hair.

She looked so much like how I'd dreamt her over the last couple of weeks that I knew at once who she was. She shaded her eyes, a tired smile crossing her face. "I told you that I was close, that I was coming."

"So it was you who left that message on my wall. It was pretty cryptic."

She shrugged, trying to sit up straighter. "Trying to communicate directly in dream time is not my forte. But I did find you."

I went to her, kneeling to examine her, taking care to not aggravate any of her injuries, both seen and hidden. Except for the few scrapes that I could see, she appeared unharmed. Still, I wanted to get her to the hospital in Wickerman Falls.

If possible, in the same room with Claire.

"I need to get you out of here," I said, shifting my position. "Can you walk?"

She nodded, said, "Yes, I'm more stiff than anything else, little sister."

I grinned. "You're going to have to explain how you knew about me."

Cat took my hand. "When I get a shower and some clean clothes."

"I'm thinking after an overnight in the hospital with Claire," I said, "maybe then would be the time, so you're not repeating yourself."

She looked up sharply to protest, winced. "The hospital sounds like a plan. What happened to Claire?"

I explained quickly, bringing her up to date. "She's fine, more shaken up than anything else, which is understandable." Glancing over my shoulder, I added, "I'm going up top, then help you out." I moved back to the stairs, supporting her weight until she felt steady on her own. Then I climbed up and turned back for her. She shielded her eyes again from the sudden change in light, then reached for me.

I took her hands and pulled my oldest sister out of the dark.

Acknowledgements

An extra special thank you goes to Eric and Henry at Ojai Business Center, who used their collective skills to add the titles and graphics to the front cover photo.

And to David Reeser of Ojai Digital for his help in making sure my books were properly formatted.

About the Author

J.J. Brown lives in Southern California, surrounded by an eclectic assortment of books, two cats and several horses.

She is currently at work on several projects.

You can follow her at J.J. Brown, Wordslinger on Twitter, Facebook, and Instagram.

You can also follow her blog: jjbrownwordslinger.com.

CPSIA information can be obtained
at www.ICGtesting.com
Printed in the USA
FSHW022204191021
85450FS